LOVEDEATH

DAN SIMMONS

LOVEDEATH

WARNER BOOKS

A Time Warner Company

Frontispiece: "Love and Death" by G. F. Watts. By permission of The Tate Gallery.

"Hugh Selwyn Mauberly" by Ezra Pound. By permission of New Directions.

Excerpt from "The Glory of Women" by Siegfried Sassoon. From *Siegfried Sassoon's Long Journey,* edited by Paul Fussell, © 1983, Oxford University Press. By permission of George Sassoon.

Excerpt from "Dulce et Decorum Est" by Wilfred Owen. From *The Poems of Wilfred Owen,* edited by John Stallworthy, The Hogarth Press. By permission of the Random Century Group.

Excerpt from "The General Inspecting His Trenches" by A. P. Herbert. From *Somme* by Lyn McDonald. By permission of A. P. Watt Ltd. on behalf of Crystal Hale and Jocelyn Herbert.

Excerpt by C. H. Sorley. From *Marlborough and Other Poems* by C. H. Sorley, Cambridge University Press, 1915.

"The Great Lover" by Rupert Brooke. From *Collected Poems* by Rupert Brooks, published by Papermac. By permission of Sidgwick & Jackson.

Table from *Death's Men—Soldiers of the Great War* by Denis Winter, Allen Lane, 1978. Copyright © Denis Winter, 1978.

Soldier's Doggerel, "The World Wasn't Made in a Day," and excerpts by A. G. West, S. Sassoon, Wilfred Owen, and Charles Sorley from *Eye Deep in Hell: Trench Warfare in World War I* by John Ellis. Published by The Johns Hopkins University Press, Baltimore © 1976. By permission of Pantheon Press.

Warner Books, Inc., 1271 Avenue of the Americas, New York, NY 10020

W A Time Warner Company

Printed in the United States of America

First Printing: November 1993

10 9 8 7 6 5 4 3 2 1

Library of Congress Cataloging-in-Publication Data

Simmons, Dan.
    Lovedeath / Dan Simmons.
        p.   cm.
    ISBN 0-446-51756-9
    1. Horror tales, American. I. Title.
PS3569.I47292L68   1993
813'.54—dc20   92-51031
                                                               CIP

Book design: H. Roberts

This book is dedicated to Richard Harrison and Dan Peterson, good friends, good traveling companions.

Acknowledgments

I would like to acknowledge the following people:

To Richard Harrison, a sincere thank-you for sharing his treasure trove of books, materials, and personal expertise on the Battle of the Somme and for the conversation on the Normandy beach that rainy August day, from which the entire project grew.

To Dan Peterson, a double debt of thanks for his interest in the Sioux (which may have rubbed off a bit on the author) and for traveling with me through the gardens of Japan, the back alleys of Hong Kong, and the *klongs* of Bangkok in search of a story.

To Richard Curtis, my agent and friend, a sincere thank-you made no less sincere for its repetition, for again helping me to write what I wanted, when I wanted.

And finally, as always, to Karen and Jane, for their love, patience, and unwavering support.

"Love, thou art absolute sole lord
of life and death."
                    —Richard Crashaw (1613–1649)
                    "Hymne to St. Theresa"

"Never, never, never, never, never"
                    —William Shakespeare
                    King Lear

Contents

Foreword   *xiii*

ENTROPY'S BED AT MIDNIGHT   *1*
DYING IN BANGKOK   *33*
SLEEPING WITH TEETH WOMEN   *79*
FLASHBACK   *153*
THE GREAT LOVER   *201*
  Notes   *307*

Foreword

I wanted to call this collection of five novellas "Liebestod," but was gently reminded that not many Americans are fond of or familiar with opera, that not everyone would instantly translate the German as "lovedeath" and know that it was from Act II of Wagner's *Tristan und Isolde,* and that even if everyone *did* know all this . . . it still might not be a good idea to associate my book with the image of a huge lady in a brass brassiere belting out an indecipherable dirge for her dead boyfriend. That is what my advisors said. Of course, I think they're all philistines. But then again, I don't care that much for Wagner myself.

I have heard Mark Twain credited with saying, "Wagner's music is not as bad as it sounds," but I've never seen the source of that quote. I *did* recently run across a letter from Twain written during a trip to Europe in which he attended his first Wagnerian opera and the following excerpt shows some of his enthusiasm at the experience:

> Each sang his indictive narrative in turn, accompanied by the whole orchestra of sixty instruments; and when this had continued for some time, and one was hoping they might come to an understanding and modify the noise, a great chorus composed entirely of maniacs would suddenly break forth, and then during two minutes, and sometimes three, I lived over again all that I had suffered the time the orphan asylum had burned down.

I considered changing the title of this collection to *Burning Down the Orphan Asylum,* but, despite the delicious ring that phrase has to it, my literary advisors again won out.

Lovedeath it is, then.

Novels and novel-length projects are, for me at least, labors of love even at the worst of times, but *Lovedeath* was most especially so, at least in part because it demanded to be written at precisely that . . . the worst of times. When the labor pains began in earnest for this book, I was happily embarked upon one novel and arranging a deadline for a second one. I had not planned to write these novellas *now,* it was not convenient to do it, and there would be repercussions if I took the time and energy to do so. *Tough cookies,* came the muffled message from within as the familiar literary contractions began. *Here I come.*

It is odd how living things rarely arrange their births to fit conveniently into our busy schedules.

It was time for *Lovedeath* to be born and now it has been. Since you are holding it in your hands right now, you might do me a favor and count the fingers and toes. If anything is missing, tell me later. I'm resting at the moment.

I had considered writing something superficially profound here about the themes of Eros and Thanatos which circle through these five tales like hungry sharks in a crowded pool, but truth be told, almost all successful stories include some element of the twin themes of love and death. What make these tales distinctive—if anything does—are, perhaps, the different angles at which I approach the topic. After publishing a dozen or so books, I know my own work well enough to be aware that the themes of love, death, and the act of dealing with the sense of loss so common to both these human experiences, are almost obsessive topics in my fiction. I do not plan it so. It is what stirs me deep within and I write about it. I have no choice in the matter. In these novellas, however, I did choose to approach the topics from a variety of perspectives in the hope that some useful parallax would emerge.

I believe it has for me. I can only hope it does for the reader.

A word here about novellas. Fiction of this intermediate length—too long to be called a short story, too short to claim the title of novel—is well loved by most writers and loathed by editors and publishers.

For the writer, the novella can be the perfect length in which to observe a fictional universe without suffering the inevitable diffusion of focus that the large lens of the novel necessarily brings to the process. A novella allows the writer—and, with luck, the reader—to breathe deeply of character, setting, theme, and unrushed narrative without the added pollutants of subplot, ancillary characters, chapter breaks, and the inevitable digressions which cloud the atmosphere of all but the most perfect of novels. A novella, as with a short story, demands that each sentence—no, each *word*—has at least a double reason for existence. Writers love novellas, both as challenge and change of pace.

Editors and publishers hate novellas because they are hard to sell. Despite the enormous popularity of novellas by such diverse writers as Ernest Hemingway, J. D. Salinger, Saul Bellow, and Stephen King, publishers still lie awake nights worrying about how to package the things. The publishers and readers of "serious fiction" tend to take their novellas straight and solo (i.e., *The Old Man and the Sea*), throw in a lot of blank pages fore and aft, pretend it is a novel, hope that no one important will notice that it is not, and wait for the Nobel Prize.

Other writers tend to return to a theme again and again, exorcising in the process whatever demons drive them to the topic, and then publish these medium-length tales over the moans, groans, and whimpered entreaties of their editors. For some writers this approach has several strengths: firstly, the novella seems to be the perfect length for a work of horror; secondly, overt genre-fiction novellas can coexist comfortably with straight-fiction novellas in a way which no other type of collection allows; finally, if the author is capable of multiple styles and a variety of narrative tones, such a collection can be a showcase for the writer and a treasure trove for the reader.

Or at least that is how *I* respond as a reader when confronted with a collection of novellas from a writer I trust. I remember reading Stephen King's novella "The Body" for the first time and thinking *Yes!*

And now, having belabored the point about whimpering, moaning, groaning editors, I would like to thank my editor at Warner— John Silbersack—for his enthusiasm and total support for this project. John understood why I chose the twin themes of love and death as well as the form of the novella for their delivery. He was a good midwife and I recommend him to other writers who are expecting novellas.

Now a few words about the novellas themselves:

"Entropy's Bed at Midnight" is my attempt to explore the role that accident plays in death, love, pain, and laughter. It is a paean to the human side of Chaos theory. The "Orange File" insurance cases are real. Trust me.

"Dying in Bangkok" may be my final word on the horror of AIDS, that "Liebestod" pairing of love and death that has transformed our world . . . and which will continue to do so into the next century even if a cure were to be found tomorrow. To research the setting, I arrived in Bangkok in May of 1992 mere hours after the government saw fit to shoot scores of young demonstrators in a country that had always tried to avoid such overt violence. Bullet holes were still visible on the bloodstained street near the Democracy Monument. People were eager to tell me of their experiences. But as tragic as the civil terror had been, as disquieting as the public bullet holes and bloodstains were, it still was the knowledge of the coming AIDS epidemic there, as silent and stealthy and unstoppable as the Red Death, that saddened me most as I walked the raucous streets of Patpong District.

"Sleeping with Teeth Women" is my celebration of the richness of Native American lore—specifically Sioux, although the folktales of a dozen tribes are subsumed in this narrative—and it was a pleasure to research. Even for an inveterate spiritual nonbeliever such as myself, the Black Hills of South Dakota exert a strange and persuasive power. It is easy to see why the *Paha Sapa* are sacred to the Sioux and to other tribes . . . and why the young men of the Sioux still choose to go there for their visions. Finally, this long

In 1969 and 1970, as I approached the end of my undergraduate experience at Wabash College and the inevitability of being drafted and sent to Vietnam, my own obsession with the war led me to the antiwar writings of the 1920s and 30s. Largely forgotten now by the general public, the body of literature about the Great War and the description of the experience of war that was published in those years may be without equal. The young British men who were being wasted by the millions in World War I included some of this century's finest writers. Present at the Battle of the Somme alone were the poets Robert Graves, Siegfried Sassoon, John Masefield, Edmund Blunden, and Mark Plowman. The romantic poetry of Rupert Brooke, whose poem and title "The Great Lover" I have borrowed, best exemplified the romantic idealism of these men as they entered the war. But Brooke died of fever on the Greek isle of Skyros in 1915, before most of the great battles of that war were fought . . . before the death of innocence . . . before the death of much of his generation. The trench verse of Sassoon, Blunden, and the others showed the descent from romantic abstraction to vivid battle-field horror and cynicism. Those poets who survived the war wrote prose narratives such as Robert Graves's *Good-Bye to All That* and Siegfried Sassoon's *Memoirs of an Infantry Officer* and Ernest Hemingway's *A Farewell to Arms* and Erich Maria Remarque's *Im Westen Nichts Neues* (which I remember reading in German the week that my low draft number—84—was drawn in the lottery).

This poetry and prose was important to me in 1969 and 1970 as I came to grips with my own possible involvement in the nightmare that was Vietnam. Years later, thinking of the brilliant war literature of the 1920s and 1930s, I agreed with the reviewer who said that, in comparison, most of the "literature of the Vietnam War reads like whining letters from kids at summer camp who found the experience less agreeable than they had bargained for."

This is not to say that the horrors of Vietnam were any less terrible to those who suffered them than the horrors of trench warfare were to the Tommies and Doughboys of the Great War . . . only that the poets and novelists of that earlier conflict were better writers.

For me, there was added to the forceful clarity of their writing

story of an unwilling young Messiah who wants only to get la
instead ends up being chosen as the savior of his people,
antidote to what I consider the saccharine condescension of
travesties as *Dances with Wolves.* I have only a trace of Indian b
but even if I were a full-blooded Sioux, I think that I would r
be hunted and exterminated as a feared enemy than be patronize
Hollywood as a weak, whimpering, idealized, politically cor
victim. *Mitakuye oyasin. All my relatives.*

"Flashback" is science fiction. Sort of. There are very few g
whiz, high-tech goodies in this tale of memory and loss, of love a
death. It is, rather, an exploration of the point where the ability
recapture the past—and those lost to us in the past—becomes
sickness rather than a source of solace. While the tale itself ha
modest goals, I have found that the mere mention of a druglik
flashback has stirred people to share their own thoughts about usin
it—if, when, why, how much. Even friends who have never used
recreational drugs say that they might become flashback addicts in
short order. And, with all of us still emerging from the Reagan era in
which the nation seemed to be dreaming only of its past while
mortgaging its future, flashback addiction seems more than an idle
fantasy.

Finally, "The Great Lover." I need to talk a minute about this
unorthodox tale.

I have a fictional poet in "The Great Lover," but the poetry he is
supposed to have written is actually the genius of such World War I
poets as A. G. West, Siegfried Sassoon, Rupert Brooke, Charles
Sorley, and Wilfred Owen. Normally, the use of actual poetry—
unattributed except as footnotes—would be awkward. Creating the
illusion that these poems come from the imagination of a fictional
poet would seem to be unthinkable . . . inefficient at best, unethical
at the worst.

But there is a reason for this approach. In a real sense, I had
little or no choice in the matter. The fact is that the poems were not
included to add to the verisimilitude of the story—rather, the *story*
was written as a personal form of illuminating and explaining the
power of this particular poetry.

Let me explain.

the simple fact that the thought of World War I had always frightened me. For some reason, the form of life and death in that war—mud, claustrophobic trenches, gas, bayonets, shelling, the casual wasting of millions by foolish, foolish commanders—had been my particular *bête noire*. Rather than continue to read obsessively on the subject, I avoided it for years. It made me sick and it made me angry; and it brought back deep fears of my own.

Two events conspired to change that attitude. First, my family and I happened to be visiting friends in England during the national Remembrance Day there in November of 1991, and I saw firsthand how fresh the wounds of that seemingly ancient war were on the minds and hearts of the British people. Second, almost a year later, I was touring the Normandy invasion battlefields with my friend Richard Harrison—a headmaster by profession but a military historian by vocation—and we discussed, over the bones of Hitler's *Festung Europa,* what more terrible sacrifice of men had been demanded during the Great War.

And at that moment, on a chilly August day in Normandy, far removed in time and place from the quiet River Somme and the cemetery headstones that rise like poppies there, row on row, I decided to write about the Battle of the Somme.

The decision to write about it was easy. The way I chose to develop the novella was problematic.

Most important to me was the inclusion of some of the poetry that had so affected me two decades earlier. In creating my fictional poet, James Edwin Rooke, I wished not to diminish the brilliance of the actual poets who wrote the verse, but, rather, to combine a few of their disparate experiences into the life of a symbolic "everyman." In so doing, I hoped to be able to understand how a sensitive mind and heart could have survived—with mind and heart essentially intact— the incredible horrors of that first Great War of our bloody century.

The second condition I set for myself in this novella was to present the horrors in as factual a manner as I could manage given the rather fantastic premise of my tale of love and death. In other words, I decided that the details of the Battle of the Somme would

be as well documented as I could make them. The result—as with
the included poetry—is a montage of reported images and experiences taken from life rather than imagination. Thus, when James
Edwin Rooke has an encounter with a certain corpse, a set of
dentures, and a rat, it is an echo of a French soldier's memory of an
event as recorded in J. Meyer's *La vie quotidienne des soldats pendant la
grande guerre* (Hachette, Paris, 1966) and retold by Henrí Barbusse
and quoted in *Eye Deep in Hell: Trench Warfare in World War I* by John
Ellis (Johns Hopkins University Press, Baltimore, 1976). Similarly,
the parallax view of the Somme attack of 10 July, 1916, might
include a single incident as reported by Sergeant Jack Cross, No.
4842, C Company, 13th (S) Rifle Battalion, The Rifle Brigade (in
Somme, Lyn Macdonald, Michael Joseph Ltd., 1983), briefly commented
upon by Siegfried Sassoon *(Memoirs of an Infantry Officer,* Faber and
Faber, Ltd., 1930) and perceived quite differently by Lieutenant Guy
Chapman *(A Passionate Prodigality,* Buchan & Enright, London,
1933).

I mention this not to pretend some scholarly precision—my
readings are too haphazard, my research twice removed, my methods
less than stringent and more than suspect—but to share the complex
game I played, which was, to the best of my ability, *to get it right.*

This is not to say that I did get it right. (Sometimes I chose not
to, as when I have mustard gas used experimentally some months
before it actually appeared on the Western Front in the spring of
1917.) But I do believe that those who witnessed these events and
wrote about them so eloquently, in prose and poetry, did seem to
come closer to the terrible beauty and terror of combat than most of
the war chroniclers since Homer. Knowing that memory is faulty at
best, I still trusted the persistence of their memory.

Strange things happened during this immersion period of research for "The Great Lover." A casual mention by a 1916 line officer
of a painting titled "The Happy Warrior" by the nineteenth-century
artist George Frederick Watts sent me into the dusty stacks of the
University of Colorado (at Boulder) library to find an example of the
art that seemed to appeal to both the romantic and morose side of
this officer. Going through books published in the 1880s and not

checked out since 1947, I came across a photograph of Watts's allegorical painting "Love and Death" and knew at once that it would become the central metaphor of my Somme tale. I went so far as to contact my agent and editor requesting that a print of this obscure painting be used as a frontispiece in the novella collection.

Only later, when reading a previously ignored section of Siegfried Sassoon's autobiographical novel trilogy, *The Memoirs of George Sherston*, did I come across this passage:

> I felt as if I had changed since the Easter holidays. The drawing-room door creaked as I went softly in and crept across the beeswaxed parquet floor. Last night's half-consumed candles and the cat's half-empty bowl of milk under the gate-legged table seemed to belong neither here nor there, and my own silent face looked queerly at me out of the mirror. And there was the familiar photograph of "Love and Death," by Watts, with its secret meaning which I could never quite formulate in a thought, though it often touched me with a vague emotion of pathos.

Finally, I have to say that my reading of these novelists and poets in 1969 and 1970 did more than simply confirm my antiwar feelings of the time. Seeing the impact of their verse and literature on the generation that came of age between the wars, observing how an Oxford class in the late 1930s could be so moved by the word-memories of the Great War that they could ignore Hitler's rise and take a pledge that they would not fight for their country *under any circumstance* . . . all this added a disturbing and enlightening perspective to an already complex issue. Even with Vietnam festering and the antiwar intellectualism beckoning, I understood that perceiving the horrors of war was not enough . . . that there *were* things worse than warfare . . . death camps for one, the darkness of a Thousand Year Reich for another, trading a Vietnam for a nuclear exchange for a final thing . . . and that while nothing could excuse the stupidities that led to a Battle of the Somme, events could explain the honest need for the next generation to return to its own front. And the next generation. And the next.

Does all this answer the question of why I chose to include actual poetry in "The Great Lover" and why I worry so much about the details? Probably not. But I appreciate your attention.

Oddly enough, I did not consider using the single piece of post–Great War poetry that most moved me during those dear, dead, waiting-for-the-draft days of the late sixties. The poet was Ezra Pound, who—by great coincidence—had been fired some sixty years earlier, in 1908, from his post as instructor at the same Wabash College I was attending. Reputedly he had been harboring a chorus girl in his room. Like Mark Twain's Sandwich Island cannibals who ate the missionary, Pound said that he was sorry. He said that it was an accident. He said that it would not happen again. The college fired him anyway. (Pound went on to better things, sailing to Italy to join his literary friends, exclaiming, as he stepped down the gangplank, that he had been "saved from the Ninth Circle of Desolation!" which anyone who has attended my little college in Crawfordsville, Indiana, can understand.)

The poem is "HUGH SELWYN MAUBERLY." I thought twenty-two years ago that it was a good parable not only for the horror of the Great War, but for the tragedy of America's experience in Vietnam. I still think that is true.

IV

These fought in any case,
and some believing,

          pro domo, in any case...

Some quick to arm,
some for adventure,
some from fear of weakness,
some from fear of censure,
some for love of slaughter, in imagination,
learning later...
some in fear, learning love of slaughter;

Died some, pro patria

          non "dulce" non "et decor"...

walked eye-deep in hell
believing in old men's lies, then unbelieving,
came home, home to a lie,
home to many deceits,
home to old lies and new infamy;
usury age-old and age-thick
and liars in public places.

Daring as never before, wastage as never before.
Young blood and high blood,
fair cheeks, and fine bodies;

fortitude as never before

frankness as never before,
disillusions as never told in the old days,
hysterias, trench confessions,
laughter out of dead bellies.

V

There died a myriad,
And of the best, among them,
For an old bitch gone in the teeth,
For a botched civilization,

Charm, smiling at the good mouth,
Quick eyes gone under earth's lid,

For two gross of broken statues,
For a few thousand battered books.

And so we return to "Liebestod." To love. And to death. And, I
hope, to love again. And perhaps the final word should be borrowed
from my fictional poet James Edwin Rooke, who may have heard
Lieutenant Guy Chapman quote Andrew Marvell as the young
lieutenant watched his comrades prepare to die at the Somme:

My love is of a birth as rare
As 'tis for object strange and high:
It was begotten by Despair
Upon impossibility.

—Dan Simmons
Colorado, January, 1993

LOVEDEATH

ENTROPY'S BED
AT MIDNIGHT

We'd just gotten out of Denver, headed west during Friday rush hour, up the first major hill and Caroline had asked what the runaway truck ramp was for, when I saw the semitrailer in trouble on the eastbound, downhill lanes. At the time I thought he merely was going too quickly for the four-mile, six-percent grade, but the next morning in Breckenridge I saw the photos of the wreckage on the front pages of both the *Denver Post* and the *Rocky Mountain News;* the truck driver had survived but three women had died in the Toyota Camry he'd smashed into and forced over the concrete restraining wall.

At the time, I told Caroline what the runaway truck exits were for and we'd watched for other ramps during the hour drive to the little ski-resort town. "It looks scary," she said, looking at one of the steep cul de sacs of deep gravel. "Do trucks run out of control very often?" Caroline had turned six just three months earlier, in May, but she was precocious both in her vocabulary and her anxiety about a world with too many sharp edges. If Kay and others were to be believed, I'd helped create that anxiety in her.

"No." I lied, "It's very rare."

Breckenridge in August was not the most exciting place I could have taken my daughter after not seeing her for several months. The small ski town was more "real" than Vail or Aspen, but other than a few upscale shops and a single Wendy's—disguised as an old Victorian home but still featuring a menu suitable for kids—there wasn't a hell of a lot to do there in the summer. I'd planned on camping Friday

1

night, but after three months of dry heat in Colorado this weekend turned cold and blustery with heavy rains. I found us a small suite with a kitchenette at a lodge below the ski area and that evening we settled in to watch George Pal's *War of the Worlds* on a tiny TV.

Tucking Caroline in that night in the little daybed in the dining area, the rain running noisily from the gutters outside, I couldn't help but notice how much she looked like Kay. In the five months since the two of them had moved back to Denver, Caroline had thinned out, her face was beginning to reflect Kay's elegant bone structure as the baby fat receded, and her brown hair was shorter, not much longer than Kay's when I met her that summer after I'd returned from Vietnam and hit the Pepsi truck. Caroline's dark eyes showed the same vulnerable intelligence as Kay's, and I noticed that she rested her cheek on her palm rather than the pillow, in the same way.

The great tragedy of being separated from your children, even briefly, during the early years is that when you return they're different people. Perhaps that's always true, whatever age. I don't know.

"Daddy, can we go see the Alpine Slide in the morning?"

"Sure, kiddo. If the weather improves." I was sorry that I'd grabbed the brochures from the lobby. It would have been all right if Caroline hadn't taught herself to read before she was five. As it was, she'd read aloud the glowing descriptions of the Alpine Slide from each of the five "What-to-Do-in-Breckenridge" brochures. To say that I was less than enthusiastic to have her slide down a mountainside would have been an understatement.

"That movie about Martians was silly, wasn't it, Daddy?"

"It sure was."

"I mean, if they were smart enough to build spaceships, they'd be smart enough to know about germs, wouldn't they?"

"Absolutely," I said. I'd never thought about it. *War of the Worlds* had been the first non-Disney movie I'd ever seen—I was five when it was released in 1953—and all the way back from the Rialto I'd clung to my older brother's hand. "Didja see the wires holding up those stupid Martian machines?" Rick had asked, probably trying to allay my fears, but I had only blinked in the gray Chicago snowfall and held on more tightly to his mittened hand. I'd slept with a night-light for months after that and couldn't look at the night sky from our third-floor landing without waiting for the meteor trails of the invading Martian cylinders. A year later, when we moved to a small town thirty miles from Peoria, I reassured myself that the Martians would attack the big cities first, leaving us rural folks enough time at least to commit suicide before their heat rays were turned on us. Later when my fears had turned from Martians to nuclear war, I used the same logic to find some peace of mind.

"Good night, Daddy," said Caroline, nestling her cheek on her palm.

"Good night, sweetheart." I went into the other room, slid the door half closed, and tried to read from Raymond Carver's last collection of stories. After a while I gave it up and listened to the rain.

I never liked Kay's dad much—he'd been a civil engineer before he retired and still held a black-white view of every issue—but he'd surprised me by coming to visit me at the clinic where I was drying out and recovering from whatever kind of breakdown I'd had just after Kay and I were separated.

"Kay tells me that you watched Caroline go to school every morning and were waiting for her when she came out," said the old man. "Were you thinking about kidnapping her?"

I smiled and shook my head. "You know better, Calvin. I was just making sure she was okay."

He nodded. "And you almost punched that lady who was baby-sitting Caroline while Kay worked."

I shrugged, wishing I was wearing something other than a bathrobe and pajamas. "She was driving Caroline and the other kids around in her van without having them wear seatbelts."

He looked at me. "What are you afraid of, Bobby?"

"Entropy," I said without taking time to think.

Calvin frowned slightly, rubbing his cheeks. "It's been a hell of a long time since my college physics," he said, "but isn't entropy just the energy you can't get at to do work?"

"Yes," I said, amazed that I was talking about this to Kay's father, "but it's also a measure of randomness. And the certainty that everything which can get fucked up, will. It's the operative force behind Murphy's Law."

"The Brooklyn Bridge," he said.

"What?" I said.

"If entropy scares you, Bobby, think about the Brooklyn Bridge."

I shook my head. It hurt. Being sober was not all it was cracked up to be.

"John Roebling and his son designed that bridge to last," said Calvin. "Built in the 1870s for a tenth its current traffic, finished years before the first car would cross it, but all stresses were figured, all tolerances multiplied by a factor of five or ten, and look at it today. They gave it a complete inspection a few years ago and decided all it needed was a new coat of paint."

"Great," I'd said at the time. "If you're a bridge."

But I went to New York after I was released from the clinic. My cover story was that I was going back to confer with Centurion, Prairie Midland's parent company, about transferring back to the Denver area, but in reality I'd gone to stare at the bridge. I wondered if I'd been factoring tolerances for Caroline's life by a margin of five, or ten, or more, and in so doing turning things which should have been growing in the sun into brick and iron.

Stupid idea. There was a great bar right near the base of the bridge, but I only had a beer before going back to the hotel.

The rain let up sometime after midnight but a strong wind still blew down from the mountains and I was grateful for the extra blankets on the shelf. Several times I went out to check on Caroline. She was fine, sprawled in one of the impossible contortions six-year-olds prefer for sleep, and I pulled the spread and blanket back over her and went back in to try to sleep.

One of my favorite Orange File reports was the claim of Farmer McDonald and his son Clem. Those aren't their real names, of course. I don't know what I'll do if I ever get around to collecting these in some sort of book or something. So often the claimants' names are so perfect to their stories—like that lecherous dentist in Salem, Oregon, named Dr. Dick—that I can't imagine changing them. Also, to enjoy the files the way I have all these years, you'd have to read them in the full insurancese, complete with police reports, field adjustors' forms, accident diagrams, and the statements and depositions taken from the victims, claimants, primary participants, and witnesses.

Every once in a while I get an echo of claims-file insurancese when they interview a deputy sheriff or state trooper or someone on TV after a shooting or somesuch. I used to prod Kay from her book and make her watch. "Uh . . . at approximately this point in time," the fat deputy would be saying into the camera, "uh . . . the alleged suspect exited his *ve*-hicle and proceeded on foot . . . uh . . . at a high rate of speed until myself and Officer Fogerty intercepted and proceeded to restrain the suspect. At this time . . . uh . . . the suspect offered some physical resistance which, between Officer Fogerty and I, we successfully succeeded in overcoming."

I translated for Kay. "That means the crook got out of his car and ran like hell until those two knocked him down and stomped him."

Kay would smile dutifully. "Bobby," she'd say, "every pseudo-profession and level of bureaucracy has its double-talk quotient."

"Like what?" I'd say. The only jobs I'd ever held were in the Army and insurance. They were about the same thing.

"Take my field," she'd say. "Education. What we lack in technical terms we make up for in useless jargon. A child can't be retarded, he has to be labeled SLIC . . . a Significantly Learning-Impaired Child. We can't hire a coordinator to take care of a growing drop-out problem . . . we advertise for a TOSA—Teacher On Special Assignment—for Discontinuers. Instead of tutoring a slow child, we design elaborate IEP's—Independent Education Profiles for non-autonomous learners. Instead of high groups for fast learners, we have to fund TAG programs."

"Yeah," I'd say, waving at the screen where our local, attractive, Eurasian-female anchorperson had taken the place of the fat deputy, "but cops talk so wonderfully *stupid*."

Anyway, Farmer McDonald had been reshingling his barn roof when the events of the aforementioned automobile insurance claim proceeded to occur.

Wait a minute, you say. *Automobile* claim? While reshingling a barn? Wait. Listen.

This was when I was working out of the Oregon office of Prairie

Midland. Farmer McDonald owned a large place thirty miles southeast of Portland. I remember it was raining when I went out to take measurements and statements. It's always raining in my memories of Oregon.

So anyway, Mr. McDonald was about a third finished with the shingling job on the north side of the barn when he grew a bit nervous about the increasingly steep pitch of the roof. He went down, found a long bit of rope, went back up, tied one end securely around himself, and went higher to attach it to something solid. He decided that the cupola was too rotten and the lightning rods and weather vanes were too flimsy. That's when he saw Clem, his grown son, in the yard near the house. McDonald tossed the rope over the roof ridge and down to him, ordered Clem to tie the line to something "real solid," and then went back to the north roof to get on with his shingling.

Clem weighed about 280 pounds when I interviewed him and he grinned a lot. I had no doubt that Kay would have staffed him as a SLIC student and given him the strongest IEP a non-autonomous learner could receive. Clem had been one of the Discontinuer TOSA's failures. He also could have used a bath.

Clem used a double half-hitch to lash the rope to the rear bumper of their 1975 GM pickup parked between the rear porch and the chicken coop. Then Clem went back to his chores.

Mrs. McDonald emerged approximately nineteen minutes later, got in the truck, and proceeded to drive to town to get groceries.

She didn't get all the way to town. According to the local sheriff's report: ". . . At this point in time, Mr. McDonald's spouse was waved to a stop by Mr. Floyd J. Howell, an employee of the U.S. Postal Service, approximately 2.3 miles from the McDonald domicile on County Road 483, who at that point in time drove alongside Mrs. McDonald and succeeded in conveying, through an assortment of verbal and nonverbal communications, the fact that Mrs. McDonald was dragging something behind her vehicle and should pull over at her earliest convenience."

Prairie Midland, my company, ended up paying. The judge's final ruling had to take into account the indisputable fact that Mr. McDonald was attached to a vehicle under full coverage by us at the time of the accident. If I remember correctly, the settlement included replacing the cupola Farmer McDonald took out on his way over the top. We also had to pay for the completion of the roofing job.

In the morning it was cool but the storm had blown over, so Caroline and I had breakfast at Wendy's and drove up to the base of Peak 8 where the Alpine Slide was.

"Oh, Daddy, it looks like fun."

"Uh-huh."

"Don't you wish Mommy was here?"

"Mmmm," I said. In the months since the separation I hadn't gotten over wishing Kay was there for every new experience, but I'd gotten use to it the way one gets used to a missing tooth. I wished Kay were there now so she could help me think of a graceful way of keeping Caroline off the damned Alpine Slide.

"Can we go on it?"

"It looks a little scary," I said.

Caroline nodded and regarded the mountainside for a minute. "Yeah, a little," she said, "but I don't think Scout would be afraid of it."

"No," I agreed. My son would have loved it all right. Of course Scout would have thought it was a great ride if someone had taped him in a cardboard box halfway up a mountainside and thrown him over the edge. "What do you say we walk around a minute and check things out?"

The area had been open for less than half an hour but already the parking lot was two-thirds full and a steady stream of children and adults were lined up at the ticket booth and the lift lines. There were two lifts—something called the Colorado Super Lift, triple-wide chairs which ran far up the mountain to the Vista Haus restaurant at 11,600 feet, and the smaller, two-person Alpine Slide lift which ran less than a mile up a steeper slope. Already we could hear the scrape of brakes and screams as riders came down the last curves of the winding concrete trough of the Slide. I couldn't see the top of the Slide through the trees. The bigger scenic lift was almost empty as it traveled sedately above a slope which looked like a fairway tilted almost vertical in the rich morning light.

"Why don't we go on the big one?" I suggested. "We could get a great view."

"Aw, no," said Caroline, "I'd rather go on the *Slide*." My daughter whined the least of any six-year-old I'd ever met, but this was perilously close.

"Let's see how much."

We joined a line moving toward the ticket window. Despite the intense high-altitude sunlight, the air was chill and the breeze made it even colder. Caroline and I were wearing jeans and sweatshirts, but most of the families in sight were shivering and grinning in shorts and T-shirts, as if proclaiming, By God, it's August, it's still summer, and we're on *vacation*. Clouds were beginning to come into sight above the summit of Peak 8. The tickets were $4.00 for an adult, $2.50 for Caroline. She would have ridden free six months earlier when she was five.

I looked again at the Alpine Slide. Two sinuous concrete runs had been lain in parallel down the ski slope. A flimsy, split-rail fence bordered it on either side, zig-zagging down the steep hillside like brown lightning strokes. I couldn't see the beginning of the slide but sledders were visible and audible as they hurtled into the lower third of the run, their colorful sleds riding high on the banked curves. Most of the sledders were screaming.

"Please, Dad?"

"I'm thinking," I said, conscious that I was holding up the line.

The woman behind the glass looked at my ten-dollar bill and said, "If you're gonna want to ride more than once, it's cheaper to buy one of the five-ride specials."

"Probably just once apiece," I said.

"The two-rides for six dollars for you and two for four dollars for the little girl would be cheaper."

"Just one ride apiece," I said, more sharply than I'd intended.

"You wear these around your neck," said Caroline, slipping the elastic cord of the ticket over her head as we walked toward the base of the lift.

Mine was too tight. It cut into the flesh of my throat like a garroter's wire. The line to the lift was shorter than I'd thought.

*   *   *

Prairie Midland was a high-risk company. Our insureds paid more because of poor driving records, histories of defaulting, felony records, past DUI's, or a hundred other reasons. Anybody in this country can get insured if he or she has the money. The day after that drunk wiped out a school bus and killed twenty-seven people, he could have gotten coverage from Prairie Midland or twenty other companies and pool-coverage fronts like us. This country depends upon the automobile. We can't leave consumers sitting at home.

Sometimes after I'd just changed from State Farm to Prairie Midland, I'd be driving somewhere with Kay and see a wino politely vomiting into a gutter or a bag lady conversing with the sky, and I'd say proudly, "One of our insureds there. Probably on the way to a Mensa meeting."

I hadn't intended on going into the insurance business. In high school I wanted to be a comedian—some sort of stand-up comic. My favorite albums were the early Bill Cosby and Jonathan Winters. Cosby was funny then. He hadn't traded his childlike humor for all the childish smirking and mugging and self-congratulation I see him doing now every time I turn on the TV.

Jonathan Winters was even better—a truly insane genius. I would do entire monologues from his early albums. Sometimes my brother Rick wouldn't want to do some stupid stunt I'd dreamed up—jumping our bikes off a fifteen-foot ramp, say, or waiting on Hendlemann's Trestle for the 4:10 southbound to blow its whistle on the curve above—and I'd say in perfect Jonathan Winterese: "Okay then, Senator, chicken out then, go back to your car. I'll talk Ace down by myself."

In college I no longer wanted to be a comedian, but I didn't want to be anything else, either. I took liberal arts courses, protested the war, and spent an inordinate amount of time trying to get laid. In Vietnam I sometimes thought about what job I was going to find when I returned to the World, but I don't think I ever considered insurance adjusting. I spent a lot of time over there thinking about getting laid, too.

I once figured out that during the six months and twelve days that I was "in-country" during my abbreviated tour in the late, unlamented Republic of South Viet Nam, I never got farther than seven miles from where I'd first landed at the Tan Son Nhut Airport outside of Saigon. I was, in the parlance of my comrades-in-arms who actually hiked out into the boonies and got shot at, a REMF—a Rear-Echelon Motherfucker. That was all right with me at the time. I suppose it still is, although sometimes I think about it.

Anyway, it's sort of funny that I never thought about getting into automotive insurance since Dad did it for so many years. One of my earliest memories of going anywhere with him alone was when I rode with him on an adjustor's errand—I suspect it was somewhere barely out beyond Chicago's ring of forest preserves in the suburbs but to me it seemed like wilderness—and I played in one of the wrecks while he was estimating the other one.

I remember sitting in the passenger seat and looking through a Little Golden Book that had been on the floorboards. It was *Bambi.* I remember the page where Bambi met Flower was warped and still moist with a dark stain. In the windshield directly in front of me there was an oval hole which the top of my four- or five-year-old skull would have fit perfectly.

No one thought about seat belts for cars in those days. As late as the early sixties I remember flying somewhere with my dad and people not knowing how to buckle the lap belts in the plane. Dad had to buy the belts for our Chrysler from a USAC racing supply store and everyone thought we were nuts for wearing them.

I remember the car with the Bambi book was a Renault. Imported cars were relatively rare in the early fifties. This one seemed like a fragile toy. The turn indicator broke off in my hand when I played with it. I didn't tell Dad.

Most of the Orange File cases were mine, but some of them were sent to me by other agents and field people who learned that I was keeping the File.

One of my favorites about the time Scout was born was the Safeway Parking Lot Claim. Kay and I'd just moved from Indianapolis to Denver to be near her family. I wasn't Claims Manager yet and had to do the interviewing myself.

I'll call them Casper and Mrs. Casper. The wife was built like an oversized howitzer shell which had been wrapped in a print dress.

Casper was tall and skinny with thick glasses, bow tie, suspenders a decade before the movie *Wall Street* brought them into style, a nervous mouth, long, twitchy fingers, and Ichabod Crane-ish feet in polished Florsheims.

The couple had just come out of a Safeway in the Denver suburb of Littleton and had gone around to the driver's side to set the groceries in the backseat of their Prairie Midland–insured 1978 four-door Plymouth. Casper was carrying the two bags of groceries. Mrs. Casper unlocked the driver's door, reached in to unlatch the rear door, and opened it for him, talking at him all the while. The parking lot was crowded. Casper stepped out a bit, his back to his own car, as she opened the door.

As the Fates always seem to have it in our business, the Ford Bronco parked next to them was also covered by our agency, even though Prairie Midland is small enough that it insures only one out of every thousand cars on the road. Our insured, a temporarily out-of-work construction worker, wasn't in the Bronco. Nor was the only other driver in the household (his common-law wife) covered under our policy. The Bronco had been driven there—allegedly unknown to our insured—by his fourteen-year-old son Bubba, who unerringly chose that instant to slam the Bronco into reverse and to roar out of the parking space, rolling over both of Casper's feet with the right rear and front wheels of the Bronco as he did so.

Casper screamed and threw $86.46 worth of groceries into the air. The Bronco drove away. In some agony, Casper collapsed against his own car, holding himself up only by the strength of his hands.

"What I did next, I swear, I did because I was flustered," his wife later said in her statement to me. What she did next was slam the rear door shut. On Casper's fingers.

Pain isn't funny, but taking Casper's statement in that little house in Littleton was one of the most painful things *I'd* ever done. Both of his feet were heavily swathed and elevated on a Naugahyde ottoman. Eight of his fingers were in splints. He didn't seem to care about the driver of the Bronco—who still, six days after the accident, hadn't gone home—but he couldn't stop talking about his wife. "If that bitch comes back," he said, waving his splints in the air, "I'll *strangle* her!"

I took as much of the statement as I could and got out of there, pausing on the street corner to hang onto a mailbox until the worst of the laughter had passed. The image of Casper strangling anyone with those stiff, splayed finger splints was more than I could handle.

Caroline had never been on a chair lift before and we had an awkward moment boarding. I had to pull her upright on the seat before she slid off. The gum-chewing teenager at the boarding area was no help, saying something in an unintelligible monologue as she threw two of the plastic sleds on hooks at the back of the chair.

We rode up the hillside twenty or thirty feet above rocks and brown stubble. I'd ridden lifts in the winter when the slopes were white and gave an illusion of snow-covered softness below; now it was more like riding a rocking porch swing suspended thirty feet above rocks and tree stumps.

Caroline was delighted. "It's so *quiet*. Look, Daddy, a chipmunk."

"Ground squirrel," I corrected, keeping my right arm around her as we ascended. The Alpine Slide was longer than I'd thought. We caught a glimpse beneath us of adults and youngsters careening down the troughs, their sleds rasping against the concrete sides. Their hands gripped some sort of control stick, their eyes were wide, their hair and shirttails flapped in the breeze of their passage, but no one looked especially alarmed. As we watched, a heavyset man with red hair came barreling down the slide, his body hunched forward, eyes intense, both hands on the stick like a fighter pilot trying to pull out of a dive. His sled slashed high into a curve and made an ominous racket on the very lip of high-banked concrete, as if considering flying out of control into the ravine beyond. The wedge of blue plastic and steel wavered, shook, and dropped back into the groove, rocketing out of sight behind and beneath us.

It was odd that Kay, who grew up in Colorado, had never skied. She used to joke that there were a dozen non-skiing natives who met in weekly support groups during the winter. Gwen, my ex-secretary, had grown up in the flattest section of Indiana, but had loved to ski. Once when she was leaving early on a Friday, Gwen told me how her father had died. "We were in New Hampshire for a long weekend and Daddy'd just done a real hard double-black diamond run and was standing there near the pool area on his skis, proud as a peacock, when he gets a sort of surprised look on his face and pushes up his goggles and then his face turns as gray as a mouse's belly and he sort of leaned forward on his poles, like he was a ski jumper, sort of, until his nose was almost touching the snow between his tips. Then he went plop. Tony, he was my boyfriend who was with me that weekend, he and I sort of laughed. But Daddy just laid there. When we turned him over, his face was almost black, his tongue was all swole up, and he was stone cold dead. But like I told Momsy on the phone that night, well, he went when he was happy."

I'd gone skiing with Gwen. Not that weekend, but later. Telling Kay I had a conference in Louisville and flying out to Vermont or Utah. Gwen was a nice person in a myriad of small ways—she wept when the goldfish in the outer office died—but she probably never would be accused of needing one of the TAG programs for gifted people which Kay had described to me.

"Hang on, kiddo," I told Caroline, taking her hand as we approached the end of the chair-lift ride. The lift didn't slow appreciably as we came onto the ramp, and the gum-chewing teenager on this end was more intent on unloading the sleds from the hook than helping the passengers, so Caroline and I jumped, half-stumbled, and scurried out of harm's way by ourselves.

There were other sleds leaning against a wall with names such as SKYWALKER, X-15, and BLUE LIGHTNING inked on their undersides. I chose one named OLD POKEY and joined the shorter of the two lines at the top of the Slide.

"Am I going down by myself, Daddy?"

"Not this time," I said. I squeezed her hand. It was colder this high up. Clouds were building up above the shoulder of the mountain. "Let's try it together."

Caroline nodded, returning the pressure of my hand. The line grew shorter ahead of us.

From the time he was old enough to stand, Scout would throw himself headfirst into space toward Kay or me, trusting that we would catch him. Caroline has never done that. Even with piggyback rides she is cautious, warning her "horse" not to fall backward or trip. Scout used to love being thrown high in the air and being caught—even as a baby—and when I saw the opening title shots of *The World According to Garp* a few years ago, I had to laugh. Caroline wanted to be cuddled, cradled, enfolded . . . protected.

Kay and I hated to think it was just the difference between male and female children. We said it was just personalities, different and distinct little people, but I wonder. The last couple of years have been worse.

Believe what you want, I know precisely what Death looks like. It's a Pepsi truck with black sidewalls.

The summer I got back from Vietnam I was living in Indianapolis, taking insulin for the diabetes that hadn't been discovered or diagnosed until I went into the infirmary at Tan Son Nhut and which got me discharged five months early. I was living with three other guys, two of them ex-medics from Vietnam who'd gone into medical school, and our townhouse looked like a set out of *M*A*S*H* . . . the movie, not the TV show. We all wore fatigues most of the time and olive-drab underwear all of the time and two of us slept on army-surplus cots. We were all Donald Sutherland–cool and Elliott Gould–smartass and the pot and booze were taken for granted. All four of us drove motorcycles.

The first road accident I ever saw—I was four and we were on Route 66 coming out of Chicago—was a motorcycle fatality. I remember the unique and heavy sound of the man and bike hitting the left rear quarterpanel of the Studebaker as they both came through the intersection at the same time. Since then I've been on the scene of at least thirty motorcycle deaths, read the details of several hundred more, and had half a dozen spills of my own. The first time I ever *rode* a cycle I put it up the side of a Conoco station. I'd been doing fine until I pulled into the station lot to turn around—still moving fast in third gear—and simply forgot where the brakes were. I was thirteen. Three old farts had come out of the station after I'd slid into the wall, climbed the bay doors, and dumped it. They stood over me while I lay under the gas tank and twisted handlebars of Rick's new 250cc machine. Finally one of them spat and said, "Whatsamatter, boy," his mouth still full of tobacco and Illinois drawl, "don't ya know how to ride that thing?"

But by the time of the Pepsi truck I'd been riding for years; I'd logged more time on a bike than behind the wheel of a car. Even while in 'Nam I'd bought a Kawasaki from a Marine on his way home.

So one day in Indianapolis I was riding my roommate's 450 Honda—my own bike was in the shop—heading west on 38th Street a few miles north of the Speedway. An Econoline van, no windows in the back, was in front of me and slowed after pulling away from a stoplight at 38th and High School Road. I leaned and accelerated around him in the left lane, really kicking it the way you do after a few years of gaining confidence on a bike before your first big spill. It's as if by blowing away all the heaps of Detroit pig iron bogged in traffic, we could get rid of the sense of inferiority and vulnerability those same heaps gave us on the open road.

Anyway, I must have been doing forty-five or fifty when I swerved around the Econoline. And then I discovered the reason for his slowing.

The Pepsi truck had pulled out of the corner Shell station and had been stopped by traffic from pulling into the eastbound lanes. The truck was white and as massive as a metal rhinoceros with an old Pepsi label on its side. Its high racks were filled with bottles. The truck took up the entire left lane and most of the right lane with a blue Chevy ahead of the Econoline van filling what was left. The van was a green wall to my right. Thick traffic rushed the other way three feet to my left, and the cab of the Pepsi truck stuck six feet further into their lane. A Camaro was slamming on its brakes behind me.

Usually, when in doubt, you lay the bike down as gently as you can, count on losing some skin, and hope for the best. I always wore a helmet—even back then in my stupid days—and usually wore boots and leather, but this was mid-August. I was in sneakers, cut-off fatigues, and my standard-issue olive-drab undershirt.

The underside of the Pepsi truck seemed to come down to the ground—mufflers, transmission housings, low steps, pipes, teeth, I don't know what fuck-all—and it was moving slightly, creeping, not enough to get out of my way, but enough to give me a clear image of those left-rear double wheels rolling over whatever remained of me and my roommate's Honda after I slid into the junk underneath. In Vietnam we called trucks like that a deuce-and-a-half. Now I was going to die under one. I decided to stay upright. I don't think I hit the brakes hard enough to leave a skid mark. The left front wheel of that Pepsi truck was all I could see now and it was higher than my head. I figured that it might be softer than steel and headed straight for it.

Of course, all this wasn't a linear thought process. Accidents that give you time to *think* aren't real accidents. But everyone who has screwed up, looked at Death, and lived through it can remember the clarity of it all, the surreal quality of time slowed and stretched to near infinity. I'm convinced that the last fading thoughts in accident victims' dying brains are of this phenomenon of stretched time, the almost painful acuity of perception, and astonishment at it all. It's as if violent death were an astronomical black hole and entering it gives rise to all the slowed time, multiple realities, and stretched space that guys like Stephen Hawking talk about. That and four-letter words. A friend of mine on the National Transportation Safety Board air-crash review team once told me that of the hundreds of cockpit recorder tapes he'd listened to after airline tragedies, only a handful didn't have a four-letter epithet in the last second or two.

Anyway, I roared around the van, saw the Pepsi truck, said "Oh fuck," and hit him dead on.

Elisabeth Kubler-Ross and those other ghouls give us glowing reports of the newly dead sweeping down long tunnels, seeing light, hearing familiar voices, and feeling a benevolent warmth.

Crap.

Death is a Pepsi truck with no place to go. Dying is *wham,* feeling like the world's biggest fuck-up and being jerked up and out of it all. Like a puppy being lifted out of its box by the nape of its neck. Like a chess piece being removed from the board by an angry player. *Wham,* jerk, gone.

Dick Pennington, one of my roommates, happened to be on duty at the ER when I was brought in and was sitting there when I came to the next morning. "Bobby," he said gently, using the bedside manner they drill into residents at Methodist Hospital, "you're a fucking mess." I was just glad it hadn't been Kurt on duty; he was the roommate whose Honda I'd just totaled.

A hundred and eighty stitches in my right leg, sixty-three in the left. Multiple fracture of the right arm. Concussion. Broken collar bone. When I met Kay a few weeks later at the Simon and Garfunkel concert, it was because she couldn't see around me for all the casts, braces, and bandages.

Years later when I was discussing the insurance merits of state helmet laws with her, Kay surprised me with the opinion that motorcyclists shouldn't be required to wear helmets or any other safety equipment. Usually Kay was so Ralph Naderish about such things that I had to ask her why. "Gets the feebs out of the gene pool," she said with only a hint of a smile. "Motorcycles are as close to a force for natural selection as we can get in a civilized society."

I still ride occasionally. I never took Scout anywhere on my bike and I wouldn't dream of letting Caroline on one.

The kid working at the top of the Slide wasn't chewing gum but his mouth hung open and his jaw muscles rippled slightly as he if were keeping in practice. "Both goin' together?" he said. He sounded vaguely disapproving.

"Yeah." I'd wrestled the sled into the groove of the trough, crawled in, and was getting Caroline settled in between my knees. The sled ahead of us had disappeared and the teenagers behind us were shifting from foot to foot in impatience.

"Yeah, okay, been on it before?" asked the kid who worked there. He didn't wait for a response. "Okay, pull back on that stick to test your brakes, yeah, fine, forward makes it speed up, back slow, don't crowd the sled in front of you, you gotta get off quick when it comes to a full stop at the bottom, Okay? Go!" He slapped me on the back. Caroline filled the cusp of my arms and legs, her hands below mine on the control stick. We rolled forward and down.

A lot of accidents are caused by too much caution. One of my earliest Orange File claims was from when I'd just started in the business and was working for State Farm in Indianapolis. Kay was still in the public schools then, working in a little high school in a town named Brownsburg about ten miles out, and I was driving all over the state looking at wrecks. Jesus, we were happy for some reason.

This particular claim—hell, I'll just use their real names, the Johnsons—happened near the intersection of I-70 and I-465 and 74, not far from the airport. Mr. and Mrs. Johnson had both taken early retirement in order to realize their lifelong dream of traveling around America for a year or two before settling down in Florida or Arizona or somewhere. They were taking Mr. Johnson's eighty-one-year-old mother with them, figuring that when it came time to put her in a nursing home they'd just leave her somewhere nice and go on about their travels. The problem was, both Mr. and Mrs. Johnson hated to drive and hadn't been more than twenty-five miles from their tidy little suburban ranch house in more than a decade.

They'd bought a serious piece of traveling equipment—the largest camper then made, set on the back of a GM pickup that could have dragged six tons to the moon and back. Mrs. Johnson later told me that they would have bought a motor home—a full-sized RV—but that it had "looked too big and powerful" in the showroom. As it was, they passed up a Labrador in favor of a pit bull.

They never really got to test their new vehicle's power. When I saw the GM after it had been towed, the odometer had 8.9 miles on it and 7.5 of that was the delivery from the dealer. The entrance to I-465 was 1.4 miles from the Johnson house.

Mr. Johnson was driving and he'd been doing fine until he got to the bottom of the curved entrance ramp and stopped. Mrs. Johnson had been calling the traffic from the passenger side and said it was "Okay to go." Mr. Johnson didn't go. He didn't trust the accuracy of the pickup's right-side exterior mirror. He was worried whether the truck would accelerate properly. It was harder to handle than his Ford Crown Victoria.

Meanwhile, the Johnsons and their new camper sat at the bottom of the on-ramp while traffic increased on the southbound Interstate lanes and backed up behind them all the way to Morris Street above. Horns began honking. Mr. Johnson later admitted that he had sweated through his new JCPenney shirt.

"It looks better!" Mrs. Johnson called. She meant, she said later, that it looked like it might clear after the next cluster of high-speed traffic had passed.

Mr. Johnson did not wait to hear more. Without checking his mirrors he gunned it, flooded it, restarted it, and swerved out into traffic at a speed which the Indiana Highway Patrol later estimated at between seven and nine miles per hour.

At least three cars in the far left lane where the entrance ramp merged managed to change lanes. Two of those vehicles contacted at least three other cars, which caused a small chain reaction of fender benders, but none of that is relevant because none of *them* were insured by State Farm. The final vehicle in that particular high-speed cluster had neither time nor room to change lanes. That vehicle was an eighteen-wheel semi leased by Mother's Own Baked Goods, Inc. out of Saginaw, Michigan. Every time I heard Mr. Johnson's voice on the tape-recorded depositions referring to that "gol-durned Mother's trucker," I thought he was saying something else.

The Mother's trucker had been on the road for nine hours and was doing approximately seventy-five miles per hour when he saw the Johnson's pickup and oversized camper pull out in front of him. "The goddamned thing seemed to hop sideways and damn near stop in front of me," he said later. "I've seen quadriplegics move faster than that old fart was going."

The lanes to the right of the Mother's trucker were filled with colliding automobiles. The left lane was clogged with traffic from the entrance ramp backed up behind the Johnsons. The Mother's trucker did what he could—swerving as far right as possible without squashing a '78 Volvo and repeatedly hitting his airhorns.

The blast from the approaching semi's horns had an effect on our insureds. Mr. Johnson braked the camper to a full stop. Mrs. Johnson screamed.

The truck's cab missed the Johnson's camper, merely taking off the right outside mirror. The semitrailer *almost* missed. It was a matter of inches.

The state trooper I spoke to later over the after-hours drinks at the 911 Lounge on Washington Street said, "That rig opened up that camper like a big fuckin' can opener going to work on a tin of tuna. Cleanest bit of highway surgery I've ever seen."

The Johnsons were shaken but unhurt. They heard a sound— "Sort of like a giant can opener," said Mrs. Johnson—felt a heavy vibration, and turned in time to see the Mother's trucker's semi and part of their own camper pass them on the right. "That's when I remembered Mama," Mr. Johnson said later.

It's against Indiana state law to carry passengers in a separately configured or towed camping or recreational vehicle. The Johnsons said they hadn't known that. They only knew that Mama had a headache, she'd planned to sleep for the first few hours of the trip, and that they hadn't paid $32,000 to have Mama in the cab with them for their entire tour of America.

Mama wasn't in the cab with them. She wasn't in any of the camper's four beds, or in the dining booth, or in one of the seats back there either. Mama had chosen that moment to use the bathroom.

The commodes in that brand of camper were chemical toilets set in a prefabricated, self-contained metal unit which was dropped into the right rear corner of the camper during the last stages of manufacture. "That son-of-a-bitchin' little outhouse come out of there slick as you please," said the state trooper at the 911 Lounge. "Only thing left behind was the door. Truck'd given a spin to the unit like one of them gyroscopes my kid used to play with at Christmas."

"Mama," Mr. Johnson said as his mother and toilet unit spun by him at a speed later estimated as only slightly less than the Mother's trucker's.

The driver of the '78 Volvo later said in his statement: "I could see these two skinny white legs sticking straight out, horizontal. I think she had those pink, puffy slippers on that old ladies wear, but all I could see was this pink and white blur as the whole thing skipped down the highway."

Two hundred and eighty-six feet. I know it's not an exaggeration because I walked it myself with a measuring wheel while the state trooper paced it off beside me and his partner stopped traffic in that lane. For a while that stretch of I-465 always had a cop car parked along the median breakdown lane while some new guy was being told the story.

I don't know the resolution of that claim because we moved to Denver not long after that. I know that the Mother's trucker carrier sued State Farm, we sued them, several of the other involved cars' drivers sued the Johnsons, Mr. and Mrs. Johnson sued the Mother's trucker, and—this was the best part—Mama sued her son and his wife, not only for payment of medical bills resulting from the broken hip and bruised ribs, but for "reckless endangerment and grievous embarrassment resulting from public humiliation."

I think it's still in the courts.

Caroline and I came down the Slide as slowly as I could without bringing the sled to a stop. It was fast enough. The slope slanted at forty degrees or more much of the way and we must have been going thirty miles per hour on the straightaways. That's negligible in a car but can be felt viscerally when you're hurtling down a hill in the open with your rump two inches off the concrete. The teenagers behind us were shouting at us to speed up. I ignored them and concentrated on braking before the next corner so we weren't too high on the curve.

"How do you like it?" I called to Caroline over the wind and the roar of rollers under the sled.

"*Love* it!" she screamed back. Her hair blew up against my chin.

A final set of curves, a lessening of steepness, an absence of trees, and we were braking to a stop on the long, level section at the bottom of the slope. I helped Caroline up and out, clumsily got to my feet, and lifted the bulky sled out of the trough. The teenagers passed us, grumbling and slouching.

"Again, Daddy, please? *Please?*" said Caroline.

"No way," I said. The trick is to know when to be firm.

"Six-fifty, please," said the woman behind the glass. "I told you it would've been cheaper to buy the ten-dollars-for-two-rides-each special."

The dead bodies were kept in PSF-1, the Primary Storage Facility at Tan Son Nhut. There was a morgue at the base and another refrigerated portable unit near the main hangar, but PSF-1 was where the bodies waited between final processing and the flight home. Some of the idiots in the battalion called it the DEROS Hilton or Preboarding for Stupid Fuck-ups-1.

A lot of the young men I processed to be sent home from Vietnam were accident victims. Some of the accidents were combat or weapons related, but most were the result of mishaps with Jeeps or heavy equipment or those damn mopeds you saw everywhere in and around Saigon. Prairie Midland would have made a fortune selling premiums in Vietnam.

I remember being called out of the trailer I was using as an office to look at the body of a kid who'd been screwing around with his buddies, pretending to attach some C-4 explosive to an ARVN APC. This kid had lain down and pretended to stick grenades in the tread wheels as the APC rolled past, something his buddy said they'd seen in a movie called *Darby's Rangers,* when the South Vietnamese driver'd gotten fed up. Seven tons of armored personnel carrier had backed over this young Spec-4. On reinforced asphalt, not mud.

I didn't look at the body, but I remember that the body bag had looked as limp as my garment bag with only one suit in it. Later, doing the paperwork on him, I noticed that the kid was being shipped to Princeville, Illinois, a little town only a few miles from where I'd lived in Elmwood after we moved from Chicago.

It was in Elmwood that I first realized that I was really going to die someday. It was a Saturday evening in late August of the summer of 1960, only a few days before school was scheduled to start again. I was twelve and ready to start seventh grade and had forgotten to get my "junior high physical," even though the junior high was nothing more than some new classrooms tacked onto the same elementary school I'd been attending. Still, you couldn't sign up for seventh grade unless you'd had your physical.

I have no idea how or why I'd been able to see our town's only doctor late on a Saturday afternoon, but I had. Things were weird then. Physicians even used to come to sick people's homes.

This particular doctor had fled from Hungary two years earlier. He blended right into life in Elmwood except that he dressed bizarrely, smelled really weird, combed his hair strangely, looked different, and spoke so almost no one could understand him. He was also a mean bastard. His name was Dr. Viskes but every kid in town called him Dr. Vicious.

I remember I'd received several shots—the old fashioned kind with the dull needles that went back into the autoclave. I suspect Dr. Viskes reused his until they were too dull to break the skin. Anyway, I was on my way to War Memorial Park to watch the Free Show.

Elmwood's only movie theater—forty-six seats—was closed in the summer because Don and Deedee Ewalt, the owners, always went up to their place on Big Pine Lake in Minnesota. But their son, Harmon, even though he was a successful dentist in Peoria, almost an hour's drive away, had made a tradition out of bringing a 16-mm projector and film canisters of some recent release to give the Free Show against a white canvas screen stretched across the front of the bandstand in Memorial Park. Families picnicked on blankets or watched from their cars pulled up to the curb, and it was an infinitely more pleasant experience than going to Ewalt's Theater.

This was the last Free Show of the summer and I was rushing there after my physical, sore arms and all, when it suddenly struck me that I was going to die.

Not then, probably. Not that night, perhaps. But someday. Inevitably. Irrevocably.

I felt as if the wind had been knocked out of me. I stumbled backward and sat on a low stone near where the grass met the asphalt of Third Street. I could hear the sound track of the cartoon from the Free Show a block away.

Death was real. It was unavoidable. We all knew it and pretended to accept it but nobody *believed* it. I didn't. Death was something we put off in our minds the way we contrived not to think about scheduled trips to the dentist or the resumption of school after a summer of freedom. Something might come up to change things . . . events would postpone the dental appointment . . . there would be other vacations.

But death was *it.* I lowered my forehead to my knees, stared at my sneakers, and tried to breathe.

One of the days of the week I was tripping blithely through would someday be *the* day. The day on which I died. It *had* to be one of those seven days. Which one? *Saturday?* It didn't seem fair to die on a Saturday. *Sunday? Monday? Tuesday? Wednesday?* Wednesday . . . my favorite TV show, "Man Into Space" with William Lundigan, was on Wednesday evening. *Thursday? Friday?*

The warehouse and our administrative battalion HQ were on the opposite side of the airfield from the civilian and military terminal complexes. The outward bound C-130's and C-5A's would taxi away from the main hangar area, cross the head of the main runway as if they were ready to fly out, and then taxi over to our side of the field where they'd load up with their real cargo.

The Tan Son Nhut warehouse was always very hot. The steel transport boxes were supposed to be hermetically sealed, airtight, but the air was always heavy with the sweet smell of decay. It reminded me of the renderer's truck that used to come by on the evening streets of Elmwood.

Years after I came back from Vietnam, I began to think of the place as just another accident, as if the entire U.S.A. had been a Ford Fairlane or Buick Regal and Vietnam just a wall or tree that had gotten in the way when the driver's attention was elsewhere. Or maybe it was a DUI-related wreck. Who cares now? Minor damage. Hell, everybody knows that we kill as many Americans on the highway each year as we managed to obliterate in almost a decade of effort in Vietnam. Only we don't erect black walls to commemorate the highway victims. Or bring all the bodies to a single warehouse.

That night in Elmwood twelve years before PSF-1, I sat for a while until the sense of having been belted in the solar plexus faded and went away. But the sense of something having changed forever did not fade.

Eventually, I rose, dusted off my jeans, rubbed my aching arms, and walked the rest of the way to the last Free Show of the summer.

Riding the chair lift toward the beginning of our second slide, Caroline said, "Daddy, do you believe in God?"

"Mmm?" I said. I'd been watching the dark cumulus appearing and building above Peak 8.

"Do you believe in God? Mommy doesn't, I don't think, but Carrie down the street does."

I cleared my throat. I'd rehearsed my answer to this dreaded question so many times in the past few years that my prepared answer, if printed in full, could have served as a curriculum for a semester-long philosophy course with a comparative religion course thrown in. "No," I said to Caroline, "I guess I don't."

Caroline nodded. We were nearing the end of the lift ride. "I guess I don't either, at least from what Carrie says about God, but sometimes I think about it."

"About God?"

"Not exactly," said Caroline. "But about how if there's no God then there's no heaven and if there's no heaven . . . then where's Scout?"

We were approaching the unloading platform. The male teenaged attendant was busy talking to two female teenaged attendants. "Here," I said to Caroline as we approached the tricky part, "give me your hand. Don't let go."

There was no claim, but let's treat it as if there were. Call the family Family X. Mr. and Mrs. X, a son five-and-a-half, and a daughter not quite four.

The move from Indianapolis to Oregon was good for Mr. and Mrs. X. The father was becoming an independent adjustor after years of working for a large company. The mother was going to use her new degree to teach at a local college rather than in public schools. The kids were looking forward to a bigger yard, woods nearby, a lake in the neighborhood, new friends, all the things kids look forward to.

The new house was in a suburb of Portland called Lake Oswego and both house and suburb were beautiful. The yard was landscaped, rain-forest lush, and a delight after the years of Colorado near-desert. There was a small building behind the main house where Mr. X was going to have his office. He never used it.

As with all accidents, a change in any one of a hundred small decisions could have avoided it. As with all accidents, nothing did.

Mr. X was busy in the house with the movers but took time to tell the kids they could play in the lower garden area of the backyard but to stay away from the moving van. Mrs. X was in the bedroom at the far end of the house, supervising the unpacking. She said later that she thought the children were in the front yard.

On his previous load, one of the movers had taken out the son's new bicycle and left it in the driveway. The boy had just received a twenty-inch bike because he had worn out his sixteen-incher. The boy was made for wheels. Friends said that the boy had his father's eyes and hair. But his headlong courage was his own.

The two children came up out of the lower garden area and the boy saw his new two-wheeler waiting for him just beyond the stoop. He ran for it at the same instant the driver backed the van up—just a yard or so—to get a better angle for moving the piano in.

It was Caroline's screaming that told me something was wrong. When I first came out, I thought something had happened to the driver—he was on his knees by the side of the truck, sobbing almost hysterically. Caroline was silent by then, but I followed the path of her horrified gaze and saw what had happened.

Scout had not been run over. The rear of the truck had barely connected, or so it seemed for a moment until I felt the terrible softness under his hair at the base of his skull. I lifted him without thinking, turned toward the house, then turned away as if I was going to run down the driveway and carry him all the way to the hospital. I held him while Kay came closer, saw how serious it was, ran in to call the authorities, and then came back out to brush the hair off his face while I stood there holding him. I was still holding him, rocking him, when the ambulance arrived.

I remember that Kay put her arm around the driver at one point as if *he* were the one who needed consoling. For a second I hated her for doing that. I still do.

The moving company's insurance carrier later offered a cash settlement. Money changed hands. As if it mattered.

"Can I do down by myself?"

"I'm not sure, kiddo. You have to pull back very hard to slow the sled down once it gets going. I'm not sure you're strong enough to do it by yourself."

"Please, Daddy. I'll be careful."

"Let me think a second, Caroline."

"Okay, let's keep it moving," called the kid at the head of the Slide. There was no one behind us. I noticed for the first time that the chair lift had stopped bringing people up, probably because of the dark clouds massing over the mountain.

"Daddy?"

"All right." I lifted her into the blue sled. She looked very small in it.

I pulled an orange sled into the trough for myself and clambered in. The attendant went through his bored litany and tapped Caroline on the back. She looked back once, pressed the stick forward, and began moving down the steep incline. Too late, I realized that I should have gone in front of her, to slow her down if things got out of control.

My heart pounding, I leaned forward and followed her.

When I was in the clinic, I'd have the same dream almost every night. Perhaps it was the medication.

I would dream that I was in front of a class teaching geometry, pointing to a diagram painted on a red wall. The diagram was of an inverted cone. I pointed to the circle at the top of the cone. "The diameter is in units of potential," I said. "The circumference in units of available choices. At birth both are nearly infinite."

I ran my pointer down the outside of the cone in a descending spiral. "Imagine," I said, "that the vertical distance is comprised of units of time which also correspond to the units of choice in the dwindling circumference. As time passes, as an increasing number of choices is made, it is obvious that a nearly infinite number of alternate choices are thus eliminated."

The pointer would descend, spiraling down the outside of the cone. "Please note," I would say, "how the rapid descent through time and the increasingly smaller set of choices bring one *here*." I tap the lowest point of the cone. "Time left—zero. Choices remaining—zero. Potential from which to draw—zero." I pause. "It is, of course, a diagram of life."

The students nod and busily scribble their notes. All the students are Scout. Every one.

Caroline isn't using her brake very much. We are going down much faster than we did the first time. I shout for her to slow down. Lightning flashes somewhere behind us. The thunder is almost lost under the roar of our sleds. I try to catch up.

She is going much too fast.

A lot of unexplained single-vehicle highway deaths are suicides. Police put "unexplained" or "lost control" or "possible insect in vehicle caused driver to lose control" but I suspect that more often than not it's a combination of high speed, a bridge abutment, and the sudden knowledge of opportunity. Homicide is also popular. Quite a few of Prairie Midland's messier files were cases of vehicular homicide that couldn't be proved.

My last file in Oregon was a possible Orange File case about a woman who'd followed her husband to his girlfriend's house, waited all night, then trailed him to work. When he left the building for lunch, she roared across the parking lot and two lanes of traffic to run him down with her 1987 Taurus.

The husband was more wary than most. He saw her coming and jumped back through the revolving doors. His wife couldn't stop the Taurus before it smashed into the wall.

Neither our insured nor his wife were injured. The lawsuit came from a forty-six-year-old computer programmer working in the basement office below. One of the bricks from the wall the driver destroyed fell through the acoustical tile and klonked the programmer right on the forehead. He's asking for $1.2 million. If the trial goes to jury, he'll probably get a good chunk of it. Those who say America will never go socialist overlook the fact that our legal system has already discovered a way to rearrange the wealth in this country.

For the first few months it wasn't too bad—Caroline needed me at least when she woke screaming in the night—but eventually I knew I had to leave.

I'd follow her to school in the morning even though I wasn't living at home any longer. Sometimes I would sit in the park across the street and look at the windows of her classroom, trying to catch a glimpse of the top of her head. I'd greet her at the end of each day and walk her home, returning later with my car to watch the house from across the street. Sometimes I would come back to stay a few days, a week, but I knew how impossible it was to *really* protect them while I was there. To see what's going on you have to be outside, close but outside.

Caroline and I are the only ones on the Alpine Slide. She isn't slowing so I try to speed up to catch her. There is nothing I can really do. We are on separate sleds. But if she crashes, if she flies off, if she goes sliding up and over the wall, I have to be right there to follow her.

She looks back when we come rushing out of a stand of aspen trees, their leaves shimmering against the black backdrop of sky. I shout at her to slow down, knowing even as I do so that my words have been lost in the wind.

Not long before things really came unraveled for me, I went to one of Kay's faculty parties. I'd never really liked most of her public school teaching colleagues. I liked her college colleagues even less.

This night some asshole in the regulation uniform of a tweed sportscoat with leather patches at the elbows asked me what business I was in and I said, "Entropy."

"Interesting," said the asshole, twitching his granny glasses. "I teach physics. Perhaps our interests overlap."

"I doubt it," I said. I'd had several double Scotches since I'd arrived at the party but I felt nothing. I said, "I only get involved when entropy's out of its bed at midnight."

A second asshole, one I vaguely recognized as Kay's department chair, joined the conversation without being invited. "What an interesting phrase," he said, his accent making me think of someone from Brooklyn who'd spent years in England. "Is it yours?"

"Uh-uh," I said, delighted to show these guys up. "Shakespeare's." I'd heard the phrase in some Shakespearean play I'd attended when I was in college and it had stuck with me. I was certain it was Shakespeare.

"Oh, I doubt that," said asshole number two, laughing politely.

"Doubt it all you want," I snapped, suddenly angry. "Shakespeare wrote it. I can't help it if you don't know the classics."

The physics guy adjusted his glasses. His voice was soft but I was sure that I could hear the smugness underneath. "It's a neat phrase," he said, "but it doesn't seem likely that Shakespeare coined it. Entropy really wasn't a concept in the sixteenth century."

"Could it have been another word, perhaps?" asked the English department asshole.

"Or another playwright?" said the physics man.

"It was Shakespeare," I said, trying to think of a truly witty, college faculty–level zinger to leave them with. I settled for throwing my Scotch glass on the floor and stalking from the room.

I spent about four months reading through Shakespeare's plays, starting with *Hamlet* and *Macbeth*—ones that I remembered attending for courses I was taking—and then going through the others. I discovered something interesting. There was tragedy in most of his so-called comedies and definitely comedy—no matter how brief—in the worst of his tragedies.

I finally found it. The line was from *King Henry IV.* Part I, Act II, Line 328. Only it read—"What doth gravity out of his bed at midnight?"

Well, I figured as philosophically as I could, *the hell with it.*

We are less than halfway down the Slide and Caroline shows no signs of slowing.

We bank high around curves, slam onto straightaways, and ride higher into even sharper curves. It is like tobogganing on concrete.

Our velocity increases as we go lower. I dread the last part.

The Orange File was born back in Indianapolis when I pulled the Johnson file and a few others and couldn't find a file folder for them. Some temporary secretary—I think it was Gwen—had ordered some absurd orange folders, so I retrieved one from the waste basket and slid the file in my drawer.

It's very thick now.

Two weeks ago, before I left Oregon to give things one more try in Colorado, two cars were going opposite directions on a narrow county road near the coast. Thick fog rolls in. No center stripe. Guy driving the southbound '88 BMW decides to roll his window down and stick his head out for a better view just as the guy in the northbound '87 Audi decides to do the same thing . . .

Last week Tom called with the claim file of a dentist named Dr. Dick who'd take his mistress for a long lunch-hour ride in his brand-new Jag convertible, leather interior. . .

Shit.

Most accidents are like the one Caroline and I just missed yesterday. Broken glass gleaming in the light of flares. Possessions scattered across a hillside. Glimpses of bodies under sheets or still caught in a vice of twisted metal or lying impossibly contorted among the weeds. More blood than you can imagine. There'd been so little blood with Scout. I noticed that as I held him, reassured myself with that fact even as he cooled in my arms.

Caroline is going very, very fast, but I'm heavier and I catch up. The front of my sled almost touches the back of hers. She is very intent upon what she is doing, caught up in the ecstasy of controlled speed. She concentrates very intensely on the coming curve. As we rocket around it, the front of my sled inches from the back of hers, I see that she is smiling, cheeks flushed.

Accidents are like death. Waiting for us everywhere. Inevitable. Unavoidable. Plan as we might, they defy our planning.

But I'm beginning to see that there is a difference between gravity and entropy. The contents of the Orange File are all true, but the Orange File is a lie. My lie.

"Hi, Daddy!" Caroline takes a second look over her shoulder and waves, then returns her attention to the control stick, preparing for the next series of curves. It has been a long time since I've seen her this happy.

I wave back when she isn't looking and pull back on the stick, slowing slightly. The distance between her sled and mine widens.

A bunch of brain-dead fundamentalists are picketing and pamphleteering the high school near where Kay and Caroline live. Where I may be living soon. Last year, Kay says, it was for hiring "secular humanists." This year it's because some science teacher worked up enough conviction in his profession to tell the kids that all research suggests that life on this Earth is an accident, that if you take a kettle of primordial soup and shake it enough, shock it enough, even freeze it enough, you get organic compounds. Allow these compounds to suffer random accidents long enough and you get life.

That's life with a capital L.

The fundamentalists are outraged that something as sacred and important as Life could be an accident. They want it to be a result of a command, a plan, a blueprint, a simple, orderly, well-engineered, easily understood project designed by a deity who, like Kay's dad, would figure all tolerances and fudge them by a safety factor of five or ten.

Well, fuck them. Accidents happen. We're one of them. But our loving each other's not an accident. Nor our enjoyment of the days we have together. Nor our anxieties for each other and our fear of sharp edges when our children learn to walk.

But, like Scout, sometimes we have to be brave and hurl ourselves headfirst into space, knowing that someone we love will be there to catch us if they can.

Caroline's far ahead of me now. Her yellow sweatshirt is very bright as she flashes around the curves and roars ahead on the straight stretches.

I pull back on my stick, slowing to a more sedate descent, one which matches my mood. I want to look from side to side, to see the country go by. I may not be on this particular mountain again.

I hear Caroline's happy laughter ahead of me and the love I feel for her expands to painful dimensions. I don't mind the pain. We've outrun the storm but I hear the sky rumble and feel moisture touch my cheek.

We're farther down than I had realized. I can see the bottom now, but we're far enough away that there's ride enough left to enjoy. Caroline is flying now. She takes a second to lift a hand my way, then looks ahead. I lose sight of her for a moment as she passes through a grove of trees but I have confidence that she will reappear and she does, much farther down the mountain, a blue and yellow blur, her sled in perfect balance between gravity and speed, her spirit in perfect balance between control and joy.

Knowing that she's not looking, I lift a hand and wave.

And wave again.

DYING IN BANGKOK

I fly back to Asia in the late spring of 1992, leaving one City of Angels which had just exorcised its evil spirits in an orgy of looting and flame and arriving in another where the blood demons are gathering on the horizon like blackened monsoon clouds. My home city of Los Angeles had gone up in flames and insane looting the month before; Bangkok—known locally as Krung Thep, "the City of Angels"—is preparing to slaughter its own children on the streets near the Democracy Monument.

All of this is irrelevant to me. I have my own blood score to settle.

The minute I step outside the air-conditioned vaults of Bangkok's Don Muang International Airport terminal, it all comes back to me: the heat, over a hundred and five Fahrenheit, the humidity as close to liquid air as atmosphere can get, the stink of carbon monoxide and industrial pollution, and the open sewage of ten million people turning the air into a cocktail thick enough to drink. The smell and the heat and the humidity and the intense tropical sunlight combine to make breathing a physical effort, like trying to inhale oxygen through a thick blanket moistened with kerosene. And the airport is twenty-five *klicks* from the center of town.

I feel myself stir and harden just to be there.

"Dr. Merrick?"

I nod. A yellow Mercedes from the Oriental Hotel is waiting for me. The liveried driver tries to make small talk during the ninety-minute ride until he notices that I am not responding. Then he settles into a sullen silence while I listen to the hum of the air conditioner and concentrate on watching Bangkok unfold like the petals of some cement-and-steel flower.

There is no scenic way into Bangkok today unless one were to ride a *sampan* upriver into the heart of the city. The commute into the old section of Bangkok now is pure capitalist madness: traffic jams, Asian palaces that are really new shopping malls, industrial clutter, new elevated expressways being built, ferro-concrete apartment towers, billboards hawking Japanese electronics, the roar of motorcycles, and the constant arc-flash and jackhammer-thud of new construction. As is the case with all of Asia's new megalopolises, Bangkok is tearing itself down and rebuilding itself daily in a frenzy that makes Western cities such as New York look as permanent as the pyramids.

David, my driver, makes a last bid for tourist advice and to sell his own services as a driver during my stay at the Oriental, and then we are in the heart of the city, cruising down the tree-lined lanes of Silom Road amidst the two-stroke roar of *tuk-tuks* and the more aggressive scream of Suzuki motorcycles.

Silom Road is jammed with people but looks empty and lethargic compared to its usual crush of manic crowds. I glance at my watch. It is 8 P.M. on a Friday night Los Angeles time: eleven o'clock Saturday morning here in Bangkok. Silom Road is resting, waiting for the evening excitement which emanates from Patpong like the scent of a bitch in heat. One final turn down a nondescript *soi,* or sidestreet, and we are slowing in the main drive of the Oriental Hotel and more uniformed men are rushing to open the door of the Mercedes.

In crossing the ten yards or so from the driveway to the air-conditioned interior of the Oriental, I can smell it. Through the pollution and the stink of the river just out of sight beyond the hotel, through the heavy miasmal mix of human sewage and hibiscus bordering the hotel drive, and the carbon monoxide swirling like an invisible fog, I can smell it: an urgent scent like a subtle blend of exotic perfume, the Clorox tang of semen, and the coppery taste of blood.

I hurry through the courteous greetings and the bowed *wais* and the gracious registerings of the world's finest hotel, wanting only to get to my room and shower and feign sleep, to lie there and stare at the teak and plaster ceiling until the sunlight fades and the night begins. Darkness will bring this particular City of the Angels alive—or at least stir the corpse of it into slow, erotic motion.

When it is well and truly dark, I rise, dress in my Bangkok street clothes, and go out into the night.

The first time I saw Bangkok had been almost exactly twenty-two years earlier, in May of 1970. Tres and I had chosen Bangkok as our destination for the seven days of out-country R&R we had coming to us. Actually, I don't know many grunts who called it R&R back then: many called it I&I . . . intercourse and intoxication. Married officers used their leave to meet wives in Hawaii, but for the rest of us grunts the Army offered a smorgasbord of destinations ranging from Tokyo to Sydney. A lot of us chose Bangkok for four reasons: 1) it was easy to get to and didn't use up a lot of our time in travel 2) the cheap sex 3) the cheap sex and 4) the cheap sex.

To tell the truth, Tres had chosen Bangkok for other reasons and I followed along trusting in his judgment, much the way I did when we were out on a LURP: a long-range reconnaissance patrol. Tres—Robert William Tindale III—was only about a year older than I was, but he was taller, stronger, smarter, and infinitely better educated. I'd dropped out of my Midwestern college in my junior year and just rattled around until the draft sucked me in. He had graduated from Kenyon College with honors and then enlisted in the infantry rather than go on to graduate school.

Tres' nickname came from the Spanish word for "three" and was pronounced *tray*. Most of us had nicknames in the platoon—mine was Prick because of the heavy PRC-25 radio I'd carried around during my short stint as RTO—but Tres came to us with his nickname in place. Someone had got a peek at his papers and before his first week was out, we were all shaking our heads at the fact that—with all of his education and typing skills, attributes that generally allowed even a draftee to be a happy REMF (Rear Echelon Mother Fucker)—Tres *had enlisted in the infantry as a line grunt.*

Tres had a deep interest in Asian cultures and was good at languages. He was the only grunt in the company who could speak any real Vietnamese. Most of us thought that *beaucoup* was Vietnamese and felt clever to know *didi-mau* and half-a-dozen other corrupted local phrases. Tres *spoke* Vietnamese, although he kept that fact from reaching any officer other than our own L-T. "I wouldn't let them make me a typist or officer," he used to say to me. "I'll be goddamned if I'll let them turn me into some pissant interrogator."

Tres had never studied the Thai language, but he learned quickly.

"Just tell me what the Thai word is for 'blow-job,'" I'd said to him during the MAC flight from Saigon to Bangkok.

"I don't know," said Tres. "But the phrase for hand-job is *shak wao.*"

"No shit," I'd said.

"No shit," said Tres. He was reading a book and didn't look up. "It means 'pulling on the kite string.'"

I thought about that image for a minute. The transport was losing altitude, jouncing through clouds toward Bangkok. "I think I'll hold out for a blow-job," I said. I was not quite twenty years old and had only experienced oral sex once, with a college girlfriend of mine who had obviously never tried it before either. But I was full of hormones and macho posturing I'd picked up from the platoon, not to mention the sheer adrenaline rush of being alive after six months in the boonies. "Definitely a blow-job," I said.

Tres had grunted something and kept reading. It was some dusty book about Thai customs or mythology or religion or something.

I realize now that if I'd known what he was reading about and why he had chosen Bangkok, I probably wouldn't have stepped off the plane.

The floor valet, elevator doorman, concierge, and main doormen of the Oriental do not raise eyebrows at my wrinkled chinos and stained photographer's vest. At 350 American dollars a night their guests can wear whatever they want when they venture out into the city. The concierge does, however, step out to talk to me before I leave the air-conditioned sanity of the hotel.

"Dr. Merrick," he says, "you are aware of the . . . ah . . . tensions that exist in Bangkok at the current time?"

I nod. "The student riots? The military crackdown?"

The concierge smiles and bows slightly, obviously grateful at not having to educate the *farang* in what seems an embarrassing topic to him. "Yes, sir," he says. "I mention it only because while the problems have been concentrated near the University and the Grand Palace, there have been . . . ah . . . disturbances on Silom Road."

I nod again. "But there's no curfew yet," I said. "Patpong is still open."

The concierge smiles with no hint of a leer. "Oh, yes, sir. Patpong and the nightclubs are open for business. The city is very much open."

I thank him and go out, ignoring the huckstering for boat tours, taxi rides, and "good night fun" from the gaggle of small businessmen just beyond the hotel driveway. It is dark but the heat has not diminished and the traffic noise from the *soi* is louder than ever. I turn left on Silom Road and head for Patpong through jostling throngs of people.

It is not hard to recognize when I get there: the narrow streets connecting Silom and Suriwong roads are awash with cheap neon signs: MARVELUS MASSAGE, PUSSY GALORE, BABY A-GO-GO, SUPERGIRL LIVE SEX SHOWS, PUSSY ALIVE!, and a score of others. The lanes of Patpong are narrow enough to be pedestrian only, but the roar and pop of the three-wheeled *tuk-tuks* in the boulevards beyond provide a constant background to the rock-and-roll music blaring from speakers and open doors.

Young men or women—sometimes it is hard to tell in androgynous Thailand—begin plucking at my sleeve and gesturing toward doorways the moment I turn into the lane called Patpong One.

"Mister, best live sex shows, best pussy shows . . ."

"Hey, Mister, this way prettiest girls, best prices . . ."

"Want to see nicest shave pussy? Meet nice girl?"

"You want girls? No? You want boys?"

I stroll on, ignoring the gentle tugs at my sleeve. The last query had come as I entered the lane called Patpong Two. The night zone is divided into three areas: Patpong One serves straights,

Patpong Two offers delights to both straights and gays, and Patpong Three is all gay. The majority of the action here on Patpong Two is still for heterosexuals, although most of the bars have smiling boys as well as girls.

I pause in front of a bar labeled PUSSY DELITE. A little man with one arm and a face turned blue by the flickering neon steps forward and hands me a long plastic card. "Pussy menu?" he says, his voice the epitome of an upscale maître d's.

I take the grubby plastic card and study it:

> PUSSY BANANAS
>
> PUSSY COCA-COLA
>
> PUSSY CHOPSTICKS
>
> PUSSY RAZORBLADES
>
> PUSSY SMOKING

Nodding, I start into the busy nightclub. The one-armed maître d' hurries forward and retrieves his card.

The club is small and smoky with four bars set in a square around a crude stage. The girl on the stage—she looks to be no more than sixteen or seventeen—is arched completely backward, so that the top of her head almost touches the rough wood of the stage, her legs and arms supporting her in a crablike backbend. She is naked; her crotch has been shaved. Colored lights shaft down through the smoke and fall on her like soft lasers. The center of the stage is a turntable and the girl holds the arched position while her body rotates so that everyone can see her exposed genitals. There is a lighted cigarette set between her labia. As the stage revolves toward each section of the bar, smoke puffs from her vulva as if she is exhaling. Occasionally one of the drunker patrons applauds.

Most of the men in the bar are Thai, but there are plenty of *farang* scattered around: arrogant German-types in khaki with their hair slicked back, beaky Brits paying more attention to their drinks than to the girl on the stage, an occasional frowning Chinese from Hong Kong squinting through glasses, and a few fat Americans with untouched drinks and protruding eyes. There are no Japanese here; there is an exclusive area to the east of Patpong that the Japanese maintain for their businessmen on sex vacations. I've never seen the street, but I have heard that it is Ginza-clean, kept off-limits to others by security guards, and that the girls who serve the Japanese businessmen are required to take weekly HIV tests. At any rate, there are no Japanese here tonight.

I move up to the central bar and take an empty stool. The girl's upside-down face revolves three feet from me. Her eyes are open but unfocused. Her small breasts seem little more than swellings. I can count her ribs.

A bartender slides forward in the narrow space between the stage and bar and I ask for a cold Singha: the local beer costs fifty *baht* more here than in a regular bar, but it is still the cheapest thing I can order. The glass and can are no sooner set in front of me than a young Thai woman slides close, her left breast touching my bare forearm through her thin cotton tank top. Although she is no older than the girl whose genitals even now rotate our way again, she looks older because of the heavy makeup that now glows a necrous color in the shifting blue light.

She says something but the blare of rock and roll is so loud that I have to lean closer so she can repeat it. Her breast presses harder against my arm.

"My name Nok," she says again, almost shouting this time. "What your name?"

She is so close that I can smell the sweet talcum-and-perspiration scent of her through the cigarette smoke. Thais are among the cleanest people in the world, bathing several times a day. Ignoring her question, I say, "Nok . . . means bird. Are you a bird, Nok?"

Her eyes widen. "Do you speak Thai?" she asks in Thai.

I show no comprehension. "Are you a bird, Nok?" I ask again.

She sighs and says in English, "Yes, I a thirsty bird. Buy me drink?"

I nod and the bartender is there a fraction of a second later, pouring her the most expensive "whiskey" in the place. It is 98 percent tea, of course.

"You from States?" she asks, a bit of animation coming into her dark eyes. "I like States very much."

I brush her long hair out of her eyes and sip my beer. "If you're a bird," I say, "are you a *khai long?*" The phrase means "little lost chicken" but is often applied to street girls in Bangkok.

Nok pulls her head back and folds her arms as if I have slapped her. She starts to turn away but I grip her thin arm and pull her back against me. "Finish your whiskey," I say.

Nok pouts but sips the tea. We watch her friend on the stage as the girl's hairless vulva rotates our way again. The cigarette has burned down to the exposed labia. Sipping my beer, I marvel—not for the first time—at how human beings can turn the most intimate sights into the most grotesque. At the last second before the cigarette would burn her, the girl reaches down, retrieves it, takes a drag on it with the appropriate lips, tosses it between the stage and the bar, and wriggles out of her yoga backbend. Only one or two of the men along the bar applaud. The girl bounces offstage and an older Thai woman, also naked, steps onto the revolving platform, squats, and fans four double edged razorblades in the light.

I turn back to Nok. "I'm sorry I hurt your feelings," I say. "You are a very pretty bird. Would you like to help me have fun tonight?"

Nok forces a smile. "I love to make you fun tonight." She pretends to frown as if she has just thought of something. "But Mr. Diang . . ." she nods toward a thin Thai man with dyed red hair who stands in the shadows, "he be very mad at Nok if Nok not work all shift. Him I must pay if I go make fun."

I nod and take out the thick roll of *baht* I had changed dollars for at the airport. "I understand," I say, peeling off 4 five-hundred *baht* bills . . . almost eighty dollars. Even the highest-class bar-whores in Bangkok used to charge only two or three hundred *baht,* but the government ruined that a few years ago by bringing out a five hundred *baht* note. It seems cheap to ask for change, so now most girls charge five hundred for the act with another five hundred to pay their "Mr. Diangs."

She glances toward the old man with red hair and he nods ever so slightly. Nok smiles at me. "Yes, I have place for much fun."

I pull the money back. "I thought we might try to find someone to have fun with," I shout over the blasting rock and roll. In the corner of my vision I can see the woman on stage inserting the blades.

Nok makes a face; sharing the evening with other girls will cut down on her profit. *"Sakha bue din,"* she says softly.

I smile quizzically. "What does that mean?"

"It means you have enough fun just with Nok, who love you very much," she says, smiling again.

Actually, the phrase is shorthand for a northern village saying that goes "Your cock is on the ground, I tread it like a snake." I smile my appreciation at her kindness.

"This money would be just for you, of course," I say, setting the two thousand *baht* closer to her hand. "There would be more if we find exactly the right girl."

Smiling more broadly now, Nok squints at me. "You have girl in mind? Someone you know or someone I find. Good friend who also love you much?"

"Someone I know of," I say and take a breath. "Have you heard of a woman named Mara? Or perhaps her daughter, Tanha?"

Nok freezes and for an instant she *is* a bird—a frightened, captured bird. She tries to pull away but I still hold her arm.

"Na!" she cries in a little girl's voice. *"Na, na . . ."*

"There's more money. . ." I begin, sliding the *baht* toward her.

"Na!" cries Nok, tears in her eyes.

Mr. Diang takes a quick step forward and nods toward a huge Thai near the door. The two men cut through the crowd toward us like sharks through shallow water.

I let go of Nok's arm and she slips away through the crowd. I hold both hands up, palms out, and Mr. Diang and his bouncer stop five paces from me. The old man with the red hair tilts his head toward the door and I nod my agreement.

I drink the last long swallow of beer and leave. There are other places on my list. Someone's love of money will be greater than their fear of Mara . . .

Perhaps.

Twenty-two years earlier, Patpong had existed but American grunts could not afford it. The Thai government and the U.S. Army had cobbled together a red-light district of cheap bars, cheaper hotels,

and massage parlors on New Petchburi Road, miles from the more
businesslike Patpong.

We didn't give a shit where they sent us as long as the girls and
booze and drugs were there. They were.

Tres and I spent our first forty-eight hours trolling the bars and
clubs. Actually, we didn't have to leave our flophouse hotel to find
prostitutes—there were a dozen hanging around the lobby—but
somehow it didn't seem enough of a challenge just to take the
elevator downstairs. Like shooting sparrows in the barn after shining
the flashlight beam on them, Tres said. So we trolled Petchburi
Road.

During the first day and night in Bangkok I discovered what a
no-hands bar was. The food was lousy and the booze was overpriced,
but the novelty of having the girls feed us and lift the glasses to our
lips was memorable. Between feeding us bites and sips, they cooed
and winked and ran long-nailed fingers up the insides of our thighs.
It was hard to reconcile all of this with the fact that twenty-four
hours earlier we had been humping our rucks up the red-clay jungle
hillsides of the A Shau Valley.

That first six months of Vietnam were beyond anything in my
brief experience on this planet. Even now, with more than forty years
of life behind me, the heat and terror and exhaustion of jungle
warfare stands separate from everything else in my mind.

Separate from everything except what happened in Bangkok.

At any rate, we drank and whored our way through the
red-light district for forty-eight hours. Tres and I had taken separate
rooms so that we could bring girls back, and this we did. The cost
then for an evening of sexual favors was less than what I would have
paid for a case of cold beer from the firebase PX . . . and that wasn't
much. A T-shirt or pair of jeans given to our little girls would pay
for a week's worth of *mai chao* or "hired wives." They'd not only
screw or give head on command but they'd wash our clothes or tidy
up the hotel room while we were out looking for other girls.

You have to remember that this was in 1970. AIDS wasn't even
dreamt of then. Oh, the Army had made us bring rubbers along and
watch half a dozen films warning us about venereal diseases, but the
biggest threat to our health was Saigon Rose, a tough strain of

syphilis brought into the country by GIs. Still and all, our girls were so young and innocent looking, and stupid, I realize now, that they didn't even ask us to wear rubbers. Perhaps they thought that having a child by a *farang* was good luck or would somehow miraculously get them to the States. I don't know. I didn't ask.

But four days into our seven days of R&R, even the attraction of cheap Thai marijuana and cheaper sex was paling a bit. I was doing it because Tres was doing it; following his lead had become a form of survival for me in the boonies.

But Tres wanted something else. And I followed.

"I've found out about something really cool," he said early on the evening of our fourth night in the city. "Really cool."

I nodded. Tang, my little *mia chao*, had been pouting that she wanted to go out to dinner, but I'd ignored her and gone down to meet Tres in the bar when he called.

"It's going to take some money," said Tres. "How much do you have?"

I fumbled in my wallet. Tang and I had been smoking some Thai sticks in the room, and things were a bit luminescent and off-center for me. "Couple hundred *baht*," I said.

Tres shook his head. "This is going to take dollars," he said. "Maybe four or five hundred."

I goggled at him. We hadn't spent a fraction of that during our entire R&R so far. Nothing in Bangkok cost more than a couple of bucks.

"This is special," he said. "Really special. Didn't you tell me that you were bringing along the three hundred bucks your uncle sent you?"

I nodded dumbly. The money was stuffed in a sneaker in the bottom of my duffel upstairs. "I wanted to buy my ma something special," I said. "Silk or a kimono or something..." I trailed off lamely.

Tres smiled. "You'll like this better than a kimono for your mom. Get the money. Hurry."

I hurried. When I got downstairs there was a young Thai man waiting at the door with Tres. "Johnny," he said, "this is Maladung.

Maladung, this is Johnny Merrick. We call Johnny 'the Prick' in the platoon."

Maladung smirked at me.

Before I could explain that a PRC-25 radio was called a Prick-25 and that I'd humped it around for a month-and-a-half before they found a bigger RTO, Maladung had nodded at us and led the way out into the night. We took a three-wheeled *tuk-tuk* down to the river. Technically the broad river that had flowed all the way from the Himalayas to bisect the heart of old Bangkok was called the Chao Phraya, but all I ever heard the locals call it was Mae Nam—"the River."

We stepped out onto the darkened pier; Maladung snapped something at a man who stood on a long, narrow boat that was a mere shadow beneath the pier. The man answered something in response and Tres said, "Give me a hundred *baht* note, Johnny."

I fumbled in my wallet, trying to keep the dollars and colored *baht* separate. Only the light from a passing barge allowed me to find the proper note. I handed it to Tres, who gave it to Maladung, who handed it to the dark form in the boat.

"In, now," said Maladung and we climbed down into the boat. Tres and I sat on a narrow seat near the bow. Maladung sat halfway between us and the driver, whose face was visible only from the glow of his cigarette. Maladung snapped something in Thai, the huge engine roared behind us, and the boat leaped out into the river, its narrow bow pounding against the barge's wake.

I know now that these small boats are called "long-tailed taxis" and are for hire by the hundreds. They get their name from the long propeller shaft that has a full-sized automobile engine mounted on it. I noticed that night Tres and I boarded one that the shaft was so well counterbalanced that our driver could lift the prop out of the water with one hand, the heavy engine seemingly weightless in the center.

Bangkok is a city of small canals, or *klongs*. Guidebooks like to refer to it as "Venice East," but that is a typical guidebook oxymoron. The last time I was in Venice I did not notice thousands of *sampans* tied up along the canals, or rickety bamboo structures hanging out over the water like shacks on stilts, or a canal surface so thick with filth and storm debris that one could almost walk across it without getting wet.

I noticed all these things in the Bangkok *klongs* that night.

We headed downriver past the lights of the Oriental Hotel, a place Tres and I had heard of but could never dream of affording, and passed under a busy highway bridge. Our long-tailed taxi darted in front of a huge ferry with a roar of its V-6 engine, crossed toward the west bank, and then turned into a *klong* no wider than one of the narrow *sois* in the Patpong district. The little canal was pitch dark except for the weak glow of lantern light from the tied-up *sampans* and the overhanging shacks. Our driver had lit his own red lantern and hung it from a stanchion near the stern, but I had no idea how other boats avoided colliding with us as we roared around blind turns and under low bridges. Sometimes I was sure that the canvas roof of our taxi was going to collide with the underside of the sagging bridges, but even as Tres and I ducked we cleared the rotting timbers with inches to spare. The few other water taxis roared past us like noisy wraiths, their wakes slapping across our bow and splashing our knees. I looked at Tres as we passed a dimly lighted *sampan* and his eyes were wild. He was grinning broadly.

Just as I was about to shout a query as to where we were going, the driver throttled back and swung our boat directly toward a high pier with its tall pilings rising ahead of us like a slammed portcullis. I expected him to stop, or at least to throttle back so we could glide up to the dark barrier, but the driver opened the throttle with a roar and we leaped straight at the line of pilings.

"Jesus!" I yelled, but the cry was lost in the echo of our engine rattling back from the underside of the rotted pier above us. Then we swung right again and the shroud of our exhaust was bouncing off listing *sampans* that had the look of having been abandoned years earlier. The *klong* here was the canal equivalent of a back alley; there was not enough room for two boats to pass in opposite directions. There were no other boats.

For half an hour or more we twisted our way through these narrow one-way *klongs*. The stink of sewage was so strong here that my eyes watered. Several times I heard voices coming from the lightless and listing *sampans* that lined the canal like so many waterlogged wrecks.

"People *live* in those," I whispered to Tres as we passed a blackened mass where tumbledown shacks and half-sunken *sampans* had narrowed the *klong* to the point that even our suicidal driver had been forced to slow the boat to a crawl. Tres did not answer.

Just when I was sure that the driver had become lost in the maze of canals, we came to an open area of water bound about by abandoned warehouses on stilts and the backs of burned-out shacks. The effect was of a large, floating courtyard hidden from the city's streets and public canals. Several barges and black *sampans* were congregated in the center of this watery square, and I could see the dim running lanterns of several other long-tailed taxis that were tied up to the nearest *sampan.*

The driver cut the engine and we glided to the makeshift dock in a silence so sudden that it made my ears ache.

I had just realized that the "dock" was only a float comprised of oil drums and planks lashed to the *sampan* when two men stepped out through a ragged hole in the canvas side of the boat and stood balancing on the planks, watching us bump to a stop. Even in the dark I could tell that the two were built like wrestlers or bouncers. The closer of the two men barked something at us in Thai.

Maladung answered and one of the men took our line while the other stood aside to let us climb onto the small space. I stepped off the taxi first, saw a faint glow of lantern light through the ragged opening, and was about to step through when one of the men touched my chest with three fingers that seemed stronger than my entire arm.

"Must pay first," hissed Maladung from his place on the taxi.

Pay for what? I wanted to ask, but Tres leaned close and whispered, "Give me your three hundred bucks, Johnny."

My uncle had sent me the money in crisp fifties. I gave them to Tres, who handed two bills to Maladung and the other four to the closest man on the dock.

The men stepped aside and gestured me toward the opening. I had just bent to fit through the low doorway when I was startled by the sound of our boat's engine roaring to life. I straightened up in time to see the red lantern disappearing down a narrow *klong*.

"Shit," I said. "Now how do we get back?"

Tres' voice was tight with something greater than tension. "We'll worry about that later," he said. "Go on."

I looked at the ragged doorway that seemed to open to a corridor connecting the series of *sampans* and barges. Strong smells came from it and there was a muted sound rather like a large animal breathing somewhere down at the end of that tunnel.

"Do we really want to do this?" I whispered to Tres. The two Thai men on the dock were as inanimate as those statues of Chinese lion-dogs that guard the entrance to important buildings throughout Asia. "Tres?" I said.

"Yes," he said. "Come on." He pushed past me and squeezed through the opening.

Used to following his lead on patrol and night ambush and LURP, I lowered my head and followed.

God help me, I followed.

It is my second night in Patpong and I am watching a live sex show at Pussy Galore's when the four Thai men surround me.

The sex show is typical for Bangkok; a young couple screwing on twin Harley-Davidsons hanging from wires above the central stage. The two have been engaged in intercourse for over ten minutes. Their faces show no feigned passion, but their bodies are expert at revealing their coupling to every corner of the bar. The audience seems to find the primary tension not in the fucking but in the chance that the two might fall off the suspended motorcycles.

I am ignoring the show, interrogating a bar girl name Lah, when the brawny Thai shove in around me. Lah fades into the crowd. It is dark in the bar but the four men all wear sunglasses. I take a sip of flat beer and say nothing as they press closer.

"You are named Merrick?" asks the shortest of the four. His face is axe-blade thin and pockmarked with old acne or smallpox scars.

I nod.

The pockmarked man takes a step closer. "You have been asking about a woman named Mara here tonight and in other clubs last night?"

"Yes," I say.

"Come," he says. I make no resistance and the five of us move out of the bar in a flying wedge. Outside, a gap opens a bit between the burly men on my left and I could make a run for it if I choose. I do not so choose. A dark limousine is parked at the head of the lane and the man on my right opens the rear door. As he does so, I see the pearl-handled grip of a revolver tucked into his waistband.

I get in the backseat. The two tallest men sit on either side of me. I watch as the pockmarked man moves to the front passenger seat and the man with the revolver settles himself behind the wheel. The limo moves off through side streets. I know that it is sometime after 3 A.M. but the *soi* are still strangely empty this close to Patpong. At first I can tell we are moving north, parallel to the river, but then I lose all sense of direction in the maze of narrow side streets. Only the darkened signs in Chinese let me know that we're in the area north of Patpong known as Chinatown.

"Avoid *Sanam Luang* and *Ratchadamnoen Klang*," the pockmarked man says to the driver in Thai. "The army is shooting protesters tonight."

I glance to my right and see the orange glow of flames above rooftops. The staff at the Oriental had urged me not to go out tonight. Now the distant, almost soft, rattle and pop of small-arms fire can be heard over the hiss of the car's air conditioner.

We stop in an area of abandoned buildings. There are no streetlights here and only the orange glow of flames reflected from low clouds allows me to see where the street ends in vacant lots and half-demolished warehouses. I can smell the river somewhere out there in the darkness.

The pockmarked man turns and nods. The Thai on my right opens the door and pulls me out by my vest. The driver stays in the car while the other three drag me deep into the shadows near the river.

I start to speak just as the man behind me laces his fingers through my hair and pulls my head sharply back. The third man grabs my arms as the man holding my hair lifts a stiletto blade to my throat. The pockmarked face suddenly looms so close that I can smell fish and beer on the man's breath.

"Why do you ask about a woman named Mara with a daughter named Tanha?" he asks in Thai.

I blink my incomprehension. The blade draws blood just below my Adam's apple. My head is pulled so far back that I find it almost impossible to breathe.

"Why do you ask about a woman named Mara with a daughter named Tanha?" he asks again in English.

My words are little more than a rasping gargle. "I have something for them." I try to free my right hand but the third man restrains my wrist.

"Inside left pocket," I manage.

The pockmarked man hesitates only a second before tearing open my vest and feeling for the hidden pocket there. He brings out the twenty bills.

I can smell his breath on my face again as he laughs softly. "Twenty thousand dollars? Mara does not need twenty thousand dollars. There *is* no Mara," he concludes in English. In Thai, he says to the man with the knife, "Kill him."

They have done this before. The first man bends my head further back, the other man pulls my arms down sharply, while the pockmarked man steps back, fastidiously getting out of the way of the arterial spray that is coming. In that second before the knife slashes across my throat, I gasp out two words. "Look again."

I feel the tension increase in the knife-wielder's hand and arm as the blade cuts deeper, but the pockmarked man holds up one hand in a command. The blade has drawn enough blood to soak the collar of my shirt and vest now, but it cuts no deeper. The short man holds a bill high, squints at it in the dim light, and then flicks a cigarette lighter into flame. He mutters under his breath.

"What?" says the third man in Thai.

The pockmarked man answers in the same language. "It is a ten-thousand-dollar bearer's bond. They are *all* ten-thousand-dollar bonds. Twenty of them."

The other two hiss their breath.

"There is more," I say in Thai. "Much more. But I must see Mara."

My head is bent back far enough that I cannot see the pockmarked man now, but I can feel the intensity of his gaze on me. The temptation must be there for the three of them to kill me, dump my body, and keep the two hundred thousand dollars.

Only the fact that they answer to Mara gives me hope.

We stand there motionless for at least a full minute before the pockmarked man grunts something, the blade is lowered, my hair is released, and we walk back to the waiting limousine.

Tres had led the way through the tunnel carved through the arched canvas roofs of *sampans*. The first three boats were empty, the bottoms wet and the interiors smelling of rot and Asian cooking, but stepping through the wall of the third boat led us into dim light and loud noise. I realized as I stepped into the broader space that this was the barge we had seen tied up in the center of the *sampans*.

Several Thai men glanced at us as we stepped into the covered barge, and then they looked again, obviously surprised that *farang* were allowed there. But then their attention was drawn back to the makeshift stage in the center of the barge. I stood there blinking, peering through the heavy cloud of cigarette and marijuana smoke; the stage was no more than six feet by four feet, illuminated only by two hissing lanterns hanging from overhead trusses. It was empty except for two women performing cunnilingus on one another. Crude benches ran four deep around the stage and the twenty or so Thai men there were little more than dark shapes in the haze of smoke.

"What . . ." I began, but Tres hushed me and led the way to an empty bench to our left. The women on the stage were joined by two thin Thai men, little more than boys, who ignored the females as they caressed each other into an excited state.

I was tired of being hushed. I leaned closer to Tres and said, "What the hell did we have to pay three hundred American dollars for this when we can watch it for a couple of bucks in any bar on Petchburi Road?"

Tres just shook his head. "This is just the preliminary stuff,

Johnny," he whispered. "Warm-up acts. We paid for the main event."

A couple of men in front of us had turned and frowned, as if we were making too much noise in a movie theater. On the stage, the two boys had finished their preparations and had become involved with the young women as well as each other. The combinations were complicated.

I sat and crossed my legs. We didn't wear underwear in Nam because it caused crotch rot, and like a lot of grunts I'd gotten out of the habit of wearing it even while in civilian clothes on R&R. I wished I'd pulled on some jockey shorts under my light cotton slacks tonight. It seemed bad form to have a visible hard-on around all these other men.

The four young people on the stage explored combinations for another ten minutes or so. When they came—almost simultaneously— the women might have faked it, but there was no doubt that the men's orgasms were sincere enough. One of the Thai girls caught the semen on her breasts, while the other girl spread the second boy's jism on the buttocks of the first boy. The bisexual stuff disturbed me and excited me at the same time. I didn't understand myself well then.

Finished, the four young people simply stood and exited through a tunnel-door in the far wall. The patrons did not applaud. The stage was empty for several minutes and I thought that perhaps the night's program was over despite all of Tres' talk about main events, but then a short Thai man dressed in black silk shirt and trousers stepped onto the stage and said something in low, serious tones. I caught the word "Mara" twice. There was a sudden tension in the room.

"What did he . . ." I began.

"Shhh," said Tres, his eyes riveted on the stage.

"Fuck that," I said. I'd paid for this crap, I deserved to know what I was getting for my money. "What's a Mara?"

Tres sighed. "Mara is *phanyaa mahn,* Johnny. The prince of demons. He is the one who sent his three daughters—Aradi, discontent . . . Tanha, desire . . . and Raka, love . . . to tempt the Buddha. But the Buddha won."

I squinted through smoke at the empty stage and slowly

swinging lantern. A boat had passed through the hidden lagoon and its wake rocked the barge ever so slightly. "So Mara's a man?" I didn't know if I could take any more of this queer stuff.

Tres shook his head. "Not when the spirit of the *phanyaa mahn* combines with the *naga* in a demon-human incarnation."

I stared at Tres. We'd each smoked some good shit since we arrived in Bangkok—the Thai stick was almost free here—but Tres'd obviously been doing more than was good for him. He noticed my stare and smiled slightly. "Mara's the part of the world that dies, Johnny. . . the death principle. The thing we fear more than Charlie when we're out on night patrol. *Naga* is sort of a snake god that's associated with water. The river. It can take or give life. When the spirit of the *naga* is given to someone possessed by the power of the *phanyaa mahn*—Mara—the demon thing can be male or female. But what we paid to see was a female Mara that's supposed to be *phanyaa mahn naga kio.* That doesn't happen once in a thousand incarnations . . ."

I stared at Tres. His whisper was so soft that I could barely hear him, but some of the Thais had also turned to stare. I hadn't understood a fucking word he'd said. "What's a *kio?*" I said. I had the sinking feeling that I'd blown three hundred bucks on nothing.

"A *kio* is a . . . shhh," hissed Tres, pointing to the stage.

A woman came out onto the stage. She was dressed in traditional Thai silk and was carrying a small baby. Her face was sharp, almost masculine, and her hair was a nimbus of tangled black. She was older than the sex performers we had seen earlier, but still not much more than twenty. The baby mewled and tugged at the silk over her small breasts. I realized that the Thai men in the room were bowing slightly from where they sat. Some were making the traditional palms-together *wai* of obeisance. It seemed an odd thing to be doing toward a sex performer. I frowned at Tres but he was *wai*-ing too. I shook my head and looked back at the stage. Most of the men had put out their cigarettes now, but there was so much smoke in the covered barge that it was like peering through a fog.

The woman had gone to her knees on the stage. The baby hung limp in her arms. The man in black silk came onto the stage and said something in low, flat tones.

There was a long silence. Finally a fat Thai in the front row stood, turned to look once at the crowd, and then stepped onto the low stage. There was a general expulsion of breath and I could feel the tension in the room shift focus, if not actually lessen.

"What . . ." I whispered.

Tres shook his head and pointed. The fat man was handing over a thick roll of *baht* to the man in black silk.

"I thought everyone had to pay to get in," I whispered to Tres. He wasn't listening.

The man in black silk took a minute to count the money—there had to be many thousand of *baht* there—and then he stepped off the stage. As if on cue, the two young women we'd seen earlier came back out. They were dressed in some sort of ceremonial garb that I associated with a formal Thai dance I'd seen photos of; each wore a tall, peaked hat, weird shoulders, and a blouse and pants of gold silk. I began to wonder if I'd paid three hundred dollars to see four people have sex with their clothes on.

The two boys came onto the stage wearing costumes of their own and carrying an ornate chair. I was afraid we were going to get into more of the gay and lesbian stuff, but the boys merely set the chair down and disappeared. The two girls began to undress the fat man while the woman named Mara stared out at nothing, paying no attention to either the man, his attendants, or the crowd.

Having undressed the patron in an almost ritual manner and folded his clothes away, the girls pushed him back into the chair. I could see sweat beading the man's upper lip and chest. His legs appeared to be shaking slightly. If he had paid for some sort of erotic services, he certainly didn't seem to be in the mood for it all. The poor guy's cock was shriveled to almost nothing and his scrotum looked like it'd shrunk to walnut size.

The girls bent over and began to work on him with their hands and mouths. It took a while, but they were very good and within a few minutes the fat man's cock was hard and lifted high enough that the glans almost touched his belly. It still wasn't anything to write home about. Meanwhile, the ugly one named Mara was still staring out at nothing, the baby wiggling slightly in her arms. The woman seemed disinterested to the point of catatonia.

My heart began to pound then. I was afraid that they were

going to do something to the baby and the thought made me physically sick. If Tres had known that there would be an infant involved...

I glanced at him but he was looking at the hag named Mara with an expression of what might have been a mixture of fear and scholarly interest. I shook my head. This was weird shit.

The two girls left and the stage was empty except for the seated man with his modest erection and the woman with her child. Slowly Mara turned toward him and a trick of the lantern light made her eyes gleam almost yellow. It suddenly seemed too quiet in the barge, as if everyone had stopped breathing.

Mara stood, took three steps toward the man, and then went to her knees again. She was far enough away that she had to bend forward just to set her hand on his thigh. I noticed that her fingernails were very red and very long. The fat man's erection began to visibly flag at that point and I could see his balls rising again as if they wanted to hide in the protection of his body.

Mara seemed to smile at the sight. She leaned forward, still cradling the infant, and opened her mouth.

I expected oral sex then, but her head never came closer than eighteen inches to the man's genitals. Instead, her tongue slid out from between sharp and perfectly white teeth until it arched to a point where it could touch her own chin. The fat man's eyes were very wide now, and I could see his arms and belly quaking slightly. His erection had returned.

Mara shifted her head slightly, shook it as if loosening her neck, and her tongue continued to glide out. Six inches of it. Then eight. A foot of fleshy tongue sliding out of her open mouth like a pink adder uncoiling from its dark nest.

When eighteen or twenty inches of thin tongue had slid into sight, draped across the fat man's thigh, and began to wrap itself around his cock, I tried to swallow and found I could not. I tried to shut my eyes and found that my eyelids refused to close. Mouth open, breathing harshly, I just watched.

Mara's tongue slid around the head of the man's uncircumcised cock, pulling down the foreskin as it went. The lantern light reflected off the pink moistness of that tongue and glistened where it had lubricated the man's erection.

More tongue uncoiled, the tip of it spiraling down and around like the probing head of a wide-bodied serpent. The fat man closed his eyes just as the long tongue completely encircled his shaft, the narrow tip of that fleshy ribbon swaying and bobbing toward his tightened testicles. Mara's lashes also lowered but I could still see the glimmer of white and yellow under the heavy eyelids as the man's hips began to move.

The sight of that moist tongue in the yellow lantern light was terrible—nausea-inducing—but it was not the worst. The worst was the glimpse I had caught of the lesions on that tongue: openings, oblong slits in the fleshy inner part of the tongue as if someone had taken a very sharp scalpel and made a series of bloodless, centimeter-long incisions.

But these were no incisions. Even in the weak light I could see the fleshy lesions pulse open and then close of their own volition, like the feeding mouths of some hungry anemone surging in a soft tidal current. Then the tongue wrapped more tightly around the man's straining penis and I could see almost peristaltic contractions as the ribbon of pinkish flesh pulled and tightened, tightened and pulled. Mara closed her lips, pulled her head back like a fisherman with a hook deeply embedded, and the fat man moaned in ecstasy. He gripped the arms of the chair and pumped his hips more wildly, eyes half open now but seeing nothing but the red surge of his own pleasure.

Now, after years of experience as a physician, I know precisely what was occurring. It helps to think of it in clinical terms.

The overweight Thai man had experienced normal sexual arousal and had passed through the excitement phase to the plateau phase very quickly. Inside his penis, three spongy columns of tissue—the two long *corpora cavernosa* and the *corpus spongiosum* at the head of his penis—had become almost completely engorged with blood. All during the stimulation the penis continued receiving arterial blood from the dorsal, cavernous, and bulbourethral arteries while valves in the dorsal veins that drain blood from the penis shut off, allowing little or no blood to escape back into the body during the period of plateau excitement.

Meanwhile, that excitement continued to build. Involuntary tension included semispastic contractions of the Thai's facial, abdominal, and intercostal musculature. At the time, I witnessed that as a pained scowl on his straining, sweaty face and a rapid pumping of hips in the smoky light. If I had been taking his pulse, I would have found his heart rate climbing to somewhere between a hundred and a hundred seventy-five beats per minute. His systolic pressure shot up to somewhere close to 80mm Hg while his diastolic elevated to 40mm Hg or higher. At the same time, his rectal sphincter would be contracting and a maculopapular rash was beginning to spread across his face, neck, and chest.

Normally such symptoms meant the onset of orgasm, a brief spike into higher systolic and diastolic regions, and then a quick recovery as the body shifted to a resolution phase and blood flowed out of the now-open veins of the penis.

There was no such resolution.

Mara's tongue wrapped in tighter coils and continued to tug and flex. The fat man's face grew redder as he continued to pump his hips. His eyes were still open, but only the whites showed now. The head of his cock, just visible in the lantern light, seemed engorged to the point of bursting. A thick coil of tongue slid across it and around it.

The man went into what I now know are the final stages of ejaculatory response: muscle group spasms, loss of voluntary control of facial muscles, respiratory rates exceeding forty-per-minute, massive body flush, and a frenzied pumping of hips. In those days I just thought of it as coming.

Mara's head lowered as if she were reeling in her extended tongue. Her eyes were open now and very yellow. Eight or more inches of tongue were still wrapped around the man's thrusting cock as Mara lowered her red-lipped mouth to his groin.

The Thai man continued to writhe in the throes of orgasm. There was not a sound from the twenty or so men in the smoke-filled room. The man's groans were the only noise. His orgasm went on and on, far beyond the time it took for any male to ejaculate. Mara's distended face rose and fell, and each time it rose we could see the tongue still wrapped tightly around the man's still-rigid member.

"Jesus Christ," I whispered.

I know now that resolution-phase penile detumescence is rapid and involuntary. Within seconds of expelling seminal fluid, the penis begins a two-stage involution that begins with loss of about fifty percent of the erection in the first thirty seconds or so. Even when some vasocongestion remains—"keeping a hard-on" I would have called it in my 'Nam days—it is not, cannot be, a full pre-ejaculatory erection.

This Thai still had a full hard-on. We could see it every time Mara's mouth lifted above her coiled tongue. The Thai seemed to have succumbed to an epileptic fit: his legs and arms thrashed wildly, his eyes had rolled back in his head, his mouth was open and drool ran down his chin and jowls. He kept on coming and coming. Minutes passed—five, ten. I rubbed a hand across my face and my palm came away greasy with sweat. Tres was breathing through his mouth and staring with an expression suggesting horror.

Finally Mara pulled her mouth away. Her tongue unwrapped itself from the Thai's cock and slid back between her lips as if it were on a tension reel. The Thai let out a final groan and slid out of the chair; his erect penis was still thrusting into empty air.

"Christ Almighty," I whispered to myself, relieved that it was over.

It was not over.

Mara's lips looked swollen, her cheeks as puffed out as they had a second before. I had a momentary image of her mouth and cheeks filled with the huge, coiled tongue and I almost lost my lunch right there in the smoke-filled darkness.

Mara pulled her head back farther and for a second I noticed that her rouged lips seemed to be growing redder, as if she had somehow managed to apply a thick layer of glossy lipstick while performing oral sex. Then her mouth opened a bit more and the red slid down off her lips, dribbled across her chin, and spilled onto her gold silk blouse.

Blood. I realized that her cheeks and mouth were filled with blood; her obscene tongue gorged with blood. She choked it back and something like a smile filled her sharp features.

I fought back the nausea, lowered my head, and thought: *It's over now. It's over.*

It was not over.

The baby had been cradled in her left arm all during the endless fellatio, hidden from sight by Mara's head and the fat man's thigh. But now the infant was visible as its small arms clawed at Mara's blood-spattered blouse. Even as the woman arched her head further back as if sloshing the blood around in her mouth like a fine wine, the baby began pulling itself up her chest with its tiny fists sunken in gold silk, its mewling mouth pursing and opening.

I looked at Tres, found myself unable to speak, and looked back at the stage. The Thai boys had carried the still-unconscious fat man off the stage now and only Mara and her infant remained in the lantern light. The baby continued climbing until its cheek touched her mother's; I thought of a film I had seen of a tiny kangaroo baby, half-formed and almost embryonic, pulling itself through its mother's fur in the live-or-die trek from the birth canal to the pouch.

The baby began licking its mother's cheek and mouth. I saw how long the baby's tongue was, how it slid like some pink worm across Mara's chin and lips, and I tried to close my eyes or look away. I could not.

Mara seemed to come out of her trance, lifted the baby closer to her face, and lowered her mouth to the infant's. I could see the baby girl open her mouth wide, then wider, and I thought of baby birds demanding to be fed.

Mara vomited blood into the baby's open mouth. I could see the infant's cheeks fill and its throat work as it tried to swallow the sudden onslaught of thick liquid. The process was amazingly neat; very little of the heavy blood spilled onto the baby's gold robes or Mara's silk.

Spots danced in my vision and I lowered my head to my hands. The room was suddenly very hot and my vision tunneled to a narrow range. The skin of my forehead felt clammy to my touch. Next to me, Tres made a noise but did not look away from the stage.

When I looked up, the baby was almost finished feeding. I

could see its long tongue licking at Mara's lips and cheeks for any residue of the regurgitated meal.

Years later I stumbled across a *Scientific American* article titled "Food Sharing in Vampire Bats," dealing with reciprocal-altruism in donor bats regurgitating blood for roostmates. Vampire bats, it seemed, starved to death if they did not get a meal consisting of twenty to thirty milliliters of blood within sixty hours. It turned out that after the proper stimulus—the roostmate's licking under the donor bat's wings and on her lips—the donor would regurgitate blood only for those roostmates who would die within twenty-four hours without a blood meal. This reciprocal-exchange system was survival beneficial, said the article's author, because it allowed the recipient bat another night or two to search for blood, while only drawing twelve hours' worth of blood from the donor bat's sixty-hour reservoir.

But it was that *Scientific American* drawing of the smaller bat licking its donor's lips, leathery wings entwined, slash-lipped mouths moving toward each other in the blood-vomit kiss, that made me vomit into my office wastebasket twenty years after that night in Bangkok.

I remember little of the next few hours of that night. I remember the man in black silk returning to the stage and another Thai—a younger, thinner man in an expensive suit—stepping onto the stage and paying his money. I remember dragging Tres from that place and have vague memories of pressing a roll of *baht* into the hands of the driver of a long-tailed taxi on the pier outside. I would have swum from that place if I'd had to, leaving Tres behind. I vaguely remember the wind from our passage up the Chao Phraya River reviving me a bit, settling the nausea and inhibiting the surge of hysteria that threatened to engulf me.

I remember going alone to my room and locking the door that night. Tang, my *mia chao,* had disappeared, and for that I was grateful.

I remember staring at the slowly turning fan in the hour before sunrise and giggling as I worked out a simple translation. Unlike Tres, I had never been good at languages, but this translation was suddenly obvious. *Phanyaa mahn naga kio.* If *phanyaa mahn* were

Mara, the prince of demons, and if *naga* were the female serpent-demon incarnation of the *phanyaa mahn,* then *kio* could only mean one thing: vampire.

I lay there and giggled and waited for the sun to rise so that I could sleep.

The city is still burning and I can hear isolated automatic weapons fire from the government troops killing students as the four men take me to Mara.

There is no torturous trip through back *klongs* this time. The limousine crosses the river, drives south along the bank opposite the Oriental Hotel, and stops at an unfinished high-rise somewhere near the Tak Sin Road highway bridge. The pockmarked man leads us to an outside construction elevator, throws a switch, and we rumble into the night air. The elevator has no sides and I see the river and the city across the river in dreamlike clarity as we rise thirty stories and more into the thick night air. The river is as empty of traffic as I have ever seen it; only a few ferries fight the dark current downriver. Upriver, toward the Grand Palace and the universities, flames light up the night.

We rise toward the fortieth floor and a wind ruffles my hair. I am the one nearest the edge of the open, grinding platform. All the pockmarked man has to do is push me from behind and I would tumble to the river four hundred feet below. I wonder idly if falling will feel like my dreams of night-flying in the seconds before I strike.

We reach one of the top levels and the crude elevator squeals to a stop. A gate slides up and the pockmarked man beckons me out.

Somewhere above us, a welding torch flashes arc-strobes and drips magnesium-white sparks. Construction does not stop for sleep in modern Bangkok. The building has no sides here, only clear plastic draped from open beams to separate sections of the cement expanse from one another. A hot wind rustles the plastic with a sound not unlike the stirring of leathery wings.

Trouble lights hang from girders and more lights are visible through walls of plastic to our left. The five of us walk toward the light and sound. At the entrance, a sort of tunnel made from rustling plastic sheets, the three bodyguards stay behind and only the pockmarked man lifts the plastic, beckons me forward, and follows me in.

There is no stage here, but a dozen or so folding chairs are set up around an open area where an expensive Persian rug has been set on the dusty cement floor. The lamp overhead is shielded so that the space is more in shadow than direct light. Six men, all Thai and all in sleek tuxedos, sit on the folding chairs. Their arms are crossed. Two of them are smoking cigarettes. They watch me as the pockmarked man leads me forward.

I have eyes only for the two women sitting across the open space in heavy rattan chairs. The older woman might be my age or a little older; she has aged well. Her hair is still black, but now swept up in a fashionable arc. Her Asian features are unlined, her cheeks and chin still strong, and only a certain corded look in her neck and hands suggests that she is in her forties. She wears an elegant and obviously expensive gown of black and red silk; a gold-and-diamond pendant hangs across her red vest and stands out against the black silk blouse.

The younger woman next to her is infinitely more beautiful. Olive-skinned, dark-eyed, with lustrous hair that has been cut short in the newest western style, gifted with a long neck and elegant hands that exude grace even in repose, this young woman is beautiful in a way that no actress or model could ever achieve. It is obvious that she is content in herself, simultaneously aware and oblivious of her own beauty, and that whatever passions rule her, the seeking of admiration or acceptance of others is not one of them.

I know that I am looking at Mara and her daughter Tanha.

The pockmarked man steps closer to them, goes to his knees in the way that the Thai do to show deference to royalty, performs an elaborate *wai,* and then offers Mara my roll of twenty bonds without lifting his bowed head. She speaks softly and he answers respectfully.

Mara sets the money aside and looks at me. Her eyes catch the yellow gleam of the shielded lamp above.

The pockmarked man looks up, nods me forward, and reaches to pull me to my knees. I genuflect of my own accord before he can grasp my sleeve. I lower my head and keep my eyes on Mara's slippered feet.

In elegant Thai, she says, "You know what you are asking for?"

"Yes." I answer in Thai. My voice is firm.

"And you are willing to pay two hundred thousand American dollars for it?"

"Yes."

Mara purses her lips. "If you know about me," she says very softly, "then you must know that I no longer perform this . . . service."

"Yes," I say, head bowed in deference.

She waits in a silence that I realize is a command to speak. "The Reverend Tanha," I say at last.

"Raise your head," Mara says to me. To her daughter, she murmurs that I have *jai ron*—the hot heart.

"Jai bau dee," says Tanha with a soft smile, suggesting that the *farang*'s mind is not good.

"It would cost three hundred thousand to know my daughter," says Mara. There is no hint of negotiation in her voice; the price is final.

I nod respectfully, reach into the hidden pocket at the back of my vest, and remove a hundred thousand dollars in cash and bearer's bonds.

One of the bodyguards takes the money and Mara nods sightly. "When do you wish this to happen?" she says in liquid tones. Her eyes show neither boredom nor interest.

"Now," I say. "Tonight."

The older woman looks at her daughter. Tanha's nod is almost imperceptible but there is something in those lustrous brown eyes: hunger perhaps.

Mara slaps her palms together and two young Thai women come through the rustling folds of plastic, move to my side, urge me to my feet, and begin to undress me. The pockmarked man nods and his thugs bring another rattan chair forward and set it on the Persian carpet.

The six men in tuxedos lean forward with bright eyes.

Tres and I finally saw each other again over breakfast in a cheap place near the river late the next morning. I didn't really want to talk to him about it, yet I had to.

Eventually we got to it and I found our tones low, embarrassed, almost like when someone from the platoon got blown away and no one wanted to say his name for a while unless it was in the form of a joke. We didn't joke about this.

"Did you see that guy's cock . . . after?" Tres said.

I blinked, shook my head, and looked over my shoulder to make sure that no one was listening. Most of the tables near the river's edge here were empty. The temperature must have been over a hundred.

"It had these . . . lesions," whispered Tres. "Like marks I saw once when I was a lifeguard on the Cape and this guy swam into a jellyfish . . ." His voice trailed away.

I sipped cold coffee and concentrated on not shuddering.

Tres took off his glasses and rubbed his eyes. It looked like he hadn't slept either. "Johnny, you wanted to be a medic. How much blood does the human body have in it?"

I shrugged. I'd had some half-assed idea about being a medic so I could get into medical school when I got back to the World; despite my lackadaisical approach to school, my folks expected me to finish college and become something when I got home. I never told them that after a week in 'Nam I knew that I'd never get home.

"I dunno," I said. I don't think Tres saw my shrug.

He set his wire-rimmed glasses back in place. "I think it's about five or six liters," he said. "Depending upon someone's size."

I nodded, not able to picture a liter. Years later when they began selling soft drinks in liter bottles, I always imagined five or six of those bottles filled with blood equaling what we carried around in our veins every day.

"Imagine an orgasm where you're ejaculating blood," whispered Tres.

I looked over my shoulder again. I could feel my cheeks and neck flushing.

Tres touched my wrist. "No, think about it, Johnny. That guy was still alive when they took him out. These guys wouldn't pay big bucks for it if they knew it'd kill them."

Wouldn't they? I thought. It was the first time that I realized that someone might fuck even if it meant certain death. In a way, that revelation in 1970 prepared me for life in the eighties and nineties.

"How much blood could someone lose and still stay alive without a transfusion?" whispered Tres. I knew from his tone that he wasn't expecting an answer from me, just thinking aloud the way he did when we were planning an ambush site.

I did not know the answer then, but I've had the opportunity to learn it many times since, especially during my residency as an ER intern. A wounded person can lose about a liter of blood volume and recover to make it up themselves. More than about a sixth of blood volume gone, and so is the victim. With transfusions, someone can lose up to 40 percent of their blood volume and hope to recover.

I didn't know any of this then and I wasn't too curious. I was too busy trying to imagine ejaculating blood in an orgasm that went on for long minutes rather than seconds. This time I did shudder.

Tres waved the waiter over and paid the check. "I've got to get going. I need to get a cab over to Western Union."

"Why?" I said. I was so sleepy that the hot, thick air seemed to slur my words.

"I'm getting some money wired from the States," said Tres.

I sat straight up, no longer sleepy. "Why?"

Tres took his glasses off again to polish them. When he looked at me, his pale eyes looked myopic and lost. "I'm going back tonight, Johnny."

The young women have undressed me and the creature named Tanha has come closer to caress me when suddenly everything stops. Mara has given a signal.

"We have forgotten something," Mara says. It is the first time she has spoken English. She makes a graceful but ironic gesture. "The times now demand extra caution. I am sorry we did not think of it earlier." She glances at her daughter and I can see the mocking half-smile on both of their faces. "I am afraid that we must wait until tomorrow night so that the proper testing can be done," sighs Mara, switching back to Thai. I can tell that the two have played this scene many times before. I can only guess that the real reason is to inflame desire through delay, thus driving up the price again.

I also smile. "For the Health Identity Card?" I say. "For one of the clinics to certify that I am free of the HIV virus this month?"

Tanha is sitting gracefully on the Persian carpet near me. Now she shifts in my direction, smiles mockingly, and makes a small *moue*. "It is regrettable," she says, her voice as delicate as a crystal wind chime, "but necessary in these terrible times."

I nod. I have seen the statistics. The AIDS epidemic has started late in Thailand but in 1997—less than five years from now—150,000 Thais will have died from the disease. Three years later, in the year 2000, five and a half million people out of the fifty-six million Thais will be carrying the disease and at least a million will be dead. After that, the logarithmic progression is relentless. Thailand—with its lethal combination of ubiquitous prostitutes, promiscuous sexual partners, and resistance to condoms—will rival Uganda as a retroviral killing ground.

"You'll send me to one of the local clinics that do a thousand slapdash HIV tests a week," I say calmly, as if I am used to sitting naked between two beautiful, fully dressed women and an audience of strangers in tuxedos.

Mara opens her slender fingers so that the long, red nails catch the light. "There are few alternatives," she whispers.

"Perhaps I can provide one," I say and reach for my vest where it has been folded carefully atop my other clothes. I unfold the three documents and hand them to Tanha. The girl frowns prettily at them and gives them to her mother. My guess is that the younger woman cannot read English . . . perhaps not even Thai.

Mara does look over the documents. They are certificates from two major Los Angeles hospitals and a University medical clinic attesting to the fact that my blood has been repeatedly tested and repeatedly found free of HIV contamination. Each document is signed by several physicians and carries the seal of the institution. The papers on which they are typed are thick, creamy, and expensive. Each document is dated within the past week.

Mara looks at me with narrowed eyes. Her smile shows her small, sharp teeth and only the faintest hint of tongue. "How do we know these are valid?"

I shrug. "I am a doctor. I wish to live. It would be easier to bribe a Thai clinician for a Health Identity Card if I wished to deceive. I have no reason to deceive."

Mara glanced back at the papers, smiled, and handed them back to me. "I will think about this," she says.

I lean forward in my chair. "I am also at risk," I say.

Mara arches an elegant eyebrow. "Oh, how can this be?"

"Gingival blood," I say in English. "Bleeding gums. Any open sore in your mouth."

Mara reacts with a small, mocking smile, as if I have made a tiny joke. Tanha turns her exquisite face toward her mother. "What did he say?" she demands in Thai. "This *farang* makes no sense."

Mara ignores her. "You have nothing to worry about," she says to me. She nods to her daughter.

Tanha begins caressing me again.

We had three days and two nights left of our R&R. Tres did not ask me to go back with him that next night and I did not volunteer.

It was against regulations to take a weapon with us on R&R, but there were no metal detectors in those days, no airport security to speak of, and quite a few of us took knives or handguns with us when we traveled out of country. I'd brought a long-barreled .38 that I had won in a poker game from a black kid named Newport Johnson three days before he stepped on a Bouncing Betty. Now I got the .38 out of the bottom of my duffel, checked to make sure that it was loaded, and sat in my locked room that evening, wearing nothing but fatigue pants, drinking Scotch and listening to the street noises outside and watching the slow turning of the fan blades above my head.

Tres returned about 4 A.M. I listened through the wall to him banging and crashing around in his bathroom for a few minutes and then I went back to my bed and closed my eyes. Perhaps now I could sleep. His scream brought me up and out of bed, the .38 in my hand. I tore down the hall in bare feet, banged once on his door, pushed it open, and stepped into the room.

Only the bathroom light was on and it cast a thin strip of fluorescent light across the bare floor and tousled bed. There was blood on the floor and a trail of torn linen that was also soaked in blood. It looked as if Tres had tried to tear up sheets to make bandages. I took a step toward the bathroom, heard a moan on the darkness of the bed, and swiveled, still holding the .38 at my side.

"Johnny?" His voice was dry, cracked, and listless. I'd heard that tone before. Newport Johnson had sounded like that in the ten minutes or so it took him to die after the Bouncing Betty had filled him with shrapnel from his neck to his knees. I stepped closer and turned on the small lamp near his bed.

Tres was naked except for his undershirt. He was sprawled on a bloodsoaked mattress, surrounded by bloodsoaked strips of dirty linen. His pants lay on the floor nearby. They were black with dried blood. Tres' hands were covering his crotch. His fingernails were rimmed with blood.

"Johnny?" he whispered. "It won't stop."

I stepped closer, set down the .38, and touched his shoulder. Tres moved his hands and I took a step back.

There's a leech that breeds in the slow-moving waters of Vietnam that specializes in boring up the urethra of men wading in the water. Once firmly lodged in the penis, the leech begins feeding from the inside until it swells to half the size of a man's fist. We'd all heard about the goddamn thing. We all thought about it every time we waded a stream or rice paddy, which was about a dozen times a day.

Tres' cock looked like that leech had been at it. No, it was worse. Besides being swollen and raw-looking, his penis had a series of small lesions spiraling around it. It looked as if someone had taken a sewing machine with a large needle and stitched a row of stigmata down his privates. The lesions were bleeding freely.

"I can't get it to stop," whispered Tres. His face was pale and clammy with sweat. I'd seen this look on the faces of wounded guys just before they floated away on the tide of shock.

"Come on," I said, getting an arm around him, "we're going to find a hospital."

Tres pulled away and fell back on the pillows. "No, no, no. Just get the bleeding to stop." He pulled something from under a pillow and I realized that he was holding the black-bladed Ka-bar knife he used on night patrols. I lifted my .38 and for a second there was silence broken only by the rustle of the fan blades and the street noises outside.

Finally I giggled. This was nuts. Here we were hundreds of miles from Vietnam and the war, me with my sidearm and Tres with his commando knife, ready to do one another. This was fucking nuts.

I put the pistol down. "I brought some first-aid shit," I said. "I'll get it."

I'd brought the smaller of two first-aid kits that I humped around the boonies in my ruck, not for the bandages but possibly for the penicillin and definitely for the LURP uppers, downers, and painkillers that we were issued for serious missions. The morphine was rationed carefully to medics, but I'd still put away quite a stash of Dexedrine and some Demerol. There were also some sulfa drugs. I took the bandages and pills back to Tres and let him try to take care of himself while I poured some water and brought the pills in.

Tres was sitting up now with the bloodied sheet over him. He took two pills and wiped the sweat off his face. "I wonder why it won't stop bleeding," he said.

I shook my head. I didn't know then. I know now.

Vampire bats and European medical leeches exude the same anticoagulant: *hirudin.* The bats secrete it in their saliva; the leeches manufacture it in their gut and smear it on the surface of the wound. It keeps the wound from closing and keeps the blood flowing freely as long as the bloodsucker wants to feed. Vampire bats will "nurse" from the neck of a horse or cow for hours, often returning with other bats to continue the meal until sunrise.

Tres went to sleep after a while and I sat in the sprung chair near the window, watching the door and holding the useless .38 in my lap. I had thoughts of forcing Maladung to Mara again, and then shooting him and the woman. *And the infant,* I mentally added.

The thought was not unsupportable. I'd seen enough dead babies in the past five months. And none of the dead gook babies had been lapping up regurgitated blood from their mommies' lips before being offed. I don't think I would have hesitated a minute to blow away both mother and child. *And then how do you get out of here?* came the question from the rational part of my mind. I doubted if the Thais would take kindly to my canceling the ticket of what might be their only resident *phanyaa mahn naga kios*. They seemed to enjoy the mother's services too much.

I put that plan out of my mind for now and tried to figure out what to do next. If Tres were still bleeding that evening, I would take him to a MACV Army liaison office that was reported to be somewhere in Bangkok. If that failed to be real, I'd find some MP's and get them to find some good medical help. If that didn't work, I'd carry Tres to the nearest Thai hospital and use the .38 to enforce priority aid.

I fell asleep mulling these options. When I awoke it was dark in the room. The fan was still turning in its desultory fashion but the street sounds outside the window had shifted to their nighttime volume. The bedsheets were soaked with fresh blood, there was blood on the floor, the bathroom was littered with bloody towels, but Tres was gone.

I ran out into the hallway and pounded down the steps to the lobby before realizing what a sight I must be: wild-eyed, barefoot and barechested, my rumpled fatigue pants smeared with blood, the long-barreled .38 in my hand. The Thai whores and their pimps in the lobby barely looked my way.

Back in the room, I changed into civilian clothes and my loose Hawaiian shirt, tucked the pistol in my belt, and went back out into the night.

I almost caught up to Tres. I saw him on the same dock we'd departed from two nights earlier. The shadowy figure with him had to be Maladung. They had just stepped down into the long-tailed taxi as I ran out onto the dock. The boat pulled away with a roar.

Tres saw me. He stood up and almost pitched out of the accelerating boat. He raised his arm in my direction, fingers splayed, as if reaching for me across fifty feet of open water. I heard him shout at the driver—"*Yout! Phuen young mai ma! Yout!*"—which I did not understand then, but now translate as *Stop! My friend hasn't come yet! Stop!*

I saw Maladung pull him back into the boat. I drew the pistol and held it uselessly as the taxi bounced across the river, disappeared between a barge going upriver, and then reappeared only as a distant lantern before disappearing down a *klong* on the opposite side of the Chao Phraya.

I knew that I would never see Tres alive again.

Mara lowers her gaze as Tanha brings her mouth to my groin. There is no caress of tongue. Not yet. The younger woman uses her mouth to bring me to full erection.

As much as men talk and write about the joys of oral sex, there is always a slight ambiguity in the male response to the act of fellatio. For some, a mouth is too nongender-specific to allow the subconscious to relax and enjoy the act. For others, it is the uncontrolled intensity of sensation which causes a flutter of alarm amidst the cascade of pleasure. For many, it is just the unbidden thought of sharp teeth.

I have to concentrate now on not concentrating even to allow an erection to begin. Luckily, the male organ is as simple a stimulus-response mechanism as nature allows anywhere. Tanha's mouth is soft and well educated; my excitement follows its inevitable arc of engorgement.

I close my eyes and try not to think about *not thinking* about the men in tuxedos behind me. Someone has dimmed the overhead light so that only the flash of sparks dribbling from the arc-welder two floors above lights the scene and the interior of my eyelids with magnesium strobes. Mara whispers something and I feel the shock of Tanha's warm mouth pulling away. There is the shock of cooler air on me for only a second before a different moistness returns.

I open my eyes just enough to see Tanha's tongue sliding from her mouth, curling around me. The flash from the welding sparks makes the mottled flesh of her tongue look more purple than pink. I catch a glimpse of pulsating slits amidst the coated texture there, like tiny feeding orifices. I shut off my thoughts before the grasping mouth-guts of leeches and lampreys come to mind. For years I have trained myself to be equal to this moment.

The sensation, when it comes above the background surge of sliding warmth, is more like a small electric shock than the sting of a jellyfish. I gasp and open my eyes. Tanha is watching me through the curtains of her lashes. The shock comes again riding down the exquisite penile nerve system straight to the base of my spine and then to the pleasure center of my brain. I close my eyes again and groan. My scrotum contracts with pleasure. The spiral of gentle shocks surges down the length of me, soars through my body, and returns to my penis like a gently moving hand gloved in velvet. My hips begin to move without volition.

My heart is pounding so wildly that the pressure from it seems to replace sound as the only noise in the universe. My skull echoes to the rhythmic surging of my own pulse. The separate, tiny shocks along my groin have grown together to form a perfect spiral of pleasurable sensation now. It is as if I am fucking the sun. Even as my hips begin to thrust in earnest and my hands grope for Tanha's head to move that warmth closer, a distant part of my mind observes the classic symptoms of the onset of orgasm and wonders about the rate of tachycardia, myotonia, and hyperventilation.

A second later any remaining clinical awareness is washed away in a new and stronger surge of pure pleasure. Tanha's tongue is contracting, tugging from the base of my scrotum to the glans of my penis, tightening as it contracts and relaxes, contracts and relaxes. The shocks have become a single, closed circuit of almost unbearable sensation.

I ejaculate almost without noticing it, so great is the pressure now. From beneath my fluttering eyelids I can see semen dropping like a band of white petals onto the hair and shoulders of Tanha. Her tongue does not desist for an instant. Her eyes are as yellow as her mother's now. The orgasm passes without releasing me from the building pressures. My heart strains to pump more blood into my distended organ.

Yes! I will it even as my head arches back, my neck strains, and my face distorts. *Yes!* I choose the thing in which I now have no choice.

A second later I come. Blood ejaculates from the tip of my penis and bathes Tanha's face and breasts. Greedily, she lowers her mouth to me again, unwilling to spill any of it. My hips pound as I continue to pulse. The moment goes on and on.

Mara leans closer.

*   *   *

It was the Thai police who came to me just after sunrise that next morning twenty-two years ago. I thought I would be arrested for wandering the hotel halls until the early hours, shouting at no one and brandishing a cocked .38. Instead of arresting me, they brought me to Tres.

The Bangkok morgue was small and insufficiently cooled. The smell reminded me of an orchard where too much fallen fruit had gone bad in the sun. There were no metal cabinets or sliding stretchers as in the American movies: Tres was on a steel slab just like the other dozen or so corpses in the small room. They had not covered his face. He looked vulnerable without his glasses.

"He's so . . . white," I said to the only policeman who spoke English.

"He was found in the river," said the brown man in the white jacket and Sam Browne belt.

"He didn't drown," I said. It was not a question.

The policeman shook his head. "Your friend lost much blood." He tugged his white glove higher, touched Tres' chin, and swiveled the corpse's head so that I could see the long knife wound that ran from under his left ear to his Adam's apple.

I resisted the impulse to giggle. "How did you know where to find me?" I asked the policeman.

The white glove went into a pocket and came out with a room key. "The only thing on his person."

I let out a breath, swayed slightly, and steadied myself against the steel platform. "The knife wound didn't kill him, Inspector," I said. "Let me show you something." I tugged off the sheet, exposing Tres' naked body.

This time I did giggle. The inspector and the other two policemen narrowed their eyes at me.

There were no stigmata. Tres' sexual organs had been crudely but completely removed. The effect was rather like a Ken doll that someone had spilled fingernail polish on. I dropped the sheet and took a step away.

The inspector came closer and seized my forearm, whether to steady me or restrain me from running I do not know. "We think that it is . . . how you say it . . . a queer thing. A fight between faggots. We have seen this type of injury before. Always it is a type of queer thing. Jealousy."

"A queer thing," I repeated, holding back the sobs or giggles. "Yeah." I could see the arrest and trial ahead of me. The thoughts that I had kept so private would be spread across newspaper headlines, whispered in barracks and latrines. Would the Thais put me in one of their prisons or ship me back for court-martial?

The inspector released my arm. "We know that you were not there at the time he was murdered, Private Merrick. The boat master at Phulong Dock saw you shouting at the boat that carried Corporal Tindale away. The manager at the hotel will testify that you returned only a few minutes later, became drunk, and remained visible and audible throughout the night. You could not have been present when the corporal was murdered, but do you have any idea who did this? Your military will demand to know."

I lifted the sheet, draped it across Tres' corpse, and took a step away from the men. "No," I said. "I have no idea whatsoever."

Mara licks the lips of her daughter. Their arms are pulled in to their sides, their hands curled as if palsied. I imagine vampire bats hanging from the cold ceiling of a cave, wings tucked tight, only their lips and tongue active and engaged.

Tanha arches her head and the heavy red liquid is propelled from her distended lips to the waiting cavity of her mother's mouth. I hear the lapping, gurgling sounds very clearly. Tanha's tongue has not relinquished its grip and I still spasm in her grasp. My heart is straining with the effort. My vision blackens and I can no longer see their feeding and sharing, only hear the thick, liquid sounds of it.

My facial muscles are still locked in the myotoniac spasm of an involuntary grimace. I would smile if I could.

I found Maladung in the autumn of 1975, not long after I graduated from medical school. The little pimp had retired rich and returned to his northern city of Chiang Mai. I paid off the Thai detective whom I'd hired with the first installment of my inheritance money and spent two days watching Maladung before picking him up. He was married and had two grown sons and a ten-year-old daughter.

He was walking to the small store he ran in the old section of town when I pulled up alongside him in a jeep, showed him the 9mm automatic, and told him to get in. I took him into the countryside, to the small house I had rented. I promised him that he would live if he told me everything he knew.

I think he did tell me everything he knew. Mara and her girl-child had dropped out of sight and were performing only for the very rich now. Tres had been killed as a simple precaution; he and I had been the first Americans allowed in Mara's presence and they feared the consequences if word of the performance got back to the platoon. They had planned to murder me that night, but the two men sent to commit the act had seen me drunk and shouting in the upstairs hallway, had noted the gun, and had decided otherwise. By the time others were sent, I had been shipped back to Saigon.

Maladung swore that he had not known about Tres' murder until after it was carried out. He swore it. Maladung had never dreamed that the *phanyaa mahn naga kio* had meant to harm the *farang* beyond the services rendered. I placed the Browning against his forehead and told him to tell me upon pain of death what usually happened to those who received Mara's services.

Maladung was shaking like an old man. "They die," he said in Thai and repeated in English. "First they lose their soul"—*khwan hai* was the phrase he used, "their butterfly spirit flies away"—and then their *winjan,* life spirit, leaks out. "They return and return until they die," he said, voice quavering. "But this they choose."

I lowered the automatic and said, "I believe you, Maladung. You didn't know that they'd murder Tres." Then I lifted the Browning and shot him twice in the head.

That same autumn I began the search for Mara.

I come to and the men in tuxedos are gone, Tanha is sitting above me on the chair next to her mother, and the two young women are finishing their chore of cleaning and dressing me. I can feel the bandages under the trousers. It feels as if I am wearing diapers. My groin is moist with blood, but I hardly notice the discomfort because of the lingering pulse of pleasure that fills me like the echo of beautiful music.

"Mr. Noi informs me that you said you have more money," Mara says softly.

I nod, too weak to speak. Any thought of attacking the women is impossible for me now, even if I did not know that her men were waiting just beyond the wind-fluttered plastic. Mara and Tanha are sources of infinite pleasure. I could never think of hurting them now, of interrupting what is to transpire in the coming nights.

"The limousine will pick you up at midnight tomorrow at your hotel," says Mara. Her fingers move and the four men come in to remove me. I am mildly surprised to find that I cannot walk without assistance.

The streets are empty and tomb-silent. Even the shooting has ended. Orange flames still burn to the north. I close my eyes and savor the fading ecstasy as they drive me back to the Oriental.

I don't think that I knew in Vietnam that I was gay. I had disguised the very real love that I felt for Tres as other things: loyalty to a buddy, admiration, even the kind of masculine love that grunts are supposed to feel for one another in combat. But it was love. I realize that now. I have known it since shortly after I returned from the war.

I never came out of the closet. Not publicly. Even while in medical school I learned how to troll the most discreet bars, meet the most discreet men, and make the most discreet arrangements for temporary liaisons. Later, as my practice and public persona grew, I learned how to keep my prowlings restricted to rare nights in cities far away from my home in L.A. And I dated women. Those who wondered why I never married had only to look at my busy practice to see that I had no time for a domestic life.

And I continued to hunt Mara. Twice a year I flew to Thailand, learning the language and the cities, and twice a year I was told by my paid operatives there that the woman had disappeared. Only two years ago, in 1990, did she and her daughter surface again, driven into accepting expensive performances as their need for money was renewed.

There was nothing I could do then. The more I learned of Mara and Tanha and their habits, the more I was certain that I could never get close to them with a weapon. My San Francisco lover of six years left me after he awakened to me calling him "Tres" while I slept.

Then, only six months ago, certain results were returned and, after a few hours of almost hysterical anger, I saw that the weapon had been put in my hands.

I began to make my plans.

The pockmarked man nods to the others to let me out and I walk from the alley to the hotel. Even at 5 A.M. there are uniformed doormen to greet me with pleasant voices and to hold the door. I manage to nod to them and walk through the old Authors' Wing to the elevators in the new wing. Another servant appears to hold the door of the elevator.

"Good morning, Dr. Merrick," says the young Thai, little more than a boy.

I smile and wait for the elevator doors to close before grasping the brass rail and struggling to hold myself upright. I can feel the bandages leaking through my trousers. Only the long photographer's vest hides the blood.

In my room I bathe, treat the lesions with a special salve I have brought, inject myself with a coagulant, bathe again, and pull on fresh pajamas before crawling into bed. It will be light in a few minutes. In fourteen hours, darkness will fall again and I will return to Mara and her daughter.

In Chiang Mai, where the whores are cheap and the young men celebrate entry into manhood by buying a fuck, 72 percent of the city's poorest prostitutes tested positive for HIV in 1989.

In the bars and sex clubs along Patpong, condoms are handed out free by a man in a red, blue, and gold superhero suit. He is named Captain Condom and he is employed by the PDA, the Population and Community Development Association. The PDA is the brainchild of Senator Mechai Viravaidya, an economist and member of the WHO Global Commission on AIDS. Mechai has spent so much of his own time, energy, and money promoting condoms that rubbers are called *mechais* by everyone in Bangkok.

Almost no one uses them. The men refuse to and the women do not force the issue.

One out of every fifty people in Thailand makes his or her living selling sex.

I think that the computer projections for the year 2000 are wrong. I think that far more than five million Thais will be infected and many more than one million will have died. I think that the corpses will fill the *klongs* and lie along the gutters of the *soi*. I think that only the very rich and the very, very careful will avoid this plague.

Mara and Tanha were—until very recently—very rich. And they have been very careful. Only their need to be very rich again has led them to be careless.

My HIV-negative documents are, of course, falsified. It was not difficult. The lab reports are real, only the dates and name were changed prior to my photocopying them onto official stationery and adding the seals. I serve on the faculty of all three of the institutions whose seals and forms I borrowed.

In the six months since I tested HIV positive, the plan grew from a scheme to an inevitability.

They are monsters, Mara and her child, but even monsters grow careless. Even monsters can be killed.

There is no fan on the ceiling of my expensive air-conditioned suite at the Oriental Hotel. As the first pale gleamings of the dawn creep across the teak and plaster ceiling of my room, I content myself with imagining that there is a fan slowly turning there as I lull myself to sleep with the image.

I smile when I imagine the coming night's activity and the night that will follow this one. I can see the older woman licking the younger woman's lips, and then opening wide her maw for the cascade of blood. My blood. Death's blood.

Before dropping off to sleep, lulled by the medication I have taken and by the final turn of things, I summon the image that has sustained me through all these years and through these final months.

I imagine Tres removing his glasses and squinting at me, his face as vulnerable as a boy's, his cheek as soft as only a lover's cheek can be. And he says to me, "I'm going back, Johnny. I'm going back tonight."

And I take his hand in mine. And I say, with the absolute certainty of conviction, "I'm going, too."

Smiling now, having found the place I have sought so long to return to, I release myself to sleep and forgiveness.

Listen to me. I am going to tell you something important.

I have not told this story before. I do not think that I will have the time or energy to tell it again before I die. So listen to me if you want to hear it.

First, I must unwrap this bundle. I have seen you glance at it as I have spoken into your machine these last few weeks. You have been polite and not asked me what it is, although the canvas bundle must have aroused your curiosity. It is, after all, the size of a man. I saw you look at it while I was describing how a *wičaśa wakan* such as myself is wrapped up like a mummy in a *yuwipi* ceremony, and I know you must have wondered if maybe this crazy old man has a corpse of another *wičaśa wakan* sitting in the corner of his shack.

No, it is not a man. Watch now as I unwrap it.

Underneath the canvas you see there are seven rawhides lashed just so. I will remove the rawhides.

Underneath the rawhides there is this wrapping of buffalo skin.

Underneath the buffalo skin, there is this wrapping of deer skin. Do you feel how supple it is despite its age? It was moistened to such softness in the mouth of my great-grandmother. Now, take these thongs as I unwrap the deer skin.

Underneath the deer skin there is this red flannel.

Underneath the red flannel is this blue flannel. This is the last layer. Sit down now as I turn out all of the lights except the candle on the table. I will remove the blue flannel.

I see your disappointment. Two old pipes, you are thinking. You are wrong to be disappointed.

Members of my tribe of the Lakota Sioux may wait an entire lifetime to see either of these pipes and even then they may be disappointed. They may be removed only at the most holy and important of times. You may wonder why I am unwrapping them now, in front of a *Wasicun* such as yourself . . . and an ignorant *Wasicun* at that.

The answer is that you are ignorant, but as with most *Wasicun* you are not stupid. You have a secretary who will take the words I say into your tape recorder and will type them exactly as I say them. This is important. I would tell this tale to my *takoja*—my fat and pampered great-grandson—but his eyes and ears have been stuffed by the excrement of the *Wasicun* television he watches six hours every day. My other *takoja,* my true grandson, is in jail in Rapid City. Even if he were not, his mind and *nagi*—his spirit—have been destroyed by alcohol.

So there is no one here on the reservation who has the patience, brains, or wisdom to hear this tale and to understand it and use it to become a *wičaśa wakan*—a holy man—or a *waayatan,* a man of vision who can see the future. Not now. Not in these bad times the *Wasicun* have offered us to eat and we have swallowed, like a stupid horse swallowing nettles that will tear its stomach until it dies.

But someday someone from the Lakota may read of this from your ignorant repetition. And maybe they will understand. So shut up and listen.

This pipe you are looking at is the *Ptehinčala Huhu Canunpa*—the Buffalo Calf Bone Pipe. It has been in my family of the Itazipcho tribe of the Sioux nation for fifteen generations. These red things hanging from the pipe are eagle feathers; these are bird skins and small scalps. I see your reaction. Yes, perhaps these are scalps of *Wasicun* children, but I suspect they are simply the scalps of Pawnee men. The Pawnee always had small heads because they had tiny brains.

It is said that the pipe keepers always live to be almost a

hundred years old, and you know that I was born before this century began.

This other pipe is our sacred tribal pipe. You see the red bowl? It is made of a pipestone that comes from only one quarry in one place in the world. Buffalo were driven over cliffs where this pipestone was quarried. The blood of the buffalo is in this stone. But it is not the buffalo blood which makes this sacred to our people.

The pipestone is the flesh of the Sioux people. I do not mean this as what you call a metaphor. The red pipestone in this bowl *is* the flesh of the Sioux people.

Almost eighty-five years ago I entered my first Catholic church—a small mission chapel on the plains, it has been gone since before the great Depression—and I remember my shock at hearing the priest explain to us the idea of the Eucharist. "This is the body of Christ," he said through the converted Brulé Sioux who spoke his words to us. "This is his actual flesh, of which we partake."

I remember my family's shock as we discussed this in our lodge that night. We had known the *Wasicun* to be greedy—the very word for white man means "fat takers"—but we had not known them to be cannibals. We had not known that they ate the blood and flesh of their God.

But then my *tunkashila* spoke up. My grandfather was very old and very wise, he was both *wičaśa wakan* and a *waayatan*, and some say that besides being a medicine man and vision man he was also a *wapiya*, a conjurer. I remember that he had a long pale birthmark on his scalp and forehead, almost like a scar, and that this birthmark was part of his *wakan*, his holy power. When he spoke we listened. I listened that night.

"This thing the *Wasicun* priest has said is not bad," said my *tunkashila*. "Perhaps the flesh of their God is turned into bread the way the flesh of our people is turned into pipestone. Perhaps the blood of their God is turned into wine the way the blood of our people flows into us through the tribal pipe and the *Ptehinčala Huhu Canunpa*. These things are not bad. This is not cannibalism as in the stories my grandmother told me about the *Kangi Wicasha*, the Crows. We will not judge this thing."

And that night the old men nodded and spat and I did likewise.

But I hold these pipes before you now and tell you that in touching these stone bowls I am touching the flesh of my people. In smoking this tribal pipe, I am mingling my blood with the blood of all Sioux who came before me.

And there is another thing. I will be smoking this pipe while I tell this story. It is a fact that if I were to lie while smoking this pipe, I would die. Think of this while I tell you this story.

Now listen to me. Do not speak. Do not ask questions. Just listen.

First, I must tell you why I am telling this story after so many years of not telling it.

Last month, my grandson—not the grandson in jail in Rapid City but my dead third wife's daughter's son—invited me to his trailer over near Deadwood to see a movie on videotape. It was a big deal. Several of his daughters and his half-sister and five of my other relatives were there. All of them wanted to see how their old *tunkashila* reacted to the movie. It was like they were giving me a big present for still being alive when I should be dead.

The movie we watched that night was called *Dances with Wolves*. It had come out sometime earlier and there had been a big premiere over in Rapid City to which many people had driven from the res, but I was in the hospital then with pneumonia and missed all the fuss. So my grandson Leonard Sweetwater had thrown this *Dances with Wolves* party so that I would not die without seeing this wonderful thing that had been done for our people.

Well, I left halfway through the videotape. Leonard and the others thought I was just going out to urinate in the bushes—which I still prefer to using outhouses and closed-in toilets—but actually I was walking toward my home some forty miles away.

The movie made me want to throw up. I *did* throw up, although that may have been from the rotten burritos that Leonard had served before putting in the tape.

My grandchildren had made a big deal out of much of the dialogue in the movie being in actual Lakota, although when I heard them speak it was terrible—exactly the way English sounds so stupid when someone from a foreign country has memorized the words without knowing the meaning of them or understanding when to emphasize one syllable over another. It reminded me of Bela Lugosi speaking English by rote in the old *Dracula* movie. Only Lugosi was supposed to be a foreigner; these people were supposed to be Lakota *speaking their own language!*

But it was not the language idiocy that made me leave. It was the contempt.

After throwing up, I wept that evening during my long walk before Leonard and the others realized that I was going home and came to find me in their pickups. I wept because my own descendants would think that such a movie showed our people as they were. I think that anyone who would make such a movie is a weasel and that the movie should be called *Dances with Weasels.* The movie star who made it and directed it and starred in it is a weasel. I think that he acted slow and stupid and weasel-like in the movie and rather than fawning over him and giving him a home and a good name such as *Dances with Wolves* and a woman, even a captured *Wasicun* woman, my ancestors would have ignored him. Or, if he had persisted in coming around, they would have cut his balls off.

No, what made me throw up and then weep was that my own people could not see the contempt in the movie. It is a contempt that only a total conqueror can show toward the totally conquered.

At first the *Wasicun* feared the Plains Indian. They were at our mercy in the earliest days of our contact. Then, when the numbers of the *Wasicun* increased and their fear was balanced by their greed for our land, they hated us. But at least it was a hatred reinforced by respect.

The simpering, peace-loving, ecologically perfect idiots I saw portrayed as Lakota Sioux in this abortion of a movie could exist only in the mind of a California-surfer *Wasicun* such as the one who made the movie. It was condescending. It was filled with the contempt that can come from having no fear or respect whatsoever for a people who had once happily cut the balls off your own ancestors. It was the condescending arrogance of one who can offer only pity because it costs nothing.

Walking home that night, I was reminded of a game I played as a child. It was called *isto kicicastakapi* and it consisted of chewing rosebush berries, spitting the pits into your hands, and then tossing them into someone's face. Usually there was a lot of spit there with the pits.

This movie was a *Wasicun isto kicicastakapi.* It was only spit and fruit pits in the face. There was nothing real there, nothing of substance.

So again—listen. There are no stupid, grinning, *Wasicun* blond surfer heroes in this story; all of the characters are of the *Ikče Wičaśa*—pronounced Ik-che Wi-cha-sha, the natural, free human beings—the people you call the Sioux.

But listen anyway.

Long ago there was a boy born to our tribe and his name was Hoka Ushte, which meant Lame Badger. He was named that because the night the boy was born a badger had come limping into the camp and had left his dung outside the tipi where Lame Badger's mother was beginning to wrestle with the birthing stick.

Now you have to understand that the badger is an animal that is considered very *wakan,* sacred . . . filled with mysterious force. A badger's bone pizzle, his penis, was used as a sewing awl, which is a bit ironic given the problems that Hoka Ushte's own pizzle would lead him into when he grew older. Also, a badger is a powerful animal, especially once it gets in its hole. Once it is in its hole, not even three men can drag it out. My grandfather told me the story of how three young men of our tribe were returning to their winter camp near the Mini Sose, the Mud Water River which the *Wasicun* called the Missouri, near where the Spotted Tail Agency and Pine Ridge Reservation would someday be, when they spotted a badger fleeing for its hole. The young brave named Spotted Tail, later known as Broken Arm, gave chase because he had just traded one of his brother's ponies for a brand-new *Wasicun* rope and he wanted to test it. Spotted Tail roped the badger just before it jumped in its hole. Both of Spotted Tail's friends helped pull, but the badger just kept going deeper, breaking Spotted Tail's arm in three places and pulling his shoulder out of its socket. Somehow in the struggle, the treacherous *Wasicun* rope became tangled around the three braves' horses, and although Spotted Tail and his friends managed to let go of the rope, all three of the horses were pulled into the badger hole. To the braves' horror, they could hear the screams of the horses for an hour or more as that badger clamped onto each of the horses' snouts in turn, smothering it with the force of its jaws.

On that day Spotted Tail lost his name, for he was forever after known as Broken Arm—because Lost His Rope and Horses to a Badger was too long to say in Lakota—but no one in the tribe ever forgot that Spotted Tail had lost those horses and his new rope. This is the truth, and I tell it only because you should know why we respect both the *wakan* power and the animal power of the badger.

A badger also has one other interesting fact about it. If you cut open a dead badger and look at your reflection in a pool of the animal's blood, you will see yourself as you will look when you die. A friend of mine tried this when I was a boy and saw only his own boyish reflection. He said that the magic had not worked, but less than a month later he was kicked in the head by a horse and died the same day. I have never wanted to look at my reflection in badger's blood, but if I had then, I would have seen the old face you see before you now and could have become a brave warrior or an astronaut or something—knowing that I would not die until I was ancient—rather than the timid *wičaśa wakan* I chose to become.

Anyway, Hoka Ushte—Lame Badger—had a powerful name from birth, but there seemed nothing special about the boy. He grew up as only a boy and showed no special abilities. He was, like most boys, a *takoja,* a pampered grandson, and showed much more interest in playing than in doing the few chores asked of our boys in the days before schools and the reservation. His favorite games were *mato kiciyapi* in the spring, where the boys threw sharp grass stems at each other until someone bled, and *pre-hes-te* in the winter where a feathered stick was slid along the ice, and the team game of Grab-Them-by-the-Hair-and-Kick-Them in the summer. No, Hoka Ushte showed no special powers or abilities when he was a boy.

You have to remember that all the things I tell you of here occurred in the golden days after the Buffalo Woman had given us the sacred pipe and after *Wakan Tanka* had gifted us with the horse, but before the *Wasicun* began to outnumber the buffalo on the plains that were our home.

It was before the *Pehin Hanska Kasata*—the rubbing out of Long Hair at Greasy Grass, that is, the killing of Custer at the Little Big Horn in 1876.

It was before the terrible Fort Laramie Treaty of 1868 which made it illegal for the *Ikče Wičaśa*—the natural free human—to be free anymore. That is, it was before the year the *Wasicun* told us to live on a reservation.

It was, I think, the year When They Brought in the Captives, or 1843 in *Wasicun* time. I know this because Hoka Ushte's father was an old man of forty-four when the boy was born. Hoka Ushte's father was named Sleeps by the Creek and was born in the year When Many Pregnant Women Died, which corresponds to your year of 1799. More amazing was the advanced age of Hoka Ushte's mother, Three Clouds Woman, at the time of his birth: it is said that she had been born in either the year They Made the Hair on the Horses Curly, 1804, or the year When They Waved Horse Tails Over Each Other, 1805, and was a crone of thirty-eight or thirty-nine winters when the boy was born.

Hoka Ushte was their only child. Both parents, I am told, thought that a child given to them so late in life would be very important, but neither parent lived to see their child old enough to talk. Three Clouds Woman left her tipi in a blizzard to get water in that same winter of the year When They Brought in the Captives and was found frozen to death. Sleeps by the Creek, despite his advanced age, left the camp the next summer after boasting that he was going to count coup on a Pawnee and was never seen again.

Hoka Ushte was raised by grandparents and all of the women in the village and became the spoiled *takoja* I described to you earlier.

But in a sense, all of the *Ikče Wičaśa* were *takoja* in those days. By that I mean that the days were rich and easy, the past existed only in stories and the future only in dreams, and despite pain, fear, hardship, and death, life was full and simple. There were no boundaries to the wanderings of the *Ikče Wičaśa* and we truly dwelt in the *maka sitomni*—the world over, the universe.

But this is just background to the story. The story itself begins when Hoka Ushte is in his seventeenth summer and begins his *hanblečeya,* the vision quest that would change him and his people forever.

Now stop your tape and write this down. The word you hear is "hanblechia" but I want you to see it: *HAN BLE ČE YA.* It is important to know the word.

"A name is an instrument of teaching and of distinguishing natures." Do you know what wise *wičaśa wakan* said that?

No, not Black Elk. His name was Socrates. Now write the word down. *Hanblečeya.* Good. Now listen again.

By the time Hoka Ushte was seventeen summers old, some of the older men of the tribe wanted to rename him Lodge Pole because his child-maker seemed to be always standing stiff and tall, like the lodgepole pines we harvest for our tipi sticks. Hoka Ushte was embarrassed by this, but he was a passionate boy. Unlike the other young men who preferred to ride and wrestle and plan the stealing of Pawnee or Crow ponies, Hoka Ushte chose to hang around the camp and watch the young girls. He was lucky that the others did not rename him Counting Coup on Girls.

Now I have to tell you that in a small camp such as the one Hoka Ushte grew up in, there were never many *winčinčalas*—attractive girls for a boy to lose his heart to. There was, however, one such *winčinčalas,* and her name was Calf Running. Fifteen years old with a sweet face and long black hair which she kept shiny with grease, Calf Running would have been a prize for any proud brave to claim, much less a callow youth like Lame Badger. But Hoka Ushte's eye was on Calf Running much of the time.

Now I have to tell you two other things about dating and sex among my people in the times before the reservations. First, we are very shy about such things. We even have a word for that shyness—*wistelkiya*—which means both bashfulness about the act and fear of incest. It is the last part that makes us nervous. Our tribes were never large, you see, and our camps were even smaller, and our ancestors had seen the effects of too much inbreeding. Thus all the taboos on marrying too close to the family. Thus our *wistelkiya* about the whole subject.

Secondly, it is hard to describe to you now how little privacy there was then. Families slept together in communal tipis, so the children grew up with the sight and sounds of father and mother going at it like dogs in the corner or copulating under their robes, but it was considered bad manners to peek and worse manners to be so obvious in front of the older children. Hoka Ushte, raised as he was by his old grandparents, had probably never seen the making of the beast with two backs. Nor had he ever been alone with a girl in his life. The way of the young *Ikče Wičaśa* was largely a life of boys among boys and girls among girls; except for the common effort of moving camp or searching for firewood or buffalo patties, the sexes were separate.

So Hoka Ushte did what he could to get close to Calf Running, most of which consisted of hanging around the creek like a hunter stalking a wily prey. Sooner or later, he realized, every woman of the village came down to the stream to fill her water skin. So Hoka Ushte would hide behind the bushes near the stream and wait from sunrise to sunset for Calf Running to come alone to fill her bag. Sometimes Calf Running would come with her fierce mother, Loud Woman, and Lame Badger would just wait there behind his yucca plant or cottonwood tree or juniper bush, scratching his leg and looking stupid. And even when Calf Running went alone to the stream, the only thing he could do was pop up and grin at her. Sometimes Calf Running would smile back at him, but at other times she would ignore him and proceed to fill her water skin. Then Hoka Ushte was left with scratching his leg and looking stupid again.

Eventually Hoka Ushte grew bored with hanging around the stream and looking stupid, so he decided to go tipi-crawling.

Now crawling into your girlfriend's house might sound like a straightforward enough solution to a *Wasicun,* but it took most of Hoka Ushte's courage. Calf Running's father was named Standing Hollow Horn and he was fabled for his bad temper. Most people assumed the bad temper was a result of his living with Loud Woman, but his temper was legendary nonetheless. Hoka Ushte's worst fear, however, was that his tipi-crawling would wake Loud Woman herself, who would tell the other women in the village.

Sioux mothers did not treat the molestation of their daughters lightly. If Hoka Ushte had been a brave living by himself, such a discovery might have meant that the women would burn his tipi down while he slept in it. Or perhaps hamstring his horse. Since Hoka Ushte still lived with his grandparents and had no horse, he quaked at the thought of what Loud Woman and her friends might do.

But his passion for the *winčinčalas* was stronger than his fear.

On a moonless night in the Moon When the Ducks Come Back—that is to say April—Hoka Ushte crept out of his grandfather's tipi and circled the camp, making sure to keep away from where the horses were kept, until he came to where Standing Hollow Horn's tipi stood. Luckily, his beloved's tipi was at the edge of the camp so Lame Badger did not have to find a way to avoid all the dogs that would have barked at him if he had crawled through the center of the camp . . . for even though he knew all the dogs by name and they knew him, dogs are nervous at night and quick to bark at someone crawling like a weasel between the lodges.

Hoka Ushte had listened to his grandfather and the other warriors speak of how they had crept into Pawnee and Shoshone camps to count coup on their enemies, and he used those skills now to creep up on Calf Running's tipi, to pull the stake flap away from the stake at the rear of the tipi, and to slide his head under the buffalo hide wall of the lodge.

The air had been crisp and wintery outside; inside was the usual thickness of campfire smoke, exhalations of the sleeping, and the homey smell of sleeping robes that had not been aired for a long time. Loud Woman was not the neatest or most hardworking of women. As he had been taught by the warriors' stories, Hoka Ushte slipped his head under the tipi wall and did not breath or stir until he located all of the sleeping figures within. Standing Hollow Horn was located immediately by the sound of his loud snoring; Loud Woman talked and snapped even in her sleep, and every time her shrill voice filled the darkness, Hoka Ushte shuddered at the thought of waking her. Calf Running slept quietly, and as Lame Badger's eyes adjusted to the dark, he could see her pale shoulders and dark hair gleaming softly in the bit of starlight coming down through the open smoke hole.

Hoka Ushte exhaled and took a breath just before he would have passed out. The snoring and sleep-talking continued. Lame Woman snorted something derisive at her dream people and then rolled over with a great tugging of robes, putting her face to the tipi wall opposite Hoka Ushte. He took this as a welcome and wiggled into the tipi, sliding his skinny behind under the heavy buffalo canvas as silently as he could. Holding his breath again, Hoka Ushte crept the four or five feet to Calf Running's side. He saw that she wore nothing but a loose shift under her sleeping robes, and both her thin shoulders were bare. His heart was beating so loudly that he was sure it would wake everyone in the camp. He was reaching out to touch her when Standing Hollow Horn's snoring seemed to stumble, the man snorted, and he sat up in his robes.

Hoka Ushte froze into perfect stillness and tried to become a heap of buffalo robe. His heart hurt his chest it was beating so hard.

Standing Hollow Horn stood up in the dark, kicked aside his robes, opened the tipi flap, and stepped outside. Hoka Ushte could hear the big man making water out there. It sounded like a buffalo pissing to the boy. An instant later Calf Running's father stepped back into the lodge and tugged at his robes. Hoka Ushte was no more than six feet away, but his head was down, his legs were curled up, his hands were tucked away so as not to catch the starlight, and he was praying hard to *Wakan Tanka* that the older brave would not sense the extra body in the tent and gut him like a deer before bothering to find out who the invader was.

Standing Hollow Horn began snoring again.

Hoka Ushte let several minutes pass before he dared to move again. As if sensing his eagerness, Calf Running turned toward him and kicked off the last of her sleeping robe. Her breath was sweet and quick against Hoka Ushte's cheek as he leaned closer and he thought, *She is awake! She welcomes me.*

He licked suddenly dry lips and raised his left hand to her leg; his other hand was lifted to clamp across her mouth at the first indication of a scream. Hoka Ushte touched his beloved's thigh. The skin there was softer than he could have imagined, the muscle more supple than he had ever dreamed. Calf Running let out a sleepy sigh but did not scream. Hoka Ushte half-swooned with the surge of passion and imminent danger he felt. He moved his hand higher, feeling the inward curve of that strong thigh muscle, her light shift sliding up as his wrist and hand progressed. He paused only when his fingers were inches away from the warmth of Calf Running's groin. Hoka Ushte's entire body quaked with excitement; only his hand was steady and still, his fingers as rigid as his raised child-maker.

Finally Hoka Ushte could wait no longer. He slipped his fingers closer to the source of all that warmth, certain that Calf Running must awaken if she were asleep, cry out if she were already awake. But she did not awaken or cry out, only murmured softly in a sleep voice that sounded too vague to be feigned.

Hoka Ushte forgot to breathe. He was touching a woman's *winyañ shan* for the first time in his life. Excitement almost made him cry out, but he clamped his teeth onto his lower lip until blood flowed. All of his attention was on his fingertips now as they explored this new phenomenon.

Hoka Ushte was surprised to find that Calf Running's maiden hair there was not soft and curly as he had imagined, but long, almost plaited like her braids. He slid his hand along the curve of her groin and the surprisingly tough hair there and he realized that it extended out over her lower thigh and that it *was* braided. This surprised him and excited him almost beyond endurance until suddenly a cold thought struck him and stopped the excitement just before it made him explode.

With a stab of suspicion that made his already trembling fingers tremble harder, Hoka Ushte lifted his hand from the *winčinčalas*'s groin to her waist under the loose shift.

The maidenhair was there also, wrapped around the girl's waist like a harness.

Hoka Ushte knew at once that he had been fooled. His hand went lower, found the braid that extended between the girl's now-closed legs, and felt along the long hair as the braid ran out under the shift, under the edge of the sleeping robe, and across the tipi floor. Hoka Ushte was lying on it. He rolled half over and felt the line of hair as it crossed the sleeping space. Straight to Loud Woman.

Calf Running's mother had outsmarted him. She had used an old *Ikče Wičaśa* mother's trick and had tied a rope made of horse's hair around her daughter's waist and run it between her daughter's legs. The end would be tied to Loud Woman's ankle. Hoka Ushte drew back his trembling hand, knowing that any pressure on the horsehair braid could awaken the old woman who lay there now suspiciously silent. Perhaps she was already awake and clutching her skinning knife.

Hoka Ushte felt the last of Calf Running's warmth against his fingers as he drew back. He took the weight off the braided rope with infinite care, sliding back away from the sleeping girl the way he had once slid away from a coiled rattlesnake on a large rock where he had been napping.

It took Hoka Ushte an eternity to cross the little space to the gap where he had entered, and it took him two eternities to work up the courage to lift the flap and slide under it again. The noise and rustling of the tipi wall seemed like thunder on top of a buffalo stampede when he did so. Crouching outside, he was trying to bring his breathing back to order when a dog outside a neighboring tipi began barking and Hoka Ushte forgot all craft as he ran for the edge of the village, slid down the bank to the stream, and hid by one of the cottonwood trees there until it was almost dawn and he could creep back to his grandfather's tipi and re-enter as if he had just stepped outside a moment to make water.

Meanwhile, Hoka Ushte's body and mind were raging with frustrated passion. It was a very long night.

Early the next morning, Hoka Ushte's grandfather, *Tunkashila* Good Voice Hawk, came into the tipi, nudged the boy awake with his moccasin, and said, *"Co-o-co-o!* Wake up. Get ready. We are going to see Standing Hollow Horn."

Well, you can imagine how frightened Hoka Ushte was. He was sure that Calf Running's father had found his track in the morning and knew about his tipi-crawling. As afraid as he was of Standing Hollow Horn, Hoka Ushte discovered that he was more afraid of Loud Woman. The entire camp joked about how miserable a life Standing Hollow Horn lived as a result of his wife's barbed voice, and now Hoka Ushte imagined that she-turtle's beak attached to his own behind for the rest of his life. Dragging his feet through the dust to Calf Running's tent behind his *tunkashila*, Hoka Ushte could think of no way out of his disgrace except for suicide or exile.

Standing Hollow Horn's tipi had been cleared out except for ceremonial robes upon which the two men and the shame-faced boy sat. There was no sign of Loud Woman except for bowls of hot *pejuta sapa* which she had obviously boiled up and which Standing Hollow Horn now offered to Good Voice Hawk and Lame Badger. *Pejuta sapa* was "black medicine," the thick, sour drink which the *Ikče Wičaśa* traded for occasionally from the *Wasicun*. Even given how strong and bad-tasting the coffee was, it was considered *wakan* by some of the Sioux—second only to *mni waken,* holy water, whiskey—and in those days before *Wasicun* crawled all over the plains like lice on a buffalo hide, *pejuta sapa* was rare indeed. Hoka Ushte was surprised by such generosity, but then realized that such formality must precede a terrible dressing down.

The formality was increased after the *pejuta sapa* was swallowed when Standing Hollow Horn filled his pipe with *kinnikkinnik* and lit it. Again Hoka Ushte was surprised when he was included in this adult ritual, and again he decided that it was merely a prelude to the terrible punishment he was about to receive. The black medicine and the strong tobacco had made his tired head dizzy. He decided that he was too timid and too tired to go into exile for the rest of his life. He would kill himself.

"Hoka Ushte!" began Standing Hollow Horn in a voice so fierce and so resonant that the boy almost levitated off his blanket. "I think you know my daughter, Calf Running?"

Lame Badger was just able to say *"Ohan."* Yes. Other words fled his mind. He had no excuses.

"Washtay," said Standing Hollow Horn and dragged deeply on his pipe, handing it to Good Voice Hawk again. "It is good. You then know why your *tunkashila* and I have called you here?"

Hoka Ushte could only blink. *I will use a skinning knife,* he was thinking. *It is sharper and opens the large vein more quickly and with less pain.*

"Calf Running is growing too old to be without a husband,"

grunted Standing Hollow Horn. "It is time she wed and gave her mother and me grandchildren. This I have said to Good Voice Hawk many times. We have agreed that you would be a good husband for my daughter."

This time Hoka Ushte was not even capable of blinking.

Standing Hollow Horn continued glaring at the boy. "And last night I dreamt of you, Hoka Ushte."

The boy's eyes stayed open. He felt as if he would never blink again.

"I dreamt that I came into my lodge on a winter's evening and you were there with my daughter and two grandchildren. This morning I went to see Good Thunder and our *wičaśa wakan* says that the dream may have been a vision. He says that I am no *waayatan*, but that the dream may have been *wakinyanpi*. He says that this thing is good."

Hoka Ushte managed to move his head so that he was looking at his grandfather. Good Voice Hawk was taking smoke from the pipe. His eyes were narrowed to slits. Hoka Ushte looked back at Standing Hollow Horn. *My father-in-law?* Suddenly he imagined Loud Woman as his mother-in-law, living in the same tipi. Luckily it is considered taboo among the *Ikče Wičaśa* to speak to one's mother-in-law or to directly acknowledge her existence in any way. Another result of *wistelkiya,* fear of incest, perhaps. But a welcome taboo to Hoka Ushte at that moment.

"*Pilmaya,*" said Hoka Ushte, his voice as thin and shaky as a willow reed in a summer storm. "Thank you very much." He realized even as he spoke how stupid it sounded.

Standing Hollow Horn made an impatient gesture. "You do not understand. Good Voice Hawk?"

Hoka Ushte's grandfather blew a cloud of smoke and looked at his *takoja*. "Standing Hollow Horn and Loud Woman are ready for a grandson," he said slowly. "A baby to pamper and spoil and make *takoja* like yourself. Calf Running is ready for a husband . . ." He paused as if Hoka Ushte could see the obvious.

Hoka Ushte nodded, seeing nothing.

Good Voice Hawk sighed. "But you are not ready to be a husband," he said softly to Lame Badger.

The boy tried to understand this.

Good Voice Hawk scratched his cheek impatiently. "You have become neither a warrior nor a good hunter nor a young man interested in the affairs of the tribe. You have neither ponies nor pelts nor eagle feathers. You have never counted coup or laughed in the face of opponents who would have your scalp."

Hoka Ushte's face fell, but Good Voice Hawk went on quickly, as if to soften his words. "You know that we do not demand all of our young men to be warriors or heroes, Lame Badger. We know that what you dream and what is in your heart will determine what kind of man you will be . . ." He set a gnarled hand on the boy's shoulders. "You know that we honor even those born to be *winkte* . . ."

"I am not *winkte!*" snapped Hoka Ushte, finally stung to anger. A *winkte* was a man who dressed and acted like a woman. Some whispered that the *winkte* had the organs of both men and women. Although *winkte* were considered *wakan* and were paid well for giving children secret names of power, no self-respecting Lakota brave would want to be one. "I am not *winkte,*" Hoka Ushte said again, his voice thick.

"No, you are not *winkte*," agreed Good Voice Hawk. "But what *are* you, grandson?"

Hoka Ushte shook his head. "I do not understand your question, Grandfather."

The young man's *tunkashila* took a slow breath. "You have chosen not to join any of the warrior's societies, nor to go on pony raids, nor to learn to be a strong hunter to provide for the tribe . . . is there anything you have thought of doing that would make you a suitable husband for Calf Running? This thing must be decided so that my friend and *kola* Standing Hollow Horn can decide his daughter's future properly."

Hoka Ushte looked at his grandfather and his beloved's father. He had never known that the two had vowed *kola* together: had tied the rawhide thongs around their wrists to become such strong friends that they were essentially one person. Hoka Ushte realized that his attempted crime against Standing Hollow Horn the night before would have been a direct crime against his own *tunkashila* and he closed his eyes in gratitude to the horsehair braid Loud Woman had tied around her daughter's waist.

"Well?" prompted Standing Hollow Horn.

Hoka Ushte realized that both men were waiting for an answer that would determine his and Calf Running's future. Lame Badger's mind was a blank.

Both of the older men looked at him with eyes gone rheumy with the *kinnikkinnik* smoke.

"I had a dream . . ." began Hoka Ushte.

Both men leaned forward slightly. Dreams were important to the *Ikče Wičaśa*.

Hoka Ushte felt giddy himself, light-headed from the sleepless night, the terror, the tobacco, and the strong *pejuta sapa*. "I had a dream where I went on *hanblečeya* and became *wičaśa wakan*," said Hoka Ushte. Despite the firmness of his voice, the boy almost fainted from surprise when he heard the words that had emerged from his mouth.

Standing Hollow Horn's head jerked back in surprise and he looked questioningly at Good Voice Hawk. "A *wičaśa wakan*," he murmured. "And Good Thunder is growing old and has turned inward, especially since his wife died of the fever this past winter. A *hanblečeya* to see if this young one is called to be a *wičaśa wakan*." Standing Hollow Horn grunted and handed the pipe to Hoka Ushte. "*Washtay!*"

Good Voice Hawk looked at his grandson smoking and then he reached for the pipe himself. His lined face had softened to something perilously close to a smile. "*Washtay*," he agreed. "It is good. *Hecetu*. So be it."

Early the next morning, when the breaths of the ponies were visible in the cold air and the barking of dogs sounded almost painful to the ear, Hoka Ushte trudged to the tipi of the camp's only surviving holy man, carrying a gift of *kinnikkinnik* tobacco in a special pouch. After sharing the smoke of the gift in the fine tribal pipe the *wičaśa wakan* was custodian of, Good Thunder finally turned to look at the boy. "*Hiyupo*, tell me why you are here."

Hoka Ushte swallowed and told the holy man of his plan to go on *hanblečeya* and see if he also would be called to become a holy man.

Good Thunder squinted at him. "This is surprising to me, Hoka Ushte. In all of the seventeen summers I have known you, you have never asked me questions or come to my tipi to inquire about *wakan* things or seemed to pay much attention to the rituals I have performed for your grandparents. Why do you have this sudden inspiration to go on *hanblečeya?*"

Hoka Ushte swallowed before saying, "A dream, *Ate.*" The boy called Good Thunder "Father" out of respect.

The *wičaśa wakan* looked piercingly at the young man. "A dream? Tell me of your dream."

Hoka Ushte swallowed again and wove together bits of various dreams to create a convincing vision-dream. He was not lying. Not totally. To lie to the *wičaśa wakan* while smoking from the tribal pipe was to invite instant death from the Thunder Beings.

When the boy was finished, Good Thunder remained squinting at him. "So you dreamed that you were on a high place and a horse came out of the clouds and came down and told you that the spirits wished to speak to you? Is this your dream, Hoka Ushte?"

Hoka Ushte took a breath. *"Ohan."*

The old holy man rubbed his chin. "It is not a dream that would have sent me on *hanblečeya* when I was your age..." He looked up at the boy. "But then, times change...dreams change. None of the other young men have had *any* dreams that would lead them to the path of the *wičaśa wakan*." He touched Hoka Ushte's shoulder. "Do you know what the *hanblečeya* will demand of you?"

Lame Badger chewed his lip a moment. "I know that I must fast for four days, *Ate,*" he said. "And there will be a sweat lodge..."

"No, no," interrupted Good Thunder, setting the sacred pipe aside. "These are things *to do*. I asked you if you knew what would be demanded!"

Hoka Ushte did not speak.

"After you are prepared and the place is prepared," said Good Thunder, his voice suddenly stronger and more sonorous than Hoka Ushte had remembered for a long time, "you will be required to think only of seeing a vision. You must empty your mind of all other things. No thinking of food. No thinking of the *winčinčalas*..."

Hoka Ushte tried not to blink.

"You must think only of the vision," continued Good Thunder. "You must offer the smoke of the *čanšaša* to the Spirit of the East, then the Spirit of the North, and if these spirits do not grant you a vision, then you must offer smoke to the Spirit of the West, and if he does not gift you with a vision, you must do the same to the Spirit of the South."

"*Ohan*..." began Hoka Ushte.

"Shut up," said Good Thunder. "Now, if these spirits do not respond and you have fasted and meditated properly for several of your four days, then you offer smoke to the Spirit of the Earth, and, if this spirit does not grant your vision, you must make the smoke offering to *Wakan Tanka,* the Great Spirit of heaven itself... but only if you are sure the other spirits have not responded. Is this clear?"

Hoka Ushte bowed his head.

"Do not be discouraged if you wait a long time before you receive a vision," said Good Thunder. "The spirits are in no hurry. When you have seen a vision, do not beseech the spirits any further, but return here and we will advise you about the meaning of the vision."

Hoka Ushte nodded slightly, his head still bowed.

"If you do not have a vision we will be disappointed, but if we find the vision not acceptable," said Good Thunder, his voice sharp, "you will be disgraced and your grandparents will disown you and you will be the shame of the tribe...."

Hoka Ushte glanced up, his head still lowered. Good Thunder's lined face was glowering like a rain cloud.

"Or, if you were so foolish as to lie to us about having a vision," continued the *wičaša wakan*, "then we would end up advising you to do things that the spirits do not want you to do... and this would bring harm upon you and all who know you."

Hoka Ushte closed his eyes and wished that he had never lusted after Calf Running.

Good Thunder touched Hoka Ushte's lowered head and the boy jumped. "And even if you have a true vision," said the older man, "things may not go well for you or the tribe. If, for instance, you dream of the Thunder Beings or your hill is struck by lightning while you are on *hanblečeya,* then you instantly become a *heyoka,* a clown, a contrary..."

Hoka Ushte opened his eyes in shock. There had been a *heyoka* in the camp when he was little. The contrary holy man's name had been Passes Water in a Horn and although respected and feared— contraries were, after all, *wakan*—the *heyoka* was also rather *onsika.* Pitiful. In the midst of winter, when all others stayed by their lodge fires and huddled in thick robes, the *heyoka* Passes Water in a Horn wandered through drifts wearing nothing but a loincloth and complaining of the heat. In the summer, when Hoka Ushte and the other boys swam naked in the stream, the *heyoka* had sat shivering under robes and griped about the cold. Hoka Ushte remembered listening to the gibberish that Passes Water in a Horn had babbled and recalled his grandmother saying, "He speaks backward and only the spirits understand him. He is, after all, *heyoka.*" The last Hoka Ushte had seen of Passes Water in a Horn had been when the contrary had ridden out onto the plains—backward on his horse—and had never returned. Lame Badger remembered his grandfather whispering to his grandmother that week that the camp had lost some *wakan* but gained some peace.

"*Heyoka?*" said Hoka Ushte, his chin coming up a bit.

Good Thunder's eyes were slightly unfocused. "Or *Wakan Tanka* may call you to be a holy man other than the *wičaśa wakan* such as me," he said softly. "You could become the healer and do *yuwipi* and be wrapped tightly in blankets in the darkness so the spirits can find you. Or you might become *waayatan,* a man of visions, and give the tribe *wakinyanpi* that will determine our fate. Or you could be called to be *pejuta wičaśa* and become a man of herbs to create our medicine. Or perhaps..."

Good Thunder paused and his face grew darker. "Perhaps you will be called to be *wapiya,* the conjurer, and will shoot at disease with *waanazin.* Or perhaps you will be the most dangerous kind of conjurer, the *wokabiyeya,* who works with the witch medicine, the *wihmunge,* and sucks the disease straight out of a dying person with his own breath."

Hoka Ushte found himself shaking his head. "No, *Ate,* I only wish to be a regular *wičaśa wakan* like you and to marry Calf Running and to live a simple life."

The holy man's gaze regained its focus and Good Thunder looked at Hoka Ushte as if surprised to find him in his tipi. "Your wishes have nothing to do with what will happen next. Come to me tomorrow with more tobacco, and we will begin preparation for your *hanblečeya.*"

In the days that followed, Hoka Ushte and Good Thunder did the things necessary to prepare for the boy's vision quest. Because Good Thunder was the only holy man in the camp and the other camps of the *Ikče Wičaśa* were too far away for the other *wičaśa wakan* to be summoned, Good Thunder deputized such elders of the tribe as Hoka Ushte's *Tunkashila* Good Voice Hawk, the one-armed old man Wooden Cup, the *blota hunka* war-leader Tries to be Chief, the *eyapah,* or crier, Thunder Sounds, and old warriors Hard to Hit and Chased by Spiders to help the boy on his *hanblečeya.* Together they supervised Hoka Ushte's *inipi,* or first sweat lodge ceremony.

First, Lame Badger cut twelve white willow trees, stuck the poles in a circle about six feet across, weaved them into a dome, and covered over the dome with skins and robes and leaves. Lame Badger dug out a hole in the center of the lodge, and saved the scooped out earth to make a little path that the spirits might follow to the sweat lodge. At the end of the path, Hoka Ushte built up a little mound called an *unci,* the same word he used for grandmother, because that is the way Good Thunder taught him to think of the whole Earth: Grandmother.

Meanwhile, his real grandmother was busy. While humming softly to herself, she cut forty small squares from the flesh of her arm and set them in a *wagmuha* rattle along with *yuwipi* stones, tiny fossils that ants had gathered in their anthill.

Wooden Cup, Tries to be Chief, and Chased by Spiders took Hoka Ushte to the stream that ran out of the hills and directed his collecting of *sintkala waksu,* the special stones with tiny "beadwork" designs that showed they were safe for use in the sweat lodge. They would not crack and explode when water was thrown on them while they glowed from the heat. Good Thunder looked over the stones that Hoka Ushte had chosen and pronounced them good. *Tunkan*, the ancient and hard stone spirit who had been present at creation, had touched these *sintkala waksu*.

All this was done almost half a day's ride from the camp, because Hoka Ushte's *hanbleceya* would take place in the *Paha Sapa*, the sacred Black Hills, and the old men were trying to make it easy on him so that he would not have so far to go to and from the sweat lodge. During this time the old war leader Tries to be Chief had loaned Lame Badger a pony of his own, so for the first time the boy felt like a man as he rode across the prairie with the wind pulling at his braids. As he basked in the attention of the older men and in the approving gaze of the women in the camp, including Calf Running who watched him always now out of the corner of her eye, Hoka Ushte wished that he had thought of this vision quest idea earlier.

Finally the sweat lodge was completed, the opening was cut out facing west—Good Thunder had warned that eastern doors were only for the *heyoka*—and the sticks were set in place to hold the sacred tribal pipe. Good Thunder set a buffalo skull near the entrance and laid six tobacco offerings around it for good luck. Then the older men came for the *inipi* ceremony itself.

All of the men were naked in the sweat lodge, and at first this disconcerted Lame Badger. He was not used to seeing his elders in nothing but their own sweaty skins, nor was he comfortable being naked before them. But soon the intimacy of the tiny lodge and the steam made him forget his bashfulness.

Hoka Ushte's grandfather, Good Voice Hawk, did not enter the lodge but was the special person who closed the flap from the outside when all of the heated stones were in place. Thus Hoka Ushte was sealed within the *inipi* with Good Thunder, Chased by Spiders, Tries to be Chief, Wooden Cup, Hard to Hit, and Thunder Sounds.

The men sang *"Tunka-shila, hi-yay, hi-yay"* until the earth seemed to rock. They inhaled the steam and inhaled the smoke from the sacred pipe. Four times they opened the flap to let cool air and light in the lodge, four times they poured the water again, and four times they smoked the red willow tobacco. And all during this, the six old men gave advice to Hoka Ushte and Hoka Ushte listened with as much concentration as he could muster. It was very hot and very dark and the tobacco was very strong.

Finally, Good Thunder set down the pipe, said, *"Mitakuye oyasin,"* which means "All my relatives, everyone, all of us," and Good Voice Hawk opened the lodge flap from the outside, the old men crawled out into the light like babies being born, and the *inipi* was over.

Then Hoka Ushte set off into the *Paha Sapa* alone for his vision.

This I must tell you: visions are not easy. Some men of the *Ikče Wičaśa* wait all of their lives and never have a vision. Others have only one . . . but the rest of their lives are lived in obedience to that single vision.

Now Hoka Ushte did not know how he felt about having a vision as he crouched in his vision pit high on a ridge in the *Paha Sapa*. He was naked except for a beautiful blanket his grandmother had given him to wrap around him during the vision quest. He was unarmed except for the pipe Good Thunder had loaned him and the rattle he carried with its 405 sacred stones and the small squares of his grandmother's flesh making a soft noise within whenever he moved his hand. He was tired and a little stupid from the smoke and steam of the *inipi,* but he felt very clean, as if someone had scrubbed him thoroughly on the outside and the inside. He was hungry but he knew that he must not eat or drink for another ninety-six hours. Four days.

Or sooner, if the vision came sooner.

Hoka Ushte tried to pray, but his mind was full of images of Calf Running. His fingers remembered the heat of her groin before he had touched the horsehair rope. Even the memory of the horsehair made him excited. As empty as he was, as clean as he felt, the excitement seemed almost a vision in itself as his *che,* his child-maker, stirred almost of its own accord.

That first day and evening up in the *Paha Sapa,* the wind blew cold for the Moon When the Ducks Come Back, the medicine flags twitched and tugged on the end of the sticks around Hoka Ushte's chosen place, and he hunkered down in his shallow vision pit, trying to pray hard to the appropriate spirits but continuing to be haunted only by the visions of Calf Running's legs and thighs and shiny black hair. After dark, the air grew even colder and the April wind carried the hint of snow in it. Hoka Ushte curled in on himself and tried to empty his mind of anything except the proper thoughts suggested by the wise old men in the sweat lodge.

Toward dawn, Lame Badger fell asleep, curled tightly against the fresh soil of his vision pit, the *wagmuha* falling from his hand with a soft rattle of sacred stones and the pellets of his grandmother's flesh. Neither the cold wind nor the soft sound of the rattle woke him.

Then Hoka Ushte dreamed this thing: he saw himself sleeping in the vision pit with the stars shaking in the cold night air above him, and between his chosen place and the stars was a great boulder set in the sacred soil on the hillside above him on the mountain. And as he watched from this strange place outside his body, this giant boulder broke loose and went hurtling down the slope toward his own sleeping form.

Hoka Ushte screamed then, but his sleeping self did not waken and the scream was like the whistling of a *wanagi,* a ghost—thin and reedlike and not at all like a true man's scream. And the boulder crashed down the hillside toward his curled and uncomprehending form until all the watching Hoka Ushte could do was close his eyes and watch his sleeping self be crushed. But the *nagi,* or spirit form of himself, had no eyelids to close, so Hoka Ushte was forced to watch what happened next.

The boulder stopped inches from the sleeping Hoka Ushte. Then a voice came from the boulder and the hillside and the trees and even from the wind: *Go away, little man,* it said. *Go away and leave this place in peace. There is no vision here for you today.*

And Hoka Ushte awoke with a start. It was almost dawn. The boulder was in its proper place far up the hillside, just a large shape against the paling sky, and the only sound was the wind humming through the pine trees. But Hoka Ushte was shaken by the vision of no-vision, and he rose and wrapped his blanket tightly about his naked flesh and walked the hillside and tried to stay warm and awake at the same time.

All that next day the sun and winds were gentle on Hoka

Ushte, but no other vision came and he considered returning to Good Thunder and the others with only the tale of his non-vision. He decided against it. He remembered Good Thunder's words about a man and the tribe being disappointed if there were no vision but the man being disgraced if it were an unacceptable vision, and Hoka Ushte could not decide which category this no-vision vision fell into. At any rate, he decided to stay there until a better vision came to him.

By nightfall of the second night, with less than a day and a half of the four days complete, Hoka Ushte's tongue was swollen with thirst and his belly ached with hunger. The wind was even colder that second night and Lame Badger was sure that he would not sleep at all. But shortly before sunrise, when mists began rising from the canyon below him and were wrapping tendrils of white around the trees on his ridge, Hoka Ushte had the following dream:

Once again he was *nagi,* pure spirit essence, and once again he was floating somewhere above where his body lay twitching in a cold sleep. This time there was no boulder, but slowly he became aware of dark shapes moving between the trees and toward his sleeping self. The shapes moved through the shifting fog until they resolved themselves into the forms of a bear—a larger bear than Hoka Ushte had ever seen or dreamed of—and a mountain lion and a deer—not just any deer but a *taha topta sapa,* a sacred deer with a black streak across its face and a single fierce horn growing from its forehead— and a badger. The watching Hoka Ushte took some cheer in seeing the badger, but he quickly saw that this animal was not lame and that it had an unpleasant expression on its face. It looked both angry and hungry.

Hoka Ushte wanted to yell at his sleeping self to wake up and run away, but he knew now that his *nagi* voice was too weak to waken anyone or anything. So Hoka Ushte watched.

Slowly the bear and the mountain lion and the deer and the badger converged on the sleeping boy. The bear was so large that one swipe of his great paw would take the young man's head off. The mountain lion was so terrible that one closing of its massive jaws would crack bones open so the marrow would flow. The deer's horn was so sharp that it would pierce the sleeping Hoka Ushte the way a hunter's arrow would pierce a buffalo's liver. And the badger looked so fierce that it would grip the skin of the unlucky human's face and pull it off in a single tug the way Grandmother would tug off the slick belly skin of a rabbit being prepared for the pot.

But inches away from the sleeping Sioux, the animals stopped and the voice came again from all places: *Go away, little man. Leave this place in peace. There is no vision for you here today.*

And then Hoka Ushte awoke with a very bad heart, *lila čante xica,* terrified of the *ocin xica,* or bad-tempered animals. But he sat up, wrapped his blanket around himself, lifted the pipe that Good Thunder had loaned him for this time, held the *wagmuha* tight in his free hand, and waited for the sun to rise and warm him and renew whatever courage remained in his heart. And he stayed and fasted all that next day long. And he sat there that night as the darkness fell again.

It was a very dark night, no moon at all, clouds covering the stars, soft snow falling but melting as it touched the hillside, and Hoka Ushte was asleep hours before the sun promised to pale the sky.

This time he saw himself sleeping in the vision pit with a clarity even greater than before and for a long time it was just that sight: the boy sleeping with his pipe held in the crook of one arm and a rattle clutched in his hand. He looked like a sleeping baby, even to himself, and he wondered why he had come on this stupid quest.

Then the earth around the pit seemed to ripple and move and before the *nagi* Hoka Ushte could shout a warning to the sleeping Hoka Ushte, the vision pit had filled with rattlesnakes. Scores of rattlesnakes, perhaps hundreds. Great-grandfather rattlers longer than a man is tall, short fat female snakes ripe with eggs and venom, and countless baby snakes no longer than the boy's forearm but already armed with fangs and rattles.

This time Hoka Ushte awoke with a start and found that the dream did not flee with the opening of his eyes. He was covered with snakes. They were real. They hissed and rattled and spat and opened the impossible jaws inches from the terrified boy's eyes.

This is your last chance, little man, came the voice that Hoka

Ushte knew so well from his dreams. *Will you go away from this place and leave it in peace?*

Hoka Ushte almost cried *"Ohan!"* and almost leapt from the snake-writhing pit, but at the last second he remembered the disgrace this would mean to his grandparents and the old men who had sponsored him on this *hanblečeya,* so instead of shouting "Yes!" Hoka Ushte closed his eyes, prepared to die, gritted his teeth, and said, "No!"

When he opened his eyes the snakes were gone. The clouds had moved away so that starlight fell on everything. The starlight was so bright that Hoka Ushte could feel it on his skin. He closed his eyes. And slept.

And finally the true vision came.

Hoka Ushte returned to the sweat lodge as instructed. Two young boys had been stationed there to await his return, and while one ran to the camp to fetch the elders, the other stoked the fire to heat the stones. By mid-morning, the six elders were sitting naked in the steam and smoke listening to Hoka Ushte describe his vision.

At first Hoka Ushte had considered not telling about the no-vision visions, but by the time he had walked back to the sweat lodge from the *Paha Sapa* he had made up his mind to tell all the truth and only the truth.

The old men in the sweat lodge circle grunted as Hoka Ushte described the dreams of the falling boulder and the angry animals, and when he came to the part where he wrestled the rattlesnakes who told him to go away, the six elders cried *"Haye!"* in unison.

"But then a vision did come to me," said Hoka Ushte. "I think."

Good Thunder passed the pipe to the young man, and as Hoka Ushte inhaled, the old *wičaśa wakan* said, *"Washtay.* Tell us, *wičaśa."*

And Hoka Ushte described his vision in these words:

"After the rattlesnakes were gone I was very shaky, and I closed my eyes and dreamed this dream. First, I dreamed that I was not dreaming but was awake, and a voice said to me, 'Hoka Ushte, come to the top of the hill. *Yuhaxcan cannonpa.* Carry your pipe. Your pipe is *wakan. Taku woecon kin iyuha el woilagyape lo. Ehantan najin oyate maka sitomniyan cannonpa kin he uywakanpelo. It is used for doing all things. Ever since the standing people have been over all the earth, the pipe has been wakan.'* And so I carried my pipe to the top of the hill.

"And the top of my hill now seemed much higher than I had remembered it, and I could see all of the *Paha Sapa* as if I were looking down from *mahpiya,* in the clouds. But I could also see things close up . . . *hehaka,* elk in the forest, birds in the branches, beavers in the stream, even insects in the grass . . . it was as if I had been given the eyes of *wanbli,* eagle eyes. Then, with my new eagle eyes, I could see a *winyañ,* a woman, and she was far away in a distant valley in the *Paha Sapa,* but I could easily make out her long hair, which was unbraided except for a bit of braid on the left side which was tied up with buffalo fur, and her dress was of white buckskin and shone so brightly that it reminded me of Grandfather's stories of *Ptesan-Wi,* White Buffalo Woman, who gave us the first *chanunpa* and who taught the people all of the ways to use the pipe to pray . . ."

At this the six elders stirred and cleared their throats and looked at each other through the steam and smoke, for White Buffalo Woman was the most holy of all the sacred beings who had visited the *Ikče Wičaśa.* But the old men held their silence and let Hoka Ushte continue.

"But somehow I do not think it was White Buffalo Woman, for reasons that I will explain later in the dream," went on Lame Badger, not taking notice of the old men's close scrutiny. He was lost in his own vision-telling. "But I followed her with my eyes until she went into a cave somewhere deep in *Paha Sapa.* And then a strange thing happened . . ." The boy closed his eyes as if trying to see the dream image better. "I saw the *Paha Sapa* begin to shake as if the hills were a buffalo robe that some woman were shaking out. I saw the trees bend and the birds fly and the rocks go tumbling down into the canyons; I saw the streams stop flowing as the ground went from down to up and back to down beneath the water's course. I saw large boulders tumble and cracks open in the earth . . ."

The six old men seemed not to be breathing as they waited for Hoka Ushte's words.

". . . and then, it is hard to describe, but the ground folded back along ridges as if Grandmother Earth were giving birth, and four huge stone heads came up through the soil until they stood as tall as my taller-than-the-mountain viewing place, and their stone eyes were looking at me and I was looking back with my eagle eyes, and I think that they were *Wasicun* heads . . ."

Good Thunder cleared his throat. "Why do you think they were *Wasichu?*" he asked, using the other word for Fat Takers, the white men.

Hoka Ushte blinked as if shaken out of his dream all over again. "I've never seen a *Wasicun,*" he said, "but *Tunkashila* Good Voice Hawk has described them as sometimes having hair on their faces, and two of these stone heads had hairy faces . . . one had hair on his chin, the other under his nose like a little sparrow's wing."

The six old men looked at each other and grunted.

"Also," continued Hoka Ushte, "there was something about these stone faces that scared me the way Grandmother's come-inside-the-tipi-now evening call used to scare me when she cried, 'Hoka Ushte, istima ye, Wasicun anigni kte . . .'"

The old warriors smiled. They had also heard the mothers and grandmothers in the camp telling the children to come in and go to sleep or the white men would come and take the children away to their homes. The children were not afraid of *wanagi,* ghosts, or the *ciciye* or *siyoko* boogeymen, but the threat of the *Wasicun* always worked.

"And so," said Hoka Ushte, "I thought that these great stone heads that were born in the *Paha Sapa* were *Wasicun.* But that is not the end of my dream." He fidgeted, obviously uncomfortable about going on.

The old men waited.

"Then I dreamed that I went down into this valley and went into the cave where the beautiful woman had gone," he said in a strained voice. "And there was a fire in there that illuminated a dry place with beautiful white robes set about the floor . . ."

The men grunted again at the thought of white buffalo robes. Hoka Ushte paid no attention. ". . . and the dress of brilliant white buckskin was hanging on a deer horn set into the wall, and . . ." He licked his lips and took a breath. "And there were three beautiful women lying asleep on the robes near the fire. They were naked, and their skin glowed almost orange from the firelight and their hair was so glossy that it reflected the light . . ." He stopped again.

"Go on," said Good Thunder sternly.

"Yes, *Ate*. In my dream I walked softly into this cave room and knelt on the robe near the three sleeping women, who did not wake. And I . . . I enjoyed looking at their breasts and their smooth skin, *Ate* . . . and I thought to myself, *kicimu kin ktelo* . . . I will do it with her, but I was not sure which one to choose to do it with, because I was sure that the one that I was going to . . . going to . . ."

"*Tawiton*," said old Hard to Hit. "Fuck." The ancient warrior had little time for subtleties.

"*Ohan*," agreed Hoka Ushte, "I was sure that the one I was going to *tawiton* would awaken and cry out and wake the other two women. So I decided to choose the most beautiful of the three, but they were . . . they were like the same woman." Hoka Ushte paused and rubbed the sweat from his dripping brow and nose. The *oinikaga tipi*, sweat lodge, was very hot and smoky and it made him feel dizzy, as if he were still flying above the *Paha Sapa* in his dream and the six old men leaning close to him in the steamy darkness were just an extension of his dream images. Also, he was sure at this point that his dream was merely another of his dirty fantasies and would never be acceptable. Or worse, it was a vision sent to him by the *wakinyan* Thunder Beings and he would spend the rest of his life as a miserable *heyoka* contrary.

But Lame Badger saw nothing to do but go on. "Just as I was about to choose the woman, I heard this noise. It was a soft, grinding and rasping noise. I leaned forward and realized that it was coming from each woman's . . . from each woman's . . ."

"Go on!" commanded Tries to be Chief.

"From each woman's *winyan shan*," whispered Hoka Ushte. "From her sex. From all of their sexes . . ."

Several of the old men pulled their heads back as if Hoka Ushte had pissed on the ceremonial stones. Chased by Spiders put his hand over his eyes. Good Thunder showed no expression. "Continue," he said.

"I leaned closer," said Hoka Ushte, sweat dripping from him

freely now, "and saw that the maidenhair of the closest woman was very soft and that the lips of her *winyañ shan* were full and soft and slightly parted..." The boy snapped his head to flick sweat out of his eyes. He realized that his future was being determined by this vision, and that the old men must be shocked and furious by now. Despite their bashfulness with the opposite sex the *Ikče Wičaśa* were not a prudish people—both men and women enjoyed bawdy tales and coarse jokes within their own circles—but Hoka Ushte had never heard of such a vision as part of a *hanblečeya*. But he had no choice but to go on now.

"And inside, between the lips of her *winyañ shan*," he whispered, "I could see teeth gleaming."

"Teeth!" exclaimed Hard to Hit, a distasteful expression on his old face. "Hnnnnrrhhh." He made an angry bear noise.

"Teeth," said Hoka Ushte. "And I looked at the other two women's sex, and they had teeth there also. I could see them. I could hear them grinding softly, as when my grandfather grinds his teeth in his sleep."

Good Thunder poured more water on the stones. Steam hissed and billowed around them. "Is this all of the dream?"

"Which one did you *tawiton?*" Hard to Hit asked gruffly.

"I do not know," said Hoka Ushte, answering the second question first. "I knew that I had to choose and that it was important that I be with only one of the women, but then in my dream I was outside again, in the heavens, above the *Paha Sapa* and looking at the stone faces of the scowling *Wasicun* again with my eagle eyes. And the wind came up, and in the wind was a voice that said..."

"What?" prompted Thunder Sounds in his deep, rich crier's voice.

"Finish," commanded Wooden Cup. The stump of his missing arm, taken by the Shoshoni more than three decades earlier, glowed almost pink in the light from the glowing stones.

"The voice said that I must choose one and only one," said Hoka Ushte, "and that I must look only with the eye of my heart. And the voice said that I must do none of this until I was purified by the Thunder Beings and was born a second time..."

The old men muttered to themselves. "Is there more?" asked Good Thunder.

"Yes," said Hoka Ushte. "The voice said that after I was born a second time, I would be given a gift from a *Wasichu* whose spirit had fled."

Hard to Hit made a rude noise. "Given a gift by a dead white man? This makes no sense."

Hoka Ushte nodded his agreement.

"If you fucked any of these women, you would have lost your dick," grunted Hard to Hit. He glanced down between Hoka Ushte's legs. "But it must have been just your *nagi che,* your spirit-dick."

"I think that these three women were just one woman and she was a *winyañ sni,*" said Tries to be Chief. "A woman-who-is-not-a-woman."

Chased by Spiders opened his mouth to speak but Good Thunder touched his arm and said, "Silence! The boy is not *tanyerci yaguna.* He is not completely finished. Continue, Lame Badger."

"I was only going to say that the end of my dream was people coming out of the cave where I had been, the cave where one woman had entered and three had been sleeping," said Hoka Ushte, his voice flat with fatigue. "I saw you come out, and my grandparents, and all the people in our camp, and others—Oglala, Lakota, Brulés, Miniconjou, and others, I think—Sans Arcs, Yanktonais judging from the feathers, Crows and Shahiyela and Susuni. There were many tribes, I think, and as people from each nation emerged, they joined the others and swarmed like ants over the stone *Wasicun* faces, and I was waking then, *Ate,* but before I left my dream I saw the stone faces crumble like piled sand in a dry riverbed, and then all the *Ikče Wičaśa* and the other tribes spread out among the trees of the *Paha Sapa* . . . and then I woke and saw no more."

The old men did not speak then after Hoka Ushte was finished, but finally Good Thunder said, "My son, I think this was a vision and I think it was not a *wakinyan* vision, not a call from the Thunder Beings, but I want you to swear now that the vision was real. Swear upon pain of death from the Thunder Beings themselves, and remember that you are holding the pipe."

Hoka Ushte did not blink. *"Na ecel lila wakinyan agli—wakinyan namahon,"* he swore. There was no flash of lightning and the Thunder Beings did not destroy him.

Good Thunder nodded. *"Washtay.* Go back to the camp and your grandfather's tipi and take a nap. We six old men will talk of this thing and see if we can understand it." He took the pipe from Hoka Ushte's hand. *"Mitakuye oyasin,"* he said. "All my relatives." And the ceremony was over.

Hoka Ushte went home with his grandfather, ate some of his grandmother's soup although he had little appetite after almost four days of fasting, drank much water, slept several hours, awoke in the afternoon feeling drained and confused, and then slept again for fifteen hours. Good Thunder and the other old men returned to the camp the next morning. Good Voice Hawk went off to talk to the *wičaśa wakan* while Hoka Ushte sat at the entrance flap of his grandfather's tipi and waited to hear the direction the rest of his life would take.

Good Voice Hawk and Good Thunder came back together an hour later, and Hoka Ushte's heart sank at the sight of their grim faces.

His grandfather set a bony hand on the boy's shoulder. "The elders have not been able to agree on what your vision means," he said. "Good Thunder is traveling to Bear Butte to find some of his fellow *wičaśa wakan* so that they can help him understand this thing."

Hoka Ushte's shoulders slumped.

"Heya!" said his grandfather, slapping the boy's arm. "They are sure that it is a real vision."

"And I am sure that it is not from the Thunder Beings," said Good Thunder. "You are not *heyoka.*"

Hoka Ushte brightened up.

"The Yanktonais, Two Kettles, Hunkpapa, and Miniconjou *Ikče Wičaśa* holy men are meeting at the bear-shaped holy hill north of the *Paha Sapa,"* rasped Good Thunder. "I will join them."

Hoka Ushte frowned. "How do you know that the holy men of

these tribes are meeting there, *Ate?"* There had been no runners or visitors in the village for months.

Good Thunder folded his arms. "I am *wičaśa wakan."* His tone lightened a bit. "If your vision means that you are meant to be a holy man, then you too shall understand these things someday, Lame Badger. *Heceutu!* I go now."

Much of the camp turned out to watch old Good Thunder with two of his adopted grandsons, Fat Pony and Tarries by the Water, leave on his mission. The ride to Bear Butte would take two days and it might be several more days until the other holy men found time to meet with Good Thunder to wrestle the meaning out of the vision. Meanwhile, Hoka Ushte went about his business in camp, but he soon became aware of a different attitude aimed toward him; the braves his age who had treated him with some contempt for not joining a warrior society now nodded politely or stopped to have conversation; the old women smiled openly at him and the younger wives peered at him from the corners of their eyes; Calf Running herself nodded and smiled as she walked toward the stream with her water skin. Hoka Ushte realized that they were no longer looking at just a young brave with seventeen summers, but at the future holy man of the camp.

And so it went for two days of Good Thunder's absence. And so it might have gone until the real *wičaśa wakan's* return, if Standing Hollow Horn and Loud Woman had not begun a premature celebration of their daughter's marriage to the young man who had just completed his *hanblečeya.*

Loud Woman began it by telling everyone that her daughter was going to marry Hoka Ushte as soon as Good Thunder returned to tie the thongs. When Lame Badger's grandmother clucked at this news, the boy said, "You are not pleased, Grandmother?"

The old woman did not look up from punching awl and sinew through the worked hide. "This thing is not right. The girl has not gone to her *isnati* for two moons."

Hoka Ushte blushed and looked down, he was so shocked. He could not believe his grandmother was talking about *isnati.* The time of a woman's bleeding was considered both *wakan* and fearful. The woman had to isolate herself during the four days she was *isnati,* more due to the fear of her power than from any sense of casting her out. Hoka Ushte did not understand *isnati,* but even he knew that a woman who was in that time could kill a rattlesnake by spitting at it. A *wičaśa wakan* who tried to treat a woman who was *isnati* could kill both himself and the woman by accident, so great was the woman's power at that time.

These things he understood, but Hoka Ushte had no idea why it should be a problem if Calf Running had taken two moons off from her *isnati.* Would this not be a good thing? He decided to ignore his grandmother's cluckings and concentrate on his newfound popularity.

After Loud Woman spread the word that her daughter and Good Voice Hawk's grandson would be married soon, her husband, Standing Hollow Horn, complicated the matter by throwing an *otuhan.* Now an *otuhan* is a big give-away where a proud father sets out his blanket and gives away prize possessions to honor a child. In this case, the usually surly Standing Hollow Horn was giving away his second-best knife, his deer-hide bow cover, his best pony blanket, and other things to celebrate the coming marriage.

Hoka Ushte began to feel anxious. Things were happening too fast.

His nervousness grew stronger on the fourth day when Standing Hollow Horn held a feast and named Hoka Ushte guest of honor. Most of the men of the village were invited. Standing Hollow Horn raised the level of importance of the feast by making the main course dog soup. For a man to sacrifice a good friend such as his dog for another man was considered almost *wakan.* Of course, Standing Hollow Horn had no dog of his own and had to buy a puppy from Tall Horse, the son of Chased by Spiders, but it was the idea that counted.

The feast lasted much of that fourth night Good Thunder was gone, but Hoka Ushte was too nervous to enjoy it. He hardly smiled when six braves paired off in teams of two for the buffalo intestine-eating contest, each team starting from opposite ends of a long string of raw buffalo gut, chewing their way toward the middle. The older braves roared as the competing braves had to pause and belch from their meals of the half-digested and fully fermented buffalo grass that filled the intestines. Later, when it was Hoka Ushte's turn to ladle out his bowl of soup, he came up with the puppy's head. This was considered good luck for Hoka Ushte and a very good omen for the coming marriage, but Lame Badger's sense of it all being too premature made him more nervous than appreciative. He did, however, appreciate the meal. Dog soup had always been a treat for him, and the puppy's head was delicious.

Then, the next morning, Good Thunder returned with his adopted grandsons and all of the celebration ended. The angry *wičaśa wakan* called Hoka Ushte and most of the older men of the village to a meeting in his tipi that afternoon. After the proper offerings were made and the pipe was passed, here is what the holy man said:

"The other *wičaśa wakans* were waiting for me at Bear Butte. Drinks Water, the prophet, had had a vision of my coming with an important message. We retired to the sweat lodge at once. Besides the prophet Drinks Water, the *wičaśa wakans* Chips, Hump's Brother, Refuses-to-Go, Fire Thunder, and Holy Black Tail Deer were there."

At this, the men in Good Thunder's tipi gasped, for these were the most famous holy men of the *Ikče Wičaśa*.

"I told them of Hoka Ushte's vision," continued Good Thunder, his voice flat, "and they smoked and meditated upon it. After some hours, we understood it."

The silence in the tipi was thick as the smoke.

"Lame Badger's vision is a true vision and an important one," said the old holy man, his tone still more one of anger than of anything else. "Drinks Water confirms that this dream is of the *wakinyanpi* . . . that Hoka Ushte was chosen as *waayatan*, as prophet, to bring a message to all the peoples of the *Ikče Wičaśa*."

Hoka Ushte set his fingers on the robe beneath him to hold himself upright. The smoke made him dizzy to the point of fainting. He saw his grandfather blink in surprise and Standing Hollow Horn puff himself up in importance. *I will be wičaśa wakan,* thought the boy. *Calf Running will have a holy man as a husband.*

Good Thunder inhaled smoke from the tribal pipe as if fortifying himself for what he had to say next. "Hoka Ushte's vision is true sight from *čante ista,*" he continued. "From the eye of the heart. Its meaning is this . . . the *Wasichu,* the *Wasicun,* will someday overrun us. The Fat Takers will take away our life on the plains, take away the buffalo, take away our weapons, and steal the *Paha Sapa*—our holy Black Hills—away from us. The stone *Wasicun* heads mean this. *Tunkan,* the stone spirit who was there at creation and who gives us the *Inyan,* the holy rocks, has sent us a vision. There is no escaping this. The *Ikče Wičaśa*'s time as natural free humans is almost over..."

The men in the tipi shouted their anger and disagreement, ignoring manners by interrupting Good Thunder.

"No!" they shouted and murmured, and *"Šiča"*—Bad!—and one warrior whispered that Good Thunder was *witko,* crazy.

"Silence!" said the holy man, and although he had not raised his voice, the entire tipi seemed to shake from the force of his command. Into the sudden silence, he said, "This is not good news but it is the truth. For a full day the other holy men and I sought our own visions, hoping against hope that *Iktomé* or Coyote were tricking us, leading us to foolishness through false visions. But the voice of *Wakan Tanka* was heard by each of us... this thing is true. The *Wasicun* will take our lives, our horses, our freedom and our future. The great stone heads foretell this. The life of the natural free humans as we know it will be finished. Rubbed out. But..." Good Thunder raised his hand to silence the renewed muttering. "But, there is some hope in Hoka Ushte's vision."

Hoka Ushte himself was barely conscious at this point. The sound of the terrible message that he had brought and the glares from the other men seemed to be far away down a long tunnel. He set his palms against the ground to keep himself from toppling over.

"The woman in the vision is not White Buffalo Woman, but she comes from the same place as White Buffalo Woman and may be her sister," continued the holy man.

Dimly, at the end of his dark tunnel of perception, Hoka Ushte thought, *But there were three women in my dream, Ate.*

Good Thunder turned his head. His old black eyes bored into Lame Badger. "There were three women in the dream, but there is really only one woman... White Buffalo Woman's sister with the shining robe. The other two women in the cave represent the evil sides of this spirit—the evil sides will want to punish us, the real sister of White Buffalo Woman will grant us salvation."

How will I know which woman is the one who will save us? thought Hoka Ushte, already believing that the old holy man was reading his thoughts.

Good Thunder grunted and looked back around the circle of red-eyed men. "The fire in Hoka Ushte's dream is the *peta-owihankeshni*, the fire without end, the same fire that has been kept burning in this tribal pipe since Buffalo Woman visited us so long ago. The presence of this flame in the dream is good. It means that there will be *Ikče Wičaśa* to hand down the flame from generation to generation. *If* Lame Badger makes the right choice..."

How, Father? Hoka Ushte pleaded mentally, already understanding that the choice was his and that the fate of his people was in his soft hands. *How?*

"The smoke from the fire in Hoka Ushte's dream was *Tunkashila's* breath," continued the holy man, evidently not hearing the boy's desperate thoughts, "and that is good. It is the living breath of Grandfather Mystery." He turned to look at Hoka Ushte again. "And if your choice is correct, the end of the dream shall be as you have seen it... the natural free human beings will be free again. The *Wasicun* will be overthrown and will crumble to dust just as their stone heads did in the dream. The buffalo shall return, the *Paha Sapa* will belong to the people who love them, and the *Ikče Wičaśa* will walk in the sunlight of their natural ways once again."

All eyes were on Hoka Ushte, but it was Good Voice Hawk who spoke. "When will this come about, Father?"

Good Thunder closed his eyes as if he were tired. "The choice must be made in this young man's lifetime. The Age of the Stone Heads will begin in the lifetime of our children. Our return from the cave of exile will happen..." The old man sighed. "I do not know. We could not see far into the dream or into the future."

"Moons?" said Without a Tipi, a brave warrior who had never been too bright.

Chased by Spiders made a rough noise. "In the time of our children," he repeated. "Years then, *Ate?*"

Good Thunder's eyes were still closed. "Perhaps hundreds of years. Perhaps a hundred hundred. Perhaps never." He opened his eyes. "It depends upon Hoka Ushte's choice."

The young man looked back at all the eyes: shocked, accusing, curious, and angry. He wanted to say, *I did not choose this vision.*

It was Standing Hollow Horn who spoke. "But his grandfather and I have chosen the wife for him. It is to be Calf Running."

Good Thunder made a dismissing motion with his left hand. "It is not to be Calf Running. This is clear from the dream."

Standing Hollow Horn stood, cursed, slapped the side of the tipi, said, "But I have held a Big Give-Away!" saw the flatness of Good Thunder's gaze, and left the tipi in anger.

Hoka Ushte sighed. Now he had made an enemy of the shortest-tempered man in the camp. All this because his child-maker wanted to stand as straight as a lodge pole.

"Is there anything we can do?" asked Hard to Hit. "Anything the people can do to change this vision?" He looked at Lame Badger and the boy could hear the unspoken question: *To give the choice to someone else?*

"No," said Good Thunder.

Hoka Ushte licked his lips and spoke for the first time. "Must I go on another *hanbleČeya, Ate?*"

"No," repeated Good Thunder. "But the other holy men and I think that you should have a time of *oyumni.*"

Hoka Ushte chewed his lip. *Oyumni* was not a vision quest, merely a time of wandering. He felt sad and frightened at the thought of leaving the camp and his grandparents.

Then, despite the fact that a thousand questions remained in the hearts of the men sitting there and ten times that number in Hoka Ushte's frightened heart, Good Thunder set down the pipe and said, *"Mitakuye oyasin.* All my relatives."

And the meeting was over.

Hoka Ushte did not sleep that next night. Everyone in the camp had looked at him strangely after the vision-explaining ceremony with Good Thunder. Even his grandparents glanced at the boy as if a strange spirit being had come to live with them. *It is all a bad dream,* thought Hoka Ushte, but when he awoke the next morning the glances were still there, the weight of responsibility on his shoulders was still there, and his vision had not been a dream.

His grandfather found him sitting on a rock near the stream late that morning and said, "You have been invited to Standing Hollow Horn's tipi for food this afternoon."

Hoka Ushte felt his heart speed up. "Must I go, Grandfather? Standing Hollow Horn frightens me with his anger."

Good Voice Hawk made a motion with his hand. "Standing Hollow Horn is not there. He left this morning to hunt buffalo. He is very angry."

Hoka Ushte felt a surge of happiness. "Is it Calf Running who invited me?"

His grandfather shrugged. "Loud Woman gave me the invitation. I do not know if her daughter will be there."

Hoka Ushte slumped at the thought of eating with the sharp-beaked older woman. "Must I go?"

"Yes," said his grandfather. "And dress well. Wear your beaded shirt with the fringed sleeves."

Two hours later, Hoka Ushte presented himself at Standing Hollow Horn's tipi. The boy was wearing his best outfit with the beads and fringed sleeves. Standing Hollow Horn was not there. Calf Running was nowhere in sight. Only Loud Woman sat near the boiling pot, cutting vegetables. She waved him to a robe set near the fire and smiled at him. Hoka Ushte could not remember ever seeing the old woman smile before.

"I am honored that the vision-seeker has accepted my invitation," said the woman, still smiling.

Hoka Ushte felt a rush of confusion. Was she being sarcastic? *Ikče Wičaśa* women are known for their sarcasm and sharp tongues. And no tongue was sharper than this crone's. Or was she trying to curry favor with him now that he was famous? "I am honored to accept your invitation," said Hoka Ushte, deciding to be polite.

Loud Woman continued smiling and continued chopping turnips. Hoka Ushte saw that she was using the large skinning knife. "What is it you are cooking?" he asked politely.

"Guess."

"Timpsila," said Hoka Ushte, since all he had seen go into the pot were turnips.

"No," said Loud Woman, brushing the last bits of turnips into the boiling broth. "Guess again."

Hoka Ushte rubbed his cheek. *"Wojapi?"* He liked berry soup, but he had never seen it with turnips in it before.

Loud Woman smiled but shook her head. "No. But it will be *lila washtay.* Very good. Do you want to guess again, or do you want me to tell you?"

"Tell me," said Lame Badger. He felt ill at ease with the woman.

"It is *itka,* egg soup," she said.

"Ahhh," said Hoka Ushte, thinking: *egg soup?*

Loud Woman's smile had grown into a broad grin. She stood. "Yes," she cooed, "your *itka.* Your eggs. Your *susu.* Your balls." And she jumped on Hoka Ushte with a wild cry.

The boy had the presence of mind to seize her wrist before the skinning knife descended on him, and the two rolled over across the robes and dirt, Loud Woman hissing and screaming like a Thunder Being, and Hoka Ushte gritting his teeth and struggling to keep his *susu* attached. The woman actually sliced through the flap of his breechcloth before Hoka Ushte freed his right hand, made a fist, and punched her hard on the jaw. Loud Woman flew backward, the knife spinning off into the high grass, and then she dropped heavily onto the embers of the fire, screamed, and rolled away onto the buffalo robes, embers still glowing in her hair and deerskin skirt.

Not a good way to treat your mother-in-law, thought Hoka Ushte, brushing himself off shakily. *No, not my mother-in-law now.*

He went back to his grandfather's tipi. Both his *tunkashila* and his *unči kunshi* were outside waiting for him. His grandmother had tears in her eyes.

"I think I will leave for my *oyumni* now," said Hoka Ushte.

Both grandparents nodded. His grandfather had one of his ponies ready; Hoka Ushte's bow, arrows, knife, medicine pouch, robe, and extra moccasins were rolled in a bundle on the pony blanket. His grandmother gave him a bag with *papa* and *wasna* in it: traveling food.

"Toksha ake wacinyanktin ktelo," said his grandfather with a touch of the boy's forearm. *I will see you again.*

Hoka Ushte hugged his grandparents, swung himself up on the pony, and rode out of camp to the stares of many people. He decided that it would be best if he were far away before Loud Woman woke up; best if he were even farther away before Standing Hollow Horn returned from his buffalo hunt.

And thus began Hoka Ushte's *oyumni*. His wandering time.

All right, I see you changing your tapes and know that this will not be recorded, but I want to explain something to you while you fiddle with the machine.

When I describe the world Hoka Ushte went out alone into, you may recognize some of the places since you know these parts of South Dakota. But you are wrong. The Black Hills which Hoka Ushte visited for his *hanbleceya* are not the ones you can drive through today. And not just because there were no stone heads then, or towns or highways or ranches or rock shops or rattlesnake reptile gardens or taxidermy studios or Indian Craft souvenir shops or Jellystone Park campgrounds or casino towns or RV parks. No, the *Paha Sapa* were a different place because they were a different place. The *Wasicun* bring more than shitty souvenir shops and barbed wire fences, they bring a darkness and a bad smell that hides the sun that shone on the Black Hills where Hoka Ushte had his vision.

Nor were the plains and badlands that Hoka Ushte is to visit in my story like the plains and badlands you may have driven to. It is not just that today's high plains are divided and parceled by fence and highway, county roads and Interstate, nor that they are littered with *Wasichu* towns and crappy tract homes or mobile homes lined up along the highway like so many six-pack empties glinting in the sun.

No, the difference is not just that the world was empty then and it is crowded with Fat Taker garbage today. Uh-uh. The world that Hoka Ushte rode his pony into that May afternoon so long ago was sparsely populated—a man could ride his horse for days without seeing a sign of another human being—but it was far from empty.

On the grasslands then were the buffalo, still numbered in the millions when Hoka Ushte was a young man, and the animals—wolf and elk not yet driven from the prairie, bears still wandering far from the mountain homes, eagles soaring overhead, badgers in holes along the riverbeds, rattlesnakes and lizards, a single prairie dog metropolis with a population greater than Rapid City today, and, of course, there were the flies and insects and hoppers such as the *ptewoyake* which used to tell the *Ikče Wičaśa* where we could find the buffalo.

But the world was full of more than animals: Hoka Ushte rode his pony into a landscape which was busy with hostile people.

The *Wasicun,* yes, but he had never seen a Fat Taker and feared them only as one would fear a boogeyman. The terrible message of his dream made white people only more unreal to him. More real were the other Indians who were out there somewhere, camping just over the horizon or lying in wait for a lone wanderer. There were the other branches of the *Ikče Wičaśa*—the Oglalas, Miniconjous, and the Brulés Sioux. And there were those who would scalp a Lakota boy on sight: the *Susuni,* whom you call Shoshoni, and the *Shahiyela,* the Cheyennes, and the *Kangi Wicasha* or Crows, who were sometimes friends and allies and frequently deadly enemies, and the Blue Clouds, whom you call Arapahoes. There were older enemies such as the Omahas, Otos, Winnebagoes, and Missouris, whose land the *Ikče Wičaśa* had stolen or had tried to steal before Hoka Ushte was born. And there were the Pawnees and Poncas, whose land we were trying to steal in the days that Hoka Ushte knew. The Pawnees were ass-kissers and the asses they chose to kiss were *Wasicun,* even then, and in exchange for smooching Fat Taker ass the Pawnees were killing *Ikče Wičaśa* with muskets and even rifles which the *Wasichu* horse soldiers gave them.

Beyond the Pawnee were the Three Tribes, the Mandans, Hidatsas, and Arikaras, and they hated our people with a blue passion since we had stolen their land, killed their braves, and burned their villages on our own expansion west. And farther west, Hoka Ushte knew, were the Santees and the Yankonais and the Hunkpapas, all of whom regularly sent war parties east and south to kill any *Ikče Wičaśa* they might run across.

And down from the mountains to hunt on the plains came the Ute and the Flathead and the Pend d'Oreille, and while they might not have the courage to raid a Lakota village, they would kill a lone Lakota brave to show what big men they were. Hoka Ushte knew that his scalp would be a prize hanging from the lance or lodgepole of any brave in a dozen nearby tribes.

And all the tribes I have mentioned and many that I will not take time to mention feared the Blackfeet. And while the Blackfeet were busy slaughtering the River Crows, the Assiniboins, the Grosventre, the Crees, the Plains Ojibwas, and the big Ojibwas—the Chippewa— during the year of Hoka Ushte's *oyumni*, they were not too busy to pass up slaughtering a lone Lakota brave who barely knew how to use his bow.

Hoka Ushte knew that the empty land was not empty. But that is not the biggest difference in what he saw then and what you or any other *Wasicun* would see today.

The landscape that Hoka Ushte wandered across was more alive than you can even imagine. *Woniya waken*—the very air was alive. Spirit breath. Renewal. *Tunkan. Inyan.* The rocks were alive. And holy. The storms that moved above the prairie were *Wakinyan,* the noise of the thunder spirit and sign of the Thunder Beings. The flowers that bloomed in the endless grass showed the touch of *Tatuskansa,* the moving spirit, the quickening power. In the rivers dwelt the *Unktehi,* monsters and spirits both. At night, Hoka Ushte would hear the howl of the coyotes and think of Coyote, who would trick him if he could. Or a spiderweb on a tree would bear a message from *Iktomé,* the spider man who was a worse trickster than Coyote. And at evening, when all of the other spirits were quiet and the sky was emptying of light and cloud, that is when Hoka Ushte could hear the breathing of Grandfather Mystery and *Wakan Tanka* himself. And at night, when the stars spread from horizon to horizon with no lights or reflected lights in all the world to dim their glory, then Hoka Ushte could trace the path of his own life, knowing that his spirit would travel south along the Milky Way when he died.

So the world was not empty.

I see the glaze on your eyes. I see the impatience in the set of your body.

But I want you to understand a little bit. The world was different for Hoka Ushte.

All right. Turn on your machine.

*   *   *

For the first two days of Hoka Ushte's wandering, he rode his grandfather's horse east and then south across the grass plains, his back to the *Paha Sapa* and the more hostile tribes he knew to live in the west. At night he built no fire but ate the *papa* and *wasna* his grandmother had prepared for him: dried meat and pemmican pounded together with berries and kidney fat. Traveling food. On the third day he shot a rabbit with his bow and cooked it over a fire so small that, if it had been winter, he could have easily huddled over it with his blanket hiding the glow of the embers. The rabbit was tough and tasted nothing like the excellent meal his grandmother made.

On the night of the third day, he lost his horse.

It happened this way. All that day he had been skirting the edge of a dried-out and dangerous place which he knew as *Mako Sicha* and which you know as the Badlands. Hoka Ushte did not like the look of this place—all dust and rock and sinuous ridges and tortuous riverbeds left over from ancient floods—but more than that he did not like the stories he had heard about it. This dry place had been the battleground between *Wakinyan Tanka,* the great thunderbird, and *Unktehi,* whom some call *Uncegila,* the great water monster who had once filled the Missouri River from end to end. Before the battle was over, *Unktehi* had drowned most of the free human beings and only an all-out war between *Wakinyan* and his little thunderbirds against *Unktehi* and her little water monsters had saved the remnants of the *Ikče Wičaśa.*

So on the third night, Hoka Ushte hobbled his grandfather's horse in a relatively sheltered spot away from the Badlands, cooked his stringy rabbit, and settled into his blanket for another night of fitful sleep. But before *hanhepi wi,* the night-sun, had risen, a blue-black wall of storm crossed the prairie, hiding the stars, and rumbling like some ancient beast out of Good Thunder's stories. Just as Hoka Ushte sat up in his blanket with a thought to soothing his horse, the air was suddenly filled with *wakangeli,* the bad-smelling electricity a storm generates, lightning flashed from sky to earth not a quarter of a mile away, and his grandfather's horse slipped its inexpertly tied hobble and bolted away toward the Badlands.

Hoka Ushte leaped to his feet and shouted, but the horse did not heed him. The two raced across a prairie illuminated by sudden explosions from the approaching storm, the horse soon leaving the panting boy far behind. Hoka Ushte's last glimpse of the animal was as it disappeared up an arroyo just before the rain began.

Lame Badger hesitated at the edge of *Mako Sicha,* thinking that it would be wiser to go back to his camp and wait out the storm before going into those steep gullies and dark shadows. But he knew that if he did so, he would never see his grandfather's horse again. The Lakota word for horse was a fairly new word since the horse had been with the *Ikče Wičaśa* for only a few generations; *sunka wakan* meant "holy dog" and the animal was still considered sacred because of its importance. Hoka Ushte could not go home again if he lost Good Voice Hawk's horse.

He entered the Badlands just as the storm struck with full force. The moon had been hidden earlier, but now the darkness was thick and absolute. It made Hoka Ushte think of the *yuwipi* ceremony where the holy man was wrapped tight in blankets and robes and left in a dark place so that the spirits could find him.

At first the rain was merely an icy blast against his face and soaked clothing, but soon the downpour was so terrible that Hoka Ushte could not stand upright. He knelt in deep mud and water. The lightning flashes came so quickly now that the boy's eyes could not adapt to either darkness or light and he was as good as blind. Thunder grew beyond thunder and became the ripping, tearing sound of *Wakinyan Tanka's* huge beak and talons, the screams of the Thunder Beings. The ravines and gulleys and arroyos had become a terrible maze that Hoka Ushte could not find the exit from even if he had been able to stand and walk in the terrible storm. The *wakangeli* filled the air and made the boy's hair stand on end.

It was several minutes before Hoka Ushte realized that he would die if he stayed where he was. The water in the narrow arroyo was rising quickly, running in torrents from some high, rocky place deeper in *Mako Sicha.* Hoka Ushte squinted upward into the icy torrent: the ridgeline seemed a hundred feet above, its serrated edge outlined by a sky filled with lightning. Even as he watched, great yellow bolts struck boulders along the ridge. If he climbed, the lightning would almost certainly strike and kill him. If he stayed where he was, the rising water would certainly drown him.

Hoka Ushte began clambering up in the steep hillside, sliding back as great sections of mud gave way and sent him plummeting back into the roaring torrent below. The water was above his waist the last time he climbed out of the gulley. The steep hillside was a maze of rivulets and muddy waterfalls. The rain had turned to hail now and was battering Hoka Ushte's face and shoulders. He felt as if he were being stoned to death by the *Wakinyan*.

Finally Hoka Ushte had to use his knife, sinking its blade deep into the hillside to find a grip against the sliding mud. He felt as if he were trying to stab the earth to death while the skies tried to kill him with icy fists. The hail tore his clothes now, ripping through buckskin and flesh. His hair was matted down over his eyes, his braids torn asunder, and blood flowed from his temples and brow. He could not open his eyes and only realized he had made it to the top of arroyo cliff when there was no more hillside to sink his blade into.

Lame Badger lay there, straddling the narrow ridge as if he were on a bucking spirit horse, letting go of his knife to sink his fingers deep in the mud, face in the wet soil, toes scrabbling to stay put as the wind shoved him and the hail continued to pummel. Lightning struck a hundred places on the ridgelines around him. At one point, Hoka Ushte raised his bleeding face to the exploding skies and howled like a wolf, teeth bared, daring the *Wakinyan* to do their worst.

Then the skies seemed to open further, the hailstones grew to the size of fists, and Hoka Ushte knew no more.

When he awoke he thought that perhaps the skies had killed him. Then he squinted into a perfectly blue sky, saw the salt-white hills and gulleys around him already beginning to dry in the mid-morning sun, heard the trickle of the streams in the narrow folds below him, and realized that he was not yet in the other world where spirits go. There, he knew, colors were dim, the sun never shone brighter than on a foggy day, and sounds were muted. Hoka Ushte sat up on the ridge and looked down at himself in wonder.

He was naked. Not even his breechcloth had survived the floods and hail. There were a hundred bruises and a thousand scratches on his bronze body. He moaned aloud when he shifted his legs, then stifled any further moans. He might not belong to a warrior society, but he was a brave of the *Ikče Wičaśa* and he must behave as one.

His knife was gone. More than that, the very soil of the ridgeline had been washed away by the night's torrent so that nothing remained except the oddly irregular stones that had lain beneath the dirt. Hoka Ushte began moving toward the edge of the Badlands by hopping from one to another of these regular stone ridges.

He had advanced several hundred stones before he realized that these rocks were *too* regular. When he glanced back, still squinting in the glare of sunlight on white rock, he knew at once it was not rock upon which he had been treading.

Hoka Ushte was standing on one curved plate of a great, exposed vertebrae: a gleaming white spine of something long buried in *Mako Sicha* and now partially uncovered by the night's violent downpour. He realized at once that he was standing on *Unktehi* . . . *Uncegila* . . . the ancient serpent god who had lost her battle to *Wakinyan Tanka* ages ago when the rocks were young.

The exposed spine stretched miles into the Badlands, disappearing where other folds covered it or revealed white rock that may have been more bones.

Hoka Ushte began to shake. *Unktehi* was *wakan,* but it was a type of sacredness that carried more power than any *Ikče Wičaśa* holy man could deal with, much less a boy of seventeen summers. Hoka Ushte could feel the *wakan* power flowing up through his bare feet as if the *wakangeli* electricity of the night before had all been stored in the bleached white bones that curved away under him. He glanced toward the edge of the Badlands still a quarter of a mile away, then looked fearfully over his shoulder as if *Unktehi* might rise up, flesh materializing around the ancient bones as she did so, her serpent's teeth the size of mountains, her eyes blazing more fiercely than the sun.

He was tempted to slide down the steep hillside away from the exposed bone-boulders, slide to the shadowed gulley below where the last of the floods were drying. But wading through that mud and following the winding arroyos would take him hours, if he did not get lost or mired to his waist down there.

Hoka Ushte closed his eyes, thought of his vision, stopped the shaking of his legs, and continued to hop from vertebra to vertebra, absorbing the power that flowed up through his feet and ankles and legs and groin. By the time he reached the grasslands and stepped from the last patch of white bone where the great skeleton seemed to burrow deeper into the earth, Hoka Ushte felt his entire body tingling and muscles jumping as if he were a *yuwipi* man filled with spirit force. Many of his bruises were gone and most of the scratches had healed.

Two hundred paces onto the grasslands and Hoka Ushte looked back. Only white rocks and white sand gleamed in *Mako Sicha*.

He could not find his camp. Not only were his horse and knife lost, but the floods had carried away or buried his bow, arrows, robe, blanket, flints, extra clothes, and the extra bits of food he had been saving. After an hour of searching, Hoka Ushte gave it up and started walking east.

Naked, muscles still twitching from the *wakan* energy, limping a bit as his bare feet trod on cactus or yucca, the Badlands first fading and then disappearing behind him, he walked toward the horizon of a perfectly flat world.

He saw them first as a shifting, four-headed creature coming toward him through the heat haze of the late afternoon. Hoka Ushte was certain that it was one of the monsters his grandmother had warned him about—a *ciciye* or *siyoko*. There was no place to hide, the grasslands stretched forever to either side, and Hoka Ushte had no intention of hiding anyway. He stood and waited for the monster to come to him.

The four-headed monster was neither *ciciye* nor *siyoko*, merely a pony with three young men riding it. Hoka Ushte realized that three braves from another tribe were probably more dangerous than a monster, but he continued to stand his ground. As they came closer, he could see that the pony was exhausted and lathered, the three braves no older than he. Their faces were streaked with war paint and when they saw Hoka Ushte standing there they whooped, raised coup sticks, and swung the laboring pony in his direction.

It is a good day to die, thought Hoka Ushte, but the brave sentiment was just a phrase. He did not want to die and his heart was pounding. More than not wanting to die, he did not want to die naked and defenseless by the hand of Shoshoni or Crow boys who were not even old enough for each to have a horse.

They were not Shoshoni or Crow. Hoka Ushte saw the face paint, heard their cries as they drew closer, and recognized them as *Ikče Wičaśa,* although their crude dialect suggested Brulé Sioux. He saw now that they were younger than he; the oldest could not be more than fifteen summers. On their part, the three boys on horseback ceased their wild coup cries and pulled their pony to a halt ten paces away when they saw Hoka Ushte standing there naked. For a minute there was no sound except for the rasping of the exhausted pony's breathing and the dry leaping of hoppers in the grass.

"Hoka hey!" said the oldest boy at last. "Are you a human being?"

Hoka Ushte glanced down at himself and realized that he must appear more frightening than the braves, naked, scratched, and bleeding as he was. "Yes," he said, and told his tribe and family.

The oldest boy swung down off the pony and advanced with his coup stick still extended as if he were going to count coup on this strange apparition after all. After merely touching Hoka Ushte as if to confirm his reality, the boy stepped back and lifted his palm. "I am called Turning Eagle, the son of Cuts Many Noses. These are my friends Few Tails and Tried to Steal Horses.

Hoka Ushte glanced at the boys, who merely blinked back.

"Yesterday we killed two *Susuni* and since then have been chased by fifty *Susuni* on horseback." There was pride as well as fear in the boy's voice.

Hoka Ushte looked to the east but could not see the fifty Shoshoni. Some haze on the horizon might have been a dust cloud.

"We were hunting," said Turning Eagle, "when we found a *Susuni* making camp near the White River. He was with his woman and a boy of five or six summers. When he saw us, the man leaped upon his horse, pulled his boy up, and ran, leaving his woman. We

killed her and gave chase, although we had just this one pony..."
Turning Eagle gestured toward the rasping pony as if this were a
point of pride. Hoka Ushte thought that the pony was near collapse.

"When he tried to ford the river," continued Turning Eagle,
"we put two arrows into him and he fell off his horse and we caught
him down river." The boy held up a bloody scalp. "He died well. We
swam the river to get his horse and the boy, but the child had his
hands wrapped tightly in the pony's mane and the horse was faster
than ours. We had chased them an hour when we came over a hill
and saw the *Susuni* war party with the boy in the valley. They chased
us. We lost them for a while near the river. Now they are behind us
again." Turning Eagle touched his chest with pride.

Hoka Ushte looked nervously to the east. The haze was definitely a dust cloud and it was closer. "Where are you going?"

Turning Eagle bit his lip. "Our camp was somewhere between
here and the river, but we missed it in the night. We can not go
back. We are going to the *O-ana-gazhee*. The Sheltering Place."

Hoka Ushte nodded. The *O-ana-gazhee* was a high place in the
Mako Sicha where a few braves could hold off an army of Shoshoni.
But it was many miles away. There was no chance that this exhausted
pony could outrun a war party. These boys were dead.

Turning Eagle stepped closer and spoke in a near whisper so
that his friends could not hear. "I am not afraid to die, but I will
miss the girl named Sees White Cow. I had promised her that I
would count coup and return to her." The boy looked at Hoka Ushte
almost regretfully. "If the *Susuni* were not going to kill you as well, I
would ask you to tell Sees White Cow that I would have come back
to her if I could have."

Hoka Ushte blinked.

Turning Eagle stepped back and said more loudly, "It is a good
day to die." He swung up on the pony. The two boys behind him
looked very young and very frightened.

"Hoka hey!" cried Turning Eagle and dug his heels into the
pony's ribs. The little horse was too tired to gallop, but it moved
away in a trot.

Hoka Ushte watched them recede slowly in the west and then

he looked toward the east. The dust cloud was very visible. Lame Badger hesitated just a second before he began walking toward it.

If the grass had been tall, Hoka Ushte might have hidden in it, but the place he was walking was mostly dry soil and low plants. One could see for miles. There were no large rocks, no trees, and no tall yucca. The dust cloud would be on him even if he ran. The only irregularity in sight was the hint of a slight dip ahead, between him and the Shoshoni war party, and Hoka Ushte walked toward it with the resignation of a condemned man. He knew that it did not matter that he was not one of the three who had killed the Shoshoni man and woman; any Lakota scalp would serve to quench the war party's anger. Hoka Ushte idly touched his loose and matted hair.

The riders were just becoming visible in the east when Hoka Ushte reached the dry riverbed. It was not deep or wide, less than a dozen paces across, and there was no water or vegetation in it. The riverbed did not wind enough to offer a hiding place, but Hoka Ushte jumped down into it anyway. It would keep them from seeing him for another minute or two. He could feel the pounding of hooves through the ground now.

Hoka Ushte paced twenty paces north, then twenty paces south, hearing the horses' breathing and the Shoshoni shouts, before he noticed the hole in the east side of the riverbank. It was small. Probably a badger's hole. This gave him the idea.

Hoka Ushte was lean. With the sound of the horses only a minute away, he began clawing at the hole, widening it just enough to get his feet and legs in. Then he lifted himself by an exposed root and forced his legs into the aperture. Only the fact that he was naked, oiled with sweat, and carried no weapons allowed him to proceed.

His hips scraped at rock and soil, but they eventually slid deeper into the narrowing hole. The upper half of his body was still hanging out in plain sight. The Shoshoni could not miss seeing him. The earth shook with the sound of war ponies' hooves. Lame Badger forced his arms down to his sides, his fingers tearing at roots and small stones, desperately trying to make room. His body slid a little deeper until only his shoulders and head stuck out of the sandy soil.

He could hear the shouts of the Shoshoni warriors now, the grunts of the war ponies.

Hoka Ushte concentrated on making himself smaller, thinner, and slicker. With a great grunt and much tearing of already-torn skin, he slid deeper until only the top of his head was visible from outside, protruding like the top of some huge black spider. He could go no deeper. Wiggle as he tried, he could not free his arms or legs or back to slip a finger's length deeper.

The first of the Shoshoni horses was almost above him now.

Hoka Ushte shook his head against the surrounding hole, trying to cover his shiny black hair with sand and gray dust.

The first pony reached the river channel and stopped directly above him. Hoka Ushte could feel the pounding of hooves and the weight of the horses on his back. More horses arrived, stopped above him and to either side along the east side bank. Loose sand dribbled downhill into his hair from the pawing hooves of the leader's pony. Hoka Ushte gritted his teeth and closed his eyes, feeling the Shoshoni looking at him now, pointing with their lances, preparing to dismount.

There came shouts in guttural Shoshoni.

Hoka Ushte would have sung his death song then, but he had never composed one. Now he regretted all those hours wasted waiting by the stream to catch a glimpse of Calf Running. A Lakota brave, he realized now, should have been busy with more important things.

Such as preparing to die.

The lead Shoshoni shouted again, let out a bloodcurdling cry, and leaped his horse into the narrow riverbed directly above Hoka Ushte's exposed head. Torrents of dirt fell on the boy, choking him, filling his mouth with sand.

Hoka Ushte resisted the impulse to struggle, defied the impulse to choke and cough and cry out. He held his breath as more horses leaped above him, more dirt collapsed onto his head, all but burying him. Lame Badger's entire body tensed and his scalp tingled as he waited for the arrow or lance or hatchet to bury its stone point in his exposed skull. The pounding of hooves seemed to go on forever.

And then they were gone. Hoka Ushte spat sand, wiggled his

head until he could find air to breathe, and began to try to free himself. It was not easy, and the sudden surge of claustrophobia and pure panic did not help. At that moment only his earlier fear of death by the Shoshonis' blades kept him from screaming for help.

The sun was throwing long shadows across the riverbed by the time he had pulled himself free. He was so exhausted by his ordeal that for a time he could only lie on the white sand of the riverbed and pant. He was covered with blood, clay, and sand. If the Shoshoni had returned then, they might have been so alarmed by his appearance that it was possible they would not have killed him right away. They did not return.

It was almost dark by the time Hoka Ushte came up out of the riverbed on shaky legs. He knew that it made the most sense to go east or north, away from the direction of the Shoshonis and their prey, but he was curious. He began following the wide swath of hoofprints through the twilight, convincing himself that it was dark enough for him to hide in the low grass if the riders returned this way.

He found the three Brulé Sioux boys not long after the half-full night-sun had risen and cast a milky glow on the earth. The stars were bright; the Milky Way prominent despite the moon.

The Shoshoni had caught the boys a short ride from the riverbed. The Sioux pony lay where it had collapsed and died. There were no marks on it. Many tracks led to the northwest. The three Lakota boys lay within an arm's reach of one another.

The youngest one, the one Turning Eagle had introduced as Tried to Steal Horses, still had a Shoshoni arrow through his neck. His chest and belly showed the marks of a dozen other arrows. His hands were spread wide as if in surprise. His open eyes caught the moonlight, as did the white bone of his bare skull. The boy named Few Tails looked as if he had been dipped from head to foot in red berry juice. Besides taking his scalp, the Shoshoni had taken his fingers, tongue, and heart.

Turning Eagle lay a bit farther from the other two, and something about his splayed posture suggested that he had actually fought his killers. The boy's throat had been cut from ear to ear and the ragged slit seemed to be smiling at Hoka Ushte. In addition to his scalp and tongue, they had cut off Turning Eagle's ears, hands, child-maker, and balls. One of his eyes now watched from some paces away, speared on the end of a yucca spine.

Hoka Ushte turned away and gasped for air. When he was able to breathe normally he looked back, wanting to sing a death song for them, wanting to help them on their way south, but not knowing the ceremony.

Someday, when I am wičaśa wakan, he promised himself, *I will be able to do these things.*

He turned away and continued his walk east in the moonlight.

They found him a day and a night and a day later. Hoka Ushte had not slept or eaten in that time. He had not devised a weapon or contrived clothing for himself. His cuts were infected, his skin burned with sun and fever, and he was concentrating on the voices which whispered in his mind. He had walked until he could no longer walk and then stood in one place until his legs could no longer support him. He was not aware that he had fallen and had the vague sense of trying to climb the cliff of the earth itself. When the horsemen surrounded him, he was aware only of large objects blocking the sun. He was sure they were spirits come to carry him south and he was surprised when they spoke Lakota with a Brulé accent.

When he awoke sometime later he was lying between soft blankets. Evening sunlight came through the scraped tipi hide with that rich yellow thickness he had loved as a child, safe in his grandparents' lodge. He thought for a moment that he had dreamed everything in a fever state—he could feel the cold sweat that followed such a fever—but then an old noseless woman leaned over him, said something to another old, noseless woman in rough Brulé tones, and Hoka Ushte knew that nothing had been a dream.

Besides the two women without noses, there was a third, younger woman whose face was intact but stern-looking. She leaned over Hoka Ushte and said, "So . . . you are alive."

Hoka Ushte did not know how to respond to this.

All three of the women left the tent and Hoka Ushte was on the verge of drifting back into sleep when a heavyset man with a fierce face entered the tipi. "Did the *Susuni* strip you naked, take your weapons, steal your pony, and leave you bleeding out there?" snapped the big man.

Hoka Ushte could only stare for a moment. "No, the storm did this. The *Susuni* did not see me." He paused. "You are Cuts Many Noses."

The big man glowered and touched his knife. "How do you know this?"

"I met your son, Turning Eagle," said Hoka Ushte.

Cuts Many Noses let out a breath. "Is he alive?"

"No."

The big man shuddered as if his body had taken a heavy blow. "The *Susuni?*"

"Yes."

"The other two . . . Few Tails and Tried to Steal Horses . . ."

"Dead."

Cuts Many Noses nodded slowly. "This explains the ghost whistling . . ." He cut off his words. "Tell me your name and tribe and explain why you were naked and bleeding and alone."

Hoka Ushte did this. He mentioned only that he was wandering after having had a vision. The big man did not ask him about the vision.

"Can you lead us to my son's body?" asked Cuts Many Noses.

"I think so."

"In the morning? As soon as the sun rises?"

Hoka Ushte felt a terrible weakness after his ordeal and fever, but he remembered Turning Eagle's mutilated body lying there undecorated and un-honored, just lying there where the animals could feed without knowing who this person had been. "Today," said Hoka Ushte. "I will lead you there before the night-sun rises."

Cuts Many Noses appeared to consider this. "No. We must not leave the women alone when the *wanagi* walks tonight. You will lead us to Turning Eagle's body after the ghost leaves." Then he left Hoka Ushte alone to contemplate sleep.

Later, just as darkness was falling, the stern-faced woman entered with soup for him. She introduced herself tersely as "Red Hail." While Hoka Ushte lapped up the thick broth, he tried conversation. "The other two women ... the ones with the slit noses ... are they sisters?"

"No," said Red Hail, "they are Cuts Many Noses' other wives."

Hoka Ushte pondered this a moment. "And did they ... had they ... was it ..." The old Lakota punishment for a wife's adultery was to slit their nostrils or cut their noses off. But Hoka Ushte did not know how to say this diplomatically. "Was it because they ..." Lame Badger trailed off lamely.

"Yes," said Red Hail. "Cuts Many Noses has had five wives and only one ... myself ... has kept her nose. The others proclaimed their innocence, but he is a jealous man."

Hoka Ushte swallowed a lump of meat in the soup.

"You have eaten enough?" said Red Hail, taking the bowl before the boy could reply. "I must leave. It is getting dark. I must not be in the tipi with you alone." And the stern-faced woman was gone before Hoka Ushte could even say *"Pilamaye."*

Hoka Ushte awoke in the dark to the sound of a whistling and of many dogs barking. He knew at once it was the ghost Cuts Many Noses had mentioned.

The whistling was lovely, haunting, beautiful. It made Hoka Ushte sit up in the night, heart pounding, and want to follow it, even though he knew it was not meant for him. The dogs were going crazy. Hoka Ushte felt around for his knife, remembered that he had lost it, realized that someone had dressed him in a new breech clout, and then he slipped out through the tipi flap to find the source of the beautiful music.

The fires were out in the camp of the Brulé. Thirty or forty tipis gleamed milk soft in the light of the night-sun. The dogs had ceased barking but were showing their teeth. The whistling seemed to be coming from the edge of the camp, not far from Cuts Many Noses' tipi. Hoka Ushte began walking toward the sound when suddenly strong arms seized him and pulled him down.

Cuts Many Noses and half a dozen other men were crouched behind a fallen log. The big man motioned Lame Badger to silence as they peered over the log to a lone tipi set out on the grass. Suddenly a tall shadow glided over the prairie toward the tipi and the whistling seemed to swell.

"*Wanagi,*" whispered Hoka Ushte.

Cuts Many Noses nodded. "It is the ghost of Turning Eagle. He has come for his *winčinčalas.*"

"Sees White Cow," whispered Hoka Ushte. "He told me."

The tall shadow was circling the tipi now. Its arms were very long and its legs floated beneath it, the feet not touching the ground. There was a glow where one eye would be; the other socket was dark. Hoka Ushte shuddered when he remembered the eyeball on the yucca spear.

"My son had learned some of the elk medicine from his uncle," whispered Cuts Many Noses, his voice sad. "His voice is of the *siyotanka.*"

Hoka Ushte grunted. He had heard of the elk-medicine flute that would make a magic sound. Any girl who heard it would follow the flute player and fall in love with him. The whistling of the *wanagi* grew louder and more haunting now. Hoka Ushte saw the tipi flap fold back and a young woman who must be Sees White Cow stepped into the moonlight.

"Now!" said Cuts Many Noses and a dozen warriors leaped from their hiding places and began shouting and making noises.

The ghost leaped higher into the air, paused like a startled deer, and then swirled like smoke on the wind. The braves rushed to Sees White Cow's tipi and continued the shouting. The whistling sounded less like a flute now and more like the wind. Hoka Ushte joined in the shouting and waving of arms, noticing a holy man with a black *taha topta sapa* streak across his face rattling the sacred gourd of a *wagmuha* to keep the ghost at bay.

Suddenly the swirling shadow twisted like a dust devil and then flew into a thousand fragments, like black dust blowing away in the moonlight. The whistling dwindled to an echo, then to nothing.

"It is gone for tonight," said the *wičaša wakan.*

Braves went to reassure Sees White Cow and her mother. Cuts Many Noses came over to Hoka Ushte. "Thus it was last night and the night before. This is how we knew that my boy was dead. We go now to bury him."

Braves brought horses, twenty men mounted, someone helped the weakened Hoka Ushte onto his pony, and the warriors rode out onto the moonlit prairie.

It was mid-morning by the time they found the bodies. Scavengers had been at the boys and all of the eyes and much of the faces were gone. Cuts Many Noses put an arrow through a carrion bird that had been working at his son's liver and that was too fat to fly.

The men had brought lodgepoles on a *travois* and these they cut into three burial platforms. Turning Eagle's mother had sent his best war shirt and special dead man's moccasins with the soles beaded with spirit-world patterns. These they dressed the boy in while relatives of Few Tails and Tried to Steal Horses did the same for their dead. Finally the three bodies were lifted on their funeral scaffolds and the holy man, whose name was Buffalo Eye, said the proper words and offered the pipe to the spirits. By midday the ceremony was done and the twenty warriors and Hoka Ushte swung up on their ponies and rode away.

"This is not the way to your camp," said Lame Badger as he realized they were headed west, toward the *Mako Sicha.*

Cuts Many Noses only grunted and began to smear war paint on himself as they rode.

Realizing that he was with a war party, Hoka Ushte said, "I have no weapons."

"This is not your fight," said the white-haired warrior next to Cuts Many Noses. "But you must identify the *Susuni* who killed our boys."

Hoka Ushte thought of how he had hidden with his face in the dirt while the Shoshoni horses had ridden over him. He said nothing.

By nightfall they had reached the edge of the Badlands. The Brulé made a cold camp while scouts fanned out to continue trailing the Shoshoni. Their hope was that they could find the enemy camp at night, approach silently, and fall upon them at first light. The Brulé, like the other Lakota, did not enjoy fighting at night.

They did not find the camp. All the next day they followed the trail but the large Shoshoni war party had broken into four or five smaller groups and their trails were all but lost on the rocky wastes south of *Mako Sicha*. After another day of hunting, Hoka Ushte was tired, hungry—they were eating only *wasna* and the cold meat of small things they killed—and eager to return to his own quest. No one had asked him, but he thought that Turning Eagle and his friends should not have killed the Shoshoni woman and her husband in the first place. He did not volunteer this opinion to Cuts Many Noses.

On the fourth day two scouts returned to the war camp. They were very excited. Hoka Ushte listened to the gabble of Brulé dialect and realized that the scouts had found *Wasichu,* not Shoshoni. They boy's pulse raced at the thought of seeing an actual Fat Taker, but he said to Buffalo Eye, "Aren't you seeking vengeance against the Shoshoni?"

The holy man squinted at him. "The Shoshoni are probably beyond the mountains by now. We will take vengence where we can find it."

By this time the war party had traveled far west, farther than Hoka Ushte's band liked to go because of the *Wasicun* place which the Lakota called Piney Creek Fort and the Fat Takers called Fort Philip Kearny, but it was near this place that Cuts Many Noses and his warriors set their ambush.

Of the group, the actual chief was named Left Hand Charger, but Cuts Many Noses was the war chief and made the battle plans. He sent his white-haired friend, "Eagle That Stretches Its Wing," and six others to lure the *Wasichu* south to the creek. This was brave work, and the warriors clamored to be chosen. Hoka Ushte did not volunteer because he was still uncertain what this had to do with his own quest and why rubbing out *Wasicun* soldiers would take vengeance for Turning Eagle's death. He said nothing.

While Eagle That Stretches Its Wing and his men lured the *Wasichu* band south by their taunts and attempts at counting coup, Cuts Many Noses set his warriors in ambush position along the north side of Piney Creek. Hoka Ushte was assigned duty holding the horses and keeping them silent in the cottonwood grove along the north side of a hill until the *Wasicun* were in killing position. From the trees there, he could hear the shouts and shooting, but could see nothing.

The plan worked. Twenty-nine *Wasichu* soldiers and a wagon they were escorting from the fort gave chase to Eagle That Stretches Its Wing and his companions, killing only one of them—a man named Tall Crow Killer. The surviving six led the soldiers into the river valley. At the end, the white-haired brave had his warriors dismount and lead their horses as if exhausted to lure the soldiers the last way to the river.

Once the *Wasichu* were near the river, where it was too deep to ford and too fast to swim easily, Cuts Many Noses and his men fell on them with their rifles, pistols, and bows. Two other Brulé fell—One Side who was shot in the eye and who died immediately, and Brave Heart who was shot in the stomach and took two days to die—but all twenty-nine of the *Wasichu* were rubbed out in the crossfire.

As I said, Hoka Ushte saw none of this happening, but he came down to the river after the shooting stopped and saw Fat Takers for the first time. Most had been stripped by the time he arrived, but a few were still in their blue shirts and pants. The first *Wasicun* Hoka Ushte came to was a boy no older than Few Tails had been. Arrows had pierced the young man's thigh, belly, and throat, but it had been the gunshot to the chest that had killed him. Hoka Ushte knelt in wonder at the sight of this *Wasicun:* the boy's hair was a bright red and his skin was so pale that it reminded Lame Badger of a white frog's flesh. The Fat Taker's eyes were wide and staring and very blue. Hoka Ushte would have looked longer at this strange sight, but a Brulé named Kicking Bear came over and said, "His scalp is mine. I killed him." It was a challenge, but Hoka Ushte merely backed away and let the brave claim his prize.

A yellow dog was circling around and around the bodies of two of the dead men. "It is a *Wasichu* dog," called Kicking Bear from his work on the red haired boy, "but we did not kill it. He is too sweet. We will take him home and train him to be a human being's dog."

The *Wasichu* near the wagon lay stripped and dead, their limbs curled in the awkward positions of death. Cuts Many Noses' men were eager to run down the horses and had done little to the bodies except count coup, retrieve their arrows, and claim scalps. Hoka Ushte noticed that the Fat Takers were ugly with their hairy faces, hairy bodies, and fish-belly skins, but they were only men—men with bellies, behinds, and child-makers like any of the real human beings.

It was the wagon that interested Hoka Ushte. He had heard of such *travois* with wheels, but he had never seen one. This one was covered with white canvas in the back and when Hoka Ushte bent to look in, the face of a dying *Wasichu* boy-soldier suddenly thrust at him as if the Fat Taker were going to bite him.

Hoka Ushte let out a cry and took a step back, but the *Wasicun* extended a hand with something metal in it, and then dropped it as he died. Hoka Ushte caught the metal thing without thinking. It was heavier than a knife, but useless as a weapon. It had two thin metal handles rather than a single hilt, and no cutting or hammering surface. Hoka Ushte found that by wiggling the handles, he could make the small metal jaws open and close. It was obviously a *Wasichu* tool for squeezing or pulling things.

The gift will be given by a Fat Taker whose spirit has left him. The words from his vision. Hoka Ushte slipped the strange tool out of sight in his breech clout and mounted the horse Cuts Many Noses had loaned him.

"We go back," said the Brulé war chief. "We are rich with horses and revenge. The *Wasicun* will blame the *Susuni* and their vengeance will be ours."

Hoka Ushte nodded, but said, "I am pleased that Turning Eagle and his friends are avenged. But I must go now."

Cuts Many Noses frowned. "Lame Badger, my wives and I had hoped that you would come live with us and marry Sees White Cow."

Hoka Ushte blinked. He had caught only a glimpse of the girl when the ghost was serenading her. Why was everyone trying to marry him off? "This would please me greatly," he said, "but the vision of my *hanbleceya* demands that I continue on." He slid off his borrowed white horse.

"Keep the pony as a present," said Cuts Many Noses magnanimously. "He is called *Can Hanpi*—white juice of the wood— what the *Wasichu* call sugar, and he was stolen by Turning Eagle himself."

"*Pilamaye, Ate,*" said Hoka Ushte, bowing his thanks.

Cuts Many Noses gestured and the warrior Eagle That Stretches

Its Wing came forward with a knife, bow, arrows, and extra blanket for Hoka Ushte. Chief Left Hand Charger handed him a strange thing: larger than a gourd, sealed, sloshing with liquid, and smooth to the touch. It was a *Wasichu* thing.

"It is a jug of holy water," said Cuts Many Noses, using the phrase *mni waken* that the Lakota give to liquor.

Hoka Ushte held the thing gingerly, knowing its power and danger.

Left Hand Charger showed his teeth. "There were a dozen other jugs in the *Wasichu* wagon. Drink it with care. It lets spirits in whether you invite them or not."

Hoka Ushte nodded his thanks again, the warriors cried "Hoka hey!" and galloped back to the northeast, and Hoka Ushte turned his white pony south and west, away from that place of death.

The Bighorn Mountains were an area hunted by the Mountain Crow, by the Shoshoni, by the Northern Cheyenne and Northern Arapaho, and even by the bands of Hoka Ushte's Oglala Sioux *Ikče Wičaśa,* but the brooding hills were controlled by none of these groups and few braves entered there alone. Hoka Ushte did so, avoiding the rivers that the *Wasichu* forts seemed to lie along like beads on a string of buffalo gut. His pony, *Can Hanpi,* swam the Powder River easily, despite its chilling cold, and climbed steadily in the hills above Otter Creek, Forest Creek, and Willow Creek until there were no more streams, only the remnants of winter snow. The nights were cold in the highest places and Hoka Ushte huddled in the single blanket the Brulé had given him. The stars were so clear that they did not seem to twinkle. Hoka Ushte saw no one.

Then for three days he did not bother to hunt or to eat, drinking only a few sips from the small brooks that ran out under the ice. It was as if he were fasting and purifying himself for a sweat lodge ceremony or a *yuwipi* vision, although he had no such ceremony in mind. He was just not hungry.

On the fourth day he found the tipi set out on a long crag of rock swept free of snow by the wind that rarely ceased to blow at these heights. The mountains and valleys rolled below the crag; the plains were a dark shelf visible to the east. Hoka Ushte's pony had not complained before this, even when he had led it into the icy river or guided it through belly-deep drifts of snow, but now *Can Hanpi* refused to go nearer than a hundred paces to the crude tipi.

Hoka Ushte left his pony and carried his bow and a handful of arrows across the crag of rock. Three women watched him as he approached.

The two peeking from the flap of the ragged tipi were the young women of his vision: twins perhaps, sisters almost certainly. They wore dresses of white doeskin, their black hair gleamed, their faces were as serene and unlined as the surface of a dream. The third woman, their mother it seemed, was something out of a nightmare.

The old hag had a face of harsh lines, old warts, and raw boils. One eye was white with blindness; the other squinted balefully at Lame Badger as he approached. Her hair was a dirty yellow-white and her scaly scalp gleamed in places. Her dress was an unfinished robe of some animal with orangish hair and a bad smell. The old woman's back was twisted like one of the gnarled trees which grew along this harshly treated ridgeline.

"Welcome," said one of the young women, stepping away from the tipi and ignoring the harsh gaze of her mother. She took Hoka Ushte's hand and led him to the lodge. "You are far from home, young *Wičaśa*. Stay and eat with us and spend the night."

Hoka Ushte nodded but did not smile. He knew that this was part of his vision and that if he did not choose the right woman this night, he would die. And with his death would die the last chance for his people to triumph over the *Wasicun* plague that would soon sweep over the world like the ancient flood in the days of the *Wakinyan* and *Unktehi*.

The two women sat with him as the old hag prepared a soup from some rank meat. The sun was setting as they ate and the wind lifted sparks from the fire and scattered them out over the dark hills spread out below and into the darkening sky until it seemed like the campfire was seeding the night with stars.

It was full dark when Hoka Ushte finished his soup. He had noticed that none of the women were eating so he also ate none of the meat, and drank only a tiny bit of the broth. It tasted bad. When the last of the sparks had blown into the sky and the only light was from starlight reflected in the two pretty sisters' eyes, Hoka Ushte stood and made as if to go.

Both of the young women touched his arm while the hag-mother glared from her good eye. Their grip was very strong.

"I am only going to hobble my pony for the night and to get my blanket," he said. "I will be right back. Here, I leave my arrows and my bow to show you that I will return."

The sisters smiled, but one of them said, "Let me walk with you."

She did not leave the wide circle of rock swept free of snow, but *Can Hanpi* showed the whites of his eyes and backed away while the woman was near. Hoka Ushte calmed his pony as best he could, hobbled him well, and took his blanket and other things back to the tumbledown tipi with him.

Crossing the rock, the young woman took his arm again and whispered, "Be careful, brave boy. My sister and my mother are not of this earth. They eat men."

Hoka Ushte pretended surprise. "How do they do this?" he whispered back, very conscious of her strong hand on his arm.

The beautiful woman's teeth gleamed in the starlight. "If you make love to my sister, she has teeth in a secret place. They will seize you until my mother kills you, drains your blood and fluids, and hangs you on the cliff behind the tipi in a sac."

Hoka Ushte stopped walking. "How is this possible?"

The girl made a graceful motion and Lame Badger noticed her long nails. "My mother and sister are cousins to *Iktomé,* the spider man. They do not like human beings . . . except for dinner."

Hoka Ushte glanced toward the tipi. The beautiful sister and terrible mother were merely shadows near the cold embers of the fire. "And you . . ." he whispered.

The girl lowered her head. "I am also cousin to *Iktomé,* and have . . . too many teeth . . . but I am not evil." She touched his hand. "Trust me."

Hoka Ushte nodded. *"Pilamaye,"* he said.

The night-sun seemed to rise below them, so high was the cliff's edge which the tipi sat upon. The wind rose to a howl now. The old woman had retired to her robes but the sisters waited just inside the flap. One of them beckoned to him.

"One minute," he said. "I have to make water." He noticed that his bow and arrows were gone, somewhere inside the lodge. He touched his back beneath his shirt to feel the knife Cuts Many Noses had given him.

The beautiful sisters glanced at each other and waited.

Hoka Ushte walked around the tipi, crossed the windswept rock to the cliff's edge, and urinated into the night. The wind felt cold on his *che*. Like teeth.

Hoka Ushte shuddered, glanced over his shoulder, and then knelt quickly to peer under the overhang. Row upon row of silken sacs hung there, attached to the rock by some sticky substance. In the dim light, Hoka Ushte could just make out a few things gleaming through the sticky webbing: a finger there, bare teeth there, an empty eyesocket here, a shred of white flesh farther back.

Lame Badger stood, adjusted his breech cloth, and turned back to the tipi. One of the sisters had come up behind him in the dark. He could not be sure, but he thought that it was not the one who had spoken to him earlier.

"My sister told you something," she whispered urgently.

"Yes."

She touched his bare arm. "It is not I who seizes my lover and holds him with hidden teeth until our mother carves him up," she whispered. "I want to go away from here. My sister is the one who shares our mother's taste for human flesh and human blood. Trust me, and together we will outsmart them and leave while we are alive."

Hoka Ushte nodded. "How does your mother do this killing?"

The girl smiled for an instant. "You saw her back? It is actually a long tail with many barbs. While you are caught in my sister's *winyañ shan,* screaming in pain, the old woman uncoils that tail and tears your flesh with it."

Hoka Ushte tried to smile but failed. The girl saw the direction of his glance. "Your pony is already gutted," she whispered. "The old woman did it while you made water here. You could not outrun them." She touched his back, her fingers tapping the small blade there. "Our only hope is for you to kill them when they least expect an attack. Choose me as your first lover and I will make sure that my little teeth do not harm you."

Hoka Ushte pulled his arm away from her powerful grip. "How will I know it is you in the dark?"

"I will touch your cheek, like this," she whispered, raising her fingers to his face. "Then, as we begin to make the beast with two backs, scream as if I have seized your child-maker with my teeth. When they come for you, kill them."

"Yes," whispered Lame Badger, although the syllable may well have been lost in the rising wind. "Go on ahead of me."

Her eyes gleamed. The night-sun was still rising cold and white in the dark abyss below them. "You truly cannot run."

"I know this is true," said Hoka Ushte. "Go on. I will come in."

When the girl had become just another shadow next to the tipi, Hoka Ushte clenched his fists, raised them to the night, and whispered to the sky, "*Wakan Tanka, onshimalaye* . . . O Great Spirit, pity me."

The wind whistled around him much like the elk flute sweetness of the *wanagi* in the Brulé camp, and a voice whispered in Hoka Ushte's mind: *Trust your vision.*

The boy nodded, lowered his fists, and went into the tipi.

The lodge was very dark—there was not even a smoke hole and the thick hide blocked the moonlight—and the air in it was very foul. He waited until his eyes adapted as much as they would, but still he could see only the ugly mother huddled farthest away and the two sisters as dark forms nearer the tipi flap. They had laid his blanket between their robes.

"What is this lump?" whispered one of the girls as she caressed the blanket.

"A gift," whispered Hoka Ushte and brought out the jug of *Wasichu* holy water. He unplugged it and offered it to the nearest shadow, but the girl held back, as if fearing that it was poison.

"Here," said Hoka Ushte and took a swallow of the *mni waken*. It burned terribly and tasted like the worst medicine his grandmother had ever made him swallow, but he managed not to choke or gag. "Here," he said again, offering the *Wasichu* gourd.

"No," whispered one of the sisters, taking the jug and setting it away. "We are not thirsty. Come to bed."

Hoka Ushte rubbed his cheek. There went his only plan: put both the sisters to sleep with the *Wasichu* holy water and then deal with the hag-monster.

Strong hands pulled him down onto the blanket. He smelled the sweet scent of girl-flesh all around him. One of the shadows lifted above him and tugged off his shirt. Other hands pulled off his moccasins and slid up his thigh. Hoka Ushte put his hand behind him and palmed the small knife there an instant before the unseen hands tugged down his breech clout. The sisters were like the ash-shadow of Turning Eagle's *wanagi* now, their two forms flowing and interchanging above and beside him. Hoka Ushte kept glancing toward the hag, but the old woman was only a gleaming eye wrapped in robes across the tipi.

See with the čante ista, his dream had said. *With the eye of the heart.*

Four hands caressed his chest and ribs. Sharp fingernails slid across his cheek, down his throat to his collarbone. Warm, sweet breath hissed in his ear.

One of them has to be lying. And unless my hanblečeya *was a lie, one of them has to be good . . . the mother of our race. A descendant of White Buffalo Woman. They can't both be lying to me.*

He could feel the sisters unrobe next to him. Their skin smelled of *wahpewastemna,* the sweet perfume used before important ceremonies. Of that and something infinitely more musky and exciting.

Hoka Ushte felt himself becoming aroused despite his fear. The girls' bare breasts touched his forearms and side now. One of them slipped down lower so that her breath was on his thigh.

The vision.

Sweat oiled their sliding against him now. The tipi was very dark, but he could make out the black hair on their heads and between their legs, the gleam of reflected starlight on eyes and lips and teeth. There came a grinding sound, as of small teeth rubbing against one another, but Hoka Ushte could not locate the source.

One of the sisters rubbed his *che* even more erect while the other slid her breasts back and forth across his bare chest. They rolled over him like otters at play.

"I am ready," whispered one, pulling his hand toward her groin. He felt moisture there before he tugged his hand away. Had there been a sharpness there among the slickness?

"Now, please, now," whispered the same sister, or perhaps the other. Both were tugging at him. A firm hand cupped his balls, then slid up his child-maker to its swollen tip. "Now," came the same voice. Or perhaps a different one.

Fingers touched his cheek. One girl rolled on her back, all sweet-scented skin and sweat, and opened her legs to him while the other slid against him and helped him rise with a strong hand on the small of his back. Hoka Ushte felt breasts compressing beneath him, other breasts against his arm. He realized that the knife was no longer in his hand. His *che* slid against the girl's slick belly, felt the wiry softness of her lower hair. Hands reached to glide him into place.

The vision. There were three sisters. The one who did not speak was the one whose voice I heard.

Hoka Ushte tried to roll away. Hands held him in place while other hands roughly grabbed his *che* and pulled it into the girl beneath him. He could hear the teeth clicking in anticipation.

Lame Badger reared back, kicked away, heard the hiss and snap of frustration, and then had both sisters swarming on him, their legs wide and strong around him. They rolled out through the tent flap into the starlight. He could *see* the nether-teeth now, gleaming and snapping at his still-erect member. The sisters' faces were no longer beautiful as they shape-changed into something black and spiderish. Too many eyes gleamed at him.

One of the sisters rolled atop him with a hiss of triumph. The other scraped his tender places with long nails, forcing him there. Hoka Ushte could see the second sister's backbone snap free of her spine, its barbs coming around like a scorpion's tail.

Hoka Ushte reached out, found a bit of log unburned, and swept it under his own thigh and up.

The sister atop him snarled something as her *winyañ shan* seized the log and began chewing it like a dog with a stick. Splinters flew between their sweaty thighs. The sisters screamed in triumph and the scream was not human.

Hoka Ushte rolled free, kicking the occupied sister away. The second one leaped at him, the force of her leap throwing both of them back into the dark tipi. The teeth in the girl-thing's mouth snapped at his neck while her other teeth scraped his thigh. Hoka Ushte's far-flung hand fell on the hilt of his knife beneath a robe and he swung it around, feeling it go deep between the scaly breast above him. The girl-thing thrashed and hissed, screamed once, and died, rolling away with the knife still embedded in it.

Its sister filled the tipi entrance. The thing's barbed tail was snapping back and forth now, shredding the tipi fabric and letting starlight in. Hoka Ushte realized that the tipi had been wrapped about in layers of human skin. He rolled away through the tumbled lodgepoles and flapping skin, into a heap of robes made of human hair. The girl-thing crouched like a spider with a scorpion sting.

Hoka Ushte sat on something sharp, felt his stolen arrows under the robe, and lifted a bunch of them, knowing that he would not have time to find the bow. The girl-thing was almost on him, hands, legs, and tail writhing.

Instead of trying to run, Hoka Ushte leaped closer and drove the bundle of arrows deep into the thing's gleaming eyes. Then he rolled away to avoid the spasming tail.

The spider-scorpion screamed so loudly that its cry echoed from the mountains for minutes. Then, still clutching the bundle of stone arrow points in its eyes, it ran blindly, stumbling over the skin of the tumbled tipi, getting to its feet again, and going over the cliff edge near where the death sacs hung.

Hoka Ushte rushed to the edge to make sure the thing was not hanging there, but he could see it in the bright moonlight as it fell a thousand feet to the rocks below. Its scream and the echoes of its scream made a terrible harmony. The silence after it struck the rocks was very loud.

The boy staggered back to the tumbled tipi, pounded the robes until he found his bow and a single arrow, and then backed away as the thickly robed hag-mother came slowly out of the lodgepole ruins.

"Stop," he rasped, lifting the bow to full pull.

"I mean you no harm," came the thick voice from within the robes.

"I believe you," said Hoka Ushte. "But come no closer now."

The old woman stopped. Hoka Ushte sat cross-legged and relaxed his pull on the bow, watching to make sure the dark form did not approach. "Who are you?" he whispered after the moon had crossed half the sky toward morning.

"I am *winyañ sni*," said the one-eyed form, "the woman-who-is-not-a-woman. I am both sister and cousin to White Buffalo Woman who visited your people some time ago. See..." And she touched the dead embers with her gnarled hand and a fire sprang up.

"That proves nothing," said Hoka Ushte. "The *Iktomé* creatures that I slew almost certainly could do such *wapiya* tricks."

"Yes," sighed the hag. "And there is no way to prove to you that this flame is the same spark that my sister-cousin gave to your people, the *peta-owihankeshni*. The fire without end."

Hoka Ushte looked at the flame and said nothing for a while. Finally he said, "If you were with White Buffalo Woman, how did you come to be here..." He nodded toward the tumbled tipi.

"I was very beautiful but very promiscuous in the spirit place," she said in her raspy hag voice. "*Lila hinknatunpi s'a*... I repeatedly had many husbands. I caused the men near me to be possessed... *wicayuknaxkin*. Possessed with desire for me. One of these men was the spider man himself, *Iktomé*. When I grew tired of him and cast him aside, he gave me to his spider sisters. It was not their attraction which drew men here, but mine. *Iyuhawica yuknaxkinyanpi*... I cause those who stand near to be possessed."

"I am not possessed," growled Hoka Ushte.

The hag showed a single tooth in her smile. "You have been since your vision. But it is not the possession magic which drew you here, but *teriyaku*... the fact that you love me."

Hoka Ushte tried to laugh at this—the hag was, after all, a bundle of wrinkles, warts, boils, and old-woman flesh—but he could not laugh. He realized that it was love that had been behind his vision and that had led him here. He put down his bow and came closer.

"If you touch me," said the hag, "I am not responsible for what will happen."

"Nor am I," said Hoka Ushte and gently touched the ancient creature.

And in that second he saw with the eye of his heart. And the old hag was no hag, but was the most beautiful maiden he had ever seen. Instead of rotting rags, she wore a dress of dazzling white doeskin. Her lips were soft and full, her skin a thousand times more beautiful than the deceptive creatures who had tried to fool him, her eyes lovely and deep under heavy lashes, and her hair alive with starlight. Their kiss flowed on and on until Hoka Ushte lifted the maiden and carried her to his blanket. There he parted the ties on her dress and slipped it off her warm skin. Her breasts were perfect; her navel was a tender hillock upon which he rested his cheek.

She pulled his face to hers. "No, Hoka Ushte," she whispered. "In one thing I am like the spider man's cousins . . ." She moved his fingers to her *winyañ shan*. It was moist with excitement, but that was not what she wished to show him. He gently parted the tender lips with his fingers and felt the small teeth there. "I married many men because none could have me when they discovered . . ."

"Hush," whispered Hoka Ushte, his fingers exploring. "This can be fixed."

The maiden sighed with passion. She curled his fingers into a fist. "Yes, if you knock them out . . ."

"What?" whispered Hoka Ushte, stroking her hair with his free hand. "And hurt you? Never."

White Buffalo Woman's cousin turned her face to the blanket. "Then we can never . . ."

Hoka Ushte reached across her to retrieve the *Wasichu* holy water gourd from where the spider girl had hidden it. "Drink this," he said, "and when the spirits have entered you so that you feel little pain, then I will use the *Wasichu* gift."

"Gift?" said the maiden. Her eyes widened as he lifted the Fat Taker soldier's pair of pliers from its place in the rolled blanket.

And so it was that the sister-cousin to White Buffalo Woman, a maiden who was later known to our people as She Who Smiles, came to be Lame Badger's first lover and only wife. And when she returned to our camp, a great meeting of holy men was called and it was confirmed that she would be the mother of the children whose children's children would someday lead the *Ikče Wičaśa* out of their cave of darkness and back into the real world.

And later, when the story was told, my great-grandfather admitted that when he pulled the teeth that were in the wrong place, he left one little tooth there because of the wonderful sensation it offered. And my grandfather, whom I have mentioned in this tale, was the first male child born to Hoka Ushte and She Who Smiles and the scar on his scalp and forehead—the birth scar caused by that single little tooth—became the *wakan* source of much of his power when he became a holy man and a vision man and a conjurer.

I never met my great-grandfather, but I have heard in the stories that he and my great-grandmother lived to be very old, and were honored by all of the natural free human beings, and were very happy, and were especially blessed to die before all of the world they knew came under the shadow of the *Wasicun*. And they died believing that someday Hoka Ushte's vision would be fulfilled and that the shadow will be lifted.

I see your expression. I know your doubt. But never doubt that I know this story to be true. And know that I never doubt that my great-grandfather's *hanblečeya* vision will someday be true. You can take your machine and go now. The story is over. This thing has been said that had to be said.

They say that my aged great-grandfather's last words to his dying wife were, *"Toksha ake čante ista wacinyanktin ktelo.* I shall see you again with the eye of my heart."

And this I also do not doubt.

Good-bye then. *Mitakuye oyasin.* All my relatives. It is done.

FLASHBACK

Carol awoke, saw the light of morning—true morning, realtime morning—and had to resist the urge to pop her last twenty-minute tube of flashback. Instead she rolled over, pulled the pillow half over her face, and tried to recapture her dreams rather than let the realtime shakes get her. It did not work. At bedtime the night before she had flashed three hours' worth of the second trip to Bermuda with Danny, but afterward her dreams had been chaotic and unrelated. Like life.

Carol felt the rush of realtime anxiety hit her like a cold wave: she had no idea what the day could bring—death or danger to her family, embarrassment, pain—*unpredictability*. She hugged her arms to her chest and curled into a tight shell. It did not help. The shaking continued. She had unconsciously opened the drawer of the bedside table and actually had the last tube in her hand before she noticed the three collapsed and empty vials on the floor beside her bed. Carol set the twenty-minute tube on the table and went in to drive the cold shakes away with a hot shower, shouting to Val to get out of bed as she turned on the water. She saw her father's open door and knew that he had been up for hours, as he always was, having cereal and coffee before the sun rose and then puttering around in the garage before coming in to make fresh coffee for her and toast for Val.

Her father never flashbacked while the others were in the house. But Carol always found the tubes in the garage. The old man was doing three to six hours per day. Always three to six hours of the same fifteen minutes, Carol knew. Always trying to change the unchangeable.

Always trying to die.

Val was fifteen and unhappy. This morning as he slumped to the table he was wearing a Yamato interactive T-shirt, black jeans, and VR shades tuned to random overlays. He did not speak as he poured milk on his cereal and gulped his orange juice.

His grandfather came in from the garage and paused in the doorway. His name was Robert. His wife and friends had always called him Bobby. No one called him that anymore. The old man had that slightly lost, slightly querulous expression that came from age or flashback or both. Now he focused on his grandson and cleared his throat, but Val did not look up and Robert could not tell if the boy was tuned to the here and now or to the VR flickerings behind his shades.

"Warm day today," said Carol's father. He'd not been outside yet, but most days in the L.A. basin were warm.

Val grunted and continued staring in the direction of the back of the cereal box.

The old man poured coffee for himself and came over to the table. "The school counselor program called yesterday. Told me that you'd ditched another three days last week."

This got the boy's attention. His head shot up, he lowered his glasses on his nose, and said, "You tell Mom?"

"Take the glasses off," said the old man. It was not a request.

Val removed the VR shades, deactivated the telem link, tucked them in his T-shirt pocket, and waited.

"No, I didn't tell her," his grandfather said finally. "I should, but I haven't. Yet."

Val heard the threat but said nothing.

"There's no reason why a young boy like you has to screw around with flashback." Robert's voice was phlegmy with age and brittle with anger.

Val grunted and looked away.

"I mean it, goddammit," snapped his grandfather.

"Tell me about not using flashback," said Val, his voice dripping with sarcasm.

Robert took a step forward with his face mottled and fists clenched, as if he were about to hit the boy. Val stared him down as the old man stopped and tried to compose himself. When his grandfather spoke again, his voice held a forced softness. "I mean it, Val. You're too young to spend your time replaying . . ."

Val slipped out of his chair, grabbed his gym bag, and tugged the door open. "What do you know about being young?" he said.

His grandfather blinked as if he had been slapped. He opened his mouth to speak, but by the time he could think of what to say, the boy was gone.

Carol came in and poured herself some coffee. "Has Val left for school yet?"

Robert could only stare at the door and nod.

Robert looks down, sees his own hands gripping the side of the dark limousine, and knows instantly where and when he is. The heat is intense for November. His gaze moves from the windows above, then to the crowd—only two deep along this stretch of street—then back to the windows. Occasionally he glances at the back of the head in the open Lincoln ahead of him. *Lancer looks relaxed today,* he thinks.

He can hear his own thoughts like a radio tuned to a distant station, the volume little more than a murmur. He is thinking about the open windows and the slowness of the motorcade.

Robert jumps off the running board and easily jogs to his position near the left rear fender of Lancer's blue Lincoln while his eyes stay on the crowd and the windows above the street. His running is relaxed and easy; his thirty-two-year-old body is in excellent condition. Within two blocks the neighborhood changes— no more tall buildings, more empty lots and small shops, the crowd no longer even lining the route—and Robert falls back and steps onto the left running board of the number one chase car.

"You're going to wear yourself out," says Bill McIntyre from his place on the running board.

Robert grins at the other agent and sees his own reflection in Bill's sunglasses. *I'm so young,* thinks Robert for the thousandth time at this instant while his other thoughts stay tuned to the windows on the taller building ahead. He hears himself think about the route as street signs pass: Main and Market.

Get off now! he screams silently at himself. *Let go now! Run up there now.*

He seethes with frustration as he ignores the internal screams. His other thoughts contemplate running up to the rear of the Lincoln, but the low buildings here and thinning crowds convince him to stay on the running board.

No! Go! At least get closer.

Robert's head is turning away from the crowds and toward the blue Lincoln. He braces himself for the sight of the familiar thatch of chestnut hair. There it is. Then Lancer is lost to sight as Robert's gaze continues to track left. There is an open area: a hilly patch of grass and some trees.

Robert knows to the instant when he will step down off the running board, but he tries to tense his body to make himself jump sooner. It does not work. He steps off the same instant that he always does.

It takes only a few seconds to jog up to the Lincoln. Robert's attention is distracted to the right as a small group of women shout something he has never been able to make out. Glen and the others in the car also swivel their heads to the right. The four women are holding small Brownie cameras and shouting at the passengers in the Lincoln. His glance appraises and dismisses them as no threat within three seconds, but Robert knows each of the women's faces more intimately than he remembers his dead wife's. Once, in the mid-nineties, he had seen a bent old woman crossing a street in downtown Los Angeles and knew at once it was the third woman from the right from that curb thirty-two years earlier.

Now. . . get on the Lincoln's running board! he commands himself.

Instead he reaches out, taps the spare tire of the blue Lincoln as if in farewell, and drops back to the following car. Ahead, the motorcycles and lead car turn right off Main onto Houston. The blue Lincoln convertible follows a few seconds later, slowing even more than the lead car so as to make the right-angle turn without jostling the four passengers in the back. Robert steps back onto the running board of the chase car.

Look up!

Glancing left, Robert sees that railroad workers are congregated atop an overpass under which the cars will pass in a moment. He curses to himself and thinks *sloppy, sloppy.* All three cars are making a slow left onto Elm Street now. Robert leans into the open chase car and says, "Railroad bridge . . . people." In the front seat, their commander, Emory Roberts, has already seen them and is on the portable radio. Robert waves to a police officer in a yellow rain slicker who is standing on the overpass, gesturing for him to clear the bridge. The officer waves back.

"Shit," says Robert. *Go now!* he commands himself.

The blue Lincoln passes directly under a Hertz billboard with a huge clock in it. It is exactly 12:30.

"Not bad," Bill McIntyre is saying. "Couple of minutes late is all. We'll have him there in five minutes."

Robert is watching the railroad overpass. The workers are well back from the edge. The cop in the yellow slicker is standing between them and the railing. Robert relaxes a bit and glances to the right at the large brick building they are passing. Workers on their lunch break wave from the steps and curb.

Please . . . dear Jesus, please . . . move now.

Robert looks back at the overpass. The police officer in the slicker is waving, as are the workers. Two men in long raincoats stand on the bridge approach, not waving. *Plainclothes detectives or Goldwater men,* thinks Robert. Beneath those thoughts, his mind is screaming. *Now! Run now!*

"Halfback to Base. Five minutes to destination." Emory Roberts is on the radio to the Mart.

Robert is tired. The night before in Fort Worth he had been up until long after midnight playing poker with Glen, Bill, and several of the others. Today's heat is oppressive. He shakes his right arm to free his sodden shirt from his arm and back. Robert hears Jack Ready say something from the other side of the chase car and he looks across at him. People are waving and shouting happily beyond the curb there. The grass is much greener here than in Washington.

There is a sound.

Go! There's still time!

Christ, he hears himself think, *one of those goddamn workers has fired off a railroad torpedo.*

Robert looks ahead, sees the pink of the woman's dress, sees Lancer's arms rise, elbows high, hands at his own throat.

Robert's feet hit the ground as the echo of the first shot is still bouncing from building to building. He tears across the hot pavement, heart pounding. Behind him, the chase car accelerates and then has to brake hard. Amazingly, incredibly, in the face of all procedure and training, the driver of the Lincoln ahead has slowed the big car. There is another sound. One of the outrider cops glances down at his motorcycle as if it has backfired on him.

Less than three seconds have elapsed when Robert dives for the trunk grip of the Lincoln.

The third shot rings out.

Robert sees and hears the impact. Lancer's head of healthy chestnut hair seems to dissolve in a mist of pink blood and white brain matter. A piece of the President's skull, as surprisingly pink as the inside of a watermelon, arches into the air and lands on the trunk of the Lincoln, trapped there by the ornamental spare tire.

Robert's left hand has seized the metal grip and his left foot is on the step plate when the Lincoln finally accelerates. His foot comes off and he is dragging. Now he is connected to the suddenly speeding vehicle only by the numbed fingers of his left hand. He hears himself think that he will be dragged to death rather than release that grip.

It doesn't matter now, he thinks at himself. *It doesn't matter.*

Incredibly, the woman in pink is crawling out onto the trunk. Robert thinks that she is trying to reach him, to help him onto the car, but then he realizes with a stab of horror that she is reaching for the segment of skull still lodged at the rear of the trunk. With a superhuman effort he swings his right arm forward and grabs her reaching arm. Her eyes seem to glaze, she pauses . . . and helps to pull him onto the trunk of the speeding car.

Too late. All too late.

Robert pushes her down into the spattered upholstery, then shoves her to the floor of the open car. He spreadeagles his body across her and the other form in the backseat. His first glance confirms what he knew at the second of the third bullet's impact.

The car is racing now that it is too late. Motorcycles cut in ahead, their sirens screaming.

Too late.

Robert is sobbing. The wind whips his tears away. All the way to Parkland Hospital he is sobbing.

Carol's Honda was only half-charged this morning, either because of another brownout during the night or some problem with the car's batteries. She hoped and prayed that it was a brownout. She could not afford more work on the car.

There was just enough charge to get her to and from work.

The I-5 guideway was jammed to gridlock. As always, Carol had the impulse to pull the Honda into the almost-empty VIP lane and flash by the traffic jam. Only a few Lexuses or Acura Omegas were using the lane, the chauffeurs' faces stoic, the Japanese faces in the rear seats lowered to paperwork or powerbooks. *It would be worth it,* she thought, *just to get a mile or two at high speed before the freeway cops cut my power and pull me over.*

She crept forward with the inching traffic flow, watching her charge gauge drop steadily. She had assumed that the holdup was the usual bridge or lane repair, but when she got to the Santa Monica Freeway exit she saw the Nissan Voltaire van with the CHP vehicles around it. The driver was being lifted out. His eyes were open and he looked to be breathing, but he was limp and unresponsive as they trundled him into the backseat of the patrol car.

Flashback, thought Carol. More and more, people were using it even while they were stuck in traffic. As if reminded of the possibility, she opened her purse and lifted out the twenty-minute vial. If her Honda had fully charged, she could have stopped at her supplier's on Whittier Boulevard before going to work. As it was, she would have to depend on her stash at work.

Carol was almost thirty minutes late when she pulled into the parking garage beneath the Civic Center complex, but she was still the first of the four court stenographers to arrive. She turned off the motor, considered attaching the charge cable despite the higher rates here, decided to try to get home on the charge she had, opened the car door, and then closed it again.

Her bosses were used to the stenographers being late. Her bosses probably weren't in yet either. No one arrived on time anymore. She probably had half an hour or forty-five minutes before any real work would be attempted.

Carol lifted the twenty-minute vial, concentrated on summoning a specific memory the way Danny had taught her the first time she had used flashback, and popped the lid. There was the usual sweet smell, the sharp tang, and then she went somewhere else.

Danny comes in from the patio and hugs her from behind as she pours juice at the counter. His hands slip under her terrycloth robe. Rich Caribbean light pours through the windows and open door of their bungalow.

"Hey, you'll make me spill," says Carol, holding the glass of juice out over the counter.

"I want to make you spill," Danny murmurs. He is nuzzling her neck.

Carol arches back into his arms. "I read somewhere that men hug women in the kitchen as just another form of male domination," she says in a husky whisper. "A sort of Pavlovian thing to keep us in the kitchen . . ."

"Shut up," he says. He tugs her robe down over her shoulders as he continues nuzzling.

Carol closes her eyes. Her body still carries the memory of last night's lovemaking. Danny's hands come around the front of her robe now, untying the belt, opening it.

"You have to meet the buyers in thirty minutes," Carol says softly, her eyes still closed. She raises a hand to his cheek.

Danny kisses her throat precisely where her pulse throbs. "That gives us a full fifteen minutes," he whispers, his breath soft against her flesh.

Inside the swirl of sensations, Carol surrenders herself to her own surrender.

Under the high span of the railroad bridge, just below where the concrete trusses arced together like the buttresses of some Gothic cathedral, Coyne handed Val the .32-caliber semiautomatic pistol. Gene D. and Sully whistled and made other approving noises.

"This is the tool," said Coyne. "You got to make the rest happen."

"Make the rest happen," echoed Gene D.

"This is just the tool, Fool," said Sully.

"Go ahead. Check it out." Coyne's dark eyes were bright. All three of the boys were white, dressed in the torn T-shirts and tattered jeans of the middle class. Their fuzzy-logic sneakers were not new enough or expensive enough or smart enough to show that the boys were members of any ghetto gang.

Val's hands shook only slightly as he turned the pistol over in his hands and racked the slide. A bullet lay snug in the chamber. Val let the slide slam home and held the cocked weapon with his finger on the trigger guard.

"It doesn't matter who," whispered Coyne.

"Don't matter at all," giggled Sully.

"Better not to know," agreed Gene D.

"But you've gotta do the trash to enjoy the flash," said Coyne. "You gotta pay your dues, babechik."

"Dues get paid, then you get frayed," laughed Sully.

Val looked at his friends and then slid the pistol into his belt, tugging his T-shirt over it.

Gene D. high-fived him and pounded out a rioter's dap on Val's head. "Better check that safety, Babe. Don't want to blow your business off before you do the deed."

Red-faced, Val pulled the pistol out, clicked on the safety, and slid it back in his belt.

"Today's the *day!*" Sully screamed at the sky and slid down the long concrete embankment on his back. The echo of his shout bounced back from concrete walls and girders.

Before they slid down to join him, Gene D. and Coyne slapped Val on the back. "Next time you flash, boy, you'll be the Flash*man.*"

Screaming until their echoes overlapped with realtime shouts, the three boys slid down the slippery slope.

* * *

Robert lived with his daughter but also had a secret address. Just six blocks from their modest suburban home, set along an old surface street that was rarely used since the Infrastructure Crash, was a cheap VR motel that catered to New Okies and illegal immigrants. Robert kept a room there. It was close to his flashback supplier and for some reason he felt less guilty about replaying there.

Besides, the motel had keyed its telem to nostalgia options for its old-fart patrons and when Robert used the VR peepers—which was rarely now—he called up his room in early-sixties' decor. Somehow it helped the transition.

Robert used the last of his Social Security card balance to score a dozen fifteen-minute vials at the usual dollar-a-minute rate. There were deals on every block between his house and the VR flop. Robert slipped the two bubble-wrap sixpacs in his pocket and moved on to the motel in his old man's shuffle.

Today he keyed the peepers. The room was a set designer's image of 1960 Holiday Inn elegant. A kidney-shaped coffee table sat in front of a low-slung Scandinavian couch; pole lamps and starburst light fixtures spilled light; black-velvet paintings of doe-eyed children and photos of Elvis decorated the walls. Copies of *Life* magazine and the *Saturday Evening Post* were fanned on the coffee table. The view out the picture window was of a park with steel and glass skyscrapers rising above the trees. Huge Detroit–built cars were visible on a highway, their I-C engines rumbling along with a nostalgic background roar. Everything was new and clean and plastic. Only the powerful smell of rotting garbage seemed incongruous.

Robert snorted and removed the peepers. The room was bare cinderblock, empty except for the cot he was lying on and the crude wireform constructs taking up space where the table and couch should be. There was no window. The garbage smell seeped in through the ventilator and under the scarred door.

He set the headset back in place and cracked the bubblewrap. Looking out the window at the Dodges and Fords and late-fifties Chevies driving past, he called back the hot Dallas day and the heat of the car metal under his hands until he was sure that the right memory synapses were firing.

Robert lifted the fifteen-minute vial to his nose and popped the top.

* * *

Carol was scheduled to record a deposition in the district attorney's offices at 10 A.M. but the Assistant D.A. who was handling the deposition was in his cubicle flashing on a favorite fishing trip until 10:20, the elderly witness was half-an-hour late, the associate from the defense attorney's office didn't show at all, the video technician had another appointment at 11:00, and the paramedic whom the law required to administer the flashback called to say that he was stuck in traffic. The witness ended up being dismissed and Carol stowed her datawriter keyboard.

"Fuck it," said Dale Fritch, the young Assistant D.A., "the old lady wouldn't agree to flashback anyway. The whole thing is fucked."

Carol nodded. A witness who wouldn't agree to being questioned immediately after flashback was either lying or some sort of religious fanatic. The elderly black woman whom they'd been trying to get a deposition from was no religious fanatic. Even though flashback depos had no legal weight, no jury would believe testimony where the witness refused to replay the event before testifying. Video-recorded flashback depositions had almost replaced live testimony in criminal trials.

"If I call her to testify live, they'll know she's lying," said Dale Fritch as they paused by the coffee machine. "Flash may be habit-forming and hurting our productivity, but we know that it doesn't lie."

Carol took the offered cup of coffee, poured sugar in it, and said, "Sometimes it does."

Fritch raised an eyebrow.

Carol explained about her father's flashbacks.

"Christ, your dad was JFK's secret service guy? That's sort of neat."

Carol sipped the hot coffee and shook her head. "No, he wasn't. That's the weird part. The agent who jumped on the back of Kennedy's car fifty years ago was named Clint Hill. He was thirty-something when the president was shot. My dad was an insurance adjustor until he retired. He was still in high school when Kennedy was shot."

Dale Fritch frowned. "But flashback only lets you relive your own memories . . ."

Carol gripped her coffee cup. "Yeah. Unless you're crazy or suffering from Alzheimer's. Or both."

The Assistant D.A. nodded and sucked on the coffee stirrer. "I'd heard about schizos having false flashbacks, but..." He looked up suddenly. "Hey, uh...Carol...I'm sorry..."

Carol tried a smile. "It's all right. The Medicaid specialists don't think that Dad's schizophrenic, but he hasn't responded to the Alzheimer's medication..."

"How old is he?" asked Fritch, glancing at his watch.

"Just turned seventy," said Carol. "Anyway, they don't know why he's having these false flashbacks. All they can do is to advise him not to take the drug."

Fritch smiled. "And does he follow their advice?"

Carol tossed her empty cup away. "Dad's convinced that everything in the country's so shitty today because he didn't get between John Kennedy and the bullet fast enough. He figures that if he just gets there a little sooner, Kennedy will survive November twenty-second and history will retrofit itself."

The Assistant D.A. stood and smoothed his tie. "Well, he's right about one thing," he said, tossing his own cup in the recycling bin. "The country's in shitty shape."

Val stood opposite his high school and considered going in to blow away Mr. Loehr, his history teacher. The reasons he did not were clear: 1) the school had metal detectors at all the entrances and rent-a-cops in the halls and 2) even if he got in and did it, they'd catch him. What fun would it be flashing on this trashing if he had to do it in a Russian gulag? Val had never lived in an age where excess American prisoners weren't shipped to the Russian Republic, so the chance of serving time in a Siberian gulag did not seem strange to him. Once, when his grandfather had mentioned that it had not always been that way, Val had sneered and said, "Shit, what else other than prison space did we ever think the Russies had to sell?" His grandfather had not answered.

Now Val adjusted the .32 in his waistband and slouched away from the school, heading toward the shopping strip above the Interstate. The trick was to choose someone at random, do them, drop the gun somewhere it wouldn't be found, and get the hell out of the area. He'd be watching ITV when the evening news told about another senseless killing which the police suspected was flashback-related.

Val keyed his shades to provide nude realtime overlays of all the women he saw as he picked up his pace toward the shopping strip.

Carol is waiting for her high school date to pick her up. She checks her frilly Madonna-blouse to make sure that her antiperspirant is working and then stands on the corner, shifting from foot to foot and watching the traffic. She sees Ned's almost-new '93 Camaro come slashing through traffic and screech to a stop, and then she is squeezing into the backseat with Kathi.

As always on this flashback, Carol marvels at the sight of herself as she checks the rearview mirror to make sure that her makeup is all right. Her hair is shaved and dyed and spiked, she has three fake diamonds in her left ear, and her lashes and eyeliner make her look like a bright cartoon. Along with the shock of seeing herself young and bold, Carol *feels* the energy of youth in herself. She *feels* the lightness in her step, the firmness in her breasts and muscles, and the enthusiasm in her spirit. More than that, she senses the bounding skitter and slide of her own thoughts, as different in their energetic optimism from the daily plod of her thinking in the future-present as her appearance is in the then-now.

Kathi is chattering but Carol tunes out the babel and merely drinks in the sight of her friend. Kathi dropped out of school in her senior year, dropped out of sight shortly after that, and dropped out of Carol's thoughts until the fall of '98 when she heard from a friend that Kathi had died in a car accident somewhere in Canada. As always, Carol feels a flood of warm feeling toward her old friend and has to fight the useless urge to warn the girl not to follow her boyfriend to Vancouver. Instead of warning her, Carol hears her own voice babbling about who wrote whom a note in study hall that day. She feels her quickened heartbeat and flushed skin as she studiously avoids talking to the strange boy in the front passenger seat.

Ned has roared back out into traffic, cutting off a Villager van and switching lanes almost at random. Now he turns around and says, "Hey, Carol babe, you gonna ignore my friend here all day or what?"

Carol raises her chin. "Are you going to introduce your friend, or what?"

Ned makes a rude noise. From the rush of fumes, it seems that he has been drinking. "Carol, this stud muffin is Danny Rogallo. He's from West High. Danny, meet Carol Hearns. She's Kathi's friend and knows our football team, uh, how do you say it? *Intimately.* Oh shit." Ned has to brake hard and change lanes to avoid a truck that slows suddenly.

Carol bobs forward, braces herself with both hands on the back of the new boy's seat, and looks at him. Danny has turned to smile at her, either from the introduction or out of embarrassment at Ned's driving. Carol hears herself thinking that the boy is handsome with his Tom Cruise–like smile, severe athlete's haircut, and diamond ear stud. "Hey there, stud muffin," Carol hears herself say.

Danny's smile broadens.

"Hey there yourself," says the new boy, still twisted in his seat to look back at her.

Carol knows that the flashback is precisely half over and the next big moment is when their hands will accidentally touch as they ride the escalator in the mall.

"Halfback to Base. Five minutes to destination."

Robert glances at the front seat to see Emory Roberts set the radio down and write something in his shift report. Robert shakes his arm to free his sweat-sodden shirt and then glances to his right as Jack Ready says something from the running board on the opposite side of the chase car.

There is a sound.

Go, goddammit! Go! You have almost two seconds. Use it!

His gaze snaps back to the railroad overpass and he hears himself think, *Christ, one of those goddamn workers has fired off a railroad torpedo.*

Lancer's arms rise almost comically. His hands go to his throat so that, from the rear, his arms seem to extend in a direct line from his shoulders and terminate at the elbows.

Robert feels himself jump from the running board. Finally.

He is running hard toward the blue Lincoln. There is a babble to concentrate during a score

' voice commanding Jack

' voice of Dave Powers,

. Service chase car for no

: President's been hit!"

ackground noise now—indistin-

che gunshot or the flap of pigeon

: the rear of the open Lincoln, his eyes

x chestnut hair.

.o slump.

. inexplicably slows.

.ives for the rear trunk grip.

.ner shot rings out.

.ancer's head explodes in a spray of pink mist.

"Goddamn," said Robert. He was weeping. For a second he did not know where he was—the sixties decor, the traffic outside the motel window—but then he raised his hand to wipe the tears away, bumped the VR headset, and remembered.

"Goddamn," he whispered again, tearing off the headset. The almost-bare room reeked of garbage and mildew. Robert pounded the cot and wept.

Val has passed the old malls, all boarded up or converted to prison space now, and then climbed the wooden scaffolding to the strip mall on the freeway.

They were called malls and were the only malls that Val had known in his short lifetime, but even he knew that in reality they were little more than glorified flea markets on the elevated stretches of Interstate Highway that had been abandoned after the '08 Big One. Today a quarter of a mile or more of brightly colored canvas rippled and fluttered in the breeze; the gypsy vendors were out in force. Val joined the midday mobs of shoppers and understood why Coyne and Gene D. had urged him to do his flashback shooting here: he could blend into the mob in a second, there were a score of stairways down which he could escape, and the maze of shattered

concrete slabs and support rods on the tumbled sect[ion]
was a perfect spot to get rid of the gun.

Val walked the white stripe between canvas bo[oths]
out the new Japanese and German merchandise and p[assed up a]
look at the old recycled Russ and American crap. The J[ap]
and interactive stuff was cool, although he knew it was g[etting]
behind the tech toys that Jap and German kids could [have. The]
problem with TV, especially interactive TV, was that it gav[e you a]
taste of how the other half lived without showing you how you['d]
ever get there. Val's mother said that this had always been the [problem]
with TV—that when she was a kid way back in the dark ages, Af[ricans]
and Spanics in the ghetto had felt that way about programs th[at]
showed white, middle-class American affluence. Val didn't give a
damn what it used to be like in his mother's day; he just wanted
some of the new Jap tech stuff.

But not today. Today Val only wanted to use the .32, get rid of
it, and get out of there.

Coyne and Gene D. swore that there was nothing in the
universe like flashing on doing someone. Sully also swore that, but
Val trusted nothing that the taller boy said. Sully used crack, angel
dust, and turbometh as well as flashback, and Val had the usual
flashbacker's contempt for someone on one of the old drugs. Still, Val
could only watch when the three others used a thirty-minute vial to
replay their own shootings. Their faces would get lax in that sort of
idiot-dreamer's expression flashback-users had, and then they would
slump and twitch, their eyes rolling in REM randomness under closed
lids. Val had seen Coyne actually get sexually excited as he approached
the shooting part of the flashback. Gene D. said that wasting someone
was better in flashback than in realtime because you get all the
adrenaline rush and physical high while you knew—the you watching
behind everything knew—that you weren't going to get caught.

Val touched the pistol through his loose shirt and wondered. He
had not enjoyed the flashback of the rape of that Spanic girl the way
Coyne had said he would: her cries and the smell of her fear while
Sully held her down made him sick each time, so that he felt his
nausea *under* his replayed nausea. So after two or three of the gang
flashbacks on that gig, Val had taken to remembering something

else—such as the time he and Coyne had stolen Old Man Weimart's cash box when they were seven—rather than replay the rape.

But Coyne said that there was nothing like flashbacking on wasting someone. Nothing.

The open-air strip mall was busy with lunchtime shoppers and flashback dropouts. Val had noticed that more and more people were just not going to work anymore; realtime interfered with their flashing. He wondered if that was the reason the garbage was always piled so high along the curbs, why the mails rarely were delivered any longer, and why nothing seemed to get done anymore except when the Japanese were there to supervise.

Val shrugged. It really didn't matter. What mattered now was finding someone to waste, dropping the gun, and getting out of there. Strolling away from the crowded booths selling Jap and German goods toward the Russ stalls, he felt his heart rate accelerate at the mere thought of what was about to happen.

He began to see how it should be done. This section of the shopping strip near the tumbled section of freeway was less crowded than the main area, but still seemed busy enough that Val could do the shooting and get away without being too visible. He noticed the narrow lanes between the booths. Moving into one of these canvas-walled alleys, he could see the shoppers without being watched by them or by the sales people inside the makeshift tents. Val pulled the small automatic out of his waistband and held it loosely by his side. The choice now was who . . .

A woman in her sixties wandered from stall to stall, peering over bifocals at the Russ artifacts and icons on the counters. Val licked his lips and then lowered the pistol again. She looked too much like photos he'd seen of his grandmother.

Two gay dudes in wraparound VR peepers strolled arm in arm, laughing at the crude Russ merchandise and using every laugh as an excuse to hug each other. One of the men had his hand in the hip pocket of the other's jeans.

This seemed good. Val held the pistol higher. Then he saw the poodles. Each of the gays had a yapping little dog on a leash. Something about the thought of those dogs barking and leaping around after he wasted the guy was not sympatico. Val set the pistol behind his back and continued watching.

An older man moved down the line of counters, giving close attention to the Russ junk. This guy was bald and liver-spotted with age, wearing neither VR shades nor peepers, but something about his baggy old-man clothes and his watery old-man eyes reminded Val of his grandfather.

Val lifted the pistol, clicked the safety off, and took a half step beneath the flapping canvas overhang. *Shoot, walk away slowly, toss the gun in the concrete tumble down below, take the J Bus home* . . . he went over Coyne's instructions in his mind. His heart was pounding almost painfully as he lifted the little .32 and sighted down the short barrel.

A shot rang out and the old man's head jerked up. Everyone was looking down the aisle toward where the gays and their poodles had gone. The old man moved away from the counter and stared with the others as the shouting and footsteps grew louder.

Val lowered the pistol with shaking hands and stepped out to look.

The woman with gray hair and bifocals was lying in a tumble on the white-stripe center of the shopping lane. A kid no more than twelve or thirteen was running toward the end of the elevated section, his leather jacket flying. One of the gay dudes had dropped to one knee and was shouting for the kid to stop. The other gay dude was holding a badge toward the crowd and yelling at them to stay back while the dude on one knee gripped a blunt, plastic tube with both hands. Val recognized the black lump from a hundred interactive movies: an Uzi-940 needlegun. He had no doubt that the clownlike VR wraparounds were giving targeting and tactical info. The cop shouted one last time for the kid to stop. Almost at the end of the staircase, the boy did not even look back. The two poodles were straining at their leashes and barking hysterically.

The boy finally looked over his shoulder just as the cop fired. The Uzi made a compressed-air noise much like a tire gauge slipping off a valve and then the boy's jacket seemed to explode into a black cloud of leather strips as several hundred glass and steel micro-flechettes hit home. The boy fell and tumbled, limbs as loose as a rag doll's, as his own inertia and the impact of the needle cloud carried his body under the rope railing and off the elevated strip. Bits of leather jacket were still coming down like confetti as the crowd rushed forward past the gay cops and the hysterical poodles to goggle at the body thirty feet below.

Val took a breath, slipped the .32 into his waistband, pulled his shirt over it, and walked slowly to another staircase. His legs were only slightly shaky.

Carol came out of her flashback of meeting Danny to find Dale Fritch waiting just outside the door of her cubicle. She had no idea how long he had been waiting. In the past few years, privacy had become an imperative and everyone who used flashback respected other people's need for a time and space beyond interruption. Now Carol used the small mirror in her desk drawer to check her makeup and to quickly run a brush through her hair before opening the door.

The Assistant D.A. seemed uneasy. "Carol . . . ah . . . I was just wondering if you . . . ah . . . might be free for a special project tomorrow."

She raised an eyebrow. She had worked with Fritch on more than a few depositions and had been court reporter for a score of trials that he had appeared at, but until their conversation about her father that morning, she did not think they had ever said anything personal to one another. "Special project?" she said, wondering if this was some sort of come-on. She knew that the Assistant D.A. was married with two small children and had thought that his only passion was one he spoke of occasionally: trout fishing.

Dale glanced over his shoulder, stepped into an empty meeting room, and beckoned her in. Carol waited while he closed the door.

"You know that I've been investigating the Hayakawa murder?" he said softly.

Carol nodded. Mr. Hayakawa had been an important corporate advisor in the L.A. area and everyone at County knew that the investigation was . . . to use a word the D.A. tended to overuse . . . sensitive.

"Well," continued Dale, running a hand through his blond hair, "I have a witness who swears that the shooting wasn't robbery the way the cops pegged it. He swears that it's drug related."

"Drug related?" said Carol. "Coke, you mean?"

Dale chewed his lower lip. "Flashback."

Carol almost laughed out loud. "Flashback? Hayakawa could have scored flashback on any corner in the city. So could anyone else. Why would they kill him for flashback?"

Dale Fritch shook his head. "No, they killed him because he was supplying it and someone disagreed on the amount. Or so my informant swears."

Carol did not hide her skepticism. "Dale," she said, using his first name for the first time, "the Japanese don't allow any use of flashback. It's mandatory death penalty over there."

The Assistant D.A. nodded agreement. "My informant says that Hayakawa was part of a delivery network. He says that the Japanese developed the drug and . . ."

Carol made a rude noise. "Flashback was first synthesized in a lab in Chicago. I remember reading about it before it hit the streets."

"He says that the Japanese developed it and have been foisting it on us for more than a decade," continued Fritch. "Look, Carol, I know it sounds crazy, but I need a good stenographer who can keep quiet about this until I show that this informant's crazy or . . . Anyway, can you do it tomorrow?"

Carol hesitated only a second. "Sure."

"Can you do it during your lunch hour? We need to meet this guy at a café all the way across town. He's paranoid as hell."

Carol smiled only slightly. "Well, if he thinks he's blowing the lid off some gigantic international conspiracy, I can see why. Sure, I usually just brown bag it. I'll meet you in your office at noon."

Dale Fritch hesitated. "Could we make it outside . . . say the corner on the south side of the parking garage? I don't want anyone in the office to know about this."

Carol raised an eyebrow. "Not even Mr. Torrazio?" Bert Torrazio was the District Attorney, a political appointee of the mayor and his Japanese advisors. No one, not even the stenographers, thought that Torrazio was competent.

"*Especially* not Torrazio," said Fritch, his voice tense. "This whole investigation has been off the record, Carol. If Bert gets a whiff of it, Hizzoner and all the Jap money-men downtown will be on me like flies on shit . . . sorry for the language."

Carol smiled. "I'll be on the corner at noon."

The Assistant D.A.'s relief and gratitude were visible on his boyish face. "Thanks, Carol. I appreciate it."

Carol felt like an idiot for thinking that his approach had been a come-on. Nonetheless, she did not think of Danny for the entire ride home. She made it to her garage with her charge dial reading zero.

Robert saw the problem in Val's face as soon as the boy returned home. The teenager was frequently manic, more frequently depressed, and often out-of-focus from the dislocation that flashback gave you, but Robert had never seen the boy quite so distressed as this evening. Val had slammed in while he and Carol were microwaving dinner and had gone straight up to his room. There was no conversation during dinner—which was not unusual—but Val's face held that slick sheen through the entire meal and his eyes continued to flicker left and right as if he were waiting for the phone to ring. The TV was on during dinner, as was their habit, to cover the lack of talk, and Robert noticed the boy watching the local news carefully, which was more than unusual, it was unprecedented.

Robert saw the boy shift in his chair, his head actually jerking up as the local anchorwoman began describing a shooting on the I-5 strip mall.

". . . the victim has been identified as Ms. Jennifer Lopato, sixty-four, of Glendale. LAPD spokesperson Heather Gonzales says that no motive has been established for the shooting and authorities suspect that it is another flashback-related murder. In this case, however, the alleged shooter was caught in the act by two off-duty police officers who responded with deadly force. CNN/LA has obtained official LAPD gun-camera vid footage of the shooting. We warn you, the vid you are about to see is graphic . . ."

Robert watched Val watching the tape. As far as Robert could tell from glancing at the screen, the footage was no different than the nightly gun-camera carnage that filled the news these days. But Val seemed mesmerized by the images. Robert watched the boy staring open-mouthed as a youngster ran through the crowd, refused to respond to the off-screen officers' shouts to stop, and then was blown to fragments by the flechette cloud. His grandson only closed his mouth, swallowed, and turned back to the table after another minute of unrelated news about L.A.'s person-on-the-net responses to the bad war news from China.

Carol did not seem to notice her son's reaction. Her own gaze was turned inward as it usually was these days.

We're all on flashback even when we're not on flashback, thought Robert. He felt a shudder of vertigo as he often did when he thought about his own flashback experiences, followed by a worse shudder of revulsion at himself. At his family. At America.

"Something wrong, Dad?" asked Carol, looking up from her coffee. Her eyes still had that myopic, distracted look, but she was also frowning in concern.

"No," said the old man, lifting a hand in Val's direction, "I just . . ." He stopped himself. While he had been lost in his own reverie, his grandson had left the table. Robert did not even know if he had gone upstairs or out the door. "Nothing," he said to his daughter, patting her hand clumsily. "Nothing's wrong."

Years ago they had caged in the pedestrian overpass to prevent people from dropping heavy objects or themselves on the twelve lanes of northbound traffic below, then—when highway shootings had first reached epidemic proportions in the mid-nineties—they had covered it with a thick Plexiglas that was supposed to stop bullets. It didn't—as evidenced by dozens of bullet holes, both outgoing and incoming, that fractured the warped plastic all along the tunnel—but it threw off the shooters' aim enough that they used other snipers' perches above the Interstate. By then, of course, most of the public figured that anyone driving in an unarmored car deserved a bullet in the ear.

In Val's lifetime, however, wonky vets from the Asian and South American mercenary wars were beginning to drop fragmentation and other types of grenades from the overpasses, and pedestrian bridges were caged-over and sealed up again, this time with welded steel doors at either end to keep people off them altogether. Gangs blew holes in the steel plates and used the long, dark overpasses as meeting places and their own private flashback parlors. It was very dark in there and Val had to use his VR shades as nightvision goggles to find Coyne, Gene D., and Sully among the dark shapes huddling, nodding, selling, and buying.

Val pulled the .32 from his waistband and held it in the palm of his hand.

"Couldn't do it, huh?" Coyne said softly, picking the pistol up. He was a radiant green figure holding a pulsing white tube in Val's amplified night vision.

Val opened his mouth to explain about the kid and the fag cops, but then he said nothing.

Sully made a disgusted sound but the green figure that was Coyne shoved him into silence. Coyne handed the pistol back. "Keep it, Val my man. Like whatshername, the Southern bitch, said in the old movie, 'Tomorrow's another day.'"

Val blinked. Someone had lit a cigarette down the bridge-tunnel and that end of the span blazed in white light. A dozen voices shouted at the figure to douse the fucking light.

"Meanwhile," said Gene D., throwing his arm around Val, "we scored some primo flash . . ."

Val blinked again. "Flash is just flash, asshole."

Sully snorted again and Coyne put his hand on Val's back. Val felt the contact with Coyne and Gene D. pulling him in, like a noose around his chest that made it difficult to breathe.

"Flash is just flash," whispered Coyne, "but this flash has like, I dunno, some sort of pheremone-exciter shit in it, so if you're flashing, like, fucking somebody like that time we did the Spanic bitch, you come harder than you did the first time."

Val nodded although he did not understand. Flash was flash. How could you experience more than you experienced the first time? Also, he had never had an orgasm except when he played with himself, and he did not like to flash on that. But he nodded and let Gene D. and Coyne pull him down to where a bit of light through one of the cracks in the blacked-out Plexiglas spilled across the grimy concrete as bright as liquid metal.

Gene D. produced four one-hour vials. Val tried to think of what he could flash on. Most of his memories were miserable. He would never tell the others, but often—when he said he was flashing on the time they fucked the Spanic kid—he was actually replaying a

Little League game he had played when he was eight. That was the first and last year he had played, after finding that none of the guys thought baseball was cool. As far as Val knew, no one played Little League anymore... no money. The fucking Reagandebt. Sending the fucking army to fight the fucking Jap wars for them wasn't coming close to paying the interest on the fucking Jap loans.

Val didn't understand any of it. He just knew that everything was shit. He started to take the sixty-minute vial from Coyne, but the bigger boy pulled him close and whispered huskily in his ear, "Tomorrow, Val my man, we'll go with you and help you get your trash so you can flash..."

Val nodded, pulled away, and lifted the tube to his nose. The Little League game didn't come when he tried to visualize it. Instead, he found himself remembering a time when he was a tiny little shit—three, maybe two—and his mother had held him on her lap to read to him. He thought it was before she began doing flash. He had fallen asleep on her lap, but not so asleep that he couldn't hear the words as she read, slow and steady.

Feeling like the world's greatest wuss and pussy wonk, Val held the memory and broke the tab on the flashback vial.

Robert did not like interactive TV, but when Carol was in bed and when he was sure that Val was gone, he brought up CNN/LA and accessed the anchorwoman persona. The attractive Eurasian face smiled at him. "Yes, Mr. Hearns?"

"The shooting on tonight's news," he said brusquely. He did not like talking to generated personas.

The anchor smiled more broadly. "Which segment, Mr. Hearns? The news is aired hourly and..."

"Seven P.M.," said Robert and forced himself to relax a bit. "Please," he said, feeling foolish.

The anchor beamed at him. "Would that be the shooting of Mr. Colfax, Mr. Mendez, Mr. Roosevelt, Mr. Kettering, the Richardson infant, Ms. Dozois, the unidentified Haitian, Mr. Ing, Ms. Lopato..."

"Lopato," said Robert. "The Lopato shooting."

"Yes," said the anchor, disappearing into a box as the video lead-in to the story filled the screen. "Do you wish the original narration?"

"No."

"Augmented narration?"

"No. No sound at all."

"Realtime or slo-mo?"

Robert hesitated. "Slow motion, please."

The gun-camera video began rolling. The CNN/LA logo was superimposed on the lower right corner of the frame. Robert watched the rough-cut jumble of images: first the victim, a woman a few years younger than Robert lying in a pool of her own blood, her glasses nearby, then the gun camera swinging up, a slo-mo jostling of people pointing toward the body and then toward a running figure. The camera zoomed on the figure and targeting data filled the right column of the image. Robert realized that he was seeing what the cops had seen through their telem peepers. It was obvious that the running boy was no more than twelve or thirteen.

Then a fire-confirm light flashed in the right column and the cloud of flechettes, easily visible in the extreme slow motion, expanded like a halo of ice crystals until it all but obscured the running child.

The boy's coat exploded into a corona of leather shreds.

The back of the boy's head expanded in a slow-motion unfurling of hair, scalp, skull, and brain.

The bit of skull on the trunk lid, thought Robert, feeling himself slide away from realtime. He forced himself back.

The boy tumbled, the back of his head gone, flechettes quite visible in his bulging eyes and protruded face; tumbled, slid under a rope railing, and was gone. The gun-camera image froze and faded. The CNN/LA logo expanded until it filled the frame and a copyright violation warning flashed across the screen. A second later the anchorperson persona was back, waiting patiently.

"Run it again," Robert said. His voice was thick.

This time he froze the image five seconds into it, after the gun-camera lens had left the victim but before it had picked up the fleeing boy. "Go . . . stop again," said Robert.

The frozen tableau showed two or three adults pointing. One

woman had her mouth open in a shout or scream. It was the shadow-within-a-shadow in an alley between two tents that interested Robert.

"Zoom there . . . no, up . . . there. Left a bit. Stop. Good. Now can you enhance that?"

"Of course, Mr. Hearns," came the anchor's simulated voice.

As the pixels began rearranging themselves into what might be a human shape, sharpening the white blur into a recognizable face, Robert thought, *Jesus, if they'd only had this in 1963 instead of the Zapruder film . . .*

Then all such thoughts fled as the image resolved itself.

"Do you wish further augmentation?" asked the smooth voice. "There will be an additional interactive charge."

"No," said Robert. "Just hold this a minute." He was, of course, looking at his grandson's face. Val was holding a pistol with the barrel vertical, only inches from his own face. The boy's expression of horror and fascination somewhat resembled his grandfather's.

Robert heard the tapping of the rear door's combination lock and the chime of the cheap security system's approval. Val came in through the kitchen.

"Off," said Robert and the screen snapped to black.

Val was back in his own bed by 2 A.M. but the pressure and tension of the day did not let him sleep. He found two twenty-minute vials and flashed on the first one.

He is four and it is his birthday. His daddy still lives with them. They are in the apartment near the Lankershim Reconstruction Projects and Val's friend from across the corridor, five-year-old Samuel, is having dinner with them because it is a special day.

Val is in the tall wooden chair that his mommy bought at the unpainted furniture place and decorated with painted animal designs just for him after he had outgrown his highchair. Even though he is four, he loves the tall chair that allows him to look across the table eye to eye with his daddy. Now the table is littered with the remains of his special dinner. . . the crusts of hot dog rolls, bits of red Jell-O, random potato chips . . . but his daddy's plate is clean, his chair empty.

The door opens and Grandpa and Grandma come in. Val is struck, as he always is during this replay, not only by the fact that his grandmother is alive and unravaged by cancer, but at how alive and young his grandfather appears, even though this flash is only a little more than a decade in the past. *Time sure kicks the shit out of people,* he thinks, not for the first time.

"Happy Birthday, kiddo," says his suddenly-young grandfather, ruffling his hair. His grandmother bends to kiss him and he is surrounded by the scent of fresh violets. Feeling his younger self's happiness and eagerness to get on to the presents, the watching Val knows that the back of his grandfather's closet, where the old man keeps a few of her dresses, still holds a bit of that scent. He wonders if his grandfather ever lifts the dresses to his face to recapture that scent. Sometimes, when the old man is out on a trip to his flashback motel, Val does that.

Val watches his own stubby hands play with the party favors and listens to Samuel's giggles. Hardly noticed at the time but all too clear to Val now is the hurried kitchen conversation that he catches bits of . . .

"He promised to be home on time tonight," his mommy is saying. "He *promised.*"

"Why don't we serve the cake anyway," his grandma says, her voice as soothing as a remembered touch or texture.

"His own boy's birthday party. . ." Robert's voice is heavy with anger.

"Let's serve the cake!" his grandma says brightly.

Val and Samuel pause in their play as the lights go out. Suddenly the world is illuminated by a richer, deeper light as his mother carries in the cake with four huge candles on it. Everyone is singing "Happy Birthday."

Val is old enough to understand that if he makes a wish and blows all the candles out successfully, the wish will come true. His mother has not said it, but he suspects that if he does not blow all of them out on the first try the wish will fail.

He blows them out. Samuel and Grandpa and Grandma and Mommy cheer. They have all just started to cut the cake for him when the door opens and Daddy sweeps into the room, his face flushed and jacket flapping. He is carrying a large stuffed bear with a red ribbon around the neck.

Little Val does not look at the gift. He glances at Mommy's face and even the watching fifteen-year-old Val shares the fear of what he may find there.

It is all right. Mommy's reaction is not one of anger but of relief. Her eyes sparkle as if the candles had been lighted again.

Daddy kisses him and lifts him and puts his other arm around Mommy and the three of them hug there above the littered table, with Grandma and Grandpa singing "Happy Birthday" again as if this time is for real, and Samuel wiggling to get at the toys and play with him, and Daddy's arm strong around him and the tears on Mommy's cheeks being all right because she is happy, they all are happy, and little Val knows that wishes do come true and he sets his cheek against Daddy's neck and smells the sweet blend of aftershave and outdoor air there, and Grandpa is saying . . .

Val came out of the twenty-minute replay to the smell of festering garbage and the sound of sirens. Small-arms fire rattled somewhere in the neighborhood. Police choppers thudded overhead and their searchlights stabbed white through the darkness and spilled through his window like white paint.

Val rolled over and tugged his pillow over his head, trying not to think about anything, trying to recapture the flashback and incorporate it into his dreams.

His face struck something hard and cold. The pistol.

Val sat up with a stab of nausea, held the loaded semiautomatic a moment, then tucked it under his mattress with the *Penthouse* magazines. His heart was pounding. He pulled the second twenty-minute vial from his jeans pocket on the floor and broke the tab—almost too quickly—he had to rush to concentrate on the memory image so the *temprolin* could access the right neurons, stimulate the proper synapses.

He is four and it is his birthday. Samuel is yelling, his mother is preparing the cake in the kitchen, and the table is a mess of half-eaten hot dog rolls, red Jell-O, and potato chips.

The door chimes and Grandpa and Grandma sweep in . . .

* * *

Carol is watching Danny come out of the blue water and run toward her up the white-sand beach. He looks handsome, lean, tanned from their five days in the sun, and is grinning at her. He throws himself down on the blanket next to her and Carol feels her heart seem to swell with love and happiness. She takes his wet fingers. "Danny, tell me that we'll always love each other."

"We'll always love each other," he says quickly, only this time, locked away in herself, the more observing Carol sees the quick glance toward her under long lashes, the glance that might have been appraising or slightly mocking.

At the time, Carol feels only happiness. She rolls onto her back, letting the fierce Bermuda sun paint her with heat. Danny has said that they are exempt from worries about the ozone layer and skin cancer on this vacation and Carol has happily agreed. She sets her fingers against the small of Danny's back, feeling the droplets of sea water drying there. Playfully, only slightly possessively, she runs her fingers under the elastic at the back of his trunks. The base of his spine and tops of his buttocks are very cool.

She feels him stir and shift slightly on the blanket. "Want to go up to the room?" he whispers. The beach is almost empty and Carol imagines what it would be like to make love right there in the sunlight.

"In a minute," she says.

Coasting on the tide of her own sensations, the realtime Carol understands a simple fact: men tend to flashback their favorite sexual incidents—Carol knows this from their conversation—while most women travel back to re-experience times when closeness and happiness were at their peak. This does not mean that she avoids sexual incidents—in a moment she and Danny will go up to their room and the next thirty minutes will be passionate enough for anyone to choose to replay—but the moments that beckon her back through time are the instants like this where her sense of being loved are absolute, her sense of closeness almost as palpable as the heat from the tropical sun overhead.

Carol turns her head and lifts a hand to her face, ostensibly to block the fierce sunlight, but actually to steal a glimpse of Danny's face so close to hers. His eyes are closed. Beads of water glisten on his lashes. He is smiling slightly.

The bastard brought along a vial of flashback on this trip. He'll show it to me on the last evening, explain how it works, suggest that we flash back to our first sexual encounters—with someone else! He turned that last night into a sort of double ménage à trois.

Carol tries to stifle these thoughts and her realtime anger as the then-Carol rubs her fingers across her eyes, ostensibly to brush away sand but actually to brush away tears of happiness.

The police officer in the yellow rain slicker is waving at the motorcade and Robert wants to have him fired. Luckily the cop is standing between the workers and the railing, so no one should be able to throw anything. Robert glances to the right at people eating their lunch on the steps of a brick building set right where the road swings left around the grassy plaza toward the railroad overpass. They are waving. Robert sees nothing amiss there and glances back at the approaching railroad bridge.

Go! Now! Get down and run!

He stays on the left running board of the chase car. It is very hot.

"Halfback to base," their commander, Emory Roberts, radios from the front seat. "Five minutes to destination."

Robert imagines the destination, the huge merchandise mart where Lancer is scheduled to speak to hundreds of Texas businessmen. The realtime Robert feels his own fatigue in the heat.

Ignore it. Go now!

A sharp sound sends pigeons wheeling above the plaza.

Christ, one of those goddamn workers has fired off a railroad torpedo. He screams over these thoughts, trying to make himself recognize the threat. All those years of training and experience fucked by these two seconds of incomprehension. But it is not until he looks ahead again, sees Lancer's arms rising in the unmistakable gesture of a gunshot victim, that the young agent moves.

The sprint across the gap that separates the two vehicles could not be faster. Robert is reaching for the metal grip just as the third shot strikes the President.

Jesus. The impact is a fraction of a second before I hear the sound. I've never noticed that before.

Kennedy's head dissolves in a mist of pink blood and white matter.

Robert seizes the metal grip and leaps onto the step plate just as the heavy Lincoln roars ahead. Robert's foot slips off the plate and he is being half-dragged behind the accelerating convertible.

Too late. Another two seconds. A second and a half. But I will never close it.

The woman in pink is crawling out onto the trunk in an hysterical effort to retrieve part of Lancer's skull so that no one can see what she has just seen.

Inside himself, Robert unsuccessfully tries to close his eyes so that he does not have to see the next minute or two of horror.

Val was out and gone before breakfast. Over coffee, Carol found herself actually talking to her father for a change.

"Today's your counseling session, isn't it, Dad?"

Robert grunted.

"You're going, aren't you?" Carol heard the parental tone in her own voice but could do nothing about it. *When is it,* she wondered, *that we become parents to our parents?*

When they become senile or neurotic or helpless enough that we have to, came her answering thought.

"Have I ever missed one?" said her father, his voice a bit querulous.

"I don't know," said Carol, glancing at her watch.

Robert made a rude noise. "You'd know. The goddamn therapy program would call you, leave messages, and keep calling you until you got in touch in person. Just like the school truancy program . . ." The old man stopped quickly.

Carol looked up. "Has Val been ditching school again?"

Her father hesitated a second and then shrugged. "Does it matter? The schools haven't been much more than holding pens since I was a kid . . ."

"Goddammit," breathed Carol. She rinsed her coffee mug and slammed it into the dishwasher. "I'll talk to him tonight."

"Busy day?" asked her father, as if eager to change the subject.

"Hmmm," said Carol, pulling on her cape. *Dale Fritch's lunch-time depo,* she thought with a jolt. She had all but forgotten it after the night's flashbacks. Perhaps after meeting him and his crazy informant for lunch she could score some more flashback in the Afric section of town before heading back to work. She was down to a single thirty-minute tube.

The Honda was down to a quarter charge. Enough to get her to work but there was no way she could get home without paying the higher charge rates at the Civic Center. And it would mean more expensive work in the shop.

"Fuck," she said, kicking the dented side of the nine-year-old heap of junk. *Great way to start the day.*

She was pulling onto the guideway before she remembered that she had not said good-bye to her father.

"These tunnels are cool," said Coyne. "Long bus ride to get here, but they're definitely cool. How'd you say you found the entrance?"

"My mom showed me a few years ago when she started working at the Civic Center," said Val. "Used to be a bunch of malls and shit down here. They used to bring prisoners through here before they shut it up after the Big One."

Sully and Gene D. looked impressed and a bit nervous. Their footfalls echoed in the dripping corridors. There were no lights, but their VR shades amplified the slightest glow from the ventilation grills.

"You say it runs all the way from where your old lady works at the Civic Center to Pueblo Park on the other side of the One-Oh-One?" said Coyne.

"Yeah." They stopped at a boarded up storefront to light up cigarettes and pass around a bottle of wine. The matches flared like incendiary explosions in VR amplification.

"I think that you should do a Jap," said Coyne.

Val's head snapped up. "A Jap?"

Coyne, Sully, and Gene D. were grinning. "Zap a Jap," crooned Sully.

Val looked only at Coyne. "Why a Jap?"

The taller boy shrugged. "It'd be cool."

"Jap's are crazy about their security," said Val. "They've got bodyguards coming out the ass."

Coyne grinned. "Makes it cooler. We can all watch you, Val my man. We can all flash on this."

Val felt his heart pounding. "No, I mean it," he said, hoping that his voice did not sound as rattled and full of pleading as he felt. "Mom says that the Jap advisors who come to visit with the mayor or the D.A. are nuts about security. Always traveling around with bodyguards. She says that they shut off all the traffic near the Civic Center when Kasai, Morozumi, or Harada visit because . . ." Val stopped but not before he realized that he had said too much. Much too much.

Coyne leaned closer. The amplification made his lean face a blaze of light and shadows. "Because then no one can get close, right, Val my man?" He gestured toward the tunnel. "But we could get close, couldn't we?"

"Nobody knows when the mayor and his tame Japs would visit," said Val, hearing the whine in his own voice and hating it. "Really. I swear."

"Don't your old lady know?" asked Gene D. His voice echoed in the darkness. "She's hot shit down here, ain't she?"

Val made a fist, but Coyne grabbed him. "She doesn't know," said Val. "Ever. Honest."

"Hey, cryo yourself, Val my man," said Coyne, patting his arm. "We believe you. It's all right. We got all the time in the world, Babe. No rush on nothing." Coyne's face looked demonic in amplified light. "We're all friends here, yeah? And this is a mean place. Our own clubhouse, like without the gang trash, you know?" He patted Val's arm a final time and smiled at the others. "A Jap would be cool, but it don't matter who the bod is as long as we got someone to trash so's you can flash. Am I right or am I right?"

They sat and smoked in the darkness.

Carol scored three vials of flashback from one of the clerks in the D.A.'s office to tide her over and spent the morning doing depositions on civil cases for several of the lawyers who used the offices there. She was always pleased to take depositions for the private firms because it meant extra money selling them copies of the transcripts.

Several of the other stenographers were out—which was usually the case—but she learned that one of them, a woman named Sally Carter whom Carol did not know too well, was home because word had just reached her that her husband had been killed in the fighting near Hong Kong. There was the usual clucking and muttering that America had no business fighting wars for Japan or the Chinese warlords, but in the end everyone admitted that the country needed the money and that there were precious few commodities other than American military technology and warm bodies that Japan or the EC would buy.

Sally Carter's absence meant more work and deposition sales for Carol.

At 11:00 A.M. she looked in her desk drawer, ready to steal a muffin from her lunch bag, remembered that she had not packed a lunch today, and then remembered the reason. She smiled at the thought of her cloak-and-dagger rendezvous with the Assistant D.A.

At 11:15 A.M., Danny called.

The phone was obviously a poorly lighted pay phone in a bar somewhere and the video quality was poor: Danny was little more than a pale blur in the shadows. But it was a familiar blur. And his voice had not changed.

"Carol," he said, "you're looking great, kiddo. Really good."

Carol said nothing. She could not speak. It had been eight and a half years since she had last seen or spoken to Danny.

"Anyway," he said, speaking quickly to fill her silence, "I was in L.A. for a couple of days . . . I live in Chicago now, you know . . . and I just thought . . . I mean I hoped . . . I mean, dammit, Carol, will you please have lunch with me today? Please? It's very important to me."

No, thought Carol. *Absolutely not. You don't just leave Val and me, no letter, no explanation, no child support, and then call me up eight years later and say you want to have lunch. Absolutely not. No.*

"Yes," she heard herself say, feeling as if she were in one of her flashbacks and wondering if she *were* flashing on this from some sad future. "Where? When?"

Danny told her the place. It was a downtown bar in which they had eaten when they first moved to L.A. fifteen years ago and used to steal lunchbreaks to be together. "Say . . . ten minutes from now?"

Carol knew that if she took the Honda it might not hold a

charge and would leave her stranded in the shitty section of the city. She would have to take the bus. "Twenty minutes," she said.

The pale blob that was Danny nodded. She thought she could see a smile.

Carol hung up but kept her finger on the button for a minute, as if caressing it. Then she hurried to reapply her makeup and get downstairs to the bus.

"Halfback to Base. Five minutes to destination."

Oh, fuck it. Fuck it all to hell. Robert is disgusted. After years of this, he knows what will not happen. It is like self-abuse without a climax.

He keeps his eyes closed ... or tries to. One cannot shut out flashback visuals without a tremendous effort of will. People are shouting and waving on the green grass to his left.

Robert tried to escape, to return to another time, another memory ... but once begun, there is no escape from a flashback episode. They glide toward the railroad bridge overpass.

There is a sound. Pigeons wheel into the canyon above the plaza.

No use. Empty. Useless.

Three seconds later he leaps from the chase car and sprints toward the blue Lincoln.

Useless. No exercise of will can make him move more quickly. Time and memory are immutable.

Not even my fucking memory. I am *crazy. Kay, I miss you.*

The second shot. He dives for the footplate and metal grip. The third shot.

Robert tries not to see, but the image of the President's head exploding is not to be denied.

Twenty years later, fifty percent of Americans polled remembered seeing this live on television. It was never on television. It was almost two years until censored parts of the Zapruder film were released ... and then only to Life *magazine. Before flashback, memories lied ... we edited them at will. Shit, Kennedy was elected with only forty-some percent of the vote, but ten years after his death seventy-two percent of the people polled said they had voted for him.*

Memory lies.

He pushes the President's wife back into the vehicle, noticing the insanity in her wide eyes but understanding the urgency in her single-minded ambition to retrieve the bit of skull. To make everything all right again.

I'm going to find Val. Make sure he doesn't do anything stupid.

He shoves the woman back down in the seat and guards her and Lancer's body all the way to Parkland Hospital. The hopelessness flows over him like a rising tide.

Val and his friends watched the I-5 guideway from their perch on the roof of a building abandoned after the Big One. Val was holding the .32, bracing it with both hands along the edge of the roof. The traffic glided by silently except for the rush of tires on wet pavement. It had rained in the past hour.

"I could wait until a Lexus comes along and blast it," said Val.

Coyne gave him a disgusted look. "With that popgun? It's thirty yards to the VIP lane. You couldn't even hit the fucking car, much less the Jap in the backseat. If there *is* a Jap in the backseat."

"Besides," said Gene D., "their cars have the best armorplating there is. A fucking ought-six wouldn't go through one of their fucking windshields."

"Yeah," said Sully.

"A fucking needlegun wouldn't hurt a Jap Lexus from here," said Gene D.

Val lowered the pistol. "I thought that it was the best if the . . . if it was a random thing you did to flash on."

Coyne rubbed Val's short hair with his knuckles. "It *was* the best, Val my man. Now a Jap's the thing."

Val sat back, leaving the .32 on the ledge. Water pooled on the sagging asphalt roof. "But it might take days . . . weeks . . ."

Coyne grinned, swept the pistol off the ledge, and offered it to Val. "Hey, we got time, don't we, my men?"

Sully and Gene D. made noises.

Val hesitated a second and then took the pistol. It started raining again and the boys hurried for shelter. Val did not see his grandfather watching them from across the street. When they left the building a few minutes later, none of the boys noticed the old man following them toward the river.

It was raining by the time Carol got to the bar on San Julian. She hustled in, holding a newspaper over her hair, and stood a minute blinking in the dark. When the heavyset man approached her, she actually took a step backward before she recognized him.

"Danny."

He took her hands and set the wet newspaper on a table. "Carol. Christ, you look good." He hugged her clumsily.

She could not say the same about her ex-husband. Danny had put on weight—at least a hundred pounds—and his features and familiar body seemed lost in the excess. Much of his blond hair was gone and his scalp was freckled with brown spots like her father's. His skin was sallow, his eyes were dark and sunken over heavy pouches, and he was wheezing softly. What she had assumed were bad lighting and poor video quality on the phone were actually shadows and distortions of Danny himself.

"I've got our old booth," he said. Without letting go of her hands, he led her to a corner near the rear. She did not remember having a special booth here, and she had never replayed this particular memory.

A glass of Scotch sat half-finished on the table. From the way Danny smelled when he kissed her, he'd had more than one.

They sat looking at each other across the table. For a minute neither spoke. The bar was almost empty this time of day, but the bartender and a man in a tattered raincoat near the front were having an argument with a sportscaster persona on an old HDTV above a line of bottles. Carol looked down and realized that Danny was still holding both of her hands in one of his. She felt strange, anaesthetized, as if the nerves in her hands conveyed no tactile information.

"Well, Jesus, Carol," Danny said at last, "you really look great. You really do."

Carol nodded and waited.

Danny swallowed the last of the Scotch, waved the bartender over for a refill, gestured to Carol, and took the slight shaking of her head as a no. Only after a full glass of whiskey was delivered did he speak again. The rush of words flowed over Carol, relieving her of any necessity to speak.

"Well, God, Carol, here I was on a . . . well, a sort of business trip actually . . . and I realized, well, I wondered . . . Does she still work down at the Hall of Justice? . . . and there you were, right on the answering persona's list of options. Anyway, I thought . . . you know, why not? So . . . Christ, did I tell you how great you look? Beautiful, actually. Not that you weren't always a knockout. I always thought you were a knockout. But, hey, you know that.

"Anyway, you probably want to know what I'm up to, huh? Been what? Four or five years since that time . . . anyway, I'm in Chicago now. Not with Caldwell Banker anymore. Sold luxury electrics for a while, but . . . you know . . . the market's really gone to shit on those. Got out just at the right time. So, where was I? I'm in Chicago . . . I'm into some deep pattern counseling . . . thought you might be interested in me getting into some counseling."

Danny laughed. It was an oddly abrasive sound and the two men at the front of the bar glanced back and then went back to their argument with the sportscaster persona. Danny touched her fingers, lifted her hands in his again as if they were a pair of gloves he had forgotten he had, and then set them down on the scarred table. He took a drink.

"So anyway, this deep pattern counseling . . . you've heard of it? No? Jesus, I thought everyone in California would . . . anyway, there's this brilliant guy in Chicago, he's a doctor . . . you know, a Ph.D. in therapeutic flashback use . . . and he had sort of, well, ashram is the word. People with serious things to work out sort of live there and tithe to him . . . well, actually it's a bit more than tithe since it involves power of attorney . . . but what it is, is, that it's not a one-shot-a-week type of thing. We live there and the counseling . . . deep pattern counseling, it's called . . . the counseling is sort of our job like. It's an all day thing . . ."

"Using flashback," said Carol.

Danny grinned as if terrifically relieved and impressed by her depth of understanding. "You got it. Right. Perfect. You probably know all about it . . . there's a million deep pattern type counseling centers out here in sunny California. But, yeah, we're in counseling with it for eight to ten hours a day. . . under the strict supervision of Dr. Singh, of course. Or his appointed therapist-counselors. It's not like, you know, how I used to use the stuff when we were together. . ." He rubbed his cheeks and Carol heard the rasp of his palm on the stubble there. "I know I was fucking around with it then, Carol. I mean, I hardly flash on the teenage sex stuff now. It's just. . . you know. . . it's just not important given the totality of the therapeutic experience, y'know?"

Carol brushed a strand of wet hair off her forehead. "What *is* important?" she asked.

"What?" Danny had finished his Scotch and was trying to get the bartender's attention. "I'm sorry, Babe. What?"

"What is important, Danny?"

He waited for the refill and then smiled almost beatifically. "I've got a chance for a real breakthrough here, Babe. Dr. Singh himself says that I've reached the point where I can turn things around. But. . ."

Carol knew the tone well. She said nothing.

Danny took her hands again and rubbed them as if they were cold. It was *his* hands that were cold.

"But I need some help. . ." he began.

"Money," said Carol.

Danny dropped her hands and made a fist. Carol noticed how pudgy, pale, and weak his hand looked, as if the muscles there had been replaced by fat. *Or creme filling,* she thought. *Like those Bavarian creme donuts he used to eat.*

"Not just money," he rasped at her. *"Help.* I'm ready to take the step to total reintegration, and Dr. Singh says that. . ."

"Total reintegration?" said Carol. It sounded like some new software telem package that Val wanted to buy for his VR shades.

Danny's smile was condescending. "Yeah. Total recall. Complete reintegration of this past life with the soul-knowledge that I've gained during my time at the ashram. It's like. . . you know. . . retrofitting an old gas-burning car for electric or methane. There are some people at the ashram who are actually at the stage where they can reintegrate their *past* lives, but. . . Jesus, you know. . . I feel like I'll be lucky to handle this one." He made the abrasive laughing sound again.

Carol nodded. "You need money for flashback that you use in this . . . therapy," she said. "How much? How long a replay?" Her voice would have betrayed her almost total lack of curiosity if Danny had been paying any real attention.

"Well," he said, excited, obviously thinking that he had a chance, "total reintegration is . . . you know . . . *total.* I've already liquidated what I had . . . the Lakeshore apartment, the Chrysler electric, the few stocks that Wally left me . . . but I'll need a lot more to . . ." He stopped when he saw her expression. "Hey, Carol, this isn't, like, a one-payment thing. It's like . . . you know . . . a mortgage or car payments. It's not really much at all when you look at it stretched out over the period we're talking about, and . . ."

Carol said, "You're talking about flashing back on your whole life."

"Well . . . you know . . . what I mean is . . . yeah."

"Total reintegration," said Carol. "You're forty-four years old, Danny, and you're going to flashback your entire life."

He sat up straight, his chin thrusting out in what Carol remembered as his belligerent posture. As pale, overweight, and soft as he looked now, the sight was a bit pathetic.

"It's easy to make fun of someone who's willing to be vulnerable," he said. "I'm trying to straighten out my life, Carol."

Carol laughed softly. "Danny, you'd be *eighty-eight* when you finished the flashback."

He leaned forward as if he were going to impart a secret to her. His voice was wet and intimate. "Carol, this is just one life on the wheel. The most important thing about it is where we are when we *end* it."

Carol stood up. "There's no doubt where you'll be, Danny. You'll be broke." She walked away.

"Hey . . ." shouted Danny, not rising. "I forgot to ask . . . how's Val?"

Carol went out into the rain, could not remember which way the bus stop was, and began walking blindly toward the Civic Center.

*　　*　　*

Val and his friends were lounging in the steel viaduct buttresses fifty feet above the concrete riverbed when Coyne suddenly sat up, grabbed Val's shoulder, and said, "Bingo!"

"Don't you have your shades wired to news?" said Coyne, nodding and grinning at something in VR.

"News?" said Val. "Are you shitting me?"

Coyne took his glasses off. "I shit you not, Val my man. We have just been delivered a Jap."

Val felt his heart sink.

"Delivered a Jap, delivered a Jap," crooned Sully.

"What's happening?" said Gene D., coming out of a ten-minute flash. From the look of the bulge in Gene D.'s jeans, Val guessed that his friend had been flashing on the Spanic girl's rape again.

"Newsflash," grinned Coyne. "Big stir at the Civic Center. The mayor's headed over there with his Jap advisor buddy, Morozumi."

"Civic Center," said Val. "My mom works there."

Coyne nodded. "We take that neat tunnel complex you showed us in from First Street. Do the deed there at that VIP plaza on Temple Street. Get our asses out through the tunnel to Pueblo Park and then *didi mau* ourselves away by bus. Leave the fucking gun in the fucking tunnel."

"Won't work," said Val, searching his mind for reasons that it would not.

Coyne shrugged. "Maybe not. But it'll be a mainline rush to check it out."

"It won't work," said Val, repeating the phrase like a mantra as he followed the others.

Robert felt more alive than he had in years as he followed the boys onto a caterpillar bus and slid into the section behind them. His pace was lighter, his vision was clearer, and he felt as if he had cleared his head of cobwebs. He stood at the front end of the second bus section, watching through the accordion doors into Val's section to make sure he did not miss it when the boys stepped out.

Robert wondered if the therapy persona was correct, if his flashback obsession was the result of a sense of failure at not protecting his wife from her final bout of cancer. "You are aware," the program had told him, "that more than fifty years after the death of President Kennedy, there are thousands of people obsessed with conspiracy theories that have never been proven."

"I don't believe in a conspiracy," Robert had muttered.

The bearded persona had smiled on the ITV wall. "No, but you perseverate in this protection fantasy."

Robert had worked hard not to become angry. He had said nothing.

"Your wife died ... how many years ago was it?" asked the counselor.

Robert knew that the program knew. "Six," he said.

"And how long ago was it that the country was so wrapped up in the fiftieth anniversary of this assassination?"

Robert did feel anger at the simple-minded obviousness of this line of questioning. But he had promised Carol and the Medicaid caseworker that he would undergo the counseling. "Five years ago."

"And the flashback obsession ..."

"About five years," sighed Robert. He had glanced at his watch. "My time's up."

The bearded persona ... Robert thought it was a persona, he was never sure ... showed white teeth through his beard. "Bobby," he said, "that's my line."

The boys got off the bus at the ruins of the old Federal Building and Robert followed.

All the way back to the Civic Center in the rain, Carol looked around her with newly opened eyes. She looked at the ten-foot-high heaps of bagged garbage, the abandoned storefronts, the unrepaired damage from the Big One years ago, the slogans in mock-Japanese touting cheap Japanese recreation electronics, the security cameras, the cheap electrics lining the curb with their security holos pulsing ominously, the people hurrying along with gray faces and averted eyes the way she had remembered seeing vid from Eastern Europe and Russ when she was a kid ... it all seemed to match Danny's fat characterless face and whining, self-absorbed tone.

I'm going to take Val and Dad and move to Canada, she thought. It was not a whim. It was the strongest resolve she had felt in years. *Or*

Mexico. Somewhere where half the population isn't zonked on flashback at any given moment.

Carol raised her face to the rain. *I'm going to quit using that shit. Get Val and Dad to stop.*

She tried to remember what the country had been like when she was a tiny little kid, looking at the kindly, grandfatherly face of President Reagan on the old-fashioned TV. *You bankrupted us forever, you kindly, grandfatherly asshole. My kid's kids will never pay off the debt. For what . . . winning the Cold War and creating the Russ Republic so it can compete with us in buying Japanese and EC products? We can't afford them. And we've all become too stupid and too lazy to make our own.*

For the first time, Carol understood why use of flashback was cause for execution in Japan . . . a nation that had not had the death penalty for sixty years before that. For the first time she understood that a culture or a nation actually had to decide whether it would look forward or allow itself to lie back and dream until it died.

Total reintegration. Mother of Christ.

Carol had walked for more than an hour when she realized that the rain had stopped but that her cheeks were still wet. It was a shock when she turned the corner near the Civic Center and was stopped by security agents. She showed her badge at two points, was frisked by a sniffer, and then approached the north entrance where the mayor's limo and several armored Lexuses sat within a cordon of police motorcycles.

She was already upstairs and had been checked by two more security people before one of the women from the secretarial pool came rushing toward her, tears streaming down the woman's heavy face. "Carol, did you hear? It's terrible. Poor Dale."

Carol pulled herself free, went into her cubicle, and keyed her phone to vid news. The bulletin was repeated a moment later. L.A. Assistant Attorney Dale Fritch, a Japanese national named Hiroshi Nakamura, and five other people had been murdered in a downtown café. There was the usual montage of crime scene video. Carol sat down heavily.

Her urgent-message phone light was blinking. Numbly, Carol killed the news feed and keyed the message.

"Carol," said Dale Fritch, his boyish image only slightly

distorted by the poor pay-phone video, "I'm sorry we missed each other, but it's all right. Hiroshi talked more freely with just me here. Carol . . . *I believe him.* I think the Japanese have been feeding this stuff to us since the late nineties. I think there's something here bigger than the EC Payback Scandal, bigger than Watergate . . . shit, bigger than the Big One. Hiroshi has disks, papers, memos, payoff lists . . ." Fritch glanced over his shoulder. "Look, Carol, I've got to get back to him. Look, I'm not coming in this afternoon. Can you bring your datawriter and meet me at . . . uh . . . say the LAX Holiday Inn . . . at five-thirty? It'll be worth it, I promise. Okay. Uh . . . don't say anything about any of this to anyone, okay? See you at five-thirty. *Ciao.*"

Carol sat looking at her phone a minute and then recorded the message to a fresh disk, slipped it in her pocket, and keyed the news feed. A live reporter was standing in front of a restaurant where bodies were being removed on gurneys. ". . . police know only that Assistant D.A. Fritch was at the restaurant in an unofficial capacity when three men in black ski masks entered and opened fire with what one witness described as, quote, 'military-type needleguns, the kind you see in the movies.' Assistant D.A. Fritch and the others died instantly. The Japanese Embassy has no comment on the identity of the man with Fritch, but a CNN/LA news source close to the embassy informs us that the Japanese national was one Hiroshi Nakamura, a felon wanted by Tokyo Police Prefecture. Sources within the L.A.P.D. speculate that Nakamura may have been meeting with Assistant D.A. Fritch to sound out Los Angeles justice authorities on a plea bargain in exchange for a promise of no extradition. These same sources inform CNN/LA that the hit bears all the marks of a Yakuza assassination. The Yakuza, as you may remember, are Japan's most lethal crime organization and a rising problem in the new . . ."

"Carol?" said a voice behind her. "Could you step into my office for a moment?" Bert Torrazio was standing there with several security men in plainclothes.

The mayor and his advisor, Mr. Morozumi, were sitting in leather chairs across from the D.A.'s desk. Carol nodded although no introductions were made.

"Bert," said the mayor, "take me down to Dale's office, would you? I'd like to offer my condolences to his staff."

Everyone left except for Carol, two Japanese security men, and Morozumi. The advisor was impeccable in a Sartori suit, gray tie, and perfectly groomed gray hair. A modest Nippon Space Agency wrist chronometer that must have cost at least thirty thousand dollars was his only concession to extravagance. Mr. Morozumi nodded and the security men left.

"You returned from lunch three minutes too soon, Ms. Rogallo," said the advisor. "The disk, please."

Carol hesitated only a second before handing him the CD.

Morozumi smiled slightly as he slipped the silver disk in his coat pocket. "We knew, of course, that Mr. Fritch had called someone, but the city's antiquated communications equipment succeeded in tracing the call only seconds ago." Morozumi rose and crossed to a rubber tree near the window. "Mr. Torrazio should take better care of his plants," the advisor murmured almost to himself.

"Why?" said Carol. *Why kill Dale? Why feed a nation a drug for twenty years?*

Mr. Morozumi raised his face. Sunlight glinted on his round glasses. He touched a leaf of the rubber tree. "It is a sign of slovenliness not to take care of those living things in one's care," he said.

"What happens next?" said Carol. When Morozumi did not answer, she said, "To me."

The little man dusted another leaf with his fingers and then rubbed his fingertips together, cleaning them. "You live with your child, Valentine, and a father who is currently receiving counseling. Your ex-husband, Daniel, is still alive and . . . I believe . . . visiting your fair city even as we speak."

Carol felt something like cold fingers close around her heart and throat.

"To answer your question," continued Mr. Morozumi, "I presume you will continue doing your fine job here at the Justice Center and that Mr. Torrazio will be pleased with your performance. From time to time I will, perhaps, have the opportunity to chat with you and hear about the continued health and well-being of your family."

Carol said nothing. She concentrated on staying on her feet and not swaying.

Mr. Morozumi pulled a tissue from a dispenser on Bert Torrazio's desk, wiped his dirty fingers, and dropped the Kleenex on the D.A.'s blotter. As if on signal, the mayor, the D.A., and the security people came back through the door. Torrazio looked at Carol and then raised his eyebrows questioningly.

Mr. Morozumi averted his glance as if Torrazio had food on his upper lip. "We had a delightful chat and it is time to get back to business," said Mr. Morozumi. He left with the slim security men. The mayor shook Torrazio's hand, nodded in Carol's direction, and rushed to catch up to the procession.

Carol and the District Attorney stared at each other for a full minute before she turned on her heel and went back to her cubicle. The file cabinet was empty and both her phone and computer had been replaced. Carol sat down and stared at a cartoon she had taped to the frosted glass of her partition four years earlier. It showed a court reporter typing furiously as a witness and lawyer screamed at each other, the judge pounded her gavel, the defendant stood shouting at the witness, the defendant's lawyer yelled at him, and two jurors bellowed at each other on the verge of a violent confrontation. A woman behind the court reporter was saying to a friend, "She's a good writer but her plots aren't very believable."

The underground mall ended at a ventilator grill between the landscaping and the Civic Center. Coyne had brought a crowbar. The boys found themselves standing with a small press contingent bristling with vid cameras and parabolic mikes. Local reporters shouted questions at the mayor and his Japanese advisor as they descended the stairs to the idling limousine. Val was within twenty feet of the VIPs. The ventilator grill was open and waiting twenty feet behind him. The security people ignored the previously searched press group and concentrated on watching the buildings and the crowd being held back across the little plaza.

"Do it," said Coyne. "Now."

Val took the pistol and cocked it.

The mayor paused just long enough to answer a shouted

question and then wave at someone in the Civic Center doorway. Obeying protocol, Mr. Morozumi waited by the open limousine door for the mayor to finish.

Val raised the pistol. It was less then fifteen feet to the Japanese man's head. The pistol barrel was just one more lens thrust toward the small knot of VIPs. Val was not aware of Coyne, Sully, and Gene D. sliding away and disappearing down the open grill.

Robert had almost not been able to pull himself up out of the opening. He thought that all of his strength was gone by the time he stood up, brushing rust and dead leaves from his pants, but then he saw Val, saw the gun, saw that he was closer to the target than to his grandson, and then Robert ran forward immediately, without thinking, without hesitating an instant.

Val pulled the trigger. Nothing happened. He blinked and then clicked the safety off. He had just raised the pistol again when one of the cameramen near him shouted, "Hey!"

Robert ran full tilt at the black limousine. To put his body between Val and the mayor he would have to jump up and over the right rear of the trunk. He did so, forgetting his age, forgetting his arthritis, forgetting everything except the imperative to be there before the boy pulled the trigger again.

Val saw his grandfather at the last second and could not believe it as the old man vaulted to the trunk of the limo, skidded across it, and landed on his feet between the mayor and Mr. Morozumi. Security men leaped on Mr. Morozumi, pushing him down. The mayor stood alone, mouth still open to answer a question.

I made it! thought Robert knowing that he was between Val and the mayor, knowing that any bullet meant for the other man would have to go through him. *This time I made . . .*

Two of the Japanese security agents crouched, braced their weapons, and shot Robert from a distance of fifteen feet. At almost the same instant, a third security man raked automatic weapons fire across the press gallery. Val and three cameramen went down.

The mayor and Mr. Morozumi were pushed into the limo and rushed away before the watching crowd had time to begin screaming. Neither the mayor nor his advisor was hurt.

*　　*　　*

Val's body was taken to the police morgue but Carol was allowed to visit her father.

"He won't know you're here," said the doctor. His voice was disinterested. "The neurological damage is too great. There is some brain activity, but it is very limited. I'm afraid that it is just a matter of how long the life support can keep things up. Hours perhaps. Days at the most."

Carol nodded and sat down in the chair next to the bed. She did not touch his hand. The room was illuminated just by the electronic monitors.

The room is illuminated just by the light of the medical monitors. Visitors do not think that Robert can hear what they are saying, but he can.

"He has been like this for some time," says the nurse to the President's visiting daughter and her son.

"My father wants nothing but the finest care for him," says Lancer's daughter. She has grown into a beautiful woman. Her son is three or four and has inherited his grandfather's healthy thatch of chestnut hair. The little boy takes Robert's fingers in his small hands. He is not frightened by the hospital room or the IV drips or the medical monitors. He has been here before.

Lancer's daughter sits by his bedside as she has so many times before. *Do not weep for me,* thinks Robert. *I am not unhappy.*

Carol sits by her father's bed until 3 A.M. when the technicians come to unhook the machines and to take his body away.

When they are gone, she continues to sit in the dark room. Her eyes are open but she does not see. After a while she smiles, takes out a thirty-minute tube, raises it almost reverently to her nose, and breaks the tab.

THE GREAT LOVER

Editor's Prologue by Richard Edward Harrison III:
The following secret wartime journal of the poet James Edwin Rooke was "discovered" in the Imperial War Museum in London in September of 1988. In fact, the journal had been correctly logged and catalogued as one of several thousand Great War diaries found or donated to the Museum almost seventy years earlier, but the small notebook had been misfiled with bureaucratic detritus of little interest to scholars through all or most of the intervening decades. Once "discovered," however, the ensuing reaction it has created in scholars might be described as nothing less than sensational.

That it is the actual writing of James Edwin Rooke has now been verified beyond question. The handwriting has been confirmed. The poems, most of them in their earliest work state, have been identified as holistic versions of several of the more famous verses in Trench Poems *by James Edwin Rooke, copyright 1921 by Faber and Faber Ltd., London. Indeed, although the diary was not signed and was one of hundreds of nearly identical cheap journals recovered at aid stations, burial centres, or on the battlefield itself, many of the passages in this journal were "signed" by Rooke's hasty symbol* 😈 *, which was to become so famous on the cover of the 1936 Faber edition of* Trench Poems.

But even when there was no further doubt as to the authenticity of this diary, there remained a shocked disbelief. The reasons are varied and profound.

*First, James Edwin Rooke's Somme diary from the Great War had already been found and published (*One Infantry Officer's Memoirs:

James Edwin Rooke's Somme Diary, copyright 1924 by George Falkner & Sons) *and while it contained some disturbing imagery of trench warfare, the tone was of the more temperate and often wryly humorous variety which so typified officers' diaries of that time. In point of truth, most of Rooke's published* Somme Diary *comments were terse operational notes with few personal asides of interest to any but the most dedicated literary scholar or military historian.*

Certainly there was nothing of the sort of shocking material present in this more recently discovered journal.

Secondly, there were the legal rights of the Rooke estate to be considered and the surviving members of the Rooke family to be consulted. The editor wishes to thank Mrs. Eleanor Marsh of Tunbridge Wells for her kind permission to reprint the following pages.

Finally, there was the factor of the contents themselves. The reputation of James Edwin Rooke, as both poet and man, has seemed secure for most of this century. While the demands of honest scholarship require full disclosure, drastically altering the reputation of an historical figure so central to British pride and British literary tradition is no light undertaking. Thus it is that this, the first publication of James Edwin Rooke's secret Somme diary, was delayed for several years due as much to this editor's concern about the effect it would have on the image and literary legacy of the famous "trench poet" as to the serious and extended effort required to verify all aspects of the journal's authenticity.

But having verified the diary's authenticity and carefully weighed the effect such revelations will have on the memory of one of this century's premiere poets, the burden of honest scholarship compels this editor to publish the journal without amendation or expurgation.

The journal itself has suffered waterstain, some damage from the terrible war environment it describes, and the inevitable decomposition from seven decades in storage under less than optimum conditions at the Imperial War Museum. More than that, several pages are missing and may have been torn out by the author. Many passages have been scrawled over or marked out. Some of these have been retrieved through various X-ray techniques; others appear to have been lost forever.

Because of the many years and cultural differences that now separate us from those terrible months along the Somme in 1916, I have inserted a few editorial comments for purposes of clarification. Where the text is illegible or ambivalent, I have noted my own best guess reconstruction of a word or phrase. I have footnoted the bits of verse in the journals.

Other than these few editorial intrusions, the words and impressions are totally those of the twenty-eight-year-old Lieutenant James Edwin Rooke, late of C Company, No. 4237, 13th (S) Battalion, The Rifle Brigade.

—REH
Cambridge
December, 1992

Saturday, 8 July, 8.15 A.M.—

Because I had been here as observer the week before during the Big Push and "knew the way" through the endless maze of trenches, I was appointed last night to lead the entire Rifle Brigade from the reserve trenches on the Tara-Usna Ridge into our section of the Front at la Boisselle. I accepted with good enough grace, despite the fact that the lines had changed dramatically along this section of the Front in the intervening week. Since la Boisselle itself had fallen, it now lies behind the front line, while the section of enemy trench we had undermined and blown heavenward with such a ferocious bang on the morning of 1 July now exists merely as a gigantic crater to the right of our new forward line. (As I write this, the crater is in the process of becoming a mass grave for our comrades in the 34th Division whom I watched go over the top so bravely and so futilely only seven days ago. Their bodies have been out in the No Man's Land since the morning of the attack, and only the successful advance this morning during which la Boisselle finally fell has allowed our troops to reach the wire where most of the bodies have lain since the previous Saturday.)

We arrived after 10 P.M. last night, in the pouring rain, and, without sleep or a proper meal, were put to the task of burying the dead before the sun rose. The Colonel explained to the officers that burial teams had been sniped at during daylight hours so that we were to begin our business at night. The other officers and I called together the NCOs in our respective companies and passed on the explanation. The NCOs explained nothing to the men, but roused them out of their muddy nooks and crannies, out from under their dripping oilsheets, and away from their midnight brew-ups to get on with the grisly business.

The trenches here are a nightmare to navigate, even in the daytime, a confusing rat's maze even before the hasty advance and the addition of new trenches in the past two days, and last night, in the rain, the maze was almost beyond human mastery. Nonetheless, I led burial parties to places along the row of old German trenches, hoping all the while not to leave our section altogether and blunder into active Boche lines. There was little to do except to direct the men in the pulling of corpses dressed in khaki off the rolls of still-standing wire. There were more bodies in the innumerable shell craters, of course, but I decided to leave those alone in the dark and rain. A living man can drown in one of those craters. The dead are in no hurry to leave them.

This entire front stinks of death and decay and the smell has already permeated my new uniform. It never leaves one and one does not seem to grow completely used to it according to my chums in the 34th who have been here since replacing the French. It was worse, of course, out among the corpse-filled craters and body-strewn wire of what only yesterday had been No Man's Land.

Our burial parties moved forward warily under the sputtering light of Very flares and the incessant heat-lightning flash of artillery. Neither the German guns nor our own had let up their dueling from the day's battle (we lost thirteen men merely moving the mile from the Tara-Usna Ridge to the forward communications trenches behind the Front) and whatever advantage we held over snipers in the dark certainly seemed negated by the effect of the heavier nighttime shelling.

There were hundreds of bodies on the wire just in our small section of line and I had the NCOs tell the men to concentrate on these, ignoring, as I said, those in the shellholes and former German trenches. Naturally there were hundreds of German bodies there as well as the British dead, and the other two lieutenants and I decided that it would be easier to sort these out in the daylight.

The procedure was rather straightforward. Each detail consisted of men to pull our comrades' bodies from the wire, often leaving chunks of the corpse behind, other men to gather identity disks, stretcher bearers to carry each corpse to the crater, and a final group of men to gather up rifles and other recoverable equipment. At the crater, the bodies were merely tipped over without memorial service or farewell. In the red light of flares, I watched as several of these dead men—some of whom I may well have met or known during my week of liaison with the 34th Division—went rolling gently, almost comically, down the muddy slope in the rain and dark. No effort was made to identify individuals at this point. Their identity disks will be perused later and the appropriate letters written and posted.

The bodies roll very slowly, usually burying themselves in the chalk and sucking mud before reaching the noxious green lake of gas and decay at the bottom of the crater. Once, as I watched, a shell struck the lip of the crater where a work party of six men were lifting corpses off stretchers and bits of the recently quick and the recently dead all went spiraling out over the hungry maw of the pit. Two wounded men were helped back toward the aid station—I do not know if their helpers ever *found* the aid station—while the rest of the mutilated burial detail (or at least as much as could be found) were merely shoved down into the crater along with the bodies they had been handling only moments before.

We are ordered to occupy the forward trenches, but these are also mass graves.

> *And clink of shovels deepening the shallow trench.*
> *The place was rotten with dead; green clumsy legs*
> *High-booted, sprawled and grovelled along the saps*
> *And trunks, face downward, in the sucking mud,*
> *Wallowed like trodden sandbags loosely filled;*
> *And naked sodden buttocks, mats of hair,*
> *Bulged, clotted heads slept in the plastering slime*[1]

But I must write of what has caused me to start this new and private diary.

I know that I will die here at the Somme. I am certain of it.

And I know now that I am a coward.

During the past few months of training at Auxi-le-Château, or the billet time before that at Hannescamps, I had suspected that my nervous tendencies and poetic inclinations indicated a lack of nerve. But I had told myself that I was merely green, that it was merely a case of the usual jitters, of the new subaltern getting the wind up during his first exposure to the Front.

But now I know better.

I am a coward. I want to live and nothing—not King, not Country, not even saving home and family and Western Civilization from the slavering Hun—seems worth dying for.

It was getting on towards dawn and I had sent back the last burial party—Sgt. Jowett, Corporal Newey, Bobby Wood, Frank Bell, and several of the other boys who had worked at W. H. Smith's in Nottingham and who had joined together—when I tried to find my way back to Battalion H.Q. via a series of low communication trenches. Any trip through these interlocking lines of zigzagging wounds in the wet earth can take an absurd amount of time—last week I became lost trying to find 34th Divisional Headquarters and spent almost an hour traversing a few hundred yards—but this morning I was completely, totally, irrevocably, irretrievably lost. And alone. Finally, when I realized that the trench system which I was traversing was deeper than any British trench I had ever seen, that the junction signs—too dim to decipher in Very light without igniting a flame on my trench lighter, which I was not about to do—were nonetheless visibly written in *Fraktur,* and that the corpses against which I had been brushing were wearing higher boots and sharper tin hats than the honest British dead, I decided that I had blundered into a section of German trench which was—I sincerely hoped—only recently captured and not yet manned against counter-attacks.

I sat down to wait for daylight.

It was several minutes before I realized that someone was sitting directly opposite me in the rain, his pale face appearing to study me quite intensely.

I admit that I started rather violently and reached for my pistol before I realized that it was only another corpse. It was helmetless, and I could not make out the color of the uniform fabric—all uniforms seem composed of mud at any rate—but the protruding legs seemed booted more in the Boche manner than in Blighty leather. *{Ed. note—British Tommies along the Somme at this time often referred to England and things English as Blighty.}*

As I sat there waiting for dawn to reach forth her rosy fingertips, or at least for the black rain to turn to grey drizzle, I studied the man—what had been a man only days or hours before—in the red light of flares and the orange and magnesium-white pulse of exploding shells. I think the rain had let up a bit, or I had become used to it. I had left my valise *{Ed. note—some officers carried their sleeping gear in a sort of portmanteau}* and oilsheet where the Brigade had come onto the line, so I merely huddled miserably against the front of the trench since my friend seemed comfortable leaning against the parados *{Ed. note—the backside of the trench, the front being the parapet}* and satisfied myself in letting the rain drip from my tin hat onto my drenched lap.

Rats had been busy with my friend. This was no surprise, since most of the corpses we had witnessed this long day and longer night had a dead rat or two as quiet company. Sergeant Jowett, who has spent more time in the forward trenches than any of the rest of us, explained that a certain number of the giant vermin literally gorge themselves to death on the flesh of our comrades. During the first days on the line, he explained, the men tend to take it personally and to use bayonets to stab the slower-moving overstuffed creatures and toss them out into No Man's Land. But soon enough, he says, one learns to ignore the living rats, much less the dead.

There were no dead rats here tonight. At least none that I could see in the rain and mud. I began to make deductions about my friend's fate. He appeared to be almost one with the trench wall, as if he had been slammed back into it by a great force of exploding shell or a tossed Mills bomb. But his clothing and limbs were visibly intact, so that presumption seemed less than probable. It was more likely that he had been shot, had slumped against this trench wall, and one or more days of rain had brought the mud packing down around him in a sort of vertical burial. His hands were visible and very white. His clothes seemed to fit him wonderfully well, better than any quartermaster had ever clothed any living German infantry soldier—or British one either for that matter—but this sartorial precision was the result of gasses bloating the body so that expanding wet wool and leather almost creaked in protest.

I had seen this before, this deceptive rotundity of the dead.

My friend's fatal wound seemed quite visible and—to me—most terrible.

The rats and carrion birds had taken his eyes, of course, but the eyelids seemed intact right down to the lashes and he seemed to gaze at me with these black oval pits. And there was a third eye precisely in the center of his pale forehead. Sometimes, when the Very flares sputtered near the end of their descending lifetime, one or more of these three eyes seemed to wink and blink at me in some sort of necromantical conspiracy, as if saying—*You too will soon know this stillness.*

A Lee Enfield such as those the men in my rifle brigade carry and which almost certainly inflicted the visible wound in my friend, does not leave a dramatic entrance hole. Usually the German shooting victims we had passed on the roads coming up had little more than a neat, bluish, bloodless, eye-sized or smaller aperture in the side that had been facing our marksmen. Of course, they—like my friend here—might have an exit hole large enough to put one's fist in, large enough to spill the entire contents of his cranium out in a widening fan of brain and blood, but these details were mercifully hidden by the trench wall of which he seemed intent on becoming a part.

I confess here that this single, simple wound caused terror in me because I have always had an abnormal fear of being struck in the face. When other boys had faced off with fists at school, I had backed away from confrontation. Not, I told myself, because I feared pain—I feel that I deal with pain as well as the next boy or man—but precisely because the thought of a closed fist *coming toward my eyes and face* made me sick with revulsion and terror.

And now this. A bullet from one of our rifles, or—more relevantly, from its counterpart German Mauser—travels at almost half a mile per second, arriving twice as quickly as the sound of the shot itself.

Directly towards one's face. At one's eyes. Sharp metal flying directly at the eyes—the "darling of one's senses." The thought is insupportable.

I watched my friend and eventually I tore my gaze away from his unblinking tripartite stare.

I believe he had been young. Younger than my twenty-eight years certainly. Through the mud, there was the hint of short blond hair. The rats had left the flesh of his face surprisingly alone, suiting themselves to only a few long strips torn away around the cheekbones and jaw. These looked like mere finger scratches in the flarelight as water dripped from his nose and brow and strong chin.

What fascinated me were his teeth. The lips themselves may once have been full, even sensuous, but a day or more in the July sun had withered these and pulled them away from the teeth and gums so that even in the dim light I could see the bulging expanse of white and pink. The teeth were too perfect and protruded as if my friend were trying to spit out some final discharge, even if only an epithet at the injustice of his own banal death here.

As I sat staring, accustomizing myself to his presence there and my own presence *here*—here in the theatre of almost certain death where pieces of sharp metal come flying at one's eyes faster than one can perceive or dodge—I realized that those teeth, that jaw, were moving.

At first I thought it a trick of the flickering light, for although the shelling had subsided somewhat, more flares were drifting down as both the Boche and British lines anticipated the pre-dawn patrols through No Man's Land.

It was not the light. I leaned forward, thrusting my own face within a yard of my friend's.

The jaw was moving. I could hear it as dried and withered tendons stretched and popped.

The great white teeth—dentures, I realized now, for although the face was young, the teeth were certainly artificial—began to part. The entire face began to squirm, as if my friend were attempting to separate himself from the muddy trench wall and lean forward to join me in an open-mouthed kiss at the center of the pit.

I could not move. I could not breathe, even as the white teeth opened further and a great hiss of escaping gas billowed out and over me, bringing a stench of internal corruption worse than mustard gas or phosgene. The jaws worked. The throat writhed as if my dead friend were struggling against all the bonds of Hades to make one final utterance, perhaps to impart one final warning.

Then the dentures fell out, tumbling and chattering across the sunken, muddy chest, the throat and jaw writhed a final time, the mouth opened wide into a purely black, hissing oval, then stretched further into some obscene simulacrum of birth . . . and then an oily black rat—huge, its sleek body as long as a weasel's, its eyes black and arrogant—forced its way out between withered lips and rotting gums.

I did not move as the rat scuttled over me in its slow escape. It was well fed and in no hurry.

I did not move for some time after the rat had gone, but sat staring at my friend's chest and belly and wondering if I perceived other movement there.

I—my kind, my comrades and I—had brought about this young man's terrible pregnancy.

Who, I wondered, *will bring this gift to me?*

I did not move until the sun was well and truly up and three men from B Company, 13th Platoon, found me while foraging for souvenirs. This trench was not a true connecting trench at all, only a fortified extension of a sunken road the Germans had defended. It was beyond our lines, but well back from the new German position and somewhat shielded by a low ridge. The boys from B Company led me back.

I returned to the Battalion H.Q., made sure that the men of my company had been billeted in their rough dugouts, and then absently joined two men from my brigade, a certain Rifleman Monckton and Corporal Hoyles, as they brewed their morning tea.

A few minutes ago, just as I finished the first part of this entry, the Colonel came along with an officer from Staff. The Staff Captain climbed onto the firestep, peered oh-so-cautiously above the parapet toward the old No Man's Land where my men had been retrieving bodies from the wire all night, spied the hundreds of sun-blackened British corpses still lying about, and said to Colonel Pretor-Pinney, "Good God, I didn't know we were using Colonial troops!"

The Colonel said nothing. Eventually they left. "Dear God,"

Monckton muttered to the Corporal near him, "hasn't that bastard ever seen a dead man before?"

I moved away from the enlisted men before duty required me to officially overhear and reprimand them. I began laughing then. I was able to stop only seconds ago. My tears of laughter have smudged some of the lines on this page.

It is just 9 A.M. So begins our first day on the line.

Sunday, 9 July—

Have not slept since Thursday. The Captain says that the Rifle Brigade has been chosen to lead the way when we go over the top—probably tomorrow.

The Colonel came up to ask me about the Big Push of July the first. He had sent me up to visit my friend Siegfried *{Ed. note— Siegfried Sassoon}* in A Company and to watch the attack so that I could later describe it to him, the Colonel, but I wasn't able to locate Siegfried or Robert *{Ed. note—Graves perhaps? James Edwin Rooke had known both of these poets before the war}*. I *did* run across another friend, Edmund Dadd, and he allowed me to watch with the other officers from their position in reserve. Dadd and his fellows in the Royal Welch Fusiliers had a brilliant view of the 21st Division advance and the Manchester Pals attack.

Colonel Pretor-Pinney came by today in the early afternoon, peered up at the mirror above our parapet—vibrating now as the enemy was dropping 5.9s near us—and said, "Well Jimmy. What did you see last week?"

In the past week I had grown confident that the Old Man would never ask. Now, with our own Big Push less than twenty hours away, I could see that he needed to know. "Where do you want me to start, Sir?" I asked.

The Colonel offered me a cigarette from a gold case, tamped his against the case, lighted both of ours with his trench lighter, and said, "The barrage. Start with the barrage. I mean, we heard it in Albert, of course . . ." He trailed off. Our bombardment of German lines had gone on for seven days. It was said in the trenches that they had heard the guns in Blighty. Everyone from Sir Douglas *{Ed. note—Sir Douglas Haig, Commander-in-Chief of British forces}* on down had said that after such a bombardment, the Big Push would be a walkover. Most of the lads I'd known in the 34th had been worried that they wouldn't get to the German trenches in time to find the best souvenirs.

"It was a sight to watch, Sir," I said.

"Yes, yes, but the *effect*," said the Colonel. His voice was still soft—I had rarely heard the Colonel raise his voice—but there was more emotion there than I had heard before. I watched him pick a shred of tobacco from his tongue while he composed himself. "What was the effect on the wire, Jimmy?"

"Negligible, Sir. The wire was uncut in most places. The Manchesters had to bunch up in the few places where there were holes in the German wire. Most of them fell then."

The Colonel was nodding. He had heard the casualty reports during the past week. Forty thousand of our finest men had fallen before breakfast that day. "So the shelling had little effect on their wire?"

"Almost none, Sir."

"How soon did the German snipers and machine guns open up?"

"Immediately, Sir. Men were hit as soon as they lifted their heads above the parapet of the New Trench."

The Colonel continued nodding but I could see that the movement was automatic. He was thinking of something else. "And the men, Jimmy? How did the Manchesters comport themselves?"

"Brilliantly," I said. It was both the absolute truth and the greatest lie I had ever told. The Manchesters had shown profound courage—walking upright into the machine-gun fire as if they were on dress parade. As if they were walking to the theatre. But is it brilliance when one advances like a lamb to slaughter? Our Battalion had buried thousands of these brilliant lads in the past twenty-four hours.

"Good," said Colonel Pretor-Pinney, absently tapping my shoulder. "Good. I know our chaps will be equally splendid in the morning."

It was the first confirmation I had heard that the Push was definitely set for tomorrow morning. I have always disliked Mondays.

After the Colonel had left, squelching down the line of trench, chatting up the lads along the firesteps as he went, I glanced down at my hand holding the burning cigarette. It was shaking as if palsied.

Monday, 10 July, 4.45 A.M.—

No sleep again tonight. I was tapped for a night patrol. Absolute waste of our time, three hours of crawling around in No Man's Land with ten of my men. All as terrified as I, only they were allowed to show it. No intelligence garnered. No prisoners gathered. But no casualties either. We were lucky to find our way back through the desolation.

The Night Patrol

[Ed. note—Several lines were crossed out here.]

> *. . . and everywhere the dead.*
> *Only the dead were always present—present*
> *As a vile sickly smell of rottenness;*
> *The rustling stubble and the early grass,*
> *The slimy pools—the dead men stank throughall,*
> *Pungent and sharp; as bodies loomed before,*
> *And as we passed they stank: then dulled away*
> *To that vague foetor, all encompassing*
> *Infecting earth and air.*[2]

[Ed. note—A page has been roughly torn out here with only two words remaining on the serrated stub—"pure terror. . ." The verse on the next page appears to be a separate poem.]

> *We had no light to see by, save the flares.*
> *On such a trail, so lit, for ninety yards*
> *We crawled on belly and elbows, till we saw,*
> *Instead of the lumpish dead before our eyes,*
> *The stakes and crosslines of the German wire.*
> *We lay in shelter of the last dead man,*
> *Ourselves as dead, and heard their shovels ring*
> *Turning the earth, then talk and cough at times.*
> *A sentry fired and a machine gun spat;*
> *They shot a flare above us, when it fell*
> *And spluttered out in the pools of No Man's Land,*
> *We turned and crawled past the remembered dead:*

Past him and him, and them and him . . .
And through the wire and home, and got our rum.[3]

Monday, 10 July, 8.05 A.M.—

A beautiful morning. I know I am to die and it seems a cruel irony to die on such a perfect day.

In the night, during the patrol, all was mud and slime and slither. Then a summer sunrise. A vapor is rising from the trenches and shell holes as the fierce summer sun strikes the pools of foetid water. Here in the forward trench, German corpses remain and I can see vapor streaming skyward from the sodden wool uniforms on several of the bodies. Like souls fleeing heavenward from . . .

. . . from Hell? It seems so banal to write that. It does not sound like Hell. I can hear a lark from the direction of la Boisselle.

Colonel Prector-Pinney and Captain Smith from D Company came by seconds ago and the Colonel said softly, "We go over at 8.45. Set your watches."

I did so, removing my father's silver watch and carefully setting it to match the Colonel's and the Captain's. It is 8.22. My father's watch had read 8.18 when I had to reset it to 8.21. I lost three minutes of life merely by setting a watch.

A strange calmness has descended upon me.

Oddly, there has been no bombardment for the past hour or so. The silence is deafening. I had overheard Colonel Prector-Pinney tell Major Sir Foster Cunliffe that the bombardment had ended ten minutes early on July the first because of a mistaken communication to the artillery blokes. I wonder if a similar mistake has been made this morning.

From my position near the periscope—actually just a mirror set on a pole above the parapet—I can see a small wood a few hundred yards ahead of the trenches. To the right of the wood—largely splintered trunks, but a few whole trees remaining—lies another copse of shattered trunks and the remnants of the village of Contalmaison. Our chaps in the 23rd Division chased Jerry out of that village yesterday evening and now our Battalion is set to chase them out of their trenches. I wish we had learned more from the patrol last night.

The nearest Germans are only a 150 yards or so ahead of us. One could kick a football there. (My friend from the 2nd Welch Fusiliers, Eddie Dadd, told me that some of the chaps *did* kick a football ahead of them on the morning of the Big Push. It was a Pals Battalion of footballers and South African ruggers who'd joined up together. Eddie said that out of one 40-man platoon, only one man returned . . .)

8.30. Sergeants Laney on my left and Cross on my right are going up and down the lines, warning the men not to bunch up. "If you bunch up, they'll pick you off like rabbits," Sergeant Laney is saying. The words are oddly calming.

Of course they will pick us off like rabbits. I remember, as a child of about six, watching my father skin a rabbit. One incision and a tug and the fur slipped off like a guest shedding a coat, with only sticky strands of thin, gummy stuff connecting it to the pale, blue flesh.

8.32. What is a poet doing here? What are any of us doing here? I would say something inspiring to the men, but my mouth is so dry that I doubt if I could speak.

8.38. Hundreds of bayonets. They gleam in the bright sunlight. Sergeant Cross is snapping at the men to keep their bayonets below the line of the parapet. As if the Germans do not know we are coming. Where the goddamn hell is the bombardment the Colonel said they promised us?

8.40. I know what might save me. A litany of life. The things I love in ways that only a living person may love and a poet can articulate—

    —white cups, clean-gleaming
    —wet roofs beneath the lamp-light
    —the strong crust of friendly bread and many-tasting food
    —the comfortable smell of friendly fingers
    —live hair that is shining and free
    —the unpassioned beauty of a great machine

8.42. Jesus Christ, Oh Jesus. I do not love God but I love life. The cool kindliness of sheets. Radiant raindrops crouching in cool flowers. The rough kiss of clean blankets.[4] Christ, to lose all this?

8.43. Women. I do love women. The clean-smell powder-and-talc scent of women. Their pale skin and pale pink nipples in candlelight. Their gentleness and firmness and the muskscent terrible wetness . . .

8.44. I will think of women. I will close my eyes and think of a litany of femaleness, scent and touch of life womanness. All things alive and vital in *{Ed. note—This line unfinished.}*

8.45. Whistles blowing down the line. I will try to blow mine. Sergeants pushing the men up and out. Other NCOs leading. Will follow in . . . *{Ed. note—illegible}* . . . not fair.

A litany of feminine life force. Muse protects.

Good-bye.

{Ed. note—It is well known that J.E.R.'s other trench diary ends here. Or, rather, with the following terse note.}

10-7–16, 8.15 A.M.—The Colonel passes among us a final time and I prepare my men to go over the top. Our big guns remain silent. Perhaps the Staff do not want to spoil the surprise we have in store for the Germans. I joked with Sergeant Cross that I hoped Jerry was cooking breakfast as I was ravished with hunger. Gave the chaps a good laugh.

{Ed. note—It might be noted that the poems seen here in rough form have often been misdated. "The Night Patrol" is often quoted as being the result of J.E.R.'s observation of a night patrol returning on 30 June while he was observing with the 2nd Welch Fusiliers. The bit of verse beginning "And clink of shovels . . ." is usually attributed to the previous Christmas when the 13th Rifle Brigade was comfortably billeted at Hannescamps and Lieutenant Rooke was assigned to his first burial detail. What has been described elsewhere as " . . . a brilliant young poet's active imagination turned toward the perceived horrors of the Front" turns out to be simple reportage rather than poetic imagination.

Finally, the segment dealing with the actual experience of a night patrol—"We had no light to see by, save the flares."—is not to be found in any edition of Trench Poems. *It is obvious, to this bibliographer at least, that J.E.R. was working toward a longer, more definitive version of* The Night Patrol *and would have realized it had not circumstances intervened.}*

Friday, 14 July—

The Lady is not with me tonight. She was here earlier, but the doctors made noise and she has not returned. I smell her scent.

Brickers, next to me, the one with half a face who has managed to moan every hour I have been conscious, died a few minutes ago. The gargle and rattle were unmistakable.

The Lady was here then. She is not here now. I pray for her return.

Saturday, 15 July, 9.30 A.M.—

I am more cognizant of my whereabouts today. I recognize the pounding of guns. Sister Paul Marie, the nicer of the two nuns who nurse us, tells me that there is another Big Push under way. The thought makes my skin crawl.

I believe my Lady was here in the night—I remember her touch—but everything else from the past few days is a strange, pain-riddled blur. When I first became aware of myself and my surroundings yesterday, on my bedside table there were two items which I had brought back from No Man's Land: my father's watch, stopped now at 10.08, and the secret diary in which I had been scribbling just before we went Over the Top. It seems that I carried these two things in my hands during the attack. When I finally reached the dressing station some two days later, the watch was still firmly gripped in my left hand and the journal had somehow been transferred to the pocket of my blouse—almost the only bit of clothing on me that had not been shredded.

Let me describe my surroundings. I am in an RAMC forward hospital {Ed. note—*Royal Army Medical Corps*} just outside of Albert. Because this village is only two miles from the Front, this place is a kind of way stop between the crude dressing stations and field surgical hospitals closer to the Front and the true Base Hospitals much further back. (Many in England herself.) This "hospital" consists of three whitewashed rooms in what may have been part of the convent here. From my window I can see the Golden Virgin. {Ed. note—*In the center of the village of Albert was a large church and on its spire was a gilded statue of the Virgin Mary holding the infant Jesus above her head. The statue was struck by a German shell in 1915 and had been leaning at right angles to the spire ever since. The journals of Sassoon, Graves, Masefield and a hundred lesser names mention marching to the Front under this bizarre landmark. A legend had grown up on both sides of the Front that if the Virgin fell, the war would end. German troops added the coda that if the statue did indeed fall, Germany would be the victor. French engineers then quickly secured the hanging Madonna and Infant with steel hawsers. It remained in that position until Germans re-occupied Albert in 1918 and began using the steeple as an observation post, at which time British gunfire brought down both steeple and Virgin.}*

Albert is all but abandoned by civilians but somehow manages to continue to exist here so close to the fighting. Some of our artillery is *behind* the village. Troops move through in both directions by day and night and sleep is almost impossible due to the noise of their tramping, the clomp of horses' hooves, and the cursing of men tugging large guns through the mud. My hospital mates here are all officers and I understand from Sister Paul Marie's comments that this place is only for those too seriously injured to travel toward Amiens and home, or for those injured so slightly that they will soon return to the Front. I count myself unlucky to be listed in the latter category.

There are about a dozen men in my ward, several of them officers from the Rifle Brigade. Most are dying. One chap, a captain, has had both legs blown off and the stench of gangrene fills the ward at all times. Another fellow, a lieutenant such as myself, was shot through the brain and talks incessantly, wooing the poor nun as if she were his lover. An older man, a major, returns to the surgical tent every day to have a bit more of his leg sawed off. He also has the smell of gangrene and death around him, but he never complains, but merely lies on his bed and stares fixedly at the ceiling.

Sister Paul Marie tells me that Colonel Pretor-Pinney is receiving special care in the field hospital next door, still too badly wounded to be sent down the rail line to hospital. She said that his left arm had been shredded by machine-gun bullets. I knew that. I saw it happen.

Almost all of the officers in our Battalion have been killed, including all four company commanders. I also saw them die. Most of the other platoon commanders were also killed. I understand that Lieutenant Fitzgibbon was a fellow survivor, but he was so badly wounded that he was sent immediately home to Blighty. Most of our sergeants were cut down—including Cross and Monckton—but there is hope that some survived. There is much confusion after a battle.

I seem to be the only "slightly wounded" in the ward, suffering as I am from what is described as "concussion paralysis" and a case of pneumonia from the two nights lying in the shell hole. The pneumonia is bothersome, especially as they come in to drain my lungs every day with a needle literally the size of a bicycle pump— they hold me in place while they insert the needle through my back—but much worse than that is the terrible pain of feeling finally returning to my numbed legs. It is as if they have been asleep for four or five days, and the pins-and-needles sensation of their awakening may well drive me mad.

The young officer with no legs has just died. First they put a screen around his bed, then men come in with a stretcher to remove his body. Covered as he is, the form under the blanket looks much too small to have ever been a man.

The lieutenant who is shot through the skull continues to call for his nurse/nun/lover in a voice that grows increasingly wild. I suspect that he will not last the night.

I think of this place as the vestibule of Hell. Obviously some other literate soul has had similar thoughts, for written in charcoal on the wall near the window through which I can see the Golden Virgin are the words "PER ME SI VA NE LA CITTA DOLENTE, PER ME SI VA NE L'ETTERNO DOLORE, PER ME SI VA TRA LA PERDUTA GENTE." Sister Paul Marie tells me that the nuns leave it there because the officer who scribbled it told them that it was a poem attesting to the gentleness of care at this place. Obviously none of the nuns know neither Italian nor their Dante.

The quote is from the Inferno, of course, and reads—"THROUGH ME THE WAY INTO THE SUFFERING CITY, THROUGH ME THE WAY TO THE ETERNAL PAIN, THROUGH ME THE WAY THAT RUNS AMONG THE LOST."

The doctors are coming with their accursed needle. I will write later.

Saturday, 15 July, almost midnight—

The guns are very loud. I can see the Virgin and Child backlighted by the gunflashes as light from the incessant bombardment falls across the whitewashed floorboards like the flickering from some unseen fireplace.

The only other person in the ward who seems to be awake is the victim of phosgene gas who lies across the aisle from me. The noise he makes is a terrible thing. I try not to look at him, but every few seconds I steal a glance.

> ... *the white eyes writhing in his face,*
> *His hanging face, like a devil's sick of sin;*
> *If you could hear, at every holt, the blood*
> *Come gargling from the froth-corrupted lungs,*
> *Obscene as cancer, bitter as the cud*
> *Of vile, incurable sores on innocent tongues* ... [5]

Each breath the poor devil takes extorts a terrible price in pain and effort. I can not imagine he can live until morning, or even through ten more of such terrible breaths . . . but I have counted ten even while I waited to write this. Perhaps he will be doomed to live until morning and even beyond, although why such pain is inflicted on any living thing is quite beyond me. It makes Christ's so-called agony on the cross a petty thing.

I have not been able to sleep because I wait for the Lady's visit. Traces of her violet perfume remain on my own wrist and pajama sleeve and I raise these to my face when the stench from the gangrene becomes too bad.

I was sure that she would return tonight.

I think that I will write about the attack while I wait. Perhaps if I write about it, I will not dream about it again.

We went up and over at 8.45. I knew that at places in front of us, the Jerries' line was a third of a mile or so away, but our objective was a bit of enemy trench only a couple of hundred yards in front of us. I convinced myself that this was a definite advantage for our chaps, and then I clambered up the side of the trench and was out.

My first impression upon leaving the trench was a sort of light-headedness at being able to walk above ground. Then I thought giddily, *There are bees up here.* The air was absolutely filled with a *zzzp-zzzp* sound, precisely like the time when I was a boy and had disturbed a large hive of bees in Mr. Alknut's garden. When I saw the tufts of dirt leaping up ahead of and to the side of me, I realized that the noise was nothing less than bullets. I almost stopped then, so terrible was my fear of a steel-jacketed bullet striking me square in the face, but I squinted until my eyes were almost closed, leaned forward a bit, and forced myself to move forward with the lads.

All up and down the line, our men were moving forward into this murderous fire—first the officers and NCOs, then the riflemen with bayonets fixed, and then the Lewis gunners and their ammunition carriers struggling under loads. I noticed then that everyone out there—myself included—walked into the enemy fire in a sort of a diagonal crouch, as if we were all leaning into a strong wind or rain. Sergeants continued shouting at members of their platoons to keep apart and not to bunch up. Men began to fall as I watched through squinted eyes.

It was strange, actually. Men just fell over, almost casually, as if they were children playing at war. I thought at first that some of this was pure funk . . . but there was no more cover where they fell, and even as I watched more bullets struck their bodies, causing them to jerk only slightly. The sound of bullets striking flesh was almost exactly like the *pat-thud* of bullets striking the sandbags which we had all heard from the trenches. And everywhere the air continued to be filled with the *zzzp-zzzp*.

My fear was so terrible at this point that it was everything I could do to stay upright and balanced as I advanced, stepping carefully over shell holes and rotting corpses. The earth leaped up in front of me and behind. Somehow, my mind stayed quite detached.

I had begun the walk with a dozen or more of the lads from my platoon, but one by one they had fallen away. I stopped by one lying prone and asked, "Are you hurt?"

"What the fuck do you think I'm doing down here, you bleeding toff bastard?" the rude fellow shouted at me. "Picking fucking daisies?" Then a machine-gun bullet struck the precise center of the man's helmet, he vomited brains, and I moved on.

Finally only a man whom I vaguely recognized as Corporal Woodlock from No. 11 Platoon, and I, were left. We were less than fifty yards from the enemy wire when Corporal Woodlock began laughing. "Jesus Christ, Sir!" he shouted, as giddy as a schoolboy.

"Jesus Christ, Sir, I think we're the only ones who're going to get through this bloody lot!" He giggled. "Jesus Christ, Sir . . ." he began again just as several bullets tore the khaki above his chest into maroon shreds. He fell sideways into a shallow crater and I put my notebook into my blouse pocket, checked my watch, and ambled forward.

There was only a single gap in the wire in front of us and No. 8 Platoon, which had preceded us, made for it. I thought then that they looked a bit like lambs filling up a chute to the slaughter. The German machine guns opened up from fifty feet away and every member of that platoon went down in a bloody heap.

My eyes almost closed, I thought of women I had known and seduced. I visualized their skin, their lips, the color of their eyes, and their sweet smell. I imagined their touch.

Shells started falling. Bits of Corporal Woodlock erupted from his shell hole, mixed with the fragments of corpses which had been there since the Big Push of July first. The Corporal's head, helmet still firmly affixed and chin strap tightened, landed at my feet and rolled.

The hole in the wire ahead of me was clogged three high with the bodies of the men of No. 8 Platoon, so I turned left and began making for a stretch of No Man's Land where I could see men of the Rifle Brigade still standing, still advancing. I knew from the maps that somewhere ahead of me was the so-called "chalk pit," a small quarry which the enemy had fortified.

At this point I glanced to my right to see the 25th Division which was supposed to have been supporting us on that flank. No one was there. I looked far to the left to see the 23rd Division who were supposed to be attacking on our left. The field was empty. I turned around, hearing the *zzzzp-zzzzp* past my ears, to see if the 13th Fusiliers had come out in the second wave as planned. There was no second wave.

"Get down, man!" It was Colonel Pretor-Pinney crouching in a shell hole. I stepped down into it with him.

"Jimmy," he gasped. "I don't believe we can . . ." A runner stumbled into the hole and thrust a message into the Colonel's hands.

"Attack canceled, Sir," panted the boy.

The Colonel stared unbelievingly at the message. "That explains the lack of bombardment. The reason the 23rd and 25th did not come out." He crumpled the message. "It was canceled before we shoved off, Jimmy. This just did not get to us in time." He leveraged himself up over the front edge of the hole. More 5.9s and whizz-bangs were falling near us now.

"Jimmy," he said, "the chaps from Thirteen Platoon have already made it into the Boche trenches. Someone will have to go forward and tell them . . ."

"I will, Sir!" said the young runner.

Colonel Pretor-Pinney nodded and the boy leapt out of the shell hole with the speed and courage of the very young who know that they are immortal. The machine guns caught him less than ten yards out and almost tore him in half.

The Colonel looked at me. "Well, there's nothing for it then, Jimmy." We clambered out of the trench and moved forward together, leaning into the noise as if breasting a strong wind.

Some men were still alive in shell holes. Most had rid themselves of pack and rifles, clutching themselves into small spheres of fear. I saw the Colonel look left, and there in one hole were all four of our company commanders and several of their aides, crouching and pointing in different directions.

"Break that up, you bloody fools!" shouted Colonel Pretor-Pinney and then an explosion absolutely filled the crater with dust and shrapnel. When the smoke cleared, only bits of men remained.

We had almost reached the bit of fortified road near the chalk pit when the Colonel spun and went down heavily. I crouched next to him for a moment. The twin bones of his forearm were clearly visible through the mangled flesh. His lips formed words but I was quite deaf to them. I knew that this was my only opportunity to live; to pick up the Colonel and carry him back to the trenches. I might even receive a medal.

Squinting even more fiercely, I turned away and walked toward the enemy trenches.

I do not remember reaching the German lines, nor dropping into their trenches, but I clearly remember the German sergeant who came around the corner of a zigzag and shouted something at me. I am not sure which of us was more startled. I remember thinking *The man is wearing his wool greatcoat . . . in July! He must be mad.* And then the heavyset sergeant stopped shouting and began fumbling for the rifle that was—inexplicably in such a context—slung over his shoulder.

One of our lads had fallen here, his face in the mud, his Lee Enfield lying just beyond the reach of his outflung hand. Without thinking, I lifted the heavy rifle and marched forward at double time, letting my father's watch dangle from the chain I had wrapped twice around my wrist somewhere between the crater where the Colonel had fallen and here.

The German had just got his own weapon to port arms when I drove the bayonet under his guard and into his chest just below his sternum. The bayonet was twenty-one inches long. It slid into the thick wool of the man's great coat and out of sight so easily that it seemed as if he and I were conspiring together in some amateur magic act. I felt the sharpened-steel tip strike the mud of the trench behind the sergeant.

The man looked at me quizzically, lifted his own rifle a bit so that he could see the point of entry where my bayonet disappeared into the wet wool over his belly, and then he sighed softly and leaned back against the trench wall. I could feel a vibration coming from the point where my steel had severed his spine. The sergeant opened his mouth as if he were about to say something, but smiled instead. When he fell more heavily against the trench wall, I dropped my rifle as if it had grown suddenly hot to my touch. The butt of it wedged in the mud and held the corpse almost upright, the rifle and his two splayed legs making a sort of tripod, his dead hands still clutching the rifle. The man's greatcoat hung in folds like a shroud.

I turned and walked back down the trench to find 13 Platoon to tell them that the attack had been canceled.

It was while coming back that the bad thing happened.

I had found the remnants of the Rifle Brigade fighting in captured trenches, unaware that the attack had been canceled or that it had been a mistake in the first place. The Germans had reinforced both the sunken road and their lines near the chalk pit so that the place was a viper's nest of concrete emplacements, machine-gun revetments, dugouts as deep as thirty feet, and a maze of duckboards and tunnels. Our lads had cleaned them out of a long stretch of this line and were holding their own against disorganized counterattacks.

Trench fighting is terrible in the best of circumstances, and in this warren, with the Battalion depleted and low on ammunition, it was worse than terrible. By early afternoon the Rifle Brigade had used up their Mills grenades and were perilously low on rounds for rifles and their two remaining Lewis guns. All of the telephone lines brought across No Man's Land at such a cost of life had been cut almost immediately by shellfire and attempts to communicate with our trenches via semaphore flasher or flags brought fire down on the signaler without fail.

I conferred with the one officer I could find, Captain Revere, and we decided to try to make our way back as soon as it was dusk.

True twilight did not deepen in this part of France until almost ten o'clock, and as soon as we thought it was dark enough to start back without drawing the attention of the Boche, Captain Revere ordered the men out of the trenches they had spilled so much blood to capture and defend through the long, hot day. They left in groups of three or four, fading away into the shadows of No Man's Land. The German machine-gunners seemed to take pity on us. Or perhaps they were as exhausted as we were.

I had shaken hands with Captain Revere and was finding my own way across when the barrage opened up. I knew immediately from the sound that they were eighteen-inchers and that they were our own guns firing on us.

The fierce and terrible bombardment which had been promised us for the attack that morning had never arrived . . . until now. The entire field of No Man's Land that separated us from our own forward lines—about a thousand yards at this point—suddenly erupted in a solid sheet of flame and shrapnel. Once again I was squinting and leaning forward as the very atmosphere filled with metal. This time the fragments screamed by with a noise like *wwhhhiiit* . . . the final consonant added when the shrapnel embedded itself in something. Many of the blasts were airbursts, which we all feared most deeply since the head was usually struck first and anything short of a dugout with a solid roof offered no cover whatsoever.

Behind us, the German machine guns opened up. The Boche

had obviously already counterattacked and retaken the trenches we had just abandoned. There was no going forward. There was no going back. I felt like giggling as Corporal Woodlock had in his final seconds.

From what I have heard yesterday and today, I think that the 13th Rifle Brigade ceased to exist as a fighting unit about this time. Thinking that it was the Germans counterattacking from Contalmaison, our own artillery tore us to shreds.

As for me, I found myself running aimlessly from shell hole to shell hole, ducking when the larger explosions came near, running through dirt and smoke when they seemed to be landing further away. I realized that my father's watch was still gripped tightly in my left hand, the chain still wound around my wrist.

This insanity could not continue forever and it did not. One minute I was running toward what I thought were friendly lines still some hundreds of yards away, and the next instant I felt a great blast behind me and I was literally flying, looking down on the battlefield as if from a great height. I thought at that second that I had been killed and that my soul had fled my body.

Then I landed and tumbled into a deep shell crater, my legs splashing into a pool of foetid green water in the bottom. I was unconscious for a while and when I awoke it was full dark and the bombardment was continuing. I had no doubt that another shell would find me at any moment, but I was beyond caring for the time being.

The blast had shredded my trousers until I was essentially naked from the waist down and I could not feel my legs where they disappeared into the brackish water. My upper tunic was also in rags, although my blouse had survived in front. My helmet was gone. I felt little pain above the great numbness that spread from my back down to my legs, but I was sure that I had to have been hit by some mortal piece of metal that even at that second lay deep in my numbed flesh. My hands were smudged as black as the rest of me, but they seemed intact and—after some moments of drifting in and out of consciousness—I used them to try to drag myself up and out of the water.

This was not a good idea. The top of my head was only inches below the edge of the steep shell crater, and as soon as I rose above

this ad-hoc parapet, bullets and shrapnel whizzed by. I gave up struggling against the mud and slipped back down so that my legs
disappeared again up to the thighs beneath dark water.

There were one or two others sharing my hole. I say one or two
because to this day I do not know if it was one body or two
lying across the six-foot pool from me. The bottom half of a torso lay
on the mud, toes almost touching the lip of the crater. The bit of
spinal cord visible glowed white each time a flare drifted down or an
explosion lit the scene. The puttees and boots were decidedly
British and I would have thought it was the lower half of my own
body lying there if I had not already glimpsed my naked legs.

The top half of some chap's head protruded from the water,
visage toward me. He had managed to keep his helmet on and the
chinstrap seemed firmly attached. His eyes were open and staring at
me very intensely indeed. I would have guessed that this was a clever
fellow lying doggo, waiting for the bombardment to ease before
lurching up for another try, except for the fact that both the man's
mouth and nostrils were under water. There were no bubbles. He did
not blink as minutes faded into hours.

With my legs useless, my wounds unable to be assessed while
the general numbness persisted, and the bombardment continuing, I
lay back in the shell-hole mud and waited to die as the barrage
continued. When it ended, if I survived it, the Germans would send
out patrols to finish the last of us with bayonets.

I admit that I lay there and tried to think philosophical thoughts,
but the best I could do was remember the faces and names of all the
girls I had bedded. It was not an unpleasant way to pass the time.

And then the pain in my back and chest began in earnest. I had
prepared for this eventuality by bringing the regulation four morphia
tablets allowed to each officer. Now I reached for them in my trouser
pocket.

I had no trousers. Only rags and lacerations there.

I patted my blouse pocket, hoping against hope that I had put the
morphia there in a fit of absent-mindedness, but all I found were this
journal, a stub of pencil, and my silver whistle.

The pain rolled in like poison gas. I would have *welcomed* poison gas at this point, if only to put an end to the pain. I am, as I have admitted in these pages, not brave.

It was sometime after midnight and before dawn, as I writhed in the mud on the pinpoint of my dead comrade's unblinking stare, that *she* came.

The Lady. The one for whom I wait this night.

But perhaps the scratch of my pen or my upright posture keeps her from visiting. I will set the journal aside until another time and wait in the darkness between the flashes of the big guns.

Post Script: the gas victim across the aisle no longer breathes.

Sunday, 15 July, 9.00 A.M.—

The Lady did not come. Or at least I do not remember her being here. I cannot express the depth of my disappointment.

The nun—the brusque one, not Sister Paul Marie—explains the frenzied sound of our big guns by saying that there is a terrible battle being waged for High Wood. Most of the casualties streaming in, she says, are from the 33rd Division, especially the Church Lads Brigade. She says that the wounds are more terrible than anything she has seen to date.

I have come to realize that this practice of filling Kitchener's quota by recruiting Pals Battalions will reap a terrible whirlwind of grief and that while it was almost certainly a grand idea from the recruitment point of view, it is leading to empty villages, churches, fire brigades, and entire professions where the cream of our generation there will have been wiped out in a single afternoon. *{Ed. note—Even now, few can have missed or forgotten the image of Lord Kitchener pointing from his poster stating unequivocally "Your Country Needs You." What modern readers may have forgotten, however, is that Kitchener did not bring in conscription to fill the ranks until January of 1916. Thus James Edwin Rooke and some two and a half million other men in khaki were volunteers. Rooke's opinion of the "Pals Battalions," where friends and acquaintances could join* en masse, *turned out to be entirely correct. Much of the impact of the carnage of WWI on Great Britain has been not just the numbers of dead, but the terrible focus of such loss on specific locales brought about by destruction of "Pals." Pals battalions suffering more than 500 casualties (out of a battalion consisting of 1,000 men) at the Somme included the*

Accrington Pals, Leeds Pals, The Cambridge Battalion, Public Schools Battalion, 1st Bradford Pals, Glasgow Boys' Brigade Battalion, and the Co. Down Volunteers. And this was on the single day of 1 July.]

The doctors and nurses came through a while ago to push the needle through my back and into my lungs. The noise it makes extracting fluid is beyond description, but rather reminds me of a circus elephant I once watched sucking up the last of a bucket of water. The circus was passing through Weald of Kent that leafy summer, and I wish to God I were there now.

The doctor left some papers he had wearily set down and I pilfered one of the forms to read. It is an autopsy report. I have been awake since before seven—the bells in the damaged steeple under the leaning Golden Virgin work very well indeed and are somehow more intrusive than the constant rumble and roar of guns—and I have been struggling with the poem I began last night about the gas victim whose breathing I still seem to hear despite his most definite absence.

The autopsy report seems more effective as poetry than my poor scribblings. I will reproduce it verbatim:

> *Case four: Aged 39*
> *Years.*
> *Gassed 4 July 1916.*
> *Admitted to casualty clearing station*
> *The same day.*
> *Died about ten days later.*
> *Brownish pigmentation present over large surfaces*
> *Of the body. A white ring*
> *Of skin*
> *Where the wrist watch was.*
> *Marked superficial burning of the face and*
> *Scrotum.*
> *The larynx much congested. The whole of the trachea*
> *Was covered by a yellow membrane. The bronchi*
> *Contained abundant gas. The lungs fairly*
> *Voluminous.*
> *The right lung showed extensive collapse at the base.*
> *Liver congested*

> *And fatty.*
> *Stomach showed numerous*
> *Submucous haemorrhages. The brain substance was*
> *Unduly wet*
> *And very congested.*[6]

Merde. Poetry does not serve as poetry in this new age. And nonpoetry cannot masquerade as serviceable verse. Perhaps poetry is dead. Perhaps it deserved to die. Perhaps the poets do also.

The bells have stopped. Perhaps the half dozen faithful civilians still living in Albert have been driven in to Mass. The guns do not hesitate for a second. I pity The Church Lads' Brigade. For what they are about to receive, may those of us who are not there be truly thankful.

It is almost time to write about the Lady. I have hesitated to do so because anyone finding and reading my journal would think me mad.

I am not mad.

And this journal will be destroyed . . . *must* be destroyed. It is a poet's place to lay bare thoughts that others must deny even having, but poetry is dead and I soon will be and I refuse to leave these thoughts where prying eyes will find them.

And yet I must write about it all or go mad.

We had attacked on the 10th, watched our Rifle Brigade be destroyed by ten P.M., on the 10th, and all that night of the 10th I lay in the shell hole, half-delirious with the pain from legs that would not work for me, half out of my mind with thirst and fear. I admit that I drank from the green slime of that corpse-littered crater. I would have drunk my own urine by that second night. I almost certainly did.

I cannot forget the sound. It started that first night and had not died away completely by the time I crawled out of that hell on the evening of the 12th.

The sound was constant, yet it rose and fell almost like the precisely composed vagaries of a wind-tossed surf or the rustling of a million leaves on an autumn evening in Kent. Only there was nothing lulling or meditative about this sound: it was the noise of a thousand teeth scraping on a hundred slabs of slate; it was the noise of broken fingernails scrabbling; it was the hiss and gurgle and blood-rasp gaspings of gas victims fighting vainly for another mucous-filled breath.

It was the sound of the hundreds of our wounded lads in No Man's Land.

I confess that I added to that chorus. My own moans and inarticulate cries seemed to come from somewhere outside of me and at times I listened to them joining the common call of pain with a feeling more of embarrassment than horror.

Occasionally, above the dull explosions and rumble of guns and hammer of machine guns, there would be audible the flintlike clarity of a single rifle shot. And then one voice in the chorus of pain would be silenced. But the rest of us sang on.

All that second day—Tuesday the 11th—I lay between the shards of wire and bone. At one point I managed to drag myself up and sideways so that my nerveless legs were out of the water; I told myself that I was afraid they would rot, but my real fear was that something would grab me from beneath the surface of green scum. The dead soldier continued to stare at me, with only the dark pits and egg-whites of his eyes visible above the waterline and beneath the helmet shadow. Those eyes receded visibly as I watched, sinking into the skull as if retreating from the sight of me. The night before, even in the unsteady light of flares and explosions, the dark of his irises and pupils had been visible, but this second day the eyes were white with the bubbled mass of fly eggs.

The bluebottle flies were so thick that sometimes I thought they were a cloud of Valkyries that had descended on us. But they were only flies. Their buzzing reminded me of the bullets; the buzzing of bullets above me reminded me of the flies. I gave up trying to brush the flies from my face and stirred only when they crawled from my lips into my open mouth.

The steady background of moaning had slackened toward dusk that second evening, but when it grew dark the volume rose again, as if the dead had joined the dying in our song. I tried pulling myself up when it was truly dark, my hands grabbing stones, my elbows digging into mud, but as soon as my head came above the lip of the shell hole, machine guns opened up. As many tracer rounds came from the British line as from the German. Our lads were obviously nervous and frightened of a counterattack.

One of these bullets took a warning nick out of my left ear. Another cut through the tattered cloth of my blouse between my left ribs and inner arm. I gave up the thought of crawling two hundred yards through this and slid back into my brackish tomb. The soldier seemed to welcome me back with a white wink. Rats were tugging at the bottom half of the torso in the dark so that the legs seemed to be attempting a feeble dance.

My hands had gained enough feeling so that I pitched stones at the vermin. They ignored me. I preferred that to being the focus of their attention.

I dozed in a half-conscious state where the growling of the big guns wove the texture of my dreams. Suddenly, sometime before dawn, I awoke. The Lady had come.

It seems insane now to admit that I felt little surprise. There had been talk of nurses coming as far as the Front lines, but this was only barracks' fantasy. At any rate, I knew this was no nurse. She did not stumble and slide down the steep crater wall; one minute she was simply *there.* I awoke to the touch of her hand on my cheek.

To describe her, even now after several of her visits, seems somehow sacrilegious. But perhaps if I do so with even a small fraction of the reverence I feel toward her, it will not harm the chances of her future coming.

She is fair. Not merely English fair as in an absence of sun, but fair with the radiance of a fine piece of white Carrara marble. There is a light about her features, which are classical but not refined to the point of what we now think of as ideal feminine beauty. Her nose is long and straight, her chin strong, her eyes set wide apart and quite dark. Her hair is not done in the current style; when I was in Paris and London last, the ladies were wearing their hair cut shorter, dressed low on the forehead and pulled back, covering only part of their ears and often ending in a coil or bun in the back. The Lady's hair is clasped somehow with combs on the side, but it still hangs loose, rather like that of a lady of my mother's generation when preparing for bed.

When she touched my cheek, I tried to speak, to warn her of the terrible danger out here in No Man's Land, but the Lady only touched my cracked lips with a finger and shook her head as if to silence me.

I noticed dully that she was wearing a gown quite unsuitable for a nurse or our environment; she wore a material which looked soft and silky such as crêpe de Chine set in a style somewhere between a chemise and nightdress. But this was no undergarment or night-dress. The Lady's outfit was perfectly suited to her stong face and full figure. I felt as if Penelope had come for me to take me home from my wanderings.

I closed my eyes then, and in my half-dream I was still with her. We were no longer on the battlefield, but on the terrace of a fine home in the moonlight. The trees and summer night scent were familiar; I thought it might be Kent. The Lady was waiting for me at a wrought-iron table under an arbor. I approached and took my seat across from her, noticing that she was no longer wearing the soft gown but a more normal outfit, two pieces of peach-colored cotton, a basqued jacket shirred at the waist, broad sleeves ending in flounced cuffs, and an ankle-length skirt. Her auburn hair—I could see the color clearly now in the moonlight—was tied up in a more conven-tional manner and partially covered by a straw hat with a furred plume and a softly curving brim.

There was a tea set on a silver tray between us. When she tried to pour my tea, I reached to touch her. She pulled away, but was smiling.

"This is an hallucination," I said.

"Do you really think so?" she said softly. Her voice excited me as much as did her eyes.

"Yes," I said. "I'm dying in some . . ." I paused before saying "bloody shell hole." I may have been hallucinating upon the point of death, but that was no reason to lose my manners in front of a lady. ". . . in some banal shell hole in France," I continued. "And all this . . ." I waved toward the arbor, the gardens from which the July scent of hibiscus wafted, and the estate dimly visible in the moon-light. "All this is the delusion of my dying brain."

"Do you really think so?" she said again. And took my hand in hers. Her fingers were ungloved.

The word "galvanized" is too inactive to describe my reaction at her touch. It is as if I had never contacted a woman's skin until that instant. It is as if I was a stammering boy again rather than the seasoned ladies' man I had allowed myself to become since my days at Clare College, Cambridge.

I tried to speak then, to say that I was certain that none of this was real, but clouds moved from in front of the moon and touched the soft curve of flesh visible above her *décolletage,* and the words stayed stuck in my throat.

"I think this is quite real," she whispered. Her fingertip traced an oval on my upturned palm. "but you will have to return to your friends before we can meet again."

"Friends?" I whispered, embarrassed that my lips were so dried and cracked. At that moment I could remember neither the names nor faces of any friends. All my comrades in the war were dust. Less than dust. Only the Lady held the firmness of my attention.

She smiled at me. It was not the simpering smile of so many of the London ladies I had known, nor the coquettish smile of so many of the French lasses, and certainly not the cruel smile of certain widows and well-off wives I had included in my acquaintance. It was a pleasant enough smile, but weighted with irony and some challenge.

"Do you wish to see me again?" she asked. The moonlight made her lashes gleam.

"Oh, yes," I said, not thinking how naïve it sounded. And not caring.

She patted my hand a final time. "We will talk again when you have returned to where you must go."

"Where must I go?" I asked. My legs were in the brackish sludge again. My hands were twitching in nervous spasms. My father's watch, its chain wrapped around my blackened wrist, gleamed in the moonlight.

"Back," she whispered. She was wearing the chemise-robe now. I worried about it. There were so many pleats. Lice bred on us everywhere here at the Front, especially along the seams of our uniforms and in the pleats of the Scots' kilts. My uniform was new—had been new—purchased at a special officers' store in Amiens only weeks before, but already I was lousy.

No, the thought of the Lady with lice was absurd. I realized that she was touching me. Her fingers were on my bare leg, rising up my bare thigh. The soldier in the water watched with his white eyes stirring in the moonlight.

"Go back," she whispered, leaning closer. Her scent was violets and a hint of jasmine. Her fingernails raked the inside of my thigh gently, more as if in testing than in teasing. "Then we will meet again."

I started to speak then, but the Lady glanced to her left as if she had been called and then rose above the edge of the crater somehow more gently than if merely walking. Then I was alone again with the staring face, the lower torso, the tugging rats, and the cloud of flies.

I crawled out of the shell hole just before dawn, was fired at as soon as the sun came up, lay doggo another long July day, and began pulling myself toward British lines as it grew dusky on Wednesday the 12th. It was almost dawn again before someone challenged me. I heard the bolt of the rifle slamming home.

I was challenged out of the darkness to advance and be recognized or to give the code word. I could do none of these things, lying as I was exhausted and bleeding within the coils of my own wires. I *felt* the muzzle of the rifle aiming at me in the dark and could feel the unseen sentry's concentration as he prepared to fire at the sound of my croaking.

With my last strength then I could have rasped out my name and unit, perhaps a stirring "God Save the King," but none of these, I think, would have been understandable through my cracked lips and parched throat. So, inexplicably, absurdly, I began singing. The tune somewhat resembled "Here We Go Round the Mulberry Bush":

> *We don't want a girl from Givenchy-le-Noble,*
> *From Givenchy-le-Noble,*
> *From Givenchy-le Noble,*
> *If you go for a walk she will get into trouble.*
> *So we don't want a girl from Givenchy-le-Noble.*

We don't want a girl who comes from les Comptes,
Who comes from les Comptes,
Who comes from les Comptes,
For they all eat onions, and their breath rather haunts,
So we don't want a girl who comes from les Comptes.[7]

I lowered my face to the mud and waited.

"Sweet baby Jesus," came the sentry's voice. "It's someone from The Rifle Brigade. Pull him out of there, lads."

They covered my semi-nakedness with a blanket, carried me back through communication trenches, and left me at what they thought was a dressing station behind the lines.

The bells have started up again, either to celebrate the end of the last mass or to drag people in to the next. Either way, I cannot concentrate. Some mule driver is cursing at his team just outside the window as they try to pull a cart out of the mud while an entire brigade waits.

I cannot concentrate. I hurt. I will write more later.

Monday, 17 July, 2.00 P.M.—

I awoke to the Lady's scent last night, but the ward was empty except for the doomed, the dying, and me. I feel certain that she had been there only seconds before.

The long needle extracted only thimblesful of fluid this morning, I was able to stagger to the latrine with the aid of two canes, and Sister Paul Marie tells me that I will be pronounced cured within a day or two to make way for more seriously injured chaps. Several of my previous wardmates have died—the Major was found this morning, staring as fixedly at the ceiling in death as he had in his last days of life—and the new fellows seem to be from the 33rd Division. As I imagined when I heard of the fighting over the weekend, the Church Lads' Brigade seems to have met the same fate as our Brigade.

Sister tells me that Colonel Pretor-Pinney was finally shipped back to Base Hospital. There is hope that he will live. Sergeant Rowlands stopped by to see me yesterday afternoon. Rowlands had been a good man, but had been ordered back here to Albert just before our 10 July attack so that he could serve Headquarters Detail as orderly sergeant. He is bitter about missing the show, but the reassignment almost certainly saved his life.

Rowlands told me that when they took roll-call of the Brigade on the 12th, more than three hundred names carried an "M." {*Ed. note*—"M" *stood for "Missing."*} Of course no one at Headquarters knew if these men were dead, dead and buried, dead and still unburied, dead and blown to atoms, captured, wounded, wounded and evacuated, wounded and lying out in No Man's Land, at dressing stations, or already sent back to hospital. According to Rowlands, no one at Headquarters was very interested in finding out. So the Sergeant himself has used most of the past week in bicycling around every field hospital and dressing station asking after our Rifle Brigade chaps. On Friday he brought his own list to the Colonel here at the big dressing station and Pretor-Pinney wept openly, which is almost unimaginable. According to Rowlands, all the Colonel could say, again and again, was, "What a mess they've made of my Battalion. What a *mess* they've made of my Battalion."

Rowlands would not have found me at a dressing station had he sought me out last Wednesday. The lads who found me at the Front had commandeered a motorcycle with sidecar and brought me back almost to Albert, dropping me off at what they were sure was a dressing station. There was a huge tent filled with casualties on stretchers, a few workers moving around under lights on the far side, and rows of overflow stretchers and blanketed wounded on the yard outside the tent. It was a warm night; the stars were clear. The sentry and his chum lifted me out of the sidecar, found me an empty stretcher, tucked a blanket to my chin, wished me luck, and returned to their duties on the line.

Fading in and out of consciousness as I was, so giddy at being alive and out of No Man's Land, it was an hour or two before I noticed that no one was checking on me. Not a doctor. Not a nurse. Not even an enlisted man taking temperatures or carrying out *triage*.

I also noticed the silence. For the first time in three days, the chorus of wounded men did not grate on my nerves and sanity. This group made no noise at all.

It was, of course, a burial station, not a dressing station, and it seemed that the enlisted men in charge of the detail had knocked off for the night just as my friends from the Front had left me to their tender mercies. I lay outside, alone, with the noble dead. My legs did not work, but I was able to sit up and look around. Many of the bodies had not been covered with blankets. Starlight gleamed from exposed bone and still-open eyes. I actually recognized a few of the lads from 13th Platoon.

Shouting did no good, as my lungs were already so congested that I could only cough hollowly. I lay back, sure that someone would come along. From time to time horses or motorcars came along the road no more than ten meters away, but a small rise separated the rows of dead from the thoroughfare, and my gasping coughs would not have been heard at any rate.

I considered crawling for help, but now, three and a half days after my last meal—and I had eaten little breakfast the morning of the attack, not only out of nervousness but due to the soldier's fear of a stomach or intestinal wound after eating—I had no strength left in my upper body. I was quite sure that I would die of thirst or my wounds before morning.

It rained sometime before dawn. The soft mist awakened me and I pitched my head back, opened my mouth, and swallowed what I could. It was not enough. I tried cupping my hands to catch the blessed moisture, but my hands were shaking too fiercely to serve me. Knowing that the soft rain would end soon, I peered around madly in the darkness trying to find some vessel with which to capture the water and save my life—a tossed-aside canteen, a jerry can, a helmet, anything. There was nothing. Then I noticed the water pooling in the folds and wrinkles of uniforms on the uncovered corpses nearby. I admit that I crawled where I could, lapping up these minuscule pools of water before they soaked in or evaporated. I remember using my tongue like a cat at a saucer of cream as I drank water pooled in the cold hollow of a young man's throat. I had no shame then and I feel none now. The gods had abandoned me and I defied them to do their worst. I would survive to spite the Fates.

She came then.

She walked between the rows of silent forms, treading lightly. I do not know if she was barefoot or in soft slippers. Her gown was the same as the previous night's—gauzy but not diaphanous, draped in Pre-Raphaelite folds which rearranged themselves in the starlight. I lay back on my stretcher then, pulling the rough blanket up around me, my thirst forgotten. I was afraid that she was searching for me in the darkness and more afraid that she was not.

I do not pretend that I did not know who she might be, must be. It did not matter. Her hair, when she bent over me, unfolded itself around us like a curtain. The scent of her neck was the hint of violets, a trace of jasmine, and all woman's warmth.

I wanted to say no, that my lips were cracked and caked, that my breath must be rank, but she touched my mouth with her cool finger to silence me. A second later she placed her lips where her finger had been. Her kiss was both firm and soft, endless and too brief. The stars seemed to circle in my vertigo. When she pulled back, I could sense the soft form of her left breast through the material.

"Wait," I rasped, but she was already stepping away, lifting the hem of her gown so that it did not touch the curled fingers or raised faces of the others lying there in the damp.

"Wait," I whispered again, but already sleep was coming. Shivering, knowing that I would have followed her at that moment if strength and the proper time had been mine, I managed to pull the sodden blanket higher as I slipped off into a sleep as dreamless as that of the dead around me.

Tuesday, 18 July, 3.30 P.M.—

A dreadful day. They make ready to discharge me but a bad night of fever and coughing kept me in bed one last day. My legs feel as if they are attached by sutures and not my own to control, but I can stand on them now with the aid of only one cane.

Fit to serve in Kitchener's Army again.

News so bad today that I can only laugh at whatever god of irony rules the universe. With The Rifle Brigade down to half strength and less, I knew that it is finished as a fighting unit. At least for some while. That meant that when I returned to the Battalion it would be to some "cushy" duty in a quiet section of the Front . . . or more probably in reserve behind the Front. Sergeant Rowlands had said yesterday that he had seen orders sending the Battalion to

Bresle today, and then on to relatively comfortable duty near Calonne. He says that the billets are in houses there and that it is away from the fighting and the Somme.

I was beginning to think that I might live to see Christmas. Today my transfer papers arrived.

I had put in for a transfer *last* Christmas when the Brigade was in Hannescamps and I was feeling left out and rather low. I've never got along with the common sort well, and the other officers in the Brigade did not seem like gentlemen. I'd approached the Colonel and filled out forms for a transfer to 34th Division, rather hoping that I might end up with Dickie, John, Siegfried *{Ed. note—Siegfried Sassoon}*, or some of the other chaps I'd known at Cambridge. The Colonel had told me how unlikely it was that any such transfer would be approved, but I sent the papers through, heard nothing, and had forgotten about it. Today I find that I *have* been transferred—to the 1st Battalion of the 1st Rifle Brigade of the 14th Division.

Wonderful. Fucking bloody wonderful. I've been in three Divisions during my short time in this fucking army: The Rifle Brigade was trained as part of the 37th, we were told that we had been moved to the 34th when we joined the line less than two weeks ago (less than two weeks?), and now I am to pack up and join the bloody fucking 14th. I know no one in the 14th. Worse than that, Sergeant Rowlands tells me that the 14th is moving *into* position on the line even while my old Brigade is leaving it.

If I had not lost my pistol in No Man's Land, I would put it in my mouth and pull the bloody fucking trigger.

Wednesday, 19 July, 7.00 P.M.—

Earlier I went outside to watch The Rifle Brigade march out of Albert. A beautiful evening. The air was actually cool and crisp, as if autumn were approaching despite the fact that it is high summer. There was only a hint of dust and cordite and the smell of decaying bodies in the air. The Golden Virgin and her child caught the light as the Battalion marched away under her.

I did not recognize many of the faces. Hundreds of new men have been incorporated into the ranks here in Albert so that the Battalion *looks* a bit like a battalion. Those faces I did recognize looked years older than when I last saw them nine days ago. An eternity ago. I stood on the hill outside the old convent here and waved, but many of the chaps I'd known from the old Brigade stared straight ahead, seeing nothing. Many wept. After they marched out of sight I came inside, expecting to sleep or perhaps write a letter to my sister, but there was a delegation if important ladies from Blighty here and we had to all be on our best behaviour. The nuns had put screens around the lads in worst condition—the new gas case, the Church Lad who's lost both legs, his right arm, and at least one eye, two or three others—so that our visitors would not be offended. I was simply not up to speaking to them, so I feigned sleep. One of them commented to another what a handsome lad I was. The brusque sister said that I was all well and would soon be returning to the Front. The Blighty lady, some old crone with her hair done up in a Gibson Girl bun—I peeked through lowered lids—said how wonderful it was that I was going back to give it another go.

I would like to give her another go.

THE GLORY OF WOMEN

You love us when we're heroes, home on leave,
Or wounded in a mentionable place.
You worship decorations; you believe
That chivalry redeems the war's disgrace.
You make us shells. You listen with delight,
By tales of dirt and danger fondly thrilled.
You crown our distant ardours while we fight,
And mourn our laurelled memories when we're killed.
You can't believe that British troops "retire"
When hell's last horror breaks them, and they run,
Trampling the terrible corpses—blind with blood.
O German mother dreaming by the fire,
While you are knitting socks to send your son
His face is trodden deeper in the mud.[8]

I do not think that *she* will come tonight. I wish to God that she would.

Still, I do not think that she has abandoned me. We will meet again soon enough.

To sleep now. My last night in hospital. Perhaps my last night ever between clean sheets.

Saturday, 22 July—

I was wrong about the clean sheets. I have slept between sheets—although not quite so clean as in hospital—each night since coming back to Amiens to join up with my new Rifle Brigade in the 14th Division.

Shells were raining down on Albert as I left on Thursday. German 5.9s were rearranging the rubble of the town centre and falling perilously close to the large field hospital and the convent hospital where I had recovered. I suspect that I look rather romantic with my limp, my cane, and my haggard expression contrasting with my new uniform; certainly the salutes I have been receiving from new troops heading toward the Front have been snappier and more respectful than I was used to. I also have begun growing a mustache. I notice grey hairs that were not there two week ago.

Amiens is some fifteen miles behind the lines, but it might as well be fifteen hundred. There is a real world here: a bookshop run by a certain Madame Carpentier whose daughter flirts with officers, restaurants with names such as Rue du Corps Nu sans Tête, la Cathédrale, Josephine's Oyster Bar, the wonderful Godebert, and one merely called "Officers Dining Room" where a veritable covey of subalterns hang out, not to mention such other Amiens wonders such as the barbershop in Rue des Trois Cailloux where one can, after a haircut, shave, and session with hot towels, receive a *friction d'eau de quinine* which makes one's scalp tingle for hours afterward.

It is a cruel respite. The 14th moves up to the line on Monday and this reminder of what human life is like will make the Front all the more unbearable.

I had the Devil's own time of trying to find the 14th—Amiens is full of billeted troops arriving and departing and the outskirts of town looks as if a thousand circuses were setting up tents—but I finally reported to an arrogant colonel whom I did not care for at all, and then to a certain Captain Brown who seemed a pleasant enough chap. Brown introduced me to my platoon sergeants and explained that the 1st Brigade was being built back up to strength because of all the "loans" they had made to more active units. I am beginning to see this entire war as one giant game of musical chairs, where the loser dies due to being in the wrong place at the wrong time when the music stops.

I think of the Lady every night, but I know that she will not visit me here. The thought of seeing her once more is the only thing attractive about moving northeast to the Front once again.

Sunday, 23 July, noon—

Word is that Australian and New Zealand troops attacked against Pozieres sometime after midnight. Captain Brown says that despite the usual rosy reports from Headquarters and the patriotic babble from the journalists, the result will probably turn out to be much the same as with the 34th on July 1st and my own Rifle Brigade on the 10th: i.e. thousands dead in the mud for nothing.

We will be heading up to Albert tomorrow, then into the Line.

The other big news today concerns the death of Major-General Ingouville-Williams, commander of the 34th Division. I remember Dickie and Siegfried telling me that the men called him "Inky Bill." It seems that he was killed yesterday by an exploding shell while hunting for souvenirs in Mametz Wood. The officers are all sombre about the loss, but I heard Corporal Cooper say to another enlisted man that "it serves him bloody right for leaving his cushy bloody dugout to go pokin' around for souvenirs where the rest of us have to fight a bloody war." At any rate, there was quite a commotion behind the lines to find a set of four matching black horses to pull the caisson carrying his body back down the line. Captain Brown says that a suitable team was found at C Battery of the 152nd Brigade.

I suppose these things are important.

> On, marching men, on
> To the gates of death with a song.
> Sow your gladness for earth's reaping.
> So you may be glad, though sleeping.
> Strew your gladness on earth's bed,
> So be merry, so be dead.[9]

The four thousand men of our brigade march toward the Front tomorrow. I suspect that there will be no black horses to carry home the thousands who do not march back this way again.

Tuesday, 25 July, 10.00 P.M.—

The Golden Virgin and her child hung over the road as we marched back through Albert yesterday and the cloud of dust our Brigade had raised set a sort of orange halo around Madonna and Child. Our way to the Front was not quite the same as when I visited the 34th for the Big Push on the 1st or where The Rifle Brigade went into line to die as a Brigade on the 10th. Our Brigade marched through Fricourt, but instead of taking either the road toward Pozieres or Contalmaison, we went by way of Sausage Valley to the right of la Boisselle and reached the new line in front of Pozieres without exposing the men to much in the way of enemy fire. The Germans know that huge numbers of men are using Sausage Valley, but they have no direct fire so we had hoped that our only worry was the occasional 5.9 dropping in blindly to welcome us.

They used gas. I suppose if I were Jerry, I would have chosen gas as well. It makes things difficult for us with very little effort on Jerry's part. Yesterday it was just tear gas, but in sufficient quantities that we all had to don goggles or gas masks. The sight was quite absurd—literally thousands of lorries, buses, messengers on bicycles and motorbikes, long lines of ambulances, artillery caissons, horse-drawn wagons, even a detachment of cavalry—all mixed in with thousands of marching men in a cloud of white dust that rose a thousand feet in the air and mixed with tear gas so thick that the valley was absolutely drenched in it. Some of the lorry and wagon drivers had no masks—evidently they were not considered combat-ants and had been issued none—and the image of them trying to drive their vehicles or teams of horses with tears streaming down their faces, mucus literally dripping from their chins, was beyond absurdity.

The number of dead horses lining the roads up Sausage Valley is absolutely staggering. It is as if someone had decided to pave the roadsides with rotting horseflesh. It is not uncommon to see the remains of two or three horses mingled so that one cannot tell which spill of intestines belongs to which carcass. And everywhere the occluded, staring eyes, so much more reproachful, I think, than the gaze of our human dead. The flies are everywhere, of course, as well as the stink. Many of us who have been this way before brought perfume purchased in Amiens so as to hide the stink of decay that sets into our skin and uniforms, but that is a losing proposition. Better to ignore it. Meanwhile, the snarl of traffic, shouts of drivers, the sobbing and slobbering of men and horses caught without masks, the muffled curses of sergeants—all viewed and heard distantly through our clumsy masks.

One old lorry driver I talked to while the Brigade was waiting an hour for the snarl ahead to lessen told me not to trust the awkward mass of mica and canvas with its clumsy nosepiece tube with which the army has issued us. Through that abomination, I asked him what he was using. It looked like an old rag but appeared to be doing the trick.

"Piss on one of me socks," he said. He held it up to show me that he was not jesting. "Works better than that bloody froggy headpiece you're peering out of. Want to give it a try?"

I restrained my eagerness.

The Anzacs {*Ed. note—Australian and New Zealand troops*} made up the bulk of the traffic both toward and away from the Front yesterday. Evidently their attack that began sometime after 1 A.M. on Sunday morning is still going on in bloody stages. At least the idiots at Headquarters have learned not to send men over the top in daylight. Little good the darkness seems to have done the Scots and Anzacs who have been fighting for Pozieres and the little copses of woods around it: the ambulances are full and there are dozens of burial centres working overtime just back of the trenches.

It seems my lot always to come to war in the command of burial parties. While the 14th is to stay in reserve behind the Australians, our first order of business is to put our lads to work burying Australians. It is dirty work, but at least the bodies have not been out on the wire for a week or more.

The shelling is very fierce. I was pleased to find that our reserve trenches were on the Front just a few days ago, so the dugouts are deep and the facilities well prepared. I am sharing a dugout that must be twenty feet below ground level with two other lieutenants named Malcolm and Sudbridge. Captain Brown is just down the trench a bit and his dugout is even deeper than ours.

We have bunks in ours, shelves, a rotty strip of burlap to keep the light in and the gas out, and even a table at which to sit and play cards. The whole place is lit by two hurricane lamps and the effect is rather cozy. It is much cooler than the cauldron of midsummer dust and heat above.

An hour or two ago Lieutenant Malcolm suggested that we level the ground under the table, which seemed a good idea since the platform was a bit wobbly. Young Malcolm and Sudbridge had set to with a will, digging out clay to make a nice flat area under each leg, when suddenly Malcolm scraped away the last layer of lime above some rotting blue cloth. "It looks like some Frog soldier lost his tunic," Malcolm said naïvely, still digging.

The smell filled the dugout a second before the remnants of the hand and arm were exposed.

I went for a walk to smoke my pipe and confer with Captain Brown. When I returned sometime later, the dirt had been filled back in and the boys were playing cards on the wobbly table.

I had chosen an upper bunk on the silly assumption that it would be more difficult for the rats to reach me up here—I hate the thought of those huge, sleek buggers crawling across my face in the dark—but a few minutes ago I noticed that the reinforcing timber above me seemed to be shimmering slightly, as if the surface of the wood were moving. I raised a lantern to the timber and found that it was literally crawling with lice. For half an hour after I turned out the light, I could feel the things falling on my chest and cheeks. Unable to sleep, I came out here to the firestep to write this by the light of the bombardment.

The Lady has not come. I would say that this place is not worthy of her, but I know that is not the reason. I have faith that I will see her again though.

Though we are in the reserve trenches, we are still within direct view and rifle shot of the German lines outside of Pozieres. Bullets strike the sandbags above my head with a familiar sound.

I can feel the lice seeking the warm folds and pleats of my

almost-new uniform. I know from experience that I will try to find and crush them for several days, then give it up and live with the constant crawling on my flesh.

It is time now to go back in to my bunk to sleep. I have my first inspection tour of the platoon in the trenches in three hours.

Friday, 28 July, 8.00 A.M.—

The Colonel called me back to his elaborate dugout yesterday and demanded to know why I had requested transfer to the 14th Division. I admitted that I had not—that I had wanted to join the 34th to be with some of my school chums. The Colonel, a dyspeptic, pale little man, slammed down some flimsies and muttered an oath. It seems that Headquarters had got wind of a screw-up—my papers *should* have specified the 34th after all—and now everyone had their bowels in an uproar over some clark's error.

"Well, what the hell do you propose we do about this, O'Rourke?" growled the Colonel, despite the fact that my name was quite plainly printed on the various forms in front of him.

I was at a loss. It seemed inconceivable to me that in the midst of all this carnage—my men had been burying Australians, Scots, and New Zealanders all week—anyone would give a tinker's damn about one junior lieutenant posted to the wrong division.

"We can't send you to the 34th," grumbled the Colonel. "They don't have any paperwork on you and are busy rebuilding. And we bloody well can't keep you here if Headquarters keeps sending up rockets."

I nodded and wished that the whole thing would just be dropped. I had begun to get to know the other subalterns—Malcolm and Sudbridge particularly—and had struck up an actual friendship with Captain Brown and several of the sergeants.

"Here, sign this," said the Colonel, sliding papers toward me across a battered table.

I looked at the forms. "A request to transfer back to The Rifle Brigade, Sir?" I said. It already seemed like an age since I had seen the few survivors of my old Brigade march out of Albert.

The Colonel had turned back to more important papers. "Yes, yes," he said, waving at me over his shoulder to sign. "You'll stay here until we can get a replacement, but that shouldn't be more than a week or two. Let's just send you back to where you belong, eh, O'Rourke?"

"Lieutenant *Rooke*, Sir," I said, but the brown-toothed little homunculus was paying no attention to me. I signed the papers and left.

It is only now, some hours later, that I think about what this might mean. Yesterday I heard from Sergeant Rowlands, and he mentioned in his note that the reserve trenches near Calonne were quite as cushy as the survivors of the Brigade had hoped. They had every wish to sit out the rest of the war there. If my transfer comes through . . .

This way lies madness. I have too much faith in the God of Irony to believe that anything as simple as another transfer will save me.

9.00 P.M., the same day—

A hot, sticky night. The sky over No Man's Land is the color of boiled lemons. Everyone here is moving slowly, desultory with the heat, almost wishing back the heavy rains that have plagued us all summer here along the Somme. Even the dugouts are too stuffy so men take their sleep shifts fully clothed, lying full length on duckboards, a sandbag for a pillow. Luckily for us, it seems that even the German snipers are too enervated to ply their trade with much enthusiasm.

Word is that the Australians tried once again to take the windmill that has been such a sticking point near Pozieres. All we see are the hundreds and hundreds of wounded men trying to get back to dressing stations. Some are on stretchers. Some are being helped along by their friends. Others stagger along by themselves until someone gives them a hand or they simply collapse in one of the trenches or supply roads.

This afternoon I was coming back with Sergeant Ackroyd and two privates from a detail down in Sausage Valley when I happened to glance aside at a line of British bodies lying alongside the trail. What caught my eye was that all seven of the men were wearing kilts. This was no surprise since the Royal Scots Brigade of the 51st Division had been taking heavy losses for two weeks. These bodies had been covered with tarps and each foot was tagged with the yellow card which meant that the burial detail would return later, but I noticed that one of the tarps had been pushed aside. The man lying under it had red hair and looked to be an officer. A large cat was lying on the man's tartan chest and was quite happily eating his face.

I stopped and shouted. The cat ignored me. One of the privates threw a rock. It struck the body but the cat did not look up. I nodded to Sergeant Ackroyd who ordered the two men to chase the cat away.

The result was quite surprising. The cat did not deign to lift its face from its meal until the two men were quite close. Then, as they shouted and waved their arms, the overfed beast leaped at them, spitting and clawing. The Irish Private—O'Branagan I think his name is—had bent down to shoo the cat away and lurched back with bloody clawmarks across his face.

The cat ran into the basement of a cottage tumbled by shell fire, and the Private hesitated. He had unslung his rifle and was holding it in the proper attitude for defense against bayonet attack.

"Oh bloody hell," muttered the Sergeant and he and I went forward and descended into the basement. It was obvious that unless we did something about the cat, it would return to its meal as soon as we had departed.

The basement was a mass of tumbled stones, charred beams, and shadowy recesses. We had to advance through the catacombs in a sort of half-crouch. What little light that made its way through the rafters, beams, and charred floorboards above was weak indeed. The Sergeant had borrowed the frightened Private's rifle; I considered taking my pistol out of its holster, but contented myself with holding my cane a bit higher. The whole thing had become laughable.

A shifting of loose rocks in the deepest regions of the sloping basement caused the Sergeant and me to turn. There was a sort of root cellar beneath the cellar. I would have given a quid at that moment to have been carrying a hand torch. I am afraid that I hesitated a second too long at the sepulchral opening to that lower circle of darkness, for the Sergeant said in a hearty voice, "Here, Sir, let me go first. I've always had crackerjack vision in the dark."

I let the burly NCO squeeze pass and crouched to see what I could see. I had the distinct image of him bayoneting that ghoulish monster and something about the thought of the blade sliding into soft fur brought back the memory of wet wool and made me a bit queasy.

Suddenly I heard the Sergeant whisper "Mother of Christ," and he stopped on the middle of six stone steps leading into the deeper cellar. I did take my pistol out then, and stepped down to stand next to him.

It took a minute for my eyes to adapt to the very dim light. There were three human bodies in there, perhaps four. They had been there long enough and the cellar was cool enough that the stench was not much greater than the constant background scent of decay this close to the Front. I could see now from the bits of rotting cloth and remaining blonde hair that it looked like a mother had brought her two toddlers and a very small baby down to escape the shelling. But the shelling had found them. That or poison gas.

But it was not the human remains that had brought the Sergeant up short and which now caused me to grip my cane and pistol with renewed strength. The five kittens—although they were too large, too fat, to be called kittens—raised their faces from their nibbling. They were *inside* the mother and the larger of the children. Nothing was left of the baby except yellowed lace and white bones.

The Sergeant let out a cry then and rushed forward with his bayoneted rifle. The kittens scattered—the backs of the corpses were as obviously hollow as the front—and before he could reach any of them, the animals were in the tumble of blackened timbers where we could not follow.

I happened to look up then at the tangle of beams above us and a larger set of yellow eyes was watching us with what I perceived as demonic interest. At that moment the cat and kittens began to yowl—or so I tell myself now—and the sound rose in volume until the Sergeant and I could only stand with our heads swiveling, not believing the intensity of the noise.

I had heard this chorus before. In No Man's Land. And I had been part of it.

"Come on," I said to the Sergeant. We returned to the surface and stood guard over the ruins until O'Branagan returned with two canvas bags of heavy Mills grenades, three wine bottles, and the jerry can of petrol I had ordered him to scrounge or steal.

The grenades threw up a huge pall of dust and rock chips. The Sergeant and I made sure that we had lobbed at least one bomb into every recess we could find there. O'Branagan had filled the bottles, we used bits of an old shirt from the other Private's pack for fuses, and then I lit each wick with my trench lighter. The explosions were impressive enough, but the fire was even more so. I noticed that the Sergeant had kept the Private's rifle and watched carefully while the ruins burned and the already-blackened timbers fell into the smoldering pit.

Nothing emerged either before or after the fire.

A platoon of the 6th Victoria Brigade were plodding toward the Front as we finished our work, and I noticed the strange looks they gave us.

Just minutes ago I was riding my bicycle back that way in the dusk to carry a message to Headquarters when I glanced up to see the smoke still rising. The tarp was intact across the Scot's body, just as it had been when we set it back in place. But it seemed that the canvas over the face was rucked too high, and moving slightly.

I told myself that it was a trick of the failing light and pedaled on.

Tuesday, 1 August, 2.30 A.M.—

Writing this on the firestep outside Captain Brown's dugout. The bombardment is heavy enough that I can see the page to move my pencil.

I have come to understand that Death is a jealous suitor.

I think of the women waiting at home—mothers, sisters, lovers, wives—and of the proprietary way they speak of us—of the dead and doomed to die. It is an arrogant conceit on their part to think that they can hold the memory of us like ashes and bones in an urn.

Even our memory is being devoured here.

> *When you see the millions of the mouthless dead*
> *Across your dreams in pale battalions go . . .*
> *Then, scanning all the o'ercrowded mass, should you*
> *Perceive one face that you loved heretofore.*

It is a spook. None wears the face you knew.
Great death has made all his for evermore.[10]
{*Ed. note—In the last line here, Rooke has crossed out "hers" and substituted the "his" we know from his published poem.*}

God Almighty, I love life. Even this vile place, where the trees are shattered stubs and where nothing grows but craters, even the sights, scents, sounds, and stirrings of this place are preferable to the unchanging nothingness of the Great Darkness.

As much as I love nature, music, exercise, riding to hounds, spring mornings, autumn evenings . . . as much as I love these things and bring them to mind when I think *life* . . . I love women more.

I was just fifteen when I took my fifteen-year-old second-cousin on a walk down in the Weald to the hop-farm there with its unusual line of white-cowled hop-kilns. Twenty tall hop-kilns, rising above the barns like the imagined Alps above equally imagined alpine chalets, the tops of the kilns tipped white like the apex of the icing-cone Mr. Leeds used at the bakery to put writing on the celebration cakes.

Her name was Evelyn, my second-cousin, and we walked into the edge of the forest near the hop-farm quite innocently. The trail there was little used, but a quicker return to our house above the Weald. I remember the heat of that day, much like the recent hot days here on the Somme but nothing at all like them as well. The air was still that day, but leaf-dappled and alive to the hop of insects in the tall grass, birds in the upper tiers of the forest, and the scrabble of squirrels and unseen wild things behind and within the hedges.

Evelyn had brought two sweet cakes and we sat to eat them in a sheltered place near the stream that was almost lost in undergrowth. The last time I had seen my cousin she had been dressed in a hand-embroidered kimono frock that was such the rage for children then; today she was dressed in a girlish version of a Gibson Girl outfit: long skirt, a shirt with pale blue stripes and long cuffs the same color as the stripes, a lemon-colored cravat, and a straw boater. Her hair was clasped near the base of her neck, her lashes were long, her blouse was gathered at her thin waist, her cheeks were rather pink—all and all she looked very grown up.

How things started between us that day, I do not recall precisely. A game. How things proceeded after they started, however, I recall absolutely. Her blouse had fewer buttons than most ladies' things, but far too many for my patience or fumbling fingers. And then it simply flowed away. She wore thin petticoats which made no sound when they moved. Her chemise was loose except where strings gathered it under the soft curve of her still-budding breasts. The sunlight and shadow seemed part of the texture of her skin there.

I remember how gently we kissed at first, how briefly, and then how urgently. Her drawers reached her thighs but once beyond the initial elastic there, they were loose and offered no resistance to my exploring hand. And somehow, inexplicably, miraculously, neither did Evelyn.

This mystery—so warm, slightly moist, and moistening more as exploration continued, the shocking humanness of the downy hair, this incredible, heart-stopping *absence*—this mystery is part of what I thought of as I crossed No Man's Land last month, squinting against the bullets.

The Lady came to me tonight while I slept. While Lieutenants Malcolm and Sudbridge slept not three feet away from me, their snores filling the dugout.

I felt her breasts pressing against me even before I fully awakened, and I admit that I started rather violently, thinking *rat*. Then I smelled her scent and felt her cheek so close to mine. I opened my eyes and made no sound.

She was standing next to the bunk, leaning forward so that part of her upper body brushed against my arm. Her face was warm against my neck. It was raining hard outside and cool in our dugout, but I could feel her warmth wherever she touched me.

She was no phantom. I could see the faint light from the flickering beyond the half-open burlap curtain playing on her lashes. I could feel the weight of her right breast against my bare forearm. Her breath was sweet.

She kissed me. Her left hand slid between the open buttons of my undershirt. I remembered Evelyn and all the girls since her. Always, except for the few times where professionals were involved, I had been the seducer. It had been I who first slipped fingers between cotton or muslin or wool.

Not this night. I saw her smile as her long, thin fingers slid down my rough undershirt and touched the drawcords of my pyjamas. She must have felt my excitement. She seemed to smile again and she lowered her face to my throat and kissed my pulse.

When she backed away I followed, sliding down off the bunk as quietly as possible. For some reason I slid my hand across my bunk, found this journal where I had tucked it, and brought it with me. It was as if this little notebook held proof of the bond between the Lady and me.

Malcolm snored on in the lower bunk. His face had been scant inches from the Lady's translucent gown when she had roused me. I was surprised that her scent had not awakened him. Sudbridge slept in the smaller bunk across the dugout, his face turned to the sweating wall. He did not stir.

My Lady parted the burlap and went up the plank steps. She was no ghost. The burlap moved to the touch of her fingers, just as I had. The orange heat lightning of the counterbombardment cast her shadow on the planks. I followed her up and out.

She was a shadow out here in the trench; then less than a shadow. I was busy pulling on my boots, and when I looked up she had blended with the other shadows near where the trench zigs to the right so that a shell there would not send shrapnel here.

"Wait!" I said aloud. At that moment I heard the distant pop of a *grenatenwerfer* being launched and I threw myself down as several "pineapples" exploded just above the trenches, showering red hot shrapnel up and down the line. A man shouted somewhere as I began moving toward the shadows where the Lady had just passed. I must have looked an absurd sight in my rough cotton pyjama bottoms, undershirt, and boots, my diary clutched to my chest like a talisman. I had forgotten my cane and I limped a bit.

Just then I heard a sound a thousand times more terrifying than a *grenatenwerfer* pop—the sound of some of our own 18-pounders falling short and dropping shells on our line with that whistle and rush that tells one that the huge piece of metal and explosive is coming *here*. Once again I threw myself face down in the mud, and this time not a second too soon. The noise deafened me. The ground seemed to reach up and smack my chest so that for a second I thought the Boche had also tunneled under us and detonated a huge mine. With that amazing alacrity of visual image in a moment of crisis, I could imagine the entire section of trench along this part of the line bubbling up a hundred meters into the air the way the explosion did opposite our line on the morning of the 1st.

Mud and timbers dropped all around. Men cursed. I dug myself out and started back to the dugout.

The 9-inch shell from the 18-pounder had been a direct hit on our dugout. Sergeant Mack and several of the others had already rushed to begin digging, but one look at the terrible concaveness of the crater told me everything that I needed to know. The Sergeant and his men continued to dig, however, until they came across the splinters of our bunks and table and a few bits and pieces of Malcolm and Sudbridge. They stopped then, merely shoveling some of the mud back in the pit. It was not a burial, but it would do until morning came.

Captain Brown was very good; he gave me a stiff tot of his own whiskey, loaned me kit, blouse, and trousers until I can get refitted, and insisted that I sleep in his batman's bed in his own dugout. I was grateful, but I prefer to sit out here until the sun rises.

The air smells slightly of violets.

Friday, 4 August, 11.00 A.M.—

The shelling has become almost intolerable. There is a continued battle for the outskirts of Guillemont—a battle in which our 14th Division has not yet been asked to take part, thank whatever god deserves to be thanked—but the artillery exchange involves us all. It has gone on day and night for four days now, and everyone's nerves are stretched to the breaking point as we huddle in our dugouts when off duty, clutching the chalky soil and sandbags of the trenches when on duty.

It is interesting how the ear becomes educated to the precise signature of approaching death. Even above the constant cacophony, one can hear the individual German guns fire. Their small field guns have a *crack* not unlike a golf ball being struck smartly. Their shells arrive with a banshee shriek. The medium guns sound like someone tearing *The Times* lengthwise while the arrival of their shells sounds rather like heavily loaded farmcarts rumbling downhill, brakes screeching. The firing of their heavy guns can be felt in one's eardrums and sinuses, it is as if someone has come up from behind and cuffed you on the side of the head, while the shell's arrival is a slow whistling across the sky, rather like a train heard distantly, until the locomotive rush and rumble of it comes roaring directly into one's living room.

The trench mortar is child's play compared to their heavier calibre guns, but I believe we all fear it most. There are so many of the damned things and they fire so quickly. One mortar can lob twenty-two shells a minute at us, eight in the air at any given time, and the explosions—although minor compared to the concussive terror of their 5.9s or larger guns—are so frequent and so well-aimed that they make us feel that a malevolent intelligence is stalking us, unlike the more disinterested malevolence of the heavy artillery.

Yesterday a German mortar shell came whistling down on our position as I sat chatting with three men at an observation post. We all ducked and cowered, knowing from the noise that this was meant for us and that there was no escape. The damned thing makes a *woof-woof* sound as it falls, and this one sounded like a rabid dog rushing at us from out of the sky.

It *was* meant for us. The shell struck not five yards from where we crouched, collapsed a sizable section of the parados, and came rolling almost to our feet. The shell was the size of a two-gallon oil drum and was dribbling yellow paste that smelled like marzipan. It was a dud. If it had burst upon impact the way it had been designed to, the concussive force would have been felt a mile away and there would have been nothing left of the three of us except bits of tatters and shoe leather in a smoking crater the size of my mother's living room in Kent.

The last four days they have been laying down mortar shells every three yards on our position at ten-minute intervals. We can hear their gunnery chief blow his whistle before each shot. And this is in addition to the howitzers that have been blasting swimming pool–sized craters up and down our lines all day and all night. It can grow to be tiresome.

We all retreat into ourselves in some way. I tend to sit and stare at whatever book I am holding in white-clenched fingers: Today it was a new book of verse by the chap Siegfried and I were so excited about—Eliot. I read not a word, turned not a page. Some of the men curse constantly, adding their frightened litany to the incredible onslaught of noise. Others shake, some just noticeably, others almost uncontrollably. No one thinks less of them for it.

Dust and atomized chalk and cordite coat everything during a bombardment like this. When we do move around, it is with white eyes staring from grimy faces. We officers stand around the table stabbing at soiled maps with filthy fingers and dirt-rimmed nails. I am amazed that our lice continue to call us home, as foul as we all are.

I heard a Cockney singing a bit of doggerel as he stood on the firestep last night about dusk during a minute's lull in explosions. It was rather fine.

> The world wasn't made in a day,
> And Eve didn't ride in a bus,
> But most of the world's in a sandbag,
> And the rest of it's plastered on us. [11]

I wait each night for the Lady but I haven't seen her since the night Malcolm and Sudbridge were blown to bits. Captain Brown has been quite nice about sharing his dugout, but tomorrow night I will be moving into less exalted quarters with two new subalterns who have just come up. They look like children.

No word about my transfer to the 13th Battalion. I am beginning to know the men of this Rifle Brigade and to think that my destiny should lie here. However limited or common these chaps may be as individuals, their common effort and good nature under these conditions makes one feel something akin to love toward them. Each death is an affront. I think that they may soon be called upon to go over the top and the wastage appalls me in a most personal way.

For some reason Marvell comes to mind as I watch the lads from my platoon eat their ration of bully beef while the bombardment rages:

> *My love is of a birth as rare*
> *As 'tis for object strange and high:*
> *It was begotten by Despair*
> *Upon Impossibility.* [12]

Tuesday, 8 August, 4.00 P.M.—

The 55th Division has gone over the top on yet another attempt to capture Guillemont. The word is that the French attacked simultaneously on their right. It is nice to know that the French are still in the war.

Captain Brown came back from Headquarters a while ago with the word that the French were stopped cold by enfilade fire and our lads in the 55th were cut to ribbons by the German counterbombardment. He says that a few of our chaps made it to the enemy trenches, seized a stretch of them, and then were annihilated to a man by machine-gun bullets directed from Waterlot Farm, Guillemont Station, and the trenches in front of the village. All afternoon the shattered remnants of the 55th and supporting groups such as the 5th King's Liverpools have been straggling through our reserve trenches, trying to find their officers or reach dressing stations. We help when we can.

A heavy mist has been hanging over the hills and fields all day, mixing with the smoke and dust from the terrible bombardment. Brown says that two of our own Battalions ended up slaughtering each other in the mist and confusion this afternoon.

All of us in the 1st Rifle Brigade expected to be thrown into this meat grinder tomorrow, but word now is that the Reserve Battalions have been chosen as sacrifice. It is terrible to feel relief because another man will die.

Wednesday, 9 August, midnight—

She came tonight.

This afternoon I had done foot inspection—our M.O. {*Ed. note—Medical Officer*} was killed yesterday by a sniper—and the act of going down the line inspecting scores of men's bare and stinking feet had put me in a somewhat Christlike mood. Since the bombardment had let up a bit, I stayed in the advanced trenches after the 9 P.M.

tour of the platoon's posts. It is a clear, cool night for a change, and the stars above the trench are very bright. I must have fallen asleep on the duckboard where I was smoking a pipe and meditating in one of the shelter niches in the sandbags.

I awoke to the scent of violets and the touch of her hand. We were on the same patio where she had taken me before for tea. It was all purple twilight. The manor house was candlelit behind us, there were candles in hurricane lamps set around the flagstone terrace, and I could hear hounds baying softly from the kennels beyond the barn. The Lady was wearing a pale evening dress with a frilly, flesh-colored chemisette covering a low *décolletage*, with matching sleeves reaching just to her elbows. Her skirt was tight to the hips and high-waisted, belted with a subtle jeweled corselet. Her head was bare except for small, jeweled combs holding her hair at the back. Her long neck caught the lamplight.

She led the way into a dining room where a table had been set for two. The china and silver reminded me a bit of my aunt's, but the napkins were a stylish pale blue. The table was set for only two. The main course had already been set out—Cornish hens under glass with a watercress salad. A fire burned in the marble fireplace, but this seemed appropriate since there had been an autumn tang to the air outside.

We joined arms and I escorted her to her seat. Her skirt rustled softly as I set her chair in place. When I sat down, I pinched the loose skin on the top of my hand under the table. I felt the pain of it, but the verisimilitude only made me smile.

"You believe that you are dreaming?" asked the Lady with a slight smile. Her voice was as low as I had imagined, but I could not have imagined the effect it had on me. It was as if her fingertips were on my skin again.

"I forgot you speak," I said stupidly.

Her smile became more pronounced. "Of course I speak. Would you have me dumb?"

"Not at all," I stammered. "It is just . . ."

"Just that you are not sure of the rules," she said softly, filling our glasses with wine from a bottle that had been set near her place.

"There are rules?" I said.

"No. Only possibilities." Her voice was just above a whisper. The fire crackled and I could hear a wind coming up in the trees outside. "Are you hungry?" she asked.

I looked at the hen, the candlelight on fine silver, the wine in sparkling crystal, and the perfectly fresh, green salad. I had not had a meal such as this in months. "No, I am not hungry," I said truthfully.

"Good," she said, the playfulness apparent in her voice now. The Lady stood, I took her cool fingers, and she led me from the dining room through an ornate drawing room, from the drawing room to the hall, up a wide flight of stairs, down a landing lined with dark portraits, and into a room which I knew at once was her bedroom. A fire had been set here as well, and the flickering light fell on the parted lace of the curtained bed. Broad doors opened to a balcony and the stars were visible above the trees.

She turned to me and raised her face. "Please kiss me."

Feeling that I should have a script, that there should be footlights rather than firelight, I stepped forward and kissed her. Immediately all thoughts of the theatre disappeared. Her lips were warm and moist, and when they opened slightly under the pressure of mine, I felt a pleasant vertigo, as if the floor were no longer so solid. I could feel her arm and hand move until her perfect fingertips touched the back of my neck just above the collar.

When the kiss finally ended, I could only stand there, caught in a surge of passion such as none I had ever known. At some time during our embrace, my arms had encircled her. I could feel the warmth of her bare back through the lace of her blouse. She lifted her fingers from my neck, put her hand behind her, and loosened her hair.

"Come," she whispered and stepped toward the high-canopied bed. Both her small hands surrounded my single large one.

My hesitation was only for the briefest second, but she turned, my hand still in hers. One eyebrow lifted ever so slightly in query.

"Even if you are Death," I said, my voice husky, "it may well be worth it."

Her smile was just perceptible in the soft light and shadows. "You think me Death? Why not your Muse? Why not Memnosyne?"

"You could be Death," I said, "and still be my Muse."

There was a moment of silence broken only by the crackling of burning logs and the renewed rustle of wind in treetops. She lifted her finger and traced a complicated pattern on the broad back of my hand. "Does it matter?" she said.

I did not reply. When she stepped toward the bed again, I followed. She had stopped to lift her face to mine again when the wind in the trees became a train whistle, the train whistle grew to a locomotive rush, and then I was falling from the duckboard, covering my face with hands as the trench mortar shell exploded not ten yards from where I had been sleeping. The five men I had visited there not twenty minutes earlier were blown to fragments. Hot shrapnel rattled on my helmet and bits of red meat decorated the sandbags of my niche like scraps set out for the kennel dogs.

Saturday, 12 August, 6.30 P.M.—

I was cycling back on the sunken road between Pozieres and Albert this noon, carrying a message from the Colonel to Headquarters, when I stopped to watch what promised to be a bit of comedy.

One of our observation balloons was hanging like the fat sausage it was when an enemy monoplane came buzzing across the lines. I considered finding a convenient shell hole to cower in, but the insect-droning machine seemed uninterested in finding a target to bomb; it made a beeline for the balloon. Usually it is funny to watch our chaps up there when an enemy machine appears. They do not wait for the attack but immediately parachute to safety. I cannot say I blame them—the balloons explode so ferociously that I doubt that I would choose to wait around to see the flicker of enemy machine guns.

Both observers jumped just as the German plane turned toward them and I nodded in satisfaction to see their parachutes open at once. The plane made a single pass, its guns hammered for less than three seconds, and the balloon did what all such hydrogen targets do when punctured by hot lead—it exploded into a giant mass of flaming gas and rubberized shreds. The wicker basket beneath it ignited like tinder.

Unfortunately, there was almost no wind, so rather than drift toward Albert or our rear lines, the observers descended almost directly under the balloon, their parachutes settling down in slow spirals like seeds from a shaken dandelion. The flaming mass caught the first man still two hundred feet above the ground. I distinctly heard him scream as first his parachute ignited and then his clothes.

The second man jerked desperately at the lines connecting him to his silk umbrella, and for a moment I was sure that he had avoided the fate of his friend, The tumbling mass of wicker, steel cable, flaming rubber and burning gas missed him by five yards— enough to singe him but not enough to ignite his parachute or pull him down. Then I saw the Medusa-like mass of ropes and cables trailing behind the central mass. These whipped about like the *flagella* of some dying creature, and it was only bad luck that one of these steel cables lashed around the lines of the parachute, tugged it and the man sideways in a terrible jerk, and pulled him down.

The umbrella did not quite fold up and the observer might have survived if the cable had not pulled him into the burning mass of debris on the ground. As it was, I and several other passing messengers ran to the edge of the great pyre, but there was no chance of running in to help the poor chap. The flame must have covered a diameter of thirty yards. He was able to stand, run a few yards, fall into the flames, stand, run again, and fall again. This happened four or five times before he did not rise. I rather thought that the boys back in the trenches could hear his screams three miles away.

I delivered the message to Headquarters, ran into a chap there whom I had known in college, and accepted his offer of a whiskey and soda before cycling back toward the Front.

Monday, 14 August, 7.45 P.M.—

Every sort of evil omen today.

After two weeks of sunny, hot August weather, the skies opened up today. It poured. As if in response to the counterbarrage of thunder and lightning, the big guns on both sides retreated into relative silence with only an occasional salvo to keep us or the Germans honest. This is not rain, it is deluge.

After an hour the duckboards were all under water. After three hours, the sandbags began to slip in places as entire trench walls became the consistency of very moist coffee grounds. Shell holes have become lakes with their deadly green scum of solidified poison gas running off in rivulets into streams and tributaries. Everywhere bodies are washing up and washing out, and a walk in any direction shows green hands and plastered clumps of hair rising from the mud as if the trumpet for the Second Coming had sounded.

Captain Brown and Sergeant Ackroyd tell me that the River Ancre has flooded its banks and is filling the valley behind us. Ahead of us, the village of Thiepval is awash, as are the German trenches. We can tell that because the lads coming back from the fighting in Thiepval Wood say that the water the Germans pump out of their cushy trenches runs downhill to our lads' precarious positions among the shattered tree trunks. Word is that the Australians have captured the windmill that has eluded them for so long, but the Anzacs are so exhausted that all the living can do is lie in the mud with their dead and dying and suffer the deluge.

The second evil omen is that early this morning we were ordered to rear billets "for rest and refitting." By noon we had marched back to the temporary camp between Pozieres and Albert and were drying off in tents rather than our leaking dugouts. This would seem to be good news, but as we have not been directly involved in any of the fighting so far, the "rest and refitting" has to fall under the category of preparation for our own go at the objectives that have eluded so many of our dead and rotting predecessors.

The final evil omen was at the 4 o'clock meal when the men received hot stew, fresh-baked bread, hot rather than tepid tea, and oranges and chestnuts. It was the oranges and chestnuts that tied it all up in a ribbon. They only serve us these delicacies when they are fattening us up for the slaughter. I would have taken the daily trenchfare of bully beef and beans, even with its usual cloud of flies, rather than this final meal.

She has not come again since I wrote last. I think she will tonight, although I share this tent with young Lieutenants Julian and Raddison, whom the others call Raddy. The rain is pounding the canvas with fists. Everything leaks. The only course of action is to eat our fine meal, smoke our new cigarettes, and crawl into our new, lice-free blankets.

*   *   *

Tuesday, 15 August, 1.20 P.M.—

She did not visit last night, nor this morning when I was alone. It may seem insane to wish for her, but I do. And I know why I do.

It is official. Captain Brown returned from Headquarters this morning, his face slack. We go over the top on Friday, the 18th.

Brown tried to put the best face on it, explaining to all the subalterns that it will be the 33rd Division with the yeoman's task ahead of it—securing ground between Delville Wood and High Wood while simultaneously securing High Wood itself. All our Brigade has to do, says Brown, is attack on the right flank of the 33rd and to the left of Delville Wood and secure an area of enemy front known as Orchard Trench. Our effort will be part of a general attack stretching from Guillemont to Thiepval Ridge, and Captain Brown says that the boffins in Headquarters cannot see how we can fail to take High Wood and Delville Wood this time.

This Friday, 18 August, will be the fiftieth day of this battle.

A while ago, alone in my tent, I took out my revolver, made sure it was loaded, and seriously considered shooting myself. It would have to be a fatal shot, since any attempt at a self-inflicted wound is punishable by execution.

The irony makes me laugh.

Wednesday, 16 August, 2.30 P.M.—

Late this morning, Brigadier-General Shute himself—the commander of our entire Brigade—showed up with the pompous Colonel and several red-tabbed Staff adjutants in tow. The men were assembled in the rain, three companies on a side of an open square. The order went out to stand at ease and there we were, several thousand men in dripping waterproofs and sodden khaki caps (we put away our tin hats this far behind the lines), with all eyes on General Shute astride his tall black horse in the centre of our square. The horse was nervous and had to be reined in, which the General did without apparent thought.

"Well, I think that . . . yes . . . ahem, it seems to be incumbent upon me . . . that is to say, all you chaps should know that action with the enemy is . . . well, imminent, shall we say?" The General cleared his throat, reined in the nervous black, and sat higher. "I have no doubt that each and every man jack of you will comport himself with, you know, courage. And uphold the honour of this Division, which has covered itself with, well, glory since the Battle of Mons."

At this point the horse wheeled around as if leaving and we thought the lecture was over, but the General reined in the recalcitrant animal, almost stood in his stirrups, and got to the crux of his address. "And one more thing, lads," he said, voice rising. "I visited your reserve trenches two days ago and I was, well, *appalled*. Simply *appalled*. Sanitary arrangements were far from satisfactory. Hygiene was as lax as the discipline. Why, I saw *human excrement* lying about in places. You all know the regulations about burying one's waste. I need to tell you that I won't have it—*I simply won't have it!* Do you hear? I know that you have been under some artillery harassment recently, but that is no reason to behave like animals. Do you hear me? After this attack, if I find anyone not keeping their section of trench clean and disinfected according to precise regulations, I shall have that man or those men *up on charges!* And I include officers as well as the lower ranks in this charge."

As we all stood stunned in the increasingly heavy rain, General Shute wheeled his black horse a final time and almost galloped to the rear, his covey of adjutants and aides-de-camp racing to their motorcars to catch up.

We were not finished. We were called to attention and made to stand there for another forty minutes as first the Colonel ticked us off with spittle flying, echoing his commander's sentiments about human waste found lying around, and then—when the Colonel had left—the Sergeant-Major gave a stern lecture about how the severest military penalties would apply to any slacker who held back during the attack. Then the Sergeant-Major read an endless list of names— names of men executed for such offenses, complete with the date of their cowardice, their rank and unit, and finally the date and hour of their execution. It was profoundly depressing, and when we returned to our leaking tents our thoughts were more on floating shit and firing squads than on covering ourselves with glory for Blighty or King.

*　　*　　*

Same day, 9.00 P.M.—

I may have found a way out of this war more clever, or at least more certain, than shooting myself.

After I penned that last entry, I sat in my tent and wrote a poem. Because I wrote it on foolscap rather than in this journal, Lieutenant Raddison—Raddy—evidently came across it later and showed it to some of the chaps. I was furious, of course, but it was too late. The poem has made the rounds of the camp by now and I have heard laughter from a hundred sources. Even the stern old NCOs are reported to be delighted by it, and many of the lower ranks have begun singing it as a marching ditty.

As of now, only a few of the other officers know that I was the wit behind this broadside, but if it is discovered by the Colonel or anyone of higher rank, I have no doubt that my name will be on the list the next time the men must hear of executions. Captain Brown knows, but he merely gave me an exasperated look and said nothing. I suspect that he secretly enjoyed the poem.

Here it is.

> *The General inspecting the trenches*
> *Exclaimed with a horrified shout,*
> *"I refuse to command a Division*
> *Which leaves its excreta about."*
>
> *But nobody took any notice*
> *No one was prepared to refute,*
> *That the presence of shit was congenial*
> *Compared with the presence of Shute.*
>
> *And certain responsible critics*
> *Made haste to reply to his words*
> *Observing that his Staff advisers*
> *Consisted entirely of turds.*
>
> *For shit may be shot at odd corners*
> *And paper supplied there to suit,*
> *But a shit would be shot without mourners*
> *If somebody shot that shit Shute.*[13]

* * *

Thursday, 17 August, 4.00 P.M.—

Marched the Brigade back to the reserve trenches by noon, then forward to the advanced trenches held by the devastated 55th until this morning. All the way back here in the rain I kept hearing snatches of the Brigade's new "marching song." But the singing died as we reoccupied our old trenches and then moved forward to the advanced line opposite Orchard Trench.

I would like to write now that I feel fatalistic about all this, that I have been through it all before and that nothing can frighten me after what I have seen, but the truth is that I am more terrified than ever before. The thought of dying is like a great void opening within me. Marching here, I look at a field mouse scurrying away from the road in the valley and I think, *Will that mouse be alive in forty-eight hours when I am dead?* The idea—no, the probability—that I will be condemned to an eternity of non-sight, non-sound, non-touch while other things continue to live and sense the universe is almost unsupportable.

For the past hour I have been trying to read *The Return of the Native.* I do not want to die before I finish this book.

The men are pooling their cash to be divided amongst the survivors after the attack. Their feeling is admirable—*If I should die, better this money goes to some chum or fellow sufferer than rot in the mud of No Man's Land or be looted by some souvenir-hunting Hun.* If the attrition is as bad as it was with my 13th Battalion, or the 34th, or the Church Lads Brigade of the 33rd, or the 51st or 55th who still lie in silent rows, their faces to the rain, in the fields behind us . . . well, there will be some wealthy chaps this time tomorrow evening.

The religious fellows in the platoon attended a communion service not an hour ago. The altar was two stretchers on which the blood of the wounded was visible on the stained canvas beneath the chalice holding the Blood of Our Savior. I envy the men who found comfort there.

This advance trench is only seven feet deep, barely deep enough to keep our tin hats out of sight. An hour ago a Lance-Corporal from D Company peeked his head up for the briefest second and a bullet caught him square in the ear and took his face quite off. We are all aware that to show any part of ourselves, for even the briefest time, would bring a bullet.

And tomorrow we will stand up there on those sandbags and walk out toward the enemy? It hardly seems sane.

Captain Brown was talking about the barrage, and how the artillery chaps will try a different approach this time—walking a "curtain" across No Man's Land in front of us. God knows they have tried everything else. For the Australians, our officers commanding the 17-pounders followed the old recipe of twenty-four hours of barrage, then the crescendo . . . and then waited ten minutes for the Germans to come flocking out of their dugouts and reinforced bunkers . . . and then resumed it again, trying to catch them in the open.

We do not know how effective this clever plan was—the Australians who went out by the thousands to capture those trenches did not, by and large, return.

Captain Brown is quite sanguine about our Brigade reaching and taking its objective. At times I want to shout at him that the objective is not worth the floating shit that General Shute found so offensive. What use is another hundred yards of bombed-out trench if it costs a hundred thousand lives . . . or three hundred thousand . . . or a million? It is common knowledge that General Sir Douglas Haig calls the deaths of thousands of us "the usual wastage" and has said that half a million casualties before this battle is over would be "quite acceptable."

Acceptable to whom, I wonder? Not to me. My life is all I have. I thought that at the advanced age of twenty-eight, I would be less worried about losing my life. Instead, I hold every second of experience to this point as sacred and detest those who would take away my chance to see another sunrise or eat another meal or finish *The Return of the Native*.

My hand is shaking so that I can hardly read this writing. What will the men think come morning if their Lieutenant cannot muster the courage to lead them over the top? Who cares what the men would think if my funk would gain me even a minute more of life and breath.

I would care. For whatever bizarre reason, I care. Perhaps it is just fear of having one's comrades think poorly of one that sends us each over the top.

It is time for high tea. Bully beef and a bulb of onion for the men tonight. The days of oranges and chestnuts are past. It is the flies' favorite meal for us tonight—and tomorrow? Many of us will be meals for flies.

Friday, 18 August, 3.15 A.M.—

She was here tonight. I am writing this by the light of Very flares. The entire Brigade are packed into these trenches and it is very crowded. Men are sleeping with their backs to the sandbags, their feet on the duckboard or in the ten inches of water beneath. Men are crouching on the firesteps, trying to sleep, or pretending to sleep. I was one of the latter until the Lady came.

The periscope above the trench here is a slanted piece of mirror on a broomstick. I had been looking up at it idly—one can sometimes see the flash of their big guns before the sound reaches us—when suddenly the surface of the mirror reflected only her face and flowing gown. I stood then, my helmet almost showing above the parapet, and would have reached for the mirror—and almost certainly would have been shot by the snipers who already tonight had culled two of the curious from our platoon—if she had not reached for me instead.

And then we were within the shelter of her curtained bed.

She was wearing only the softly translucent gown I had first seen her in. My own clothes had been removed and were lying, neatly folded, on the chair just outside the curtains. They were no longer mud-caked or lousy. Nor was I. My hair was still slightly damp, as if from the bath.

She lifted the covers slightly so that I could slide within that inviting envelope. The autumn air had turned cooler and now it ruffled the bed curtains with a sensuous languor. The light from the fireplace and a single candle filtered through the lace and fell on damask and silk with a buttery touch. We lay on the pillows, she and I, studying each other's faces in the masked light.

When she touched my cheek, I took her wrist and held it firmly.

"You are afraid," she asked, or said, for although her dark eyes were questioning, I did not hear a rising inflection.

I did not answer.

After a moment she said, "But you know me."

I held the silence another moment. "Yes," I said at last, "I know you."

In my mother's drawing room there was a mirror in which I had, in silent, narcissistic intensity, contemplated my own face a thousand times or more. And I remember the other details of my mother's drawing room: the beeswaxed parquet floor, the cat's half-empty bowl of milk under the gate-legged table, the urn of fresh flowers which the servants replaced daily... or nightly, I should say, so that when I was a small child I had thought that the invisible appearance of these blooms in season was magical, rather like the coming of Father Christmas only much more prompt and reliable.

I remember the Herndon photograph of the painting by G. F. Watts—*Love and Death*—with the attractive spectre of feminine Death, the folds of her robe elaborated in all their Pre-Raphaelite glory, her face lowered and turned away so that when I was very young I thought that she either possessed no head or had darkness for a skull... beautiful Death with her right arm raised above a cherubic boy-child whose partially concealed right arm was also raised, as if touching Her face, or perhaps attempting, futilely, to hold Her at bay. The photograph of the painting hung directly opposite the mirror which I found so endlessly fascinating, so that each time I studied my young poet's features—for I was sure even when I was seven or eight that I must be a poet—this image of Love and Death was visible above my right shoulder, Death's posture reversed from leaning right to leaning left above young Eros, so that it seemed that the form in the image had moved of Her own accord.

"Yes," I said again to the beautiful woman in whose bed I now lay, "I know you."

She smiled once more and this time there seemed less mockery and more pleasure there. I released her wrist, but rather than stroke my cheek, the Lady slid her pale hand under the bedclothes. I started ever so slightly when her fingers touched my side and she held them still there, just above the ridge of my hip, as someone does when trying not to startle an animal which might or might not allow itself to be petted.

Her eyes, I noticed, were not all black but merely very brown, the iris actually surrounded by an infinitely thin band of green that somehow added to the lustre there.

She slid her hand slowly across the bone of my hip and down my thigh, bending her fingers back slightly so that the pads of her fingers rather than her long nails would touch my skin. I admit that the tender flesh along my thigh rippled like the pelt of some forest animal as her fingers slid lower. Never had a woman been so bold with me, behaving as if my body were hers with which to play. When her fingers curved around my rigid sex, I closed my eyes.

Friday, 18 August, 5.45 A.M.—

Dawn ends this seemingly endless night. Routine takes over. Before breakfast, each company dumps its tent packs and stacks blankets into bundles of twelve.

There is reassurance here. Each man is thinking that there is safety in routine, that Death must wait if we are called on to complete the Army's tasks.

The cooks have made an effort to brew fresh coffee and tea, although the water is often bad. Sometimes they have to lower their cans into the shell holes for water. They say that boiling it kills the germs that the foetid corpses breed, but if the cooks have miscalculated and captured the green scum on the surface left from the residues of poison gas, boiling the water merely releases and reactivates the bubbles of deadly gas. Normally we would worry about this in the advance trenches, but now with only hours until we go over the top, such a bellyache would be welcomed as an excuse to go back to hospital.

There is also an attempt at a good British breakfast—sausages, baked beans, even stewed tomatoes and eggs for some of the officers—but few of us take advantage of it. The thought of a ruptured stomach or intestines, of metal and filthy cloth driven through a gut full of such food, still drives away appetite from most of us. Fear stops the rest from eating.

We know that the order to go over the top today will come later than usual—Captain Brown thought mid-afternoon—and this makes the waiting more miserable than last time for me. At least we were up and murdered and all but finished with it by 9 A.M. during the last go.

10.10 A.M.—

I have not mentioned the barrage this morning, but it is insane. Our own position here is slightly higher than that of the Germans only a few hundred yards in front of us, and this topography dictates that our guns have to lower their aim so severely that the air above is filled with shells flying literally inches above our parapets. Half an hour ago the inevitable occurred and a chap in C Company had his head blown quite off. The effect on those crowded into that section of trench was rather terrible, since blood and brain matter drenched dozens of them and two men were carried rearward with shrapnel wounds from splinters of flying skull.

The Sergeants are going around now with a bottle of rum, doling out spoonsful to the chaps and taking frequent swigs themselves. I notice that Sergeant Ackroyd's red face has grown noticeably redder.

12.30 P.M.—

For the past fifteen minutes there has been a strange diversion.

First the guns fell silent on both sides, as if our and the German artillery chaps had all gone out for dinner. At first the men became more tense rather than less, believing that the lull in the barrage meant that our attack was imminent, but Captain Brown sent the subalterns down the length of the trench, telling the men that the attack had been set for 3 P.M. We all relaxed. Some of the chaps had a brew up while others surrendered to hunger and heated up some of their bully beef.

To add to the sense of relief from both barrage and anxiety over the uncertainty of when we were to go over the top, the rain that has plagued us for the past four days finally relented. While the sun did not actually emerge, the clouds *did* lift from their low-lying sullenness to a solid but much brighter ceiling some three or four thousand feet above the trenches.

And that is when the aeroplanes appeared.

At first they were a mere droning sound in the unaccustomed silence, then two specks broke free of the clouds some miles to the west, and soon we could make out the machines themselves, although with my nearsightedness there was no question of my actually telling friend from foe. The men did, though, and when what I perceived as the smaller of the two droning crosses quickly circled into a position behind the larger, the troops along our entire section of trench sent up a cheer.

For the next ten minutes or so it was as if we were spectators to some aerial Punch and Judy show as the two machines whirled and circled and dipped and climbed into and out of the cloud ceiling. All sniping and harassing machine-gun fire stopped as both sides of No Man's Land became engrossed in the spectacle. For the first time in weeks, the Front became so silent that one could hear bird song from the river behind us or the cough of men many yards away. And then came the tiny hammering sound of the machine guns in the aeroplanes themselves—just occasionally when one had the advantage on the other—and then so briefly as to make all of us on the ground—*under* the ground—feel like wantons for our constant and endless expenditure of ammunition.

And then, just as the aerial display threatened to become repetitious and boring, one of the machines—the larger—burst into flame and went spiraling down in tighter and tighter circles until it disappeared behind the German trenches in the direction of Guillemont. A moment later a great column of black smoke rose into the sky and our lads gave a triple hurrah followed by so many whistles and shouts that I thought that I was sitting in the working class seats at a football match.

The celebration was premature. A moment later the circling smaller machine—British or French, I assumed, although I could not make out the markings—suddenly emitted a burst of smoke.

"Coo, 'e's on fire. See the bloody flames?" said a Lance Corporal near me.

I could see no flames, but I *could* hear the sputter of the aeroplane's engine as the last of the cheering in our line died away. Evidently the machine was too high to return safely to earth before the flames consumed the pilot—or perhaps there was simply no place for it to come down in our thousand square miles of cratered earth here along the Front—for rather than descend, the aeroplane appeared to climb and try several awkward sideslipping motions, as if the frenzied pilot were attempting to keep the flames away from his body. It must not have worked; a moment later even I could see the flames and thin line of smoke trailing behind the sputtering cruciform-shape.

The men along the line of trench shouted and moaned for several seconds before I could make out the reason for their lamentation. Then I saw what they had already perceived: the pilot had jumped from the machine just below the ceiling of clouds. Even someone as ignorant of the details of aerial machinery and warfare as I knew that pilots did not carry parachutes up with them as our balloon observers do, although whether this abstemiousness is from lack of room in the flying machine or a function of their code of airborne chivalry, I do not know. At any rate, even while knowing that the plummeting figure was doomed by his lack of a few yards of silk, one hoped during the entire plummeting descent that this chap might be an exception and that the circle of white would pop open at the last moment, bearing the warrior gently down to the waiting arms of his comrades.

It did not. He fell into No Man's Land a few hundred yards to the east of our position, close enough that we could see his arms and legs thrashing as if seeking purchase in the air; close enough that even I could see a white scarf trailing like the tail of an aberrant kite. There was a long silence along the trenches when he struck. I glanced up once, expecting to see the burning aeroplane descending as rapidly as its driver had, but the machine—now blossoming in full flame like Apollo's chariot—continued to fly along until it passed into the clouds, became an eerie glow through the white ceiling, and then disappeared completely, never to reappear.

A moment later the German machine guns opened up as if the schoolmaster had blown his whistle, ending our little recess. A moment after that the barrage began again.

It is after 1 P.M. We go up and over at 3.00.

2.10 P.M.—

I did not go to sleep. I did not close my eyes.

But one moment I was here, in the slimy trenches under an atmosphere of screaming metal, and the next moment I was *there*— next to my Lady between clean sheets with the cool air ruffling balcony drapes and bed curtains.

She touched me still. And I responded still.

Brusquely, I moved her hand away from my sex, thrust aside the bedclothes, and sat in the cooling air with my back to her.

I could feel rather than see her moving toward me, feel the featherbed indent as she rested on one elbow behind me. "You do not desire me?" Her voice was the softest of whispers.

I forced an ironic smile. My clean uniform still lay folded neatly over the Empire chair, but I could see no bulge of cigarette case in the pocket of my blouse. It would have helped at that moment to have had a cigarette. "All men must desire you," I said, my own voice rough and ragged, nowhere near a whisper.

"I am not interested in all men," she said. I could feel the warmth of her breath on my bare back. "I am interested only in you."

That statement should have made me shudder, but instead it increased my arousal. I *did* want her. . . more than I had wanted any woman or any thing. I said nothing.

She laid her hand flat against my back. I could feel the outline of her palm and each slender finger as a locus of warmth. Outside, the wind blew as if leading in a storm.

"At least lie next to me," she said, rising so that her lips were next to my neck. "Lie next to me and keep me warm."

I managed an ironic chuckle. "Keep you warm so that I may be cold forevermore? Or will you keep me warm by pulling a blanket of earth over us?"

She pulled back. "You are unfair," she said.

I turned to look at her then, knowing even as I did so that such a glance might seal my fate . . . although I would be Eurydice to her Orpheus.

Neither of us vanished. She was beautiful in the candlelight. Her hair lay loose, her chemise had pulled aside so that I could see the creamy skin above one elegant shoulder, and her left breast was outlined through the thin fabric by the glow behind her. Although my breath caught in my throat, I said, "How can one be unfair to a metaphor?"

She smiled then. "You think me a metaphor?" Her right hand touched my cheek.

"I think you a seductress," I said through a tightening throat.

Her laugh was soft, pleasant, and it held no scorn. "Then you would be wrong. I am no seductress." Her fingers slid along my lips. "It is you who seeks to seduce me; it is you who has courted me since birth. It is always thus." Her face came closer and we kissed before I could speak.

Outside, the storm arrived suddenly with a gust of cold air, a blast of the terrace doors being blown open, and an endless roll of thunder.

"Good Christ," gasped the Lance Corporal huddled next to me on the firestep, "that fuckin' barrage is too fuckin' close for me fuckin' peace of mind."

2.35 P.M.—

The Sergeant and I moved along the trenches a moment ago, checking a final time that the men's kit was in battle order. Normally the chaps wear their haversacks on the left side, but in preparation for the attack they move it to the back below the shoulder blade. Beneath their haversack, their groundsheet must be rolled tightly. Our objective is to seize and *occupy* Orchard Trench and we pack as if there is no doubt that this objective will be achieved. A partial list of the men's kit includes—

Entrenching tool
Pull-through
Rifle with fixed bayonet
Bootlaces
Spine protector
Gas mask
Tin of grease
Waterproof sheet
Latherbrush
Razor and case
Holdall

Housewife
Towel
Water bottle
Bottle of oil
150 rounds of rifle ammunition
Paybook
Toothbrush
Cardigan
Cap comforter
Knife, fork, spoon
Comb
Soap
Socks (3 pairs)
Shirt
Mess tin

In addition, each man now carries an extra 180 rounds of rifle ammunition in a spare bandolier over his right shoulder and a 5-lb. Mills grenade in each tunic pocket. Many of the men carry extra canisters for the Lewis gun. Other extra burdens include Very flares, wirecutters for every tenth man, periscopes, signal lamps, wire for the telephone lines, and extra water because of the heat. The Sergeant always demands that the men show him their filled water bottles carried on the right side and the white linen bag containing an extra iron ration. My grim job is to remind the men of their field dressing sewn into the lower right flap of their tunics, and to show them how to use the iodine on the wound before wrapping it with the temporary dressing. The lads look at me—at my chalky, wasted face and cane—and they listen, believing me to be a man of more experience than I actually have.

It is no wonder, with these tons of superfluous detritus, that after each battle No Man's Land looks like a gigantic garbage heap of bandages, torn papers, toilet paper, abandoned weapons, spent cartridges, and bits of the men who carried all this there.

Earlier today the men had their teaspoon of rum to give them courage during the long wait; now the Sergeant has gone around with the attack-ration of rum: one sixty-fourth of a gallon per man, carefully doled out in a small tin cup. The easy joking of this morning's ration is not matched by horseplay now—the men accept their dole in silence, as if receiving Communion.

2.48—

The barrage intensifies, if such a thing is possible. Captain Brown just came by and reminded us that the officers will be leading the attack for each company. Previously, some stayed behind until all men were out of the trenches, but this time the military police will make sure that there are no laggards. The same police will follow the attack, using their bayonets on shirkers if need be.

Captain Brown patted me on the shoulder and said, "We'll knock back a pint after all this settles, Jimmy. See you in Orchard Trench." And then he was off to reassure the men with jokes and pats on the back.

2.56—

Numbness. I am so frightened that I am as numb as when I was shellshocked during the last attack. I only pray that my legs will carry me up the side of the trench and into the killing ground.

I will bring my cane.

2.58—

I cannot hear the barrage for the pounding of my heart. I see men's mouths moving in shouts but hear nothing—perhaps I have gone death. {sic}

For some reason I recall a snatch of Byron—

> The winds were wither'd in the stagnant air,
> And the clouds perish'd; Darkness had no need
> Of aid from them—She was the Universe.[14]

My father's watch says it is only 2.59 but the barrage has moved away and whistles are blowing up and down the

* * *

{Ed. note—The next several pages of James Edwin Rooke's diary are missing and appear to have been torn out. A fragment of one page exists and has the following verse scribbled in pencil:}

> *Who are these? Why sit they here in twilight?*
> *Wherefore rock they, purgatorial shadows?*
> *Drooping tongues from jaws that slob their relish,*
> *Baring teeth that leer like skulls' teeth wicked? Stroke*
>   *on stroke of*
> *pain—but what slow panic,*
> *Gouged these chasms round their fretted sockets?*
> *And from their hair and through their hands' palms*
> *Misery swelters. Surely we have perished*
> *Sleeping, and walk in hell; but who these hellish?*[15]

{Ed. note—the journal resumes several pages later in mid-sentence with no date or time of entry}

none of this makes any sense, so will try again . . . thusly . . .

Whistles blow. I thrust my journal in my pocket, grasp my cane like a sword, and climb the ladder. The ladder. Up. For weeks, showing the smallest part of one's head above the parapet means a sniper bullet through the brain. Death, instant, inevitable. Now they order us to climb up there. Above.

I climb. The men throng like terrified cattle thrust too many to a chute above which the slaughterhouse executioner waits. Bayonets from below make retreat down the ladder impossible once the ascent has begun. Mud on the soles of the boots of the man ahead of me—Captain Brown. He is shouting. The barrage has not ended, but is moving across No Man's Land like a curtain.

Standing on the lip of our own trench, up in sunlight and still alive—miraculous! Energy flows through me like an electric current. Up here and alive!—I wave the men up and out with my cane. Then I turn to lead the advance . . .

. . . turn to lead the advance . . .

and am hit quite squarely between the eyes.

My feet fly out from under me, I feel blood fly from my shattered brow, a great weight seems to descend out of the sky to fall upon me, and I sense my body tumbling backwards, over the edge of the trench, and then down, flying blindly into my own grave with a great splintering of duckboard and splash of muck.

Blackness for minutes or seconds. Then I open my eyes expecting to see the Lady, but instead see snatches of greying sky through a film of red. Wiping blood from my eyes, I sit up. Some great heifer of a man with a red face—Sergeant McKay from B Company—is helping me up, pulling me out from under a dead weight which seems to cling to me. I see sprawling white hands, blood-soaked khaki, and for an instant I think that the Sergeant is pulling my soul from my shattered body as if he were God's midwife.

"Just bloody bad luck for him," the red-faced NCO is saying. "Are ye all right though, Sir? I think it be just a scratch on yer noggin, Sir."

I shake my head and try to focus on what the Sergeant is saying. Men are rushing by, climbing ladders. I have been unconscious for mere seconds, if at all.

"... another go, Sir?" McKay is saying, half holding me upright as we shuffle toward the ladder through the throng of frightened men. "Careful, Sir," he says, pulling me to one side, "best not to step on the gentleman's face."

I look down. Almost under my boot lies Captain Brown. The machine-gun bullets have stitched a bloody row from his groin to his forehead, shattering his teeth and Adam's apple along their route. I realize numbly that it is the brim of Captain Brown's helmet that had caught me between the eyes seconds before; the weight of his near-eviscerated body driven into mine that had tumbled me back into the trench.

"Upsy-daisy, Sir," says the Sergeant, speaking to me in a tone one would use with a child as he helps me up the ladder.

No, I scream in my mind, *there is some mistake. I have already climbed up there. No one should have to do it twice.*

"Thank you, Sergeant," I say, my voice shaky. I wipe blood from my eyes again.

Incredibly, the Sergeant finds my cane where it had fallen near the wire and hands it to me. Bullets whine past our ears. The barrage is now some hundreds of yards ahead, but enemy 5.9s are falling all around us. I see my company—Company C—some mere 20 yards ahead, advancing with rifles at port arms, heads lowered as if advancing into a strong rain. Company B, McKay's chaps, are rising out of the trenches now two platoons abreast every 200 yards, a man every two yards, all of their pacing straight from the Infantry Manual.

"Thank you, Sergeant," I say again, dusting myself off although the khaki is soaked more with mud and water than dust. I take a step, wobble, steady myself with my cane, and start toward the enemy lines.

No Man's Land is as repugnant as I remember it. Some shell holes still smoke and stink of cordite, while others resemble ancient lunar craters with their stagnant ponds and scum of poison gas. Bodies and bits of bodies lie everywhere here between the wire. The filthy litter is everywhere; I notice a clean, well-oiled rifle lying untended and consider sweeping it up before I notice the clutched hand and severed forearm still attached.

I turn to shout to Sergeant McKay but a series of explosions hides him and the rest of his platoon from sight. Ahead of me, C Company have taken shelter in a slight dip in the terrain and are lying in almost perfect battle order. Beyond them, D Company continue on toward enemy wire. I stagger the thirty paces or so to the muddy fold in the ground and collapse next to a Lance Corporal who is keeping his head down. A machine gun stitches its way across the soil inches from my head. For the first time I notice that I have lost my helmet in the tumble back into the trench.

After a few moments of sheer gratitude at being alive, I see that while our barrage continues to move forward toward the enemy lines, the German counterbarrage is now churning up the debris between the muddy depression in which we lie, and our own wire. And it is moving closer. Not wanting to appear the insufferable officer-wallah, but also not wanting C Company either to die where they have taken shelter or to fall too far behind D Company's attack, I stand up amidst the bee-hum of bullets and pace back and forth on the far side of the depression, urging the chaps to their feet with gestures of my cane since no one can hear my voice.

None of the men move a muscle. I admit that I feel a momentary surge of uncharacteristic anger at this general funk, but it passes when I realize that if I hadn't earned these damned subaltern pips due to my college and social standing, I would be lying there with the other chaps hoping that the goddamned lieutenant would either shut up or lie down or get shot.

I drop down into the low ravine next to the Lance Corporal and begin pulling him to his feet, hoping that our example will shame the other men into movement. The Corporal almost comes apart in my arms.

He is dead, of course. They are all dead, lying there in their proper battle lines, faces against the stocks of their rifles, arms thrown across their faces as if frozen in the act of flinching. I check two other men—a private named Dunham and a bantam-sized little pipefitter named Bennett—and see from the wounds that shrapnel has dropped them like leaves from a tree. It may have been our own barrage, or perhaps the first lucky counterstrokes of the German counterfire, but a hailstorm of shrapnel has cut these men down in their tracks.

Limping, using the cane now for support rather than inspiration, I hobble forward ahead of the enemy barrage.

Just before reaching the enemy wire, I drop into a smoking shell hole where Sergeant Ackroyd is arguing with Raddy—my bunkmate, young Lieutenant Raddison. Their voices are inaudible but I can see the spittle flying from the open mouths in their white faces. It takes me a moment to understand the source of their disagreement, but then I comprehend. Both men have had their guts opened as if by a butcher's knife and they kneel there in the bile-colored mud, their intestines spilled out in a common, smoking heap. Each man is attempting to tuck himself back in, as if they were schoolboys embarrassed at having been caught with their shirts outside their trousers, and each is arguing with failing strength about which strand of grey-white gut belongs to whom.

The argument ends as I watch with wide eyes; first Raddy quits shouting and heels slowly to his left, eyes showing only whites, finally tumbling into his own viscera, and then Sergeant Ackroyd leans forward with almost ballet-like grace, the scooping movement of his arms and hands slowing, slowing, until all motion halts like the last, tired movements of a worn machine. I begin pawing my way backwards, up and over the crater lip, back into the cleanliness of the machine-gun fire, but not before I see Sergeant Ackroyd stir, his bloodless face turning toward me, his bloodless lips forming words I mercifully cannot hear.

A pitiful remnant of D Company has breached the enemy wire and seized a fifty-yard section of forward trench. Twice more I am knocked down by shellfire, once blown into the wire, which is painful, but eventually I extricate myself and drop down the muddy parapet into German trenches for the second time in my life.

A beefy sergeant and a wire-thin private whirl toward me and crouch as if ready to bayonet me.

"At ease, men," I manage. My voice sounds alien to me and I cannot imagine they can hear any of it. Both the enemy and friendly barrages have joined now into a maelstrom of metal and flame falling along this mile of trench line.

But the Sergeant lowers the Private's Lee Enfield, averts his own bayonet, and leans close. "Good Christ Almighty, Sir. You're wounded bad. Lie down, Sir."

For a moment I am sure that he is right and that I am dying, perhaps already dead, but then I glance down at myself and have to rub muddy knuckles against my lips to keep from laughing or sobbing. The front of my tunic is absolutely soaked with Captain Brown's blood. My shoulders are caked with drying brain matter. And blood continues to flow from the deep scratch on my forehead from where the captain's helmet struck me. My face is caked with dried blood. I realize that I must look like a combination of a Red Indian and a demon from hell to these exhausted and shell-shocked men. Realizing that there is no time for irony, I lean forward and say, "Situation please, Sergeant."

The old NCO sags upward almost to attention. I read his lips more than hear his voice. Even above the cordite and trench stink, I can smell the rum on his breath. "We've secured this bit o' trench, Sir," he reports. "Me an' about ten o' the lads from Lieutenant Hall's platoon. Jerry keeps counterattackin', Sir, but e' don't do much but throw them stick bombs what're easy to throw back, Sir."

As if to demonstrate this piece of acumen, a German grenade on its throwing stick comes sizzling and bouncing into the trench not three yards from us. The wire-thin private calmly sets down his rifle, lifts the bomb, and tosses it back over the sandbagged revetment. The explosion follows in less than a second.

"They're set for a bloody eight seconds, Sir," reports the Sergeant with disdain in his voice. "Fritz don't like to hold 'em for no more than two seconds or so. Oodles of time, Sir."

I nod and glance around. This is not Orchard Trench. We are some distance from our objective, perhaps as much as a hundred yards. We have captured some form of forward observation trench from the looks of the hastily sandbagged emplacement, but because it is connected to Jerry's main line, he obviously wants it back. As if to demonstrate the veracity of my assumption, there is shouting around the corner and the surviving half-dozen men of D Company fall back to this small section of trench, firing and throwing Mills bombs as they go. I press against the parados as stick grenades bounce in and are thrown back. Enemy 5.9s explode in No Man's Land a few yards behind us; "friendly" 18-pounders throw up soil and bits of corpses a dozen yards to our front. The Sergeant and I bury our faces in the muddy sandbags and wait for the clods and shrapnel to settle.

When I lift my face, it is to shout at the Sergeant. "Where is Lieutenant Hall?"

The rum fumes wash over me. "He went down way back there, Sir. Near where C Company is hidin'. Why the fuck don't they come up to support us the way they was told to? Sir?"

I wave away his question. "We'll hold this section of trench until relieved or ordered to fall back," I shout. All five of the men are gathered around me now. Two have fallen just seconds ago when a stick grenade had a shorter fuse than the private and his chum had thought.

I look at their faces. They understand that my order is a death sentence. They show no anger. Two go off to the corner where the trench zigzags on our right and begin firing down it. Two others move to the corner on our left. The Sergeant begins pulling bandoliers off the dead private and the other man who has just been killed. "Ammunition won't last 'til it gets dark," he says.

I want to say something inspiring now—"We'll hold" perhaps,

or "It will last until A Company arrive"—but I merely nod and move along the trench, swinging my cane and throwing back the occasional stick bomb. Instead of letting up, the barrage increases in severity as both sides focus on this section of shallow trench. When I raise my head to look back, one of the two men guarding our left flank is writhing on the ground and holding the bloody mass that was his groin just seconds ago. His mate stares in horror. To our right, I hear shouts in German . . . *German!* . . . and the Lance Corporal at the corner there fires seven rounds in rapid succession. He seems to be praying, but as I come closer I can hear his dry-lipped litany—"I'd give me fockin' left bollock for a fockin' Lewis gun now. . . I'd give me fockin' left bollock for a fockin' Lewis gun now. . ." He squeezes off three more rounds and reloads.

I clap him on the shoulder and walk back toward the left flank, half expecting men in grey to come flying over the parados or around the corner and bayonet me before I reach the Sergeant. I am swinging my cane and whistling softly. I am very happy.

The marble bannister under my hand was cool. I was wearing only a silk robe that rustled softly against my skin. The wind continued to rise, shimmering the treetops in the darkness like a squall moving across brittle water.

"Come to bed," she said softly from the room behind me.

I glanced over my shoulder at the wind-stirred bed curtains and the glimmering firelight. "In a moment," I said, still wishing for a cigarette.

She did not wait. I heard the rustle of her long gown and she stood next to me against the railing. Starlight sketched the curve of her cheek and set soft highlights in her tumbled hair. Her eyes looked soft and moist. She set her hand on mine and I could feel the warmth of her hand above, alternating with the chill of the marble under my palm.

"It is not fair," I said at last.

"What, my love?"

I did not turn to look at her. "It is not fair that you use the act of love to steal men from life."

I thought that I could almost hear the mockery in her silence, but when I finally turned to look at her, there was no mockery in her downcast face. Her fingers trembled against the back of my hand. She asked, "How can one steal by giving?"

Pulling my hand away, I looked toward the dark woods. "Sophistry," I mutter.

"What else can one expect from a . . . metaphor?" Her whisper was just audible above distant thunder.

I turned quickly and seized her by the throat. Her neck was so slim that it fitted nicely into my one hand. Applying pressure, I could feel her breath stop suddenly. Fragile structures lay just beneath the webbing between my straining thumb and forefinger. Her eyes widened inches from my own.

"Would you like to taste death?" I whispered in her face.

The Lady did not struggle although I could sense her weakening as no breath or blood flowed above my firm grip. Her hands stayed at her sides. I think that if she had raised one to scratch or strike me, I would have snapped her neck then like a spent match. Her gaze never left me.

"Can Death die?" I breathed into her small ear and then pulled back to watch her face. Starlight and lack of blood made it pale as porcelain. Her dark eyes seemed to answer my question with a question.

"Damn," I cursed myself and dropped my hand away. She did not raise her small hands to her throat, but I could hear her labored breathing and see the red marks my fingers had left there. Beyond us, the wind died as suddenly as it had come up.

"Damn," I said again and kissed her.

Her lips were moist and open and I could feel a sense of mutual surrender flowing through and from our contact. It was exhilarating, like the instant when one has launched oneself into space before gravity's unsubtle intervention. Her fingers did rise then, finally, and migrated, hesitant and softly fluttering, to the back of my neck. Her body pressed against mine so that I could feel her thighs and the soft cusp of her belly against me through the thin layers of silk which were all that separated us.

Our kiss ended just as I grew dizzy. She pulled her head back as if also gasping for breath or equilibrium. I gave her time for neither.

Sweeping her up in my arms, her gown so low on her left breast that I could see the pale nipple above the laced border there, I carried her from the balcony into the bedroom.

The gas shells make a different sound from High Explosive, a sort of double cough, a bit like a crass tradesman loudly clearing his throat to be noticed.

"Gas!" screams the Sergeant and we scramble through our canvas kits for the masks. I pull mine on and fumble with the clumsy straps. The thing is awkward and imperfect, a thrown-together contraption of army shirt material, thick mica eyepieces, and a nosepiece tube holding sodium thiosulphate. It will not tighten properly and I frenziedly pull at straps to cinch the gaps. Someday they will invent a true gas mask, but in the meantime my life depends upon this absurdity.

The Sergeant and I peer around, attempting to see if the gas is visible. The Germans have been using copious quantities of tear gas recently, but it is a nuisance gas and one can spot the white clouds before they disperse. In the last year or so, there has been much more use of the killing gases chlorine and phosgene. In hospital, I had seen the results of German battlefield experiments with a mixture of ethylene in a solution of sodium chloride—the so-called mustard gas. In recent weeks they have loaded these various gases in shells rather than release them from canisters.

The effect, at least on the half dozen of us still alive in the forward trench, might be described as comic. The Sergeant and I are peering around like frightened frogs. The other four chaps have set down their rifles and have been digging through kit for their masks. If the Germans want the trench now, all they have to do is waltz in to take it.

I see no visible gas. Phosgene. Almost certainly phosgene.

Chlorine is bad enough—a thousand parts per million in the air means death. The gas destroys the small bronchial tubes and alveoli of the lungs so that one cannot absorb oxygen; a man then literally drowns in the water his own lungs create. Our Brigade buried a few victims of chlorine, and the skin of these men was invariably a bright blue, their stiffened arms were thrown wide with terror, and their staring eyes told all.

Phosgene is worse. Twenty times more lethal than chlorine, invisible, and much more difficult to detect. One can smell chlorine long before the dose is lethal, but phosgene, even in deadly amounts, smells only faintly of moldy hay. It does its job, though. When I was in hospital, one poor chap who had tried only a whiff of phosgene vomited four pints of a thick, yellow fluid from his lungs *each hour* for the forty-eight hours or so until he mercifully drowned in his own excretions.

I do not know much about this new mustard gas, but Captain Brown said that it blisters and burns the flesh, blinds the eyes, rots mucus membranes, seeks out and attacks the genitals, and scours right through to the bone. He said that our chaps who are developing it were delighted that the symptoms do no appear until hours after exposure. Soldiers will not know whether they are doomed or not. I remember the autopsy report I tried to set to verse. Evidently the Germans have perfected it before us. Fritz was always clever at chemistry.

The Sergeant is shouting something now, but even leaning so that my canvas mask touches his, I cannot understand him. But I look to where he is pointing.

One of our chaps cannot find his mask. His maskless face becomes a contorted mask itself. I can clearly hear *his* screams.

"I smell it! I bloody smell it!" He throws down his kit, abandons his rifle, and scrambles up over the parapet toward No Man's Land.

I am screaming at him, urging him to piss on his sock. The Sergeant is trying to grab him. Another private attempts to grip his friend's puttees while tightening the straps on his own mask. More shells are coughing near us. It is all a comic farce.

The fleeing private gets only ten yards or so before a German machine gun slams him aside like a struck ten-pin. He had forgotten that there are more common ways to die here.

The other four men in the trench lift their weapons and prepare to fight off another counterattack. I pick up the dead private's rifle, slide the bolt back to make sure that there is a cartridge in the chamber, and join the other chaps on the firestep we have erected from sandbags at the rear of the trench. I am sweating so heavily in this clumsy canvas bag of a mask that the thick mica eyepieces, barely serviceable at the best of times, are fogged up on the inside. A clip in the gas mask keeps me from breathing through my nose so only by gasping in the bit of air that makes it through canvas and filter can I get barely enough oxygen to survive. I imagine that I can smell moldy hay. I am essentially blind.

"There!" comes the Sergeant's scream through filter and mask. "They're comin'!"

Something moves, vague shapes are visible through the opaque eyepieces. Bayonets, perhaps. German bayonets. Stick bombs come bouncing and hissing into our trench but we are all too busy to deal with them. I pant through my mouth and squeeze off several shots at the attacking shadows.

The great attraction and the great danger of passion is that it is something outside of oneself, a strong wind from nowhere in the face of which the forest of everyday thought and behavior cannot stand.

She was beautiful, my Lady. I carried her from the balcony to the bedroom, across the firelit parquet floor, feeling rather than seeing the soft nap of Persian carpet under my bare feet in the second before parting the bed curtains and setting this woman, *my* woman, gently on the high mattress there. Her hair flowed back over my forearm where it remained, still cradling her. The pale-pink circles of her nipples were visible through thin fabric.

The time for subtlety was past. I cast off my silk robe, grasped her thin garment by its lacy collar, and tore it down the front. She raised her arms above her head on the pillow and the reflected firelight painted the lower curves of her breasts with warm tones. Her legs were long and smooth, her belly slightly curved, the triangle of darkness below meeting its apex at the juncture of her shadowed thighs.

She opened her arms to me as I stretched myself out against the length of her. She must have felt my rigid sex against her thigh, for a kind of gentle shivering went through her and she closed her eyes. To quiet her, I set my fingers in her hair, kissed her eyelids, and laid myself atop her like a blanket. When we kissed, she opened her legs to me and slid her nails lower on my back. I could feel the opening warmth of her against the head of my sex, and I paused a second to savor that briefest of moments where the two of us were on the verge of becoming one.

Our kiss seemed to continue on past consciousness, she opened her mouth to me, our tongues met in urgent strife, and I slid forward into my Lady.

The Sergeant dies just before darkness comes.

We have held off two attacks, fighting in our crude gas masks, the air swirling with invisible phosgene and then—before the second assault—with vaporous clouds of tear gas. The Germans are vague shapes through the fog outside and the fog inside our thick mica lenses. We fire at the shapes and some go down. I glance at a twitching corpse just around the bend of our trench and see that the German masks are not much more refined than ours. This man has been shot through the eyepiece and blood runs from the tapered snout of the mask's tube. It is as if I have killed a demon.

There were five of us counting the wounded private, the Sergeant, and myself. And then, after several stick bombs go off on the first attack, there is only the Sergeant and myself. We gather the last of the ammunition from our dead comrades, patting their pockets for more Mills bombs or cartridges. Setting our masks together so that we can be heard, the Sergeant and I decide that we cannot hold the entire section of trench with just the two of us to guard the approaches. We retreat to the right where the trench zigzags back toward the main German lines. There are grey-clad bodies stacked in the mud for the length of the next section of trench. The rats are already busy feeding.

The Sergeant rests his rifle on a niche in the trench wall to cover this approach while I stack other sandbags to create a crude revetment. Anyone coming around the far corner will have to pass down the full length of our abandoned trench under my sights.

Then tear gas and smoke billow around us. My eyes are running with tears, I cannot breathe, but this has been the case for the past half hour in my mask so I do not know if there is a leak. I peer down the sights of my Lee Enfield waiting for the first of them to come around the corner. His back to mine, the Sergeant stares down his section of trench.

They come over the top, leaping down from the parados with guttural cries. From the distant place I have gone, I calmly notice how much longer the upper sections of their boots are than those issued to our chaps.

I shoot two of them. Another throws a stick bomb at us and flees. The Sergeant kicks the hissing bomb around the corner of the trench and I shoot the running German in the back. He continues to crawl. I shoot him again and feel nothing.

Two more men leap into our trench from almost directly overhead. I shoot one in the face and my rifle jams; the bolt will not eject the cartridge. The surviving German shouts something through his gas mask and drops into the stance for bayonet attack. With no time to turn and fire, the Sergeant shifts his rifle into a defensive diagonal and steps between the German and me.

The German lunges, the Sergeant clumsily deflects the blade, and lunges back. Both men have scored. The German's thin bayonet has entered the Sergeant's throat just under where the gas mask is tightened. Four inches of the Sergeant's blade is embedded in the German's abdomen. The two men sag to their knees, still attached by steel. Each pulls the bayonet from the other as if in a single, choreographed motion. As I watch, panting, almost fainting from lack of oxygen, the two forms thrust their bayoneted rifles at each other again even while they are on their knees. Neither has the strength to penetrate the other much more than skin deep. They drop their rifles and fall together at the same second.

Ignoring the threat of other Germans coming over the top, I drop my rifle and roll the Sergeant to his side, tugging off the mask. His mouth is wide and almost filled with blood, as round as a shell crater. His eyes are wide. I never learned his name.

The German is still alive, writhing in pain. I prop him up against the front wall of the trench, pull off his mask and study his face.

He is just a man: dark stubble, brown eyes, sweat-matted hair, and a shaving nick on his throat. He gasps for water—I know the

German word for that at least—and I lift my water bottle to his lips. He swallows, starts to speak, suddenly convulses, and dies without uttering another word.

Leaving my own rifle in the mud, I lift the Sergeant's, wipe the blood from the stock as best I can, check to make sure that there is a full magazine loaded, and sag against my tumbled sandbags. Whistles are blowing in the German trenches and I guess that they are readying another attack.

Then the shells begin to fall with deadly aim, tumbling the trench walls in, exploding parts of bodies into the air, and filling the length of the trench with screaming shrapnel. I know the sound of these guns. They are British 18-pounders. There will be no relief. Headquarters has decided that no British troops have made it this far. The barrage has begun again.

Our motion is liquid, oiled with passion and sweat. Her warmth surrounds and consumes me.

Death did not claim me when I first touched her, I am able to think through the rising surge of sensation. *Nor when I kissed her. Nor when I entered her.*

We roll among the bedclothes, never allowing ourselves to lose that most intimate of contact with the other, her legs around me, thighs gripping me. When she is above me, her breasts hang like fruit I must gather, the nipples visible like rising seeds between my fingers. Her hair is a curtain around us.

It must be when I reach the ultimate ecstasy. The so-called "little death" will not be so little this time. I do not care. I roll with her until we tumble off the bed and I lie atop her on the Persian carpet amidst the tangle and drape of bedclothes, the fireplace light showing me her face contorted with the same passion I feel.

We—I—move more rapidly now, beyond thought, past stopping, beyond return, past anything except the consummation of the passion that increases our rhythm to this sliding crescendo.

Wednesday, 23 August, sometime in the afternoon—

Ten minutes ago they jammed the needle through my back and drained a pint of fluid from my lungs. They are still not sure whether it is the probably fatal pneumonia caused by the gas I inhaled, or merely a return of the pneumonia I suffered earlier.

At least the liquid is not increasing. If I am drowning, I am drowning slowly.

The wound on my right leg worries me more. They have cut away flesh all around the wound, but the smell of gangrene fills the ward and I constantly sniff at my own bandages to see if I am contributing to the stench.

"It's your own damned fault," said the curt Dr. Babington while on his rounds after the needle extracted fluid today, "for fighting in such fertile fields."

I have not spoken since entering this place, but the doctor took my silence as query. "It's the French fields," he continued, "best fertilized in the world, don't you know. Yes, tons and tons of manure. Human waste as well, don't you know. You chaps have it saturated in your uniforms. Then a piece of metal like this passes through flesh and drives all that *merde*-soaked fabric in with it. The wound itself is nothing . . . nothing." He snapped his fingers. "But the sepsis . . . ah, well . . . we will know in a few days." And he passed on down the ward.

There are no windows in this canvas field hospital, but I asked one of the overworked nurses and she said, yes, the Madonna and Child still lean over the street in Albert in the valley below us here. The small hospital I was in last time is gone, destroyed by shelling. I find myself worrying about the kind nun who had helped me there.

Thursday, 24 August, 9.00 A.M.—

Wakened early this morning, but instead of being served the gruel we receive for breakfast, I was painfully set onto a sort of wheeled cart and pushed out into a courtyard between the tents. It was raining, but they left us there—myself and two other officers I recognized from the 1st Battalion Rifle Brigade. These two men were wounded more seriously than I. One had his face tightly wrapped in gauze, but I could tell that most or all of his lower jaw was missing. The other showed no visible wounds, but was unable to sit up in the wicker wheelchair. His head lolled as if unattached to his pale neck.

We had been left there in the rain for ten or fifteen minutes when a Colonel and several aides came out of the adjoining mess tent. It was the Colonel who had spoken to the Brigade with General Shute.

Oh, no, I thought. *I do not want a medal. Just wheel me in out of the rain, please.*

The Colonel spoke for only a minute. There were no medals.

"I expect you all to know," he began with his Harrow drawl so similar to General Shute's, "that I'm damned disappointed in you chaps. Damned disappointed." He slapped his crisply trousered thigh with a riding crop. "It is important for you chaps to . . . ah . . . understand . . . that you've let down the side. That's what you've done. Just let down the side." He wheeled as if he were going to leave but then turned back, surprising his aides who had also wheeled away as if disgusted with the three of us on our carts and wheelchairs.

"One more thing," said the Colonel. "You should know that your Battalion was the only one of the Brigade to have failed . . . the only one! And I do not want to hear any complaining about the fact that the 33rd Division did not push forward on your right . . . do you hear? I shan't have that bandied about as an excuse. The 33rd's failure is the 33rd's shame. The 1st Battalion's failure is our shame. And you chaps are responsible. And I'm . . . well . . . I'm damned disappointed."

And he and the pilot fish in his wake disappeared back into the mess tent. I could smell some sort of cake or confectionery from the baking ovens. The three of us sat or lay out in the rain for another ten minutes or so, not speaking, until someone remembered to fetch us back to the ward.

Afterwards, she lies in the protective harbor of my arm while we watch the firelight fade to embers.

"Would you like to hear a passage of His Nibs's private diary?" she whispers.

I am brought back from pleasant reverie. "What? Whose?"

"General Sir Douglas Haig," she says and smiles. "You are not the only one who keeps a private journal."

I play with a strand of her hair. "How do you know what the General writes in his private diary?"

She ignores me, closes her eyes, and recites as if from memory. "Saturday, 19 August—The operation carried out yesterday was most successful. It was on a front of over eleven miles. We now hold the ridge south-east of and overlooking Thiepval. Nearly five hundred prisoners were taken here while the battalion which carried out the attack only lost forty men! During their advance our men kept close to the artillery barrage."

I look at her in the fading light. "Why do you tell me this?"

She shifts sideways so that her bare shoulder becomes a faintly lit crescent leading to her shadowed face. "I thought that you might like to know that you were part of a success."

"My battalion was destroyed," I whisper, feeling very strange at bringing the War into our bed. "More than forty men died in C Company alone."

She nods slightly against the pillow. I cannot see her eyes for the shadows. "But the leading battalion lost only forty. And gained several hundred yards of mud. General Sir Douglas Haig is pleased."

"Fuck General Sir Douglas Haig," I say.

I expect some sound of shock from my Lady, but she sets her hand playfully on my bare chest and if there is a sound, it is a soft laugh.

Saturday, 26 August, 7.00 P.M.—

It is getting dark earlier. This is the one week anniversary of my waking up in the casualty clearing station.

I remember nothing of leaving the trench or making my way back across No Man's Land. I remember no help in finding the station. I remember nothing of taking my mask off and choking on the remnants of gas, nor of receiving the shrapnel wound that has turned my right leg into a throbbing mass of suppurating pain.

I do remember awakening. After the first attack, when I thought I was waking in hospital, I found myself among the dead. After this attack, when I was sure that I would lie unwaking among the dead, I awoke to the flare of acetylene torches with a surgeon bending over me. If he is God or the Devil, I thought, then God or the Devil dresses in army-issue white smock liberally spattered with blood. His archangels on high looked to be a sister in nurse whites, and orderly with pince-nez glasses, and a tired anaesthetist with a smock as gored as the surgeon's.

And then I remember very little except arriving here on the 21st, not even being aware of time as I scribbled in my journal, trying to make sense of all those fragmented images.

And fuck General Sir Douglas Haig, and the Colonel, and Shute, and whoever else is intent upon killing me. I defy them. I defy the gods. I defy God Himself.

Sunday, 27 August, 5.00 A.M.—

Awoke coughing, retching yellow fluid, and drowning at 3.22 A.M. Had to shout for a nurse, who came slowly, obviously irritated at being wakened.

Could not breathe. Thought *All right, then . . . so this is the way of it. It was worth it. She was worth it.* And then all such rational thoughts fled as I gasped for air and flailed about like the drowning man I was. Every time I inhaled I vomited yellow bile. My throat was full, my nose was full. Black spots danced all around my vision, but blessed oblivion did not condescend to arrive as I thrashed and retched and pounded the stained mattress as if it were the ocean.

I remember my last coherent thought was *Dying is not so easy as they make it out . . . Tolstoy, this is how peasants die!* and then a bored orderly sauntered in with one of the bicycle-pump needles, they slapped it through my shoulder blade into my right lung, and a few minutes later they had extracted enough of the thick fluid that I could breathe . . . after a fashion . . . although the terrible sucking, mucusy sound must have kept many of the other chaps here awake. They said nothing.

Same day, 11.15 A.M.—

A priest came through to give Communion to the Catholic lads. I watched and listened to his gentleness for almost an hour, seeing how truly moved he was by the plight of the more seriously wounded. When he passed my bed, glanced at my chart, and saw "NONE" typed in above the line that says "RELIGION," he nonetheless stopped and asked if there was anything he could do for me. Still unable to talk, I could only shake my head and try to hide my tears.

An hour later the doctor in charge of the ward sat tiredly on the edge of my bed. "Listen, Lieutenant," he said, his voice more tired than stern, "it seems as if the gangrene may be getting better. And the orderlies assure me that the lung problem is minor." He polished his glasses and then leaned forward. "If you think these . . . minor accidents of war . . . are going to assure you of a cushy rest period back in the arms of England, well . . . the war goes on, Lieutenant. And I expect you to be back in it as soon as we can get you out of here to free up this bed for a truly wounded man. Do you understand me?"

I started to nod, but then I spoke for the first time in the week I have been here. "Yes, Sir," I said through the phlegm and fluid that filled my throat. "I expect to go back to the Front. I *want* to go back to the Front."

He cleaned his glasses and frowned at me, as if I were having some sport with him, but in the end he only shook his head and moved on.

I was not having sport with him. I was telling the truth. What I could not tell him is what the Lady told me this morning.

It is morning, a beautiful autumn morning, and we are having a light breakfast of tea and croissants on her patio. She is wearing a dark skirt and a light-blue blouse, gathered at the cuffs and midriff, fastened at the throat by an emerald brooch. Her dark hair is tied up in an intricate manner. Her eyes are smiling as she pours my tea.

"We will not meet again for a while," she says, setting the silver teapot aside. She adds the single lump of sugar I prefer.

I am stunned into silence for only a minute. "But I want . . . I mean, we must . . ." I break off, appalled at my own incoherence. I want to tell her that I used to be a poet who understood language.

She sets her hand on mine. "And we will," she says. "We will see each other again. It will be a short while for me. A bit longer for you."

I frown at my lack of understanding. "You realize that I understand nothing," I say honestly. "I had thought that our love would . . . had to . . ."

She smiles. Her hand does not leave mine. "Do you remember the photograph of the painting in your mother's drawing room?"

I nod, my face reddening. Discussing this is somehow more intimate than our night of total intimacy. "G. F. Watts," I say. *"Love and Death.* The woman figure of Death . . ." I pause, unable to say 'you,' ". . . the robed figure standing above the child . . . Eros, I presume. Love."

Her fingernails trace small patterns on the back of my hand. "You used to think it had a secret meaning." she says, very quietly.

"Yes." I can think of nothing intelligent to say. The secret meaning had eluded me then. It eludes me now.

She smiles again, but again there is no mockery there. I remember her face in the firelight. "Perhaps," she says, "just perhaps, instead of the female Thanatos looming over the threatened Eros, it is your feminine . . . metaphor . . ." She smiles more broadly now. ". . . of Love who is stopping the capricious young prankster Death from playing his tricks."

I blink, struck stupid.

My Lady laughs softly and pours herself tea, lifting the cup and saucer. The absence of her hand on mine is like a harbinger of winters to come.

"But love . . . of whom?" I say at last. "Of what? What great passion would forestall death?"

Her graceful eyebrow arches. "You do not know? You, a poet?"

I do not know. I say as much.

She leans forward so that I can hear the rustle of her starched cotton blouse and the silk beneath. Our faces are so close that I can feel the warmth from her skin. "Then you need more time to learn," she whispers, her voice as filled with emotion as when she cried out last night.

I set my own hand, shaking, on the small iron table. "And how much time will we have . . . now . . . together . . . until we part?" I ask.

She does not laugh at my redundancies. Her eyes are warm. "Time enough for tea," she says, and raises her cup to her lips.

*　　*　　*

Thursday, 31 August, 1.00 P.M.—

Discharged from the field hospital near Albert today. Can barely walk, but found a ride in an empty ambulance going back to Carnoy Valley where General Shute has pulled the brigade to rest before another offensive.

One of the other surgeons, over Dr. Babington's terse report that my wound and pneumonia were healed sufficiently to return to duty, recommended strongly that I be shipped back to Blighty for at least a month of recuperation. I thanked the other surgeon, but said that Dr. Babington's suggestion suited me.

I know very few of the chaps here in the valley camp. I did run into Sergeant McKay, the gentleman who had helped me up out of the trenches after I had been knocked backwards by poor Captain Brown, and we were so delighted to see that the other had survived the attack that I think we barely restrained from hugging one another. Most of the other faces in C and D Companies are fresh and strange.

Sergeant McKay asked me if I had heard the storm the night before. I admitted that I had slept through it.

"One 'ell of a show, Sir," he said, his red face beaming. "Soaked us all good, it did. The lightnin' was worse than the barrage on the day we went over. At the 'eight of it, Sir, it struck two of our observation balloons and blowed them right up, Sir. Quite a show. Beggin' your pardon, Sir, but I can't see how no one could sleep through such a show. No disrespect meant, Sir."

I grinned at him. "No disrespect inferred, Sergeant." I hesitated only a second. "It sounds like quite a storm, but it was just . . . ah . . . well, last night was my last night in Albert, and I . . . well, I was not alone, Sergeant."

The NCO's smile grew broader, his face screwed up in a wink worthy of the stage, and he saluted me. "Yes, Sir," he said. "Well, glad you're back, Sir. And wishin' you good health while you're here, Sir."

Now I sit on my bunk and try to rest. My chest aches, my leg aches, but I try to ignore these distractions. Word is that there will be a general attack on Delville Wood within 48 hours and that General Shute wants his lads—us—in the forefront of it.

But 48 hours is a goodly amount of time. I have books to read—*The Return of the Native* here in my locker, as is the new Eliot which I have not yet finished—and after reading a bit, I may take a stroll around the camp. The storm seems to be over. The air is clear. It is a lovely evening.

Editor's Afterword—

Here ends the newly discovered war diary of Lieutenant James Edwin Rooke.

There was an attack on Delville Wood on the 2nd of September, 1916, although Rooke's Battalion did not bear the brunt of it. The Gloucestershire Regiment, 5th Division—the so-called "Bristol City Battalion"—had the honor of leading the way. The Battalion was all but destroyed in thirty hours of fierce fighting.

Rooke did participate in the larger offensive of 15 September. This battle marked the first time tanks were used on a battlefield, although there were too few and they were poorly used. Rooke was not injured during this final attack on Delville Wood, although 40% of his platoon were reported missing, wounded, or dead after the action.

The poet did not see Thiepval finally captured on 27 September. A forgotten transfer had come through shortly after the 15 September offensive, and Rooke returned to his old unit, the 13th Battalion Rifle Brigade. There are only two letters extant from this quiet period in the "cushy" trenches near Calonne, but in both letters to his sister, Rooke appears to have been simultaneously contemplative and quietly joyful. He wrote no poetry.

The 13th Rifle Brigade returned to the Somme on 11 November, 1916, when winter was setting in and trench conditions were particularly dreadful. James Edwin Rooke participated in the terrible fighting during the attack on Serre on November 13–15. The objective was not attained. Rooke was in the field hospital near Pozieres, dealing with a third and more serious bout of pneumonia, when word came that the Battle of the Somme was "over" on 19 November, 1916.

Actually, there was no formal end to the battle. It had merely petered out amidst the mud, snow, and freezing temperatures of that particularly early and harsh winter.

More than 1,200,000 men died during the five months of fighting along the Somme in 1916. No major breakthroughs were achieved.

James Edwin Rooke returned to his unit and stayed along the Front at the Somme—where casualties still ran at about 30,000 men a month for the

British—until he was wounded again at the battle called Third Ypres, or Passchendaele, in August of 1917. Rooke was hit by two machine-gun bullets while leading an attack on a German pillbox with the strange name of Springfield Farm.

Survivors of Passchendaele later remembered and spoke mostly of the mud there; General Sir Douglas Haig himself wrote:

. . . the low-lying clayey soil, torn by shells and sodden with rain, turned into a succession of vast muddy pools, the valleys of the choked and overflowing streams were speedily transformed into long stretches of bog, impassable except by a few well-defined tracks, which became marks for the enemy artillery. To leave those tracks was to risk death by drowning."

Indeed, in one of his few letters to his sister in which he mentions details of the war itself, Lieutenant James Edwin Rooke—then convalescing in Sussex—described how a friend of his, a certain Sergeant McKay, did drown in the mud of a shell hole while the wounded lieutenant lay nearby and could do nothing to help.

Of James Edwin Rooke's life after the Great War, much has been written. Of his decision to write no poetry for publication from that time on, many have lamented. When Rooke decided to join the Roman Catholic Church in 1919, his family and friends reacted with shock. When he actually became a priest in 1921, family and friends essentially disowned him. Only his younger sister, Eleanor, continued to correspond with him during the years that followed.

While Rooke's Trench Poems *took on a fame and life of their own, the man himself retreated from the literary scene. Few of the poets of the 1930s and 40s who patterned their verse after his knew that the poet himself was still alive, although in relative seclusion, in various monasteries in France. Indeed, Rooke's literary production in those decades, while well picked-over by scholars, consists almost entirely of correspondence with his sister and the intermittent (but lively) letters he exchanged with his friend, Teilhard de Chardin. The one book he did print, privately, was the now legendary* Songs from Silence, *(John Murray Publishers, Ltd., 1938) a series of prose poems describing the contemplative life he had led in the Benedictine Abbey of St. Wandrille and the long visits he had made—some lasting years—to the Cistercian Monastery of La Grande Trappe, the Abbey of Solesmes, and the Rock Monasteries of Cappadocia.*

Scholars have shown that within the Church itself, Father Rooke seemed anything but monastic. Always expressing a love for life that sometimes bordered on the apostate, Father Rooke became as famous within his small theological circles for his theory of "life ascendent" as his friend Teilhard did for his theories of moral and spiritual evolution. These two continued their lively and impassioned correspondence until Teilhard's death in 1955.

In 1957, Rooke's sister Eleanor wrote him a letter in which she asked the aging priest why he had forsaken the comforts of wife and family for all of the years since the War. Father Rooke responded in a letter which has become famous but which, until now, has not been totally clear. I present that letter now in its entirety:

15 September, 1957
The Abbey of St. Wandrille

My dearest Eleanor,

I read your letter while strolling on the Rouen-Yvetot road this evening and it delighted me, as your letters always do, with your keen intelligence and gentle wit. But it also saddened me that you feel hesitant to ask me a question . . . "have waited these forty years," you wrote, "and know that I should wait forty more."

There is no need to wait forty more, my dear, nor even another day. The question is asked, and I take no offense.

Tonight, when the Abbot tapped his mallet and the reader ceased his reading and intoned *"Tu autem Domine miserere nobis,"* and we all rose and bowed as we chanted our thanksgiving, I was—as I have every morn and noon and evening for almost forty years—thanking not a personal or impersonal God, but merely the fact of Life itself for its gift of life.

As to my celibacy—or as you so quaintly put it—"my long denial of life's physicality," well, Eleanor, have you ever known a more physical person than your brother? Even this afternoon, as I labored to finish weeding the last patch of peas in the garden between the Abbey and the forest, can you not imagine me taking sheer physical pleasure in the sweat that ran into my eyes and trickled under my rough robes?

But I know you speak of marriage, or more precisely, of physical love.

Do you not remember that I wrote many years ago that I was

married? Not *felt* married or *acted as if I were married,* but married. I should wear a wedding ring like the nuns in Rouen who show they are wed to Christ.

Only I am not wed to Christ. I respect him and grow more interested in his teachings as each year passes—especially the idea that God is, indeed, quite literally, Love—but I am not wed to the Galilean.

Yes, my dear, I know that this is heresy, even to such a casual C of E sometime-believer as yourself. Imagine if the Abbot or dear Brother Theophylaktos or serious Father Gabriel heard me utter these words! Thank heavens for vows of silence.

I am wed, not to Christ, nor to any conventional image of God, but to Life herself. I celebrate Her daily and look forward to seeing Her even as life seems to abandon me. I find Her in the smallest things each day—the sunlight on the rough plaster of my cell, the touch of rough wool, the savor of those fresh beans I defended with my hoe for so many hot months.

Eleanor, do not think that I have abandoned God in my love of Life. It is merely that I understand—have been made to understand—that God is found in *this* Life and that to wait for another is folly.

Of course you must ask how I can shut myself away if I believe in embracing Life. The answer is difficult even for me to understand.

First, I do not consider my life in these abbeys as a retreat from life. It is—as I hope I showed in the simple little book I sent you fifteen or sixteen years ago (my God, time moves on, does it not, my baby sister?)—my way of savoring life. As imperfect as those writings were, they were my attempt to share the exquisite simplicity of such a life. It is as if I were a connoisseur of fine food, and rather than discourage my appetite through gluttony, I indulge it by ingesting only small portions of the finest cuisine.

I love Life, Eleanor. It is that simple. Had I the choice, I would live forever, accepting pain and loss as my due and learning—across time—even to appreciate the sharp seasoning of this sadness. The alternative is the Child Who Devours.

I know this makes no sense, my dear. Perhaps this poem I shall enclose, written some time ago, might cast some light on the murky cloud of verbiage I have stirred up. Poets rarely get to the point.

Please write again soon. I wish to hear about your dear husband's health (improving, I hope and will pray) and the continued fortunes of Charles and Linda in the big city. (I would not recognize London were some miracle to transport me there. The last time I saw it was during the Blitz, and while morale was very high amongst the populace, the old city itself had seen better days. Tell me, are the barrage balloons still there? Just kidding—the pub (I still call it that) near the station in the nearby village boasts a television and I caught a glance of a film set in London just last month on my way to a conference in Rouen. And there were no barrage balloons.)

Do write, Eleanor, and forgive your brother's continued obtuseness and perversity. Someday I shall grow up.

I remain—

> Your loving brother,
> James

{Ed. note—The following poem was enclosed.}

THE GREAT LOVER

I have been so great a lover: filled my days
So proudly with the splendour of Love's praise,
The pain, the calm, and the astonishment,
Desire illimitable, and still content,
And all dear names men use, to cheat despair,
For the perplexed and viewless streams that bear
Our hearts at random down the dark of life.
Now, ere the unthinking silence on that strife
Steals down, I would cheat drowsy Death so far,
My night shall be remembered for a star
That outshone all the suns of all men's days.
Shall I not crown them with immortal praise

Whom I have loved, who have given me, dared with me
High secrets, and in darkness knelt to see
The inenarrable godhead of delight?
Love is a flame;—we have beaconed the world's night.
A city:—and we have built it, these and I.
An emperor:—we have taught the world to die.
So, for their sakes I loved, ere I go hence,
And the high cause of Love's magnificence,
And to keep loyalties young, I'll write those names
Golden for ever, eagles, crying flames,
And set them as a banner, that men may know,
To dare the generations, burn, and blow
Out on the wind of time, shining and streaming . . .

These I have loved:
    White plates and cups, clean-gleaming,
Ringed with blue lines; and feathery, faery dust;
Wet roofs, beneath the lamp-light; the strong crust
Of friendly bread; and many-tasting food;
Rainbows; and the blue bitter smoke of wood;
And radiant raindrops couching in cool flowers;
And flowers themselves, that sway through sunny hours,
Dreaming of moths that drink them under the moon;
Then, the cool kindliness of sheets, that soon
Smooth away trouble; and the rough male kiss
Of blankets; grainy wood; live hair that is
Shining and free; blue-massing clouds; the keen
Unpassioned beauty of a great machine;
The benison of hot water; furs to touch;
The good smell of old clothes; and other such—
The comfortable smell of friendly fingers,
Hair's fragrance, and the musty reek that lingers
About dead leaves and last year's ferns . . . Dear names,
And thousand others throng to me! Royal flames;
Sweet water's dimpling laugh from tap or spring;
Holes in the ground; and voices that do sing:
Voices in laughter, too; and body's pain,

Soon turned to peace; and the deep-panting train;
Firm sands; the little dulling edge of foam
That browns and dwindles as the wave goes home;
And washen stones, gay for an hour; the cold
Graveness of iron; moist black earthen mould;
Sleep; and high places; footprints in the dew;
And oaks; and brown horse-chestnuts, glossy-new;
And new-peeled sticks; and shining pools on grass;—
All these have been my loves. And these shall pass.
Whatever passes not, in the great hour,
Nor all my passion, all my prayers, have power
To hold them with me through the gate of Death.
They'll play deserter, turn with traitor breath,
Break the high bond we made, and sell Love's trust
And sacramented covenant to the dust.

—Oh, never a doubt but, somewhere, I shall wake,
And give what's left of love again, and make
New friends, new strangers . . . But the best I've known,
Stays here, and changes, breaks, grows old, is blown
About the winds of the world, and fades from brains
Of living men, and dies. Nothing remains.

O dear my loves, O faithless, once again
This one last gift I give: that after men
Shall know, and later lovers, far-removed
Praise you, 'All these were lovely': say, 'He loved.'[16]

{Ed. note—James Edwin Rooke died of cancer in July of 1971. He was 83 years old.}

Notes

About the real poets:

1. Siegfried Sassoon, "And clink of shovels . . ."

Born in 1886, educated at Marlborough and Clare College, Cambridge, Sassoon served with the Sussex Yeomanry and Welch Fusiliers. He was known as an incredibly brave officer and had been seriously wounded and awarded the Military Cross even before he saw action at the Battle of the Somme.

Sassoon was the first major poet to be critical of the lack of progress in the war, and his brutal, realistic verse became the archetype for an entire generation of wartime poets. His antiwar poetry and protests were at first diagnosed as shell shock and he was committed to a sanatorium where he met Wilfred Owen, another brilliant young antiwar poet. Owen wrote of Sassoon—"I hold you as Keats + Christ + Elijah + my Colonel + my father confessor + Amenophis IV in profile."

Unlike most of the younger poets, Sassoon survived the war and became the literary editor for the *Daily Herald*. Throughout his writing career, Sassoon was obsessed with his wartime experiences and his fictional autobiography, *Memoirs of an Infantry Officer*, may be the best-known memoir of that war. Sassoon died in 1967.

2. A. G. West, "The Night Patrol"

3. A. G. West, "We had no light . . ."

4.   Images adapted from "The Great Lover" by Rupert Brooke.

Rupert Brooke was the quintessential romantic war poet. Born in 1887, educated at Rugby and King's College, Cambridge, Brooke was given a commission in the Royal Naval Division by his admirer— the First Lord of the Admiralty, Winston Churchill—saw some action at Antwerp in 1914, wrote patriotic verse about his willingness (almost eagerness) to die for his country, and died of blood poisoning while being transported to Gallipoli in 1915. He was buried on the Greek island of Scyros and his life, verse, death, and burial instantly became the stuff of legend.

Rupert Brooke's brilliant but romanticized view of the war differs wildly from the bitter verse of his contemporaries who survived to see the horrors of later battles and the high-level stupidity of the long war of attrition.

5.   Wilfred Owen, ". . . the white eyes writhing in his face"

Born in 1893, educated at Birkenhead Institute and University of London, Owen enlisted in the Artist's Rifles in 1915 and fought in France from January 1917 to June 1917, when he was invalided out. Suffering from nervous collapse, Owen was sent to the sanatorium where he met Siegfried Sassoon, who soon became his mentor. Sassoon introduced Owen to the poets Robert Graves and Robert Nichols, both of whom had been at the Somme.

Although bitter about the mishandling of the war and converted to pacifism, Owen returned to the Front and became a Company Commander dedicated to keeping his men alive. "My senses are charred" he wrote shortly before he died. "I don't take the cigarette out of my mouth when I write Deceased over their letters."

Wilfred Owen was awarded the Military Cross for exceptional bravery in October 1918, and was killed by machine-gun fire at the Sambre Canal on November 4, 1918. Many consider him the finest poet of the war.

6.   From an Official Medical History of the War (HMSO).

7.   Marching song of the 13th (S) Btn, The Rifle Brigade.

8. Siegfried Sassoon, "The Glory of Women"

9. Charles Sorley, "On, marching men, on . . ."

10. Charles Sorley, "When you see the millions of the mouthless dead . . ."

Born in 1895, educated at Marlborough, Sorley won a scholarship to University College, Oxford, but enlisted in the Suffolk Regiment in August 1914. Within a year he had obtained the rank of captain. He was killed in action at Loos on October 13, 1915. Although Sorley was only twenty at the time of his death, John Masefield and others considered him the most promising of the war poets. His *Marlborough and Other Poems* was published in 1916 and proved extremely popular. His "Song of the Ungirt Runners" is his most famous poem and has been recited by generations of schoolchildren.

In a letter home in which he had included some poetry, Sorley once wrote: "You will notice that most of what I have written is as hurried and angular as the handwriting: written out at different times and dirty with my pocket: but I have had no time for the final touch nor seem likely to have for some time."

11. Soldiers' doggerel, "The world wasn't made in a day"

12. Andrew Marvell, "The Definition of Love"

This was quoted by Guy Chapman in *A Passionate Prodigality,* published in 1933. This memoir is an excellent introduction to an officer's view of the war and the Battle of the Somme. Chapman dedicates the book to "certain soldiers who have now become a small quantity of Christian dust." Born in 1889, Guy Patterson Chapman served with the 13th Battalion and the Royal Fusiliers from 1914 to 1920. Chapman is one of the few writers who reenlisted after the war. Later becoming a barrister, writer, publisher, historian, and Professor of Modern History at Leeds University, Chapman died in 1972.

The poet Andrew Marvell lived from 1621 to 1678.

13. A. P. Herbert, "The General inspecting his trenches . . ."

An officer in the Royal Naval Division, Alan (A. P.) Herbert was present when General Shute dressed down the 63rd Division for their filthy trenches. The division had just gone into the line formerly held by the Portugese, and the men resented Shute's comments. Herbert's "poem" became a song sung to the tune of "Wrap Me Up in My Tarpaulin Jacket" and soon spread throughout the division, and then through the entire army.

The irony of the situation was that although General Shute was renowned as a spit-and-polish man and a bit of a martinet, he was admired by many of his men for his tremendous courage and willingness to crawl into No Man's Land with scout patrols. Thanks to Herbert's limerick, what tends to be remembered now about Shute is "The General inspecting his trenches..."

14.   Byron (George Gordon, Lord), "The Prisoner of Chillon and Other Poems of 1816"

15.   Wilfred Owen, "Who are these?..."

16.   Rupert Brooke, "The Great Lover"

The Cat Who Went into the Closet